a
Twisted
Ladder

RHODI HAWK

A Tom Doherty Associates Book

New York

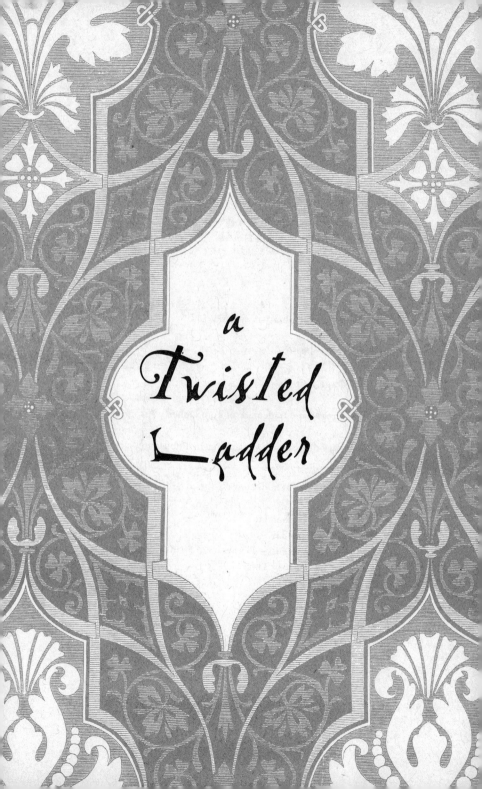

a Twisted Ladder

Haw

This is a work of fiction. All of the characters, organizations, and events portrayed in this novel are either products of the author's imagination or are used fictitiously.

A TWISTED LADDER

Copyright © 2009 by Rhodi Hawk

A Forge Book
Published by Tom Doherty Associates, LLC
175 Fifth Avenue
New York, NY 10010

www.tor-forge.com

Forge® is a registered trademark of Tom Doherty Associates, LLC.

Library of Congress Cataloging-in-Publication Data

Hawk, Rhodi.
    A twisted ladder / Rhodi Hawk.—1st ed.
        p.   cm.
    "A Tom Doherty Associates book."
    ISBN 978-0-7653-2373-6
    1. Women psychologists—Fiction.   2. Family secrets—Fiction.
3. Domestic fiction.   I. Title.
    PS3608.A884T85 2009
    813'.6—dc22

                                                    2009018761

Printed in the United States of America

0 9 8 7 6 5 4 3 2

Acknowledgments

Over the many years I've spent researching and writing my first novel, *A Twisted Ladder,* I've been looking forward to this moment above all others (OK, to be honest, maybe not as much as the actual publication of it!), when I have a chance to publicly thank those who've helped me along the way. First and foremost, I'd like to thank Peter Miller, who has become so much more than my manager. Thank you for taking a chance on an unknown entity, Peter, and thank you for your faith. You are my business associate and my friend for life.

I would also like to thank Joanna McAdam, who may very well have read this manuscript as many times as I have. In addition to being my dear friend, Joanna also helped me to pre-edit before handing off to the team, offered opinions, and has been a force of go-tell-it-on-the-mountain vigilance in spreading the word among the community. *Bardzo dziękuję, kochana.* Madly!

There have been several authors, too, who have assisted me in many ways, including offering advice, words of encouragement, making introductions, and above all, helping me to improve my skills as a writer. Thank you from the bottom of my heart, F. Paul Wilson. You are a legend in this business, and you've done so much for me and the other authors you've mentored. Your generosity boggles my mind. Special thanks, too, to Heather Graham, Jack Ketchum, Tess Gerritsen, Lou Arronica, and Joe Lansdale. And HUGE thanks to the fine folks of my writing group, Who Wants Cake: Daniel Braum, M. M. DeVoe, Nicholas Kaufmann, Sarah Langan, Victor Lavalle, K. Z. Perry, Stefan Petrucha, Lee Thomas, and David Wellington. Your no-nonsense tough love has made me a better writer.

Thank you, Eric Raab, my editor at Tor, who has shown so much patience, guidance, and faith in this project. I am so lucky to be working with you.

But at the core, I'd like to thank my family. You have wrapped a blanket of love and support around me from the very beginning. During the writing of this book I've gone through some of the biggest changes of my life, and I would never have made it through without you. Rachel, your artistic journey has mirrored mine in so many ways, and we've compared notes and bounced ideas off one another. So thank you to Friday Jones, the incomparable tattoo artist and world phenomenon, who is also my beloved sister and friend. Thank you Margaret Burns, my grandmother and guiding spirit. Thank you, Dad and Mamacita, I love you so much! And thanks to the rest of my family, including my younger brother and sister, my darling aunts, all my cousins, and all my friends. I am so grateful to have you in my life. And even Jer—you played your role in this as well, bless your heart.

Finally, I'd like to thank you, the reader. You're the reason I'm doing this. And if reading this book should prove to be an experience you value, I hope you will tell the people you care about.

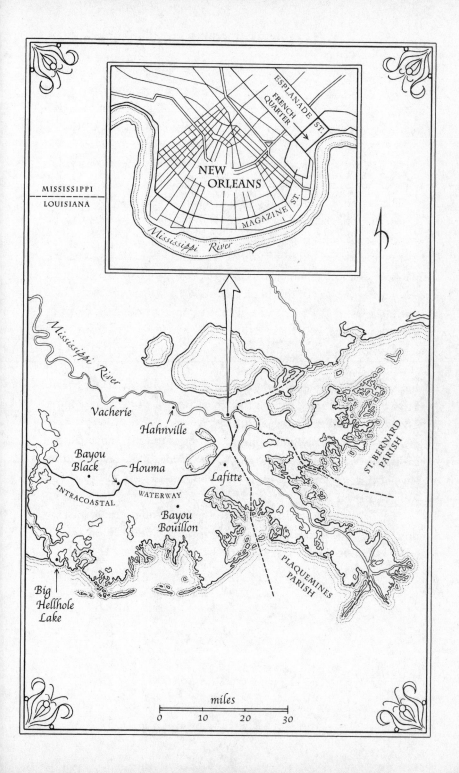

MISSISSIPPI
LOUISIANA

ESPLANADE ST.
FRENCH
QUARTER

NEW
ORLEANS

MAGAZINE ST.

Mississippi River

Mississippi River

Vacherie

Hahnville

Bayou
Black

Houma

Lafitte

ST. BERNARD
PARISH

INTRACOASTAL

WATERWAY

Bayou
Bouillon

Big
Hellhole
Lake

PLAQUEMINES
PARISH

miles

0   10   20   30

a Twisted Ladder

one

OMETHING MOVED BENEATH THE kitchen wallpaper. Madeleine was holding the phone to her ear as she tapped the spot with the back of her wooden spoon, half-expecting some kind of response under there. A skitter, perhaps, or another shift. But no. She just stared and listened to nothing while Marc waited on the line.

"It's all in your mind," he said.

She laughed and turned back to the stove, shouldering the phone to her ear so she could use both hands to stir the couche-couche. "Could be a mouse in there."

"No, it ain't no mouse," he snapped.

She paused, startled by his tone.

He said, "I'm telling you it's in your mind. You can't trust it."

Marc gave a laugh of disgust. "When you think about it, the whole damned kitchen's an illusion. What's a kitchen anyway? It ain't the walls. It ain't the floor you're standing on. It ain't even the pots or the fridge or the stove or any of that. What's a kitchen? It's air. What's any room? Air. Sectioned-off air. Trying to close off a little mess of space so you feel like there's something real there. Ain't none of it real."

Madeleine had halted in midstir on the couche and was listening, lips parted.

"You think there's something under there? You ain't gonna find it unless you do like you're putting stars to sleep. And then you'll wish you never looked."

"Putting stars to sleep?"

He was silent.

"Marc?"

His breathing sounded tense through the Nokia. She'd never heard him speak like this before. He was a simple guy, made his living wiring houses, and had strong opinions about whether you get more action baiting redfish with shrimp or with mullet cutbait. (He would swear by the former.) Marc liked to talk about *those* sorts of things. Not sectioned-off air.

Finally, he said, "Yeah."

"You all right?"

A sharp sigh through his nose. "I want you to listen to me Madeleine."

"I'm listening. I'm here. Please tell me what you would like to say to me."

"Don't you start talkin' like a shrink now. I ain't one of your patients."

She let go of the wooden spoon and the end of it fell to the side of the pan with a soft clang. "All right, I didn't mean to sound that way. I'm just listening as your sister. OK?"

When he didn't reply she added, "Mudhead?"

Another sharp breath, possibly a laugh, but it sounded more like a snort of frustration. She stared out the steamed window, nothing but vague shapes moving on the city street beyond the porch. Beads formed and chased trails of clarity down the glass.

Marc said, "I just want you to hear me when I say there ain't no goddamned mouse in that wall."

"OK. I hear you honey. Is there something else?"

He didn't reply.

She said, "Marc, why don't you tell me what's going on?"

"I want you to come on out here to Houma."

"When?"

"Now."

"You got it."

He released his breath, but when he spoke again his voice sounded more resigned than satisfied. "OK. OK. That's good. What're you cooking anyway?"

"Same old. Couche-couche and boudin."

"Should've known. You always do breakfast at suppertime, and dinner in the morning."

"You want me to bring you a plate? There's lots."

"Made extra, did you? In case Daddy shows up with a bunch of tramps off the street?"

"Tramps gotta eat, too. If they don't show up hungry now it's just a matter of time before they do."

She picked the spoon back up and gave it another stir, the smell of sausages filling her nose. Must have filled Jasmine's nose too, because the little white terrier padded in from the living room and cocked her head at the stove.

Marc said, "Well go ahead and eat. But hurry. Then come on out if you would. Don't bother with making me a plate."

"You sure you're all right?"

"It's fine. Just fine."

He was lying of course. Marc wouldn't be talking this way if things were fine. But she saw that some of the shapes through the window were looming closer, and though she could see only his outline, Madeleine recognized her father's jaunty gait.

"Speak of the devil. Daddy's coming."

"With a bunch of tramps off the street?"

She squinted. "Can't see but it looks like he's got at least one."

Marc sighed.

Madeleine said, "Look, I'm still gonna head out there to Bayou Black, OK?"

"All right, don't let'm talk you into dawdling."

"Love you, baby."

"Love you, too."

She set the phone on the counter, waiting to hear the front door open, wondering. She turned and looked at the bubble in the wallpaper again. Swollen and bloated from rot in the walls. This wasn't the first time she'd noticed movement—or at least a sense of something between the framing boards and the bulge on the old Victorian print. Once she'd even put her stethoscope to it, but had heard nothing.

"One last room to restore," she said to the wallpaper bubble, and she thought of Marc's strange words about illusions of rooms.

Trying to close off a little mess of space so you feel like there's something real there.

Jasmine barked and ran for the foyer. The front door opened.

❧

BAYOU BLACK, 2009

THE SOLUTION WAS SIMPLE: He would kill his sister. Simple, not easy.

Marc kicked the documents to the side, causing them to tear beneath his foot as he cleared the wood floor. He spread the quilt. A riot of triangles, squares, and circles, all in competing colors. He turned it over so the patterns faced the floor and the barren underside of fabric showed. The cloth now lay clean and white.

He smoothed out the corners and upon it, began to disassemble his shotgun, neatly laying each black piece in a row.

Marc and Madeleine had always protected each other before. This is how he would protect her now. He checked the clock. They'd spoken an hour ago, and the drive from New Orleans would take her about that long. Assuming Daddy didn't keep her, she'd be arriving soon. He twisted the lid from the bottle and dabbed fluid onto a cotton cloth.

"Just talk to her," the other one said. "You're acting insane."

Marc hunched his shoulders and almost laughed out loud at that one, but he was shaking too hard and needed to concentrate. A tricky matter, this . . . what do you call it? He thought hard on the word for killing your own sister. Your own beloved, ruined. . . .

And the other one said, "Don't you think this is a little extreme? Chrissake, talk to her first."

Marc did not respond, a habit he'd been striving to perfect. To be able to ignore the other one, truly ignore him—if only he could. He focused on the tools in his hand and the motion of the cloth through the barrel.

"I don't get it," the other one said. "You electrocute somebody who doesn't even die, and that bothers you. That you had a problem with. But you think you can kill your own sister *and* yourself, and that's supposed to be poetic?"

"Shut up, shut up!"

A memory of the shuddering transformer. He'd very nearly killed his own journeyman electrician—caused him terrible agony—and it had been no accident. And yet it had seemed right and just. What would Madeleine think if she knew the truth? Was she, too, capable of such a thing?

Marc forced it all out of his mind: the memory of the electrocution, the staring motifs in the records he'd read. He shoved all of it aside to the corners of his mind. He tried to ignore the other one's taunting prattle, and the damn chattering of the birds and insects outside that never, ever ceased. The metallic scent of cleaning fluid bit at his nostrils.

Marc removed even the tiniest speck of dust. The gentle movement of the cloth through the barrel. The way the parts lay cleanly organized. The trigger. The spring. The firing pin.

"You're pathetic, you know that? A stupid, sniveling—"

The words tumbled away under a sudden thunder of music. Marc hadn't moved toward the radio on the counter. Hadn't even set down the barrel brush. A pinch in his mind, and the radio came on.

But it didn't help much. The words kept coming.

"Marc, listen to me. What makes you think she's like you, anyway?"

God, those words, they keep coming and coming. The radio hadn't stopped it. The voice skipped past the filter of Marc's ears and lodged inside his mind.

"What if you're wrong, Marc? Did you ever think of that? What if you're wrong about her and you kill her?"

Marc squeezed his eyes shut, increasing the sound of the radio until it reached maximum volume. Music crackled and vibrated throughout the sinew of the tiny house. But not enough. Like a worm swaying in an ear of corn, the other one's words stood out, insisting to be heard.

No use.

"She's your sister, Marc, but that doesn't necessarily mean she's the same as you. She's different."

Not different enough, Marc thought. He had to save her, spare her what he'd gone through. Was going through now.

One by one, he fit the pieces of the .12 gauge back together. He checked the clock. A full hour since he had called—plenty of time for Madeleine to get here. Adequate time to shake his resolve.

He looked at his hands, trembling, capable of murder. Those hands were familiar with this process. He'd used them to close a circuit that sent twenty thousand volts through a human body. But he'd not yet successfully completed a kill. He'd failed, and he didn't even know whether that failure was a good thing or a bad thing.

He'd grown so weary of this oil slick in his gut, this chronic uncertainty. Wanted to be clean of it. Even the very tools that had helped him build his livelihood as an electrician—honest tools, solid and otherwise devoted to constructive work—even they had become stained. God, he wished they could be clean again.

Maddy would never know this feeling. He would save her. He could spare her this.

He would take her to the womb of the Delta. They would lie down under the gray silken depths and give their bodies to the creatures of Bayou Black, sleeping on the broad, soft bed of clay that lay beneath the forest.

"This doesn't make sense, Marc. Just talk to her."

Marc said, "Sororicide. That's what you call it when you murder your sister."

But his words were lost under the blare of the radio, and his hands kept moving as if they could guide his thoughts. Each part of the shotgun clicked into place until it once again formed a single unit. So clean now. Marc stood, fingers shaking, and loaded the shells, half of them dropping into a snowdrift of papers. He folded the quilt, allowing the geometric shapes to glare back into the room again. He walked to the front room and checked the window.

Still no sign of her. He wasn't sure how much longer he could wait like this. Perhaps he should get out his tools, try to scrub away the killing truth in them.

"Ah, Maddy," he whispered.

For all those years, Bayou Black had given them sustenance. Fish, crab, snakes. Growing up, Marc and Madeleine lived like orphans, and could not have survived without hunting and fishing. Now they would lay down their own bodies to this cycle. They would take the boat out into the bayou, to a sacred place they once shared with their childhood friend. A special place. A secret place known only to them.

He would end it for her first. He would spare her any fear. Then he would turn the shotgun on himself while the creatures waited in the shadows. Together they would honor the cycle.

t w o

✤

BAYOU BLACK, 2009

ADELEINE SPED SOUTH TOWARD Houma. She tried yet
again to call her brother, but he still wasn't answering the phone. She felt a spark in her jaw and realized she'd been grinding her teeth.

The city shrank back into the haze, an occasional wink in her
rearview mirror, and the swamp-rimmed highway drew her deeper
into the land of her childhood. She would tell her brother about the
joke Daddy played on her.

Her mind flashed an image of Daddy Blank's mischievous expression; she barked out a laugh. Yes, she'd tell Marc how their father had
gotten her good.

Daddy's bloodhound sense must have told him he'd find couche-
couche on the stove. But this time the friend Daddy'd dragged along
wasn't just some street tramp.

"This is Ethan Manderleigh," Daddy'd told her, and she'd regarded them both with restrained impatience.

She'd ladled up two plates of couche-couche with cane syrup, tucking in some steaming links of boudin, and set them on the kitchen table.

"I gotta head out," she'd said, which was the stupidest thing she might have done.

Telling Daddy you're in a hurry was like showing a year's bank statements to an RV salesman, and she'd seen his eyes alight at the opportunity to bait her. Too quick to light, in fact. She resisted the urge to start in on him: *Have you been taking your meds, Daddy?* With the upcoming testimony before the House Ways and Means Committee, he'd darn well better be taking his meds.

"Oh, we don't wanna keep ya," Daddy'd said, but his devil-tail smile was already on the curve. "You don't have any sweet tea in the fridge, do you darlin?"

She didn't, but it would only take but a minute to throw together.

She cut a look at Daddy's new captive, Ethan Manderleigh, who fidgeted like a duke forced to share a farmer's table. Like Maddy, he was dark-haired and approaching thirty. But while Madeleine's eyes were blue, his were hazel, and Madeleine suspected the only blue in him would be found in his blood. She belonged to a family of mixed race: mulattos. He looked the opposite: purebred white, old money New Orleans. He leaned over and petted Jasmine under the table.

Daddy's collection of people always proved eclectic. He could play poker with the governor at lunch and drink from a brown paper bag with parolees by supper. He'd explained that Ethan had joined the Historic Preservation Society, confirming Madeleine's suspicion that he was some spoiled trust fund recipient. Tall, square-jawed, no doubt self-absorbed and stifling. Madeleine actually preferred when Daddy brought home street people.

But to his credit, Ethan Manderleigh seemed embarrassed at having intruded.

"It goes against my upbringing to take advantage of someone's hospitality," Ethan had said. "Come on, Daddy Blank, let me treat ya at Willie Mae's. And then we can treat your daughter here another time."

"It's all right," Maddy had said, mollified. "I'm just going to put out some sweet tea and then I'll leave y'all to it."

And that's when she discovered a tree frog in the sugar bowl. Nearly broke the china when the thing leapt out at her.

Daddy'd guffawed and slapped his leg. She had no idea how he'd managed to slip a frog in there without her catching him. But once she regained composure, Madeleine had given in to a good laugh herself. Poor Ethan, unaccustomed to Daddy Blank's antics, looked positively ashen—like he feared Madeleine might swoon. As if she was some fainting belle who had never worn pigtails and caught tadpoles in the mud flats.

The shock on Ethan's face, that appalled get-the-smelling-salts-and-begin-the-rites-of-contrition look of horror, had sent both Daddy Blank and Madeleine into shuddering, tear-streaked, belly-cramping hysterics.

Daddy'd abused his chance to score a glass of sweet tea, but Maddy did pour some Coca-Cola for all of them, and had even ladled herself a plate to eat alongside her father and Ethan Manderleigh. She'd settled in, thinking a few minutes' indulgence wouldn't hurt.

"Well, at least you're not afraid of toads," Ethan had said.

"Gray tree frog, actually," Madeleine replied. "*Hyla versicolor*. Or so the field guide calls it."

Ethan raised a brow. "A woman who knows her amphibians. You sound like you have a scientific mind. Are you in that line of work?"

"Actually," Daddy said as he slipped a piece of boudin under the table for Jasmine, "you two are kind of in the same business. Madeleine's a head shrinker and Ethan here is a head cutter."

Madeleine looked at Ethan. "What on earth is that man talking about?"

Ethan said, "I'm a neurologist."

"Oh. Where do you practice? One of the hospitals here in town?"

Ethan shook his head. "On staff at Tulane."

"I am too. In the Department of Psychology."

"So I heard. I also heard you're an activist."

Madeleine smiled. "Not really. Daddy and I are gonna testify before the House Ways and Means Committee, but it's hardly activism. Just trying to get funding for a special cause."

"What cause is that?"

She'd shrugged, but Daddy said, "It's all right honey, he knows."

Madeleine said, "It's what I call cognitive schizophrenia. The same condition Daddy has. But the testimony will be broader. We're just trying to get as much support as we can for our organizational affiliate, the Association for Psychological Discovery."

"Cognitive schizophrenia," Ethan said. "You know, I've actually read about that. There was an article in *The Window Inside* a few months back."

Madeleine nodded. "That was mine. I've been trying to get the word out as much as possible before the testimony."

When they'd finished their sausage and couche (and Maddy'd rinsed the wretched frog and put him outside by the courtyard pond), she'd been surprised at how much time had passed since she'd hung up with Marc.

Now she was drumming her fingers on the steering wheel, playing over in her mind how she would tell her brother about the stunt Daddy'd pulled with the frog in the sugar bowl, so that Marc could have a laugh, too. He'd throw back his head and have a big old laugh. For some reason, it seemed ever so important to rehearse this scene in her mind, to see her brother throw back his head and have his big old laugh. With that image she could squash that strange trickle of dread that had seeped beneath the phone conversation. That odd crimp in his voice.

"You sure you're all right?" she'd asked.

"It's fine. Just fine."

Fine. She would pretend to believe everything was fine. She'd stay overnight and they'd have a nice, long visit.

❧

SHE PULLED INTO THE drive as the sun was shooting slants across the bayou, bending with the golden reeds in the Gulf wind. Even before she switched off the truck's motor she could hear Marc's radio blaring from inside the tiny cottage. She made her way up the steps to the front door, under the hip roof above the porch.

She hesitated, looking back over her shoulder. Nothing behind her but a spread of bayou. Muffled, booming music came from within the house, so loud she couldn't even hear the creak of the porch swing as it fidgeted beside her in the breeze.

She knocked on the door.

She waited.

She knocked again, then opened it.

"Marc?" she called, but her voice was swallowed by the music and the blackness within.

The only glow came from the back, where the bathroom sat opposite the kitchen. She groped for a light switch or radio switch and found the latter first, and suddenly there was silence. And in this newfound quiet, visibility also improved, as if the radio had not only monopolized her ears but also her eyes.

From the bathroom, she could hear the sound of the tub filling.

"Marc? You there? Daddy got me good!"

She picked her way over dark shapes of odds and ends now visible all over the floor.

"You're gonna have to help me think of a way to get even. That sneak put a frog in my—good gracious, baby, when was the last time you cleaned up?"

She reached the kitchen and waved her fingertips along the wall until she found the light switch. "Marc? Did you hear me? I had to dump out all that sugar!"

The light came on with a click of her fingers.

Beyond the windowsill, blackbirds called in alarm. Maddy blinked at the kitchen, trying to untangle her mind from what she saw. Piles of papers were lying strewn about; it looked like the library after the hurricane: records, books, newsprint. Most of it seemed old, and none of it had been treated with respect. A quilt sat folded on the stove. Dirty dishes littered the sink and cemented themselves to the papers, and caterpillars of mold floated in coffee mugs and open cans

of potted spaghetti. She picked up the nearest slip of something—
what looked like an old will—and saw her surname written time and
again:

Chloe LeBlanc.

Rémi LeBlanc.

Patrice LeBlanc.

She wondered who all those people were. Relatives, obviously, but
beyond her grandparents she knew little of her ancestry. Marc must
have hauled all this stuff down from the attic. She folded the will and
looked at the counter, spotting one of the names, Chloe LeBlanc,
penciled in Marc's hand on the back of a torn envelope. He'd also
written an address and phone number, along with yesterday's date
and the letters "LM," Marc's notation for "left message."

The name Chloe sounded familiar. Some distant relation, Maddy
was sure, but she couldn't place exactly where she'd heard it.

"Marc!" she called, louder this time, still scrutinizing the paper as
she walked to the bathroom. She lifted her hand to rap on the door,
but stopped when she heard a splash at her sandals and felt tepid water
between her toes. She looked down.

A broad, half-inch-deep wave was stealing from the bathroom to
the floorboards of the kitchen.

Her pulse began to buzz. Her breathing grew shallow, lips part-
ing, and her mind finally pulled a curtain to the obvious: Something
was very wrong.

She swung the bathroom door wide. No sign of Marc.

Crystal sickles of water were leaking over the rim of the tub. She
took a tremulous step, stretching her chin to see inside. A small part
of herself, the part that liked to jab needles of panic, half-expected to
find him lying under the surface.

But no, the tub was too small. And yet she did see something. She
saw her brother's tools: a screwdriver, a stud finder, a level, other things.
Even coils of wire. All heaped in dark reefs under clear ripples.

"*Sacrebleu,*" she breathed.

She lunged for the faucet, turning it off and then sidling backward
with her wrists pinned to her chest. Rushing bathwater disappeared

to the gurgle of the overflow drain. Her jaw muscle seized. The water could not have been flowing very long. Probably made its first spill as she'd entered the kitchen.

She searched the house, flipping on lights in every room. In the bedrooms, blankets had been draped over the curtains as if guarding against the possibility that any light might filter through. She regarded the paper still clutched in her hand, the LeBlanc will, and returned to the kitchen. Beyond the sill, blackbirds ruffled their feathers to hasten the end of daylight.

She paused, not sure what to do, and lifted the scrap of envelope that bore Chloe LeBlanc's name. As she did, something rolled out from beneath it. It wobbled off the counter and Madeleine tried to catch it before she even realized what it was, but she fumbled and it dropped. She reached down to pick it up. But when she saw it, her legs grew weak, her knees softening under her. She sank to the floor.

A shotgun shell.

She stared, wiping her hand as if she'd been petting a rat. Her mind cramped over this thing on the floor, its tarnished brass tip the same color as the wood boards beneath it. That it had no more business lying there than a green plastic cigar. That it was not locked away in the closet.

"Marc?"

She closed her eyes, and when she did, she saw herself as she was, kneeling on the kitchen floor of the Creole cottage. But she saw her brother too. His silhouette approached her silently from behind. And in his arms he carried—

She stopped breathing. She didn't dare open her eyes.

She saw a glistening trail down his cheek. Tears. She watched him raise the shotgun.

She squeezed her eyes tighter and buried her face in her hands. She could feel him. Could hear the heart of her brother reaching for her. See the gun form a plane beginning at his shoulder and tapering to an end at her own skull.

Still kneeling, she curled in tighter, her breath frozen. Waiting.

The blackbirds flew from their bough near the window.

She opened her eyes, turning to look over her shoulder and seeing no one there.

And then she saw the front door that still gaped, where those sideways reeds of golden light had already diffused to gray. The setting sun now offered no color, no shadow; only a withdrawal of light.

His presence lingered. She felt his need to turn the gun on himself—and his need to kill her. And his desperate, abject loneliness.

He was out there. Not in this house. Outside somewhere in Bayou Black.

She twisted to her feet, her legs sluggish as she made her way to the door. Gripping the jamb, she could see that the tiny skiff was not tethered at the boat slip. She trotted across the St. Augustine grass to the bank. The bayou stretched in a broad mirror, reflecting double-ended trees already turning black. No boat nearby. Not on the water, not at the slip. The nearest craft would be at the neighbors' place, the Thibodaux who ran the café.

She strode and then jogged the half-mile to their property, and pounded on their door. An evensong of frogs and crickets was just beginning to pulse.

"Thibby! Nida!" Maddy called.

She pressed the heels of her hands to her forehead. The yard was still but for the intermittent blaze of a firefly. Nida's old white Caddy was gone, which meant they weren't home. But Madeleine knew where Thibby kept the keys to his skiff.

She retrieved them, hands stupid and fumbling, and it occurred to her that she should have called Sheriff Cavanaugh for help. Too late now. She broke into an all-out run, feet quickening across crabgrass and then thumping over the dock. She climbed into the skiff, and as she untied the knot a snake unwound itself from the coil of rope and darted across to the other side, disappearing soundlessly into the bayou mirror.

It's their time now.

She and Marc had always associated the snakes with twilight. She

pulled the starter cord and moved the skiff into the bayou, remembering how she and Marc used to play with their friend Zenon who'd
lived nearby. The children ruled the daylight, fishing or swimming in
the steaming afternoons while the serpents coiled themselves into
lazy piles on rocks, storing up reserved heat so they could hunt in the
evening. When full darkness fell, the alligators would rule Bayou
Black. But that in-between time, that colorless screen that wasn't day
and was not yet night, that belonged to the snakes.

The skiff rumbled through the smaller artery and turned into the
broad shipping channel. Thibby's vessel was fast, but it still nodded
through the swamplands with agonizing lethargy. It slurped and
coughed, and finally rounded the bend and down a narrow waterway, and then an even narrower one.

Gray receded, allowing black to steal forth, and Madeleine snapped
on the guide light. She knew where to find her brother. Perhaps when
he saw her, Marc would lay that thing down and shake off whatever
fog had consumed him, a fog that had in some way woven tendrils into
her own lungs, enough to convince her that her brother was out here,
in their secret cove of Bayou Black. He was lying in wait for her, waiting to die.

The skiff entered their old secret burrow within the cypress forest. She switched off the light. Better in the dark. Her brother was
there. Her dear, sweet brother. She knew he was waiting for her.

She made a final turn. And she wanted to be wrong. God, how
she wanted to be wrong, and wished for the comfort of that joke,
that stupid joke she'd played on herself as she'd driven to Houma.
Pretending she could make him laugh, throw back his head and have
a big old laugh. That she herself might fall for the ridiculous joke that
he was fine.

Crack!

She felt him now in an orange burst. Felt his fear and anguish and
fury, all reaching out to her in a moment of monstrous ecstasy. The
darkness stole in around her, and eyes of the swamp creatures flashed
in slivers of moon.

She touched her hair, expecting to find blood. But no; she was unharmed. She switched on the light.

He was there. His boot and leg were still tangled in the skiff, but the rest of him hung over the side, suspended upside down in the water. Lying in wait, but no longer waiting to die.

three

HAHNVILLE, 1912

RÉMI WHITTLED ON A length of hickory and breathed the wet wind from the river. Jacob sat next to him. The gallery wrapped around the entire perimeter of the plantation house, a shelter of mortise and tenon trusses extending from the roof. The design served necessity over vanity, admitting the breeze from the Mississippi while keeping out the rain. From the rails of the gallery, Rémi could see the river, rows of sugarcane, and all the workers of Terrefleurs.

"*Il va pleuvoir,*" he said as he dragged his knife along the wood, pulling a long thin curl, then revised, "*Mais non,* I'll say it in English: It will rain."

Jacob took a sip of cherry bounce. "Now how in the hell am I ever gonna learn French if y'all insist on speaking English?"

"My friend, you will never speak French. You are too thick in the head. At Terrefleurs, we speak only English now."

"You just switchin because of my pretty little sister." Jacob offered a wink. "She always gets her way with you." He paused and eyed Rémi. "You know, I been meanin to say, I'm sorry about Mama."

Rémi shrugged. At the wedding reception, he had overheard Mrs. Chapman refer to Rémi's family as Creole savages.

Jacob sighed. "I just wanted you to know I'm glad you're part of the family now. I guess we all must seem kinda arrogant to you."

Rémi smiled. "I understand how it is. As Creoles, we have our ways, and your parents are not used to it. But with each generation, our differences get smaller and smaller."

"I s'pose eventually we won't be able to tell who's who."

The air hung thick. The sky shone in a hazy light blue and the evening sun illuminated the yellow paint of the gallery, but rain was coming. The two men sipped their drinks, Tatie Bernadette's home-made cherry bounce. And as the breeze escalated, Tatie's voice rippled from inside as she instructed the other servants to close the shutters. Rémi watched the workers of the field swinging their cane knives in time to the line boss' cadence.

"Seem like they're moving faster than usual out there today," Jacob said.

"They're excited. It's almost *roulaison,* the celebration at the end of cutting season."

"Roolay-who?"

"*Roulaison.* The people have worked hard. We'll have a big feast. They'll make hot punch of boiled cane juice and brandy."

"Sounds like my kind of tradition."

Rémi eyed him. "If you had planted cane this season, you could celebrate your own harvest."

Jacob shrugged. "I know, I know."

"If you're not going to plant, you might as well pull out altogether."

"We're gonna plant. I know you have a lot of your own assets tied up in helping us get started. We'll get around to it."

Rémi said, "I just think you should either plant or not plant. I don't know what you're waiting for. And to tell the truth, I say forget about sugarcane. It's too demanding. Even the Americans know this. They don't call it 'growing cane,' they say, 'raising cane.'"

"No, you got it all wrong. You're quotin the Bible there. It's 'raising

Cain,' as in Cain and Abel, not sugarcane. Cain was the bad seed. So
when we say 'raising Cain,' we mean raising hell."

Rémi nodded, smiling. "Yes, it's true, just as it says in the Bible.
And raising cane is the same as raising Cain."

The door to the ladies' parlor opened, and Helen emerged with
her servant, Chloe. Helen stood slender and handsome, pale-skinned
with soft black hair and clear green eyes. Chloe's wide eyes shone
from the black skin of her face, her body more skinny than slender,
her dress overworn. She carried a silver tray with a fresh carafe of
cherry bounce.

"There's my little sister," Jacob said, and he rose to kiss Helen.

Chloe set the carafe on the round wooden table without pouring. She raised her head and sniffed the air, but her gaze did not lift
toward the clouds amassing in the west. She looked instead toward
the eastern well, and as she turned her head, her dress moved to
reveal a scar at her shoulder, a long, pale zipper across her African
skin.

She had appeared at the plantation a few years ago, half-starved and
looking for work. She'd spoken only Creole. Rémi never asked about
where she came from. He set aside his whittling and brushed off his
hands.

"It's so good to see you, Jacob," Helen said as she embraced her
brother. "You'll stay for supper, won't you?"

"No honey, I gotta get back. I was just passing through and wanted
to welcome y'all home from your honeymoon." He kissed her cheek
again and turned to Rémi, shaking his hand. "Take good care of my
little sister, now, you hear?"

Jacob descended the steps, and Rémi noticed that Chloe's gaze
measured Jacob with distaste as he joined his driver by his motorcar.
For one who'd appeared from nowhere, desperate and hungry, Chloe
was not terribly deferential. A good thing, as Rémi saw it; he preferred to know the minds of those in his employ. Rémi and Helen
waved at Jacob and watched the vehicle disappear through the allée
of pecan trees.

"You are so thin, *chérie*." Rémi said as he slipped his arm around his bride's waist. "No one would even know that you are carrying my child."

He nestled his face to her neck and breathed the warmth of her skin, his knuckle gently brushing her belly.

She pushed him away. "You prefer that I were fat?"

"I wish you to be healthy, and our child to be healthy."

"All right then." She patted his cheek.

"*Eau de cerise, monsieur?*" Chloe was staring at him, her cheekbones forming chevrons in the waning sunlight.

"English, please Chloe," Rémi said. "Remember at Terrefleurs we speak English now, in honor of our new mistress. And no, I have had my share. See to Tatie Bernadette."

She paused for a moment, then retreated around to the rear gallery where he heard her open the pantry door.

Helen lifted her face toward Rémi. "By the way I meant to tell you, I'm going to have the house painted."

Rémi glanced at the outer wall in surprise. The paint was in good condition, glowing in shades of gold and coral with a red roof and teal trim.

"It's going to be painted *white,*" Helen added.

"White? But *chérie*, we've always painted the house in bright colors."

"Creole colors. You said you are ready to behave like an American. And the American houses are white."

"You use my words against me."

He stepped away from her. Perhaps the time had come to impose limits on this American homogenization.

"You are worried that our child will grow to be a Creole savage," he said.

"Now who's using words against whom? It was never I who said that!"

Her black hair shone in a clean knot at her neck. Rémi imagined how he would like to free that knot, and watch those black waves spill about her shoulders. He reached for her hand, but she pulled away and turned her face toward the river. Even out on the gallery with no one around, Helen behaved as a proper lady.

Rémi smiled. He did not mind, because he would visit her later in her parlor, in the lantern glow of night, and she would not feel compelled to be such a lady.

"Ah, well," he said. "Maybe white walls are a nice change."

The sun began to set, bringing the golden gallery to a crescendo of brilliant orange. On the horizon, a flash in the charcoal-smudged sky. Clouds channeled in from the south, and with them came the sound of thunder.

four

I GUESS YOU'RE CHLOE, then?" Madeleine said, because the old woman had still not offered her name even though Madeleine had introduced herself. "Chloe LeBlanc?"

The Victorian drawing room on Toulouse Street smelled of rot and had not undergone much restoration after the hurricane. Madeleine felt Mrs. LeBlanc's stare lingering over her blue eyes and black skin. A typical reaction, but she hadn't expected it from her own great-grandmother, stranger or not.

Mrs. LeBlanc herself seemed of purer African blood; no hint of Caucasian. With dark eyes and mottled coffee skin, the only lightness about her was in her startled-looking gray hair.

"I am one hundred and fourteen years old," the old woman replied, as if that said it all.

Madeleine gaped at the suddenness and weight of her announcement. A hundred and fourteen years. Madeleine wasn't sure she believed it. The old woman's helper, an albino black man with yellowed hair and pale skin, nodded confirmation. He settled Chloe into her seat and then abandoned them, leaving Madeleine alone with her.

Madeleine said, "A hundred and fourteen years? That's quite an achievement."

Mrs. LeBlanc nodded. If this really was her age, she was getting along remarkably well. Perhaps remarkable wasn't the word. Unsettling, more like. Madeleine decided not to believe it. They looked at one other. Madeleine shifted and regarded the sagging drapes that probably hadn't been replaced—nor drawn, nor opened, for that matter—in half a century. If she were to touch them she guessed they'd vaporize in a shimmer of dust.

"Well. The reason I wanted to meet you is—"

"I know why you're here," Mrs. LeBlanc snapped.

"You do?"

"You are Dr. Madeleine LeBlanc, my great-granddaughter. Your father is hounded by a river devil." Mrs. LeBlanc lifted a sparsely whiskered chin. "Now you have come to find out about me, eh?"

Madeleine's jaw dropped. "You already know, then?" She blinked, groping for understanding. "You know, I think I've seen you before. Around town. How long have you known I was your great-granddaughter?"

"I was notified the day each of you were born. Marc Gilbert was named for one of my sons."

Hearing this woman speak Marc's name sent a wave of shock through Madeleine's spine. Though it had only been weeks, it felt like a thousand years had passed since Madeleine had found Marc's body in Bayou Black. She recalled sharing couche-couche with Daddy and his friend, Ethan, not realizing her life was about to change.

"Marc is dead. Just recently. He killed—out on Bayou Black, he, he committed . . ." Madeleine's voice trailed off.

Mrs. LeBlanc gave a very small nod. Apparently she already knew about this too.

Madeleine's blood rose. She recalled the times she had glimpsed this shadowed old woman around New Orleans—at her grandmother's funeral, or when her father was first incarcerated—and she'd thought nothing of it. The same strangers on the street of the same neighborhood of the same town.

But the whole time, Chloe LeBlanc knew I was her great-granddaughter. And she never once spoke to me.

"Well, great-grandmother," Madeleine said, opening her hands. "I'm surprised. I never even knew you existed until a few weeks ago. I found some reference to you among my brother's things and thought I'd found a missing piece of my life. But here you knew about me and Marc all along." Her voice took a sarcastic edge. "All this time we could have been baking *cookies* and going for *walks in the park!*"

Chloe smiled, and in it a hint that perhaps Madeleine's anger was what she sought. "I do not think we would have done that, Madeleine. My daughters wanted nothing to do with me, nor did they want their children to have anything to do with me."

Madeleine folded her hands. "I see."

Chloe continued: "But I had an attendant who would go out to Houma and look in on you, and report back to me. I knew all about the three of you, from the time you were born until now."

Madeleine stared at her, absorbing that Chloe LeBlanc had just admitted to spying. The strangeness of the situation settled over her as if it lived within the very dust of the drawing room.

"Wait a minute," Madeleine said. "When Marc and I were kids, our mother abandoned us. And Daddy—" She waved her hand. "He was just *gone*. He suffers from schizophrenia and is prone to just wander off. Marc and I were basically left alone to raise *ourselves*."

Chloe nodded.

"Oh, of course," Madeleine said, her voice growing acidic. "Excuse me for repeating myself. You knew that too. You had *an attendant* looking in on us. May I ask, did it ever occur to you to intervene? Like when Marc and I were spooning mustard out of a jar because that's all we had to eat?"

Chloe's face did not change expression. "You each got along, and you're stronger for it. If you had been pampered and coddled while you were growing up you would never have survived all this. Look at yourself, Madeleine. They rely on you. You're able to stand alone. You can do that because you are strong."

"My brother most certainly did not survive. He went out to the bayou and put a shotgun in his mouth."

Laughter echoed from beyond the hall. Madeleine turned toward the sound, aware that her own throat felt like clay. She saw the albino black man watching through a reflection in the hall mirror. He looked away quickly and disappeared down the corridor. But his face was serious; he hadn't been the one laughing. The laughter sounded like a little girl's voice. Eavesdropping, tittering. Something about that voice gave Madeleine a chill of déjà vu.

Suddenly she had to get out of this place. Away from these people. She grabbed her bag as if to leave, but her hand trembled. Speaking Marc's name had caused a weakness in her legs. Despite herself, she remained fixed in her chair.

"You say my father is hounded by a kind of devil. Well you're wrong. Over the years he's come to handle his condition with dignity, and I'm proud of him."

The old woman replied with a thin sneer. "My husband had a river devil, and it drove him mad. It turned him into a puppet. For your father it is the same, Madeleine."

"I beg to differ, Mrs. LeBlanc," Madeleine said through clenched teeth. "I made psychology my life, and have been studying since I was eighteen years old. We have medications nowadays. Hospitals, support systems. Loved ones who *pull together.* Not relatives who spy on their own family!"

Chloe sat rigid.

Madeleine's anger crumbled to resignation, and she rose from the stiff drawing room chair. "Well, Mrs. LeBlanc, I think I've taken up enough of your time."

She turned and strode for the door just as her eyes began to glisten. Didn't want the old woman to see her tears.

Chloe said, "You can tell your father *you* came to see *me,* eh? I did not come for you!"

Madeleine shook her head as she reached for the door.

"Wait, Madeleine."

Mrs. LeBlanc wrested herself from her chair, and as Madeleine turned and saw her, she fought the urge to take that frail arm and help her up.

"It was for your own good. You had to be strong." Her eyes glittered black from her gnarled oak body. "Don't coddle your father. Get rid of his pills. He's no use to us as a *somnambule.*"

"No use to us as a sleepwalker? Who is *us*?"

"You waste your time with your studies and hearings. Just to keep him in his box."

And then Madeleine's voice escaped her, realizing that this bitter crone knew about the testimony in D.C. as well, the vie for funding. Chloe had invested an awful lot of energy into her spying. It made Madeleine want to go home and draw the curtains. A burning radiated from Chloe LeBlanc, an intensity that belied her age. Madeleine tried to discern whether it came from anger, or fear, or madness. Or something else.

"Who are you, exactly?" Madeleine asked.

"*Je suis seulement t'arrière-grand-mère,*" the old woman replied.

Madeleine's throat constricted upon hearing the French words for "great-grandmother." It made her long for her *mémée,* her grandmother. Hard to imagine that warm, gentle Mémée had been the daughter of this woman. Mémée had once taught her how to tie dolls out of corn husks. She passed away when Madeleine was still a little girl.

Madeleine said, "With Marc gone, I thought Daddy was all I had left. When I found out I had a great-grandmother, I came here looking for answers. Maybe even . . ."

Madeleine swallowed. She did not finish the words: a family. Instead, she lifted her chin and willed the emotion from her voice.

"I don't know why my brother did what he did. I came here thinking maybe you knew something that could shed light on all this. Because he'd tried to call you the day before and . . . Whatever was going on with Marc, I assure you, I'm going to find out."

A shadow flickered across Chloe's face, and her demeanor changed. "Madeleine, *ma p'tite,* but I want to find out too. I will help you in this."

Madeleine took a step backward, her heel grazing the door. Chloe raised her knuckles to Madeleine's hand. Not a motherly touch, more like a merchant offering a bargain.

Her eyes shone. "We begin from nothing. There is no past. You learn me and I learn you, and together we seek to understand, yanh?"

Madeleine stiffened. Her gut told her to walk out backward. Erase having fixated on a few scraps of paper that her brother had left behind, this dubious trail that had led her to Chloe. The old woman was too angry, too removed. Too . . . something. How could she possibly be of help?

But a cobweb settled over Madeleine's mind, a fragile silken thread that tugged at her, pulling her toward Chloe. After all, the request seemed so simple and clean. Innocent even.

Let her in.

The faintest tug. It almost seemed like a thought outside her own mind.

"All right," Madeleine said, and even as she uttered the words her heart sent forth a bloom of hope. "We'll start fresh from nothing. And we'll find out what went wrong with Marc."

five

*T*HE MAN IN THE video was, unquestionably, a lunatic.

Madeleine's hands were damp as she scanned ahead, making sure all the stops were in place. On the small monitor, the subject grew agitated and paced the room, making threats. He had been placed in treatment against his will, a danger to himself and to others.

That marked the first stopping point in the video. Here she would say a little something about that day two years ago when it had been filmed, and then she'd move on.

As the next frames advanced, the object of the lunatic's agitation became clearly visible: Madeleine. First Madeleine, then some unseen tormentor. The video showed the subject lunging at her. She had shoved her hands deep within her lab coat at that point, and did not bring them up to protect herself. She did not cringe. Instead, the video showed how she turned to the side and leaned back. She had known the orderlies would restrain him, and they did. She had been certain he could not harm her.

Another stopping point in the video.

"Twenty minutes, Dr. LeBlanc," an aide said, and Madeleine jumped.

"OK," she murmured, but the aide was already walking away.

Her stomach rolled. *It's just a few words. Make the introduction, explain the video, then hand over the microphone.* The back of her hand went to her forehead.

The aide paused and looked over his shoulder, then joined Madeleine where she hovered over her laptop. "You OK, Dr. LeBlanc?"

"Just a little stage fright."

"Don't worry. Mr. LeBlanc will do most of the talking."

Calling him "Mr. LeBlanc" sounded strange. In New Orleans, everyone called him Daddy Blank. The "daddy" part was natural because of his fatherly way with people, but they called him "blank" because of the last name, and also because his madness often caused him to "blank out."

The aide moved on.

The door to the screening room opened and Madeleine looked out into the federal amphitheater, then gave a start. Sitting among the onlookers, hand on her cane, was Chloe LeBlanc.

They'd spoken twice since that strange initial meeting, and Chloe hadn't expressed any intention of coming all the way to Washington, D.C. for this. As the door swung shut again, Madeleine saw that Chloe was sitting with the houseboy and on the floor by the old woman's knees sat a little blond girl who looked about eight or nine. She wondered whether this was the same child she'd overheard laughing in Chloe's drawing room. The eavesdropper's laughter, bottled in girlish innocence, and yet malicious when Madeleine spoke of her brother's suicide.

Madeleine hoped her father wouldn't notice Chloe's presence until afterward, if he even recognized the old woman at all. When Madeleine had told her father about Chloe LeBlanc, all he'd done was shudder and say, "Keep her away from me. That woman gives me the willies."

Madeleine's gaze darted to where her father stood about six feet away in the screening room. Obviously he hadn't spotted Chloe because he was watching her, his face warm and proud. He winked.

She blushed.

From the time she was a little girl, her father's smile had always given her butterflies. And now he looked so dignified in his three-piece suit, right down to his pocket watch. Another man of the same age might look old with such a thing. But on Daddy Blank it was elegance in full summer bloom. And that's exactly what the congressmen were supposed to see: That lunatic in the video and this dignified gentleman standing before them were one and the same.

Madeleine advanced the video, trying to tune out the low babble from the people, all in suits, milling about the screening room.

She had already been through this video four times over the past half hour. On the tiny screen, the "other" daddy grew more agitated; his feet suspended in midair as he strained against the men holding him. His dark face turned purple. Somewhere off-screen someone was fixing a sedative. Another doctor, not her.

This was the point where her father had broken free. He'd gotten to her in an instant.

Here, now, in the safety of the screening room, Madeleine watched a pixilated image of her own body being knocked to the ground. She could not see whether her hands ever came up in any kind of defensive gesture.

Would he really have killed me if the others hadn't been there?

At the time, she had hoped that some part of him might recognize her, that he could stop himself.

The video ended. She released her breath in a long, slow wave, trying to calm down. This was her shot to help change the way the government and society in general treated mental illness. To help Daddy. He was the only family she had left.

Her father appeared by her elbow, closing his hand over her shoulder with a warm squeeze. "It's fine kitten. Gonna be just fine."

"I know. It's just that we need the funding so badly. As it is I have to fight tooth and nail to keep them from cutting my program."

"Oh, come on now. Why are you so worried about that?"

Madeleine shot him an incredulous look. "Because this country needs it! Because of homelessness, violent crime, and countless other social issues that increased after a single stupid government decision from years ago."

"And what decision was that?" Daddy asked, shoving his hands in his pockets.

"The decision to up-end the mental health facilities and spill sick people out onto the streets."

He was beaming at her. She felt the blush return, because it occurred to her that Daddy hadn't been asking because he didn't know the answers to these questions.

"Thanks. I know you're just helping me refocus," she said.

"Listen honey, you got your head on straight and we're gonna knock this one out of the park."

"OK, you're right. I just don't want to mess this up."

"What's to mess up? We'll just do a little talkin."

She tried a smile. "Fortunately *you'll* do most of the talking."

"You did fine just now."

"That's different," Madeleine said. "Talking to you is a whole lot different from addressing Congress."

"Ain't nothin but a big room full of people, just like you and me." He patted her shoulder again and moved away.

She returned her gaze to the video. Funny how different this sort of thing was from Daddy's perspective. He was charming and loquacious and thought nothing of presenting in public. He had an excellent speech prepared, and his testimony would be about as powerful a speech as the Association for Psychological Discovery could ever hope for. But even with the video, those congressmen couldn't possibly understand the extent of Daddy's affliction. Or how difficult it was to convince a schizophrenic to stay on his meds when they made him sick and swimmy. She hoped the congressmen would be amazed at Daddy Blank's transformation. That they'd appropriate generous funding toward research and psychotropic medications like the ones that had so dramatically stabilized his personality.

"If you run that video one more time, you're liable to wear it out," the aide chided as he approached Madeleine again. "You're on in fifteen minutes."

"Already?" Madeleine glared at her watch, then glanced around the room. "Where's my father?"

The aide glanced at the door. "He ran to the men's room."

Ran to the men's room.

She stared at the door for a long moment. "Could you get him for me please?"

The aide blinked. "I'm sure he'll be right back, Dr. LeBlanc."

Madeleine leveled her gaze on him. "Please."

"Sure, but I told him to be quick. Don't worry, everything will be fine."

That's exactly what her father had told her mere minutes ago: *It's fine, kitten. Gonna be just fine.*

The aide exited through the door and Madeleine once again glimpsed the federal amphitheater. She swallowed, and then stepped through the door out into the vast room beyond. The ceiling soared high, with carved wood adorning every spare handspan above and along the four walls that rimmed the amphitheater. It was too big. Too vast. To address such an audience seemed an impossibility. Her eyes panned the perimeter, and her gaze fell on Chloe. She and her houseboy were sitting side-by-side in the same place where she'd seen them before. No sign of the child. Madeleine searched the other faces, hoping to find Daddy among them. And then she spotted the little girl.

No longer with Chloe, but instead lingering about twenty feet away, partially hidden behind a curtain in a corner of the stage where access should have been restricted. Though the child was mostly obscured, Madeleine could see that her face was smudged as she leered back.

Madeleine frowned and looked away. She groped for a sense of faith in Daddy.

And yet she knew better. Her fingers throbbed, and it felt like the inside of her stomach was sprouting brambles.

It's fine, kitten. Gonna be just fine.

But no, everything was not going to be just fine. She knew better, all right. She saw it on the face of the bewildered aide as he returned alone. Her father had left, and he had no intention of coming back.

~✦~

BATON ROUGE, 2009

ZENON LANSKY WAS SITTING with Josh, but his attention wandered from the radio to his own thoughts and then over to the apartment building and back to his thoughts again. He figured his metabolism stayed so high out of sheer mind-churning. Mostly he was thinking of Marc and Madeleine LeBlanc. The Blank sibs, his long-ago Bayou Black family. Madeleine would be in Washington, D.C. about now, he knew. Marc had left her all alone in this wide world save for her daddy. Funny how the world does you. He wondered whether Marc's suicide had knocked her off her high horse yet.

He lit another cigarette and took a drag, then hung his arm out the driver's side window. The Duster had no air conditioning and the humid Baton Rouge night crowded in close.

Headlights flashed behind them, and for a moment Zenon's gray-blue eyes shone in the rearview mirror, lids hooded in isosceles angles. The car passed and paused in front of an empty parking space along the street.

"You ain't gonna fit in that spot," Zenon said to the car.

The car maneuvered back and forth into the space until the driver gave up and drove off. Zenon and Josh both chuckled.

"You know I sit in that gun shop all damn day watching them people make asses of themselves, trying to park their cars."

Josh chewed on the end of a stick.

Filthy habit, Zenon thought.

He glanced at the flat-roofed apartment building as Radio Tirana rolled through on the shortwave. Albania, that's where he figured the broadcast was coming from. The first step was identifying the country, then the language, then if he could stand the monotony he could sift out a few cognates and get a fix on what they were actually saying.

"Anyways," Zenon was saying, "it's a cryin shame. Take somethin like an alligator, right? Stupid animal. Sloppy pickle with teeth. And yet he can haul his wide ass at thirty miles an hour to snag a hummingbird in flight. A hummingbird! And these fools cain't even parallel park an automobile? Serious! I sit in the gun shop and watch'm all damn day."

Josh chuckled.

Zenon continued, "Yesterday here come this ol' boy. Tried to park in front of the store, I swear to God, took him twenny minutes at least, and he never did get the damn thing parked. He pulled in, came in front ways, not backing up like he's s'posed to. Pulls in, then backs up. Pulls ahead, then backs it up again."

Zenon took a quick drag. "Musta gone back and forth at least ten times, and each time he's just getting fuhther and fuhther away from the curb."

Josh removed the stick from his mouth and laughed, porkpie hat hugging his scalp.

"IQ of a skunk, serious. I mean," Zenon blew out a trail of smoke. "His car end up sitting perpendicular to the damn curb!"

Josh guffawed and wiped a hand over his face. "No shit."

"I shit you not!" Zenon tapped the cigarette and let the ashes fall to the accumulating collection of butts on the pavement below his car door. "Perpendicular to the damn curb. So, you know that guy next door? The barber? Apparently he was watching the whole thing too. He couldn't take it no more and finally he come out there and told the guy to get out of the damn car. Parked it for him."

Both men were quaking with laughter now.

"You have got to be kidding me!" Josh said.

Zenon shook his head. "I swear to God. I think that barber figured the guy was gonna come in for a haircut. He didn't though." Zenon grinned. "He come into my store instead."

Josh whooped. "Oh man! He wanna buy a gun?"

"Oh yeah. He come on in, little bitty bastard, wanted a IAI rifle, standard grade."

"Did you sell it to him?"

"Hell no, I ain't sold it to'm! Like I'm'a sell a rifle to a fool like at. Anyways, his license wudn't any good. People like that can't be allowed to carry weapons."

"Yeah, no shit."

They sat quietly for a minute, then Zenon said, "That's what I'm talking about. You got some damned fool runnin around, can't even park his own car, come inna my store and wantna buy a damn rifle." He waved his hand at the apartment building. "We ought to be sitting outside *his* house right now, insteada here."

Josh shook his head. "Come on now."

The two men slipped back into silence.

Radio Tirana droned on. *Albanian, yeah. Definitely Albanian.*

The Latin-based languages were easier to figure out. Zenon had started with French because he already spoke some from the bayou, and then Spanish because that was common enough and lots of Mexicans lived in the area. But then he was fooling around and came across a station where they were speaking Farsi. And on another day, Serbo-Croatian. He'd listen in whenever he was stuck doing something mindless, like this stake-out. He never spoke any of those languages, but came to understand them easily.

Up the block, a bobtail cat moved into a pool of orange light under a street lamp. It continued at a trot until its shadow stretched long to rejoin the darkness.

Zenon cabled his mind to the cat. *Stop. Back to the streetlight.*

After a few moments, it appeared again, its silhouette distorted at the rim of shadows. It took another step toward the inner circle of light, moving slowly and with intermittent hesitation.

Come closer.

The cat looked to the left and dipped its head. It took three more hesitant steps forward before it turned and galloped for cover.

Josh said, "Good. You're getting better. Keep at it."

No street lamps glowed near Zenon and Josh. The Duster sat in relative darkness, with just enough faraway illumination to highlight ropey veins in Zenon's arm. He blew a stream of smoke out into the thick, warm air, half-expecting it to coagulate into a solid mesh when it mixed with the humidity. His face beaded with perspiration that would not evaporate.

He stole a glance at Josh. No perspiration on *his* face. Never was.

"You hot?"

Josh shrugged. "It's hot in here."

"Yeah, I know it's hot in here. *I'm* hotter'n hell. But are *you* hot?"

Josh shrugged again. "I guess. Quit givin me shit."

In the apartment building beyond, the window filled with blue light from a television, and Angel came into view.

Her long straight hair swung at her shoulders as she maneuvered through her living room. The television reflected against her skin, framing her silhouette as she passed in front of it. She poured water over plants at the sill. And though she stood right in front of the window, she did not look out. Wouldn't have seen them anyway. All the curtains stood open, even in her bedroom. The sheer fabric danced with the warm night breeze. She wore only a white button-down and panties.

"Look at that," Josh said. "Half-nekked in front of an open window. Not a lick of common sense."

Zenon shook his head.

"This one'll be easy," Josh said.

Zenon watched the figure moving inside the room beyond the windows. "I'm serious, man. I'm thinking there are better choices than this."

Josh sighed.

Zenon was not going to be put off. "I can think of about a hundred people I'd like to see go down. The governor. Hell, the moonies. Hebetudes like that fucker who cain't park."

He waved a hand at the building. "I don't even know who this woman is. I don't see why *I* shouldn't pick the mark this time."

"Zenon," Josh said, lifting his hand. "It ain't like drawing straws. She's one of them. A big one. This one's important."

"Hell on a mother." Zenon clenched his lips, his right hand working into a fist.

Josh said, "Listen, brother, you gotta carry this out according to the plan. You go out there like a cowboy picking off people you don't like, you're just some random weirdo." Josh paused, tilting his head. "And I don't got your back no more. You gotta be cool."

Zenon fell silent.

"Look man," Josh said. "I mean it, be cool. You do what I say and no one can touch you. It's for your own good. Have I steered you wrong yet?"

Zenon cut his eyes toward the street.

"No," he finally said. "You done me right."

"All right then, brother. We cool?"

"Yeah, brother, we cool."

"Good." Josh looked up at the window, then back at Zenon. "Let's get this started."

s i x

OMETIME DURING THE NIGHT, a knock at the front door startled Rémi from sleep. Before he was even fully awake his mind registered that it had to be Jacob out there. In Creole tradition, men entered a house through the men's parlor; ladies through the ladies' parlor. The only ones who used the front door were Americans and dogs. Rémi smiled, rubbing his eyes. Perhaps the Americans weren't the only ones capable of a little cultural arrogance.

Rémi sat up suddenly, emerging from the sleep fog, realizing that a knock at this hour meant something was wrong. He heard rain hammering at the tin roof above.

He donned his pants and shirt, and could hear Tatie Bernadette opening the front door. Through the thick walls of his room, he caught Jacob's voice and the muffled word "levee." A chill ran down Rémi's back. Two levees existed in this part of River Road; one across and upriver near Glory, his in-laws' plantation, and one that bordered the river here at Terrefleurs. Rémi hastily pulled on his boots and coat, and stepped outside onto the gallery. Even under the protection of the extended roof the soaking wind tore at him.

Jacob Chapman turned toward Rémi and grabbed his elbow, shouting above the buffeting gusts: "The river's gonna crest at Crow's Landing! We need every man!"

Rémi jerked his head toward the pecan allée behind the house. "Come!"

He and Jacob turned and raced toward the field workers' cottages, though Rémi felt relief knowing the levee at Crow's Landing bordered Glory, not Terrefleurs. He had personally supervised the renovation of the Terrefleurs levee, building it higher and stronger than any other in this part of the lower Mississippi. If there had to be a weak spot, let it not be at his home.

He had cautioned his in-laws to do the same when they first purchased Glory Plantation, but the Chapmans preferred to rely on the Army Corps of Engineers, refusing to invest their own funds in, as they phrased it, "the government's burden." He glanced at Jacob and noted that his felt hat had become something of a downspout, with water shearing down the center. High time his brother-in-law broke in that hat.

He roused Francois from sleep and returned to the main house with Jacob to fetch some lanterns, while Francois summoned the able-bodied men of the plantation. Rémi found Helen in her night clothes worrying on the gallery.

"Don't fret, *ma chère*," he told her. "We will bolster your parents' levee."

He led her back to her parlor door and saw her inside. And then he and Jacob pushed against the wind to the barn, and rode into the tempestuous night.

AT CROW'S LANDING, THE Glory field workers were already toiling, filling sandbags and heaving them up the mound. They waded through ankle-deep water in the rain and darkness. Elrod Chapman, Rémi's father-in-law, greeted Rémi and saw to his mare. Rémi dismounted and climbed to the top where, in the flickering glow of the lantern, he saw the water roiling a scant two feet from the crest.

"Mon dieu." He turned to work alongside the others.

Jacob and his hired hand, still atop their horses, exchanged awkward glances before following Rémi's lead.

It occurred to Rémi that perhaps the two had not intended to actually participate in the work to be done here. He shook his head and bent his back to the task.

seven

NEW ORLEANS, 2009

ADELEINE SHOOED JASMINE OUT of the truck and walked up Magazine Street to the old warehouse. Magnolia blossoms loomed heavily in the trees, and the heat caused man and beast alike to move slowly. Even Jasmine trotted at half her usual pace.

Madeleine's stomach was still knotted with anger and worry over her father, whom she hadn't seen or heard from in the weeks since he'd left her twisting in the wind in D.C. She'd had to take his place at the podium and testify alone before the House Ways and Means Committee. And God, how she'd swayed and stammered. She would never forget the feeling of cold sweaty knees in her pantyhose, and how every time she moved her arms a puff of hot, moist air erupted from the inside of her suit jacket. In the end, some money had been appropriated, but the amount was drastically lower than the Association had anticipated. This meant that the Department of Psychology at Tulane would receive nothing, and that the cognitive schizophrenia project was at serious risk for getting cut.

Madeleine hoped Daddy Blank had made his own way home to

New Orleans by now, but she couldn't be certain. He carried no cell phone, and the chances that he'd be taking his medication were pretty slim.

The bells jingled on the door as Madeleine entered the flower shop in the old brick warehouse. Jasmine saw Vinny already seated in the wicker chair, and she danced in place until Madeleine unhooked her from her leash. The little terrier vaulted into Vinny's lap.

Vinny grinned and dragged his hand through her wiry hair. "How ya doin, Jazz darlin."

Madeleine had been leasing the space inside the old brick warehouse to Samantha's Flowers for years. So many of these same flowers had arrived with notes of sympathy when Marc passed; among them, a breathtaking delivery from Ethan Manderleigh.

Near the wicker chairs, the broad farmhouse table stretched like an altar adorned with offerings of the day: the last of the marigolds and snapdragons and the season's first crop of mums. Azaleas burst from one of the racks behind the little sofa, framing Vinny's mammoth shoulders in brilliant pinks and whites. He still wore his policeman's uniform and looked like he had come straight from the graveyard shift. His muscles stretched against his shirt with skin so black it almost looked purple, and his massive, dark form loomed over Jasmine's tiny white body. When he petted her, she all but disappeared under his hands.

Samantha appeared with the percolator in one hand and a pack of cigarettes in the other.

She nodded at them, placing the cigarettes on the table, and then put her hand to her hip. "Maddy, you're wearing your shoulders for earrings again."

"What? Oh, got a bit of a headache." Madeleine forced her shoulders down though she didn't actually relax them.

"Another one?" Sam said.

Madeleine shrugged. If Daddy didn't turn up soon she'd have shoulders like a linebacker.

"Hey Vinny," Sam said as she poured coffee and then rested the percolator on the farmhouse table. "I read there was a shooting in Iberville Friday night. Were you there?"

He sighed and rubbed his face, shaking his head. "Yeah, that was a awful thing."

Madeleine sank to a wicker chair and filled her own mug. "What happened?"

"Well, you know about the Walkers' drug ring in Iberville?"

They nodded. Iberville was one of the post-hurricane ghettos that had survived, and the Walkers had emerged as one of the most notorious crime families in the area. Madeleine knew their reach all too well. The addicts landed under her care, but more poignantly, Daddy Blank had a habit of scoring heroin from the Walkers.

Vinny continued. "Ever since Jerome Walker was killed 'bout six months ago, there been all kinda trouble in Iberville. Everybody wanna take his place, be the leader and get the biggest cut of the business. So on Friday night, everything come to a head."

He rubbed his closely shaved scalp. "The gangbangers who been battling for the top slot decided to settle things once and for all. By the time it was over, we had six dead bodies. One of'm an eleven-year-old kid."

Madeleine shook her head.

"So who ended up being the last man standing?" Sam asked.

"A gang led by Carlo Jefferson." Vinny sighed. "I used to play with that boy when we were kids. Then when he was about ten years old, he got caught selling pot out of the parking lot. Guess he's running the show now."

Madeleine nodded, thinking of Carlo Jefferson. Between Daddy's former habits and her own work on the psych unit, she felt she'd had more interaction with Carlo than she needed in a lifetime.

The resident cat of the flower shop, Esmeralda, jumped onto the sofa table behind Vinny's head. Jasmine sniffed at the cat, who in turn swatted her face.

Sam regarded Madeleine with reproach. "Maddy, you were gonna go over to Iberville Friday night when you were out looking for Daddy Blank. You're lucky you didn't get caught in that shoot-out."

"I was worried Daddy might be there. He could be slipping."

"But in Iberville? . . ." But then realization dawned on Sam's face, and she seemed to register the other danger, that Daddy might have resurrected his old appetite for street drugs.

Madeleine said, "I doubt he would have slipped so far as to go back to his old ways. But the fact that he's avoiding me isn't a good sign."

Samantha nodded. "I hear ya, but you shouldn't do that sort of thing alone."

Alone. Madeleine resisted the urge to roll her eyes. Being alone had seemed a necessity. All these years she'd had her hands full building her practice and looking after Daddy and Marc. Now here she was on sabbatical from her job; no Daddy, and no Marc. The irony could turn a river red.

Madeleine turned to Vinny. "Have you seen my father anywhere over the past couple of weeks?"

"No, baby. I ain't seen Daddy Blank, and I ain't heard nothing either."

Her body sagged. She wondered how long before her father slipped into the skin of that other man. That violent man in the video.

The door to the shop flew open and a young, dark-haired Latina bustled in. "Sorry I'm late!" she called, and kept stride to the back room where she disappeared.

Madeleine and Vinny gawked. "Who was that?"

"That's Anita," Sam replied. "She's new."

Madeleine said, "Oh yeah, the new intern."

"Yup." Sam raised her voice in the direction Anita had gone. "She's studying horticulture up in Baton Rouge, but *she spends more time studying the men than the plants!*"

"I heard that!" Anita called back.

Sam and Maddy giggled.

Anita returned, wrapping an apron around her waist, and Sam introduced her around.

"You a police officer?" the girl said to Vinny. "Because I'm thinking of getting a handgun."

The group gaped at this announcement, and Anita laughed.

"I need to protect myself. My dad has me taking this self-defense class, but did you hear about that girl in the news? The one who disappeared?"

"Yeah," Sam said. "Angel Frey. The one in Baton Rouge. They still haven't found her. It's so sad."

Vinny said, "I knew that girl. She used to do volunteer work with mentally handicapped adults. I'd see her at the charity drives. She was cute. Very sweet."

"My dad's got me all paranoid now," Anita said. "I live in La Place but I go to school in Baton Rouge. I'm really thinking about getting a gun."

"Be careful," Vinny said. "Take the training and get the proper permits if you're gonna do that. No need to be in a hurry."

"You ain't gotta tell me twice. The guy who did my self-defense class has a gun shop, and he also does handgun training. And he's so cute!"

Madeleine said, "Wait a minute. I grew up with a guy who runs a gun shop in Baton Rouge. What's your trainer's name?"

"Zenon Lansky."

Madeleine gave a half laugh. "Same guy all right."

BAYOU BLACK, 2009

AMID THE SILVER GLOW of dawn, Zenon untied the rope that tethered the boat to the dock. He turned the motor over and it churned to life. A garish sound against the morning quiet. But it didn't matter because for once, Zenon was alone. He eased into the narrow byway, enjoying the solitude.

The cypress trees towered like buildings on a city street. The bayou was already coming to life. As the morning light grew stronger, the trees would fill with the sounds of birds and the sawing wings of cicadas. He followed the slate path until swamp gave way to marsh, which in turn gave way to open sea, and once again, silence. A remarkable time of day.

He sipped his coffee and savored the cool, heavy air. The trawler continued south until dawn slipped into morning and land fell from sight. At this point he knew he was far enough out, but he pressed on a bit further, if only to enjoy the peaceful moment.

Eventually, he cut the motor and drifted. The only sound came from the water lapping at the sides.

Taking great care, he lifted the long black industrial garbage bag that contained the weighted-down body of Angel Frey, and heaved it over the side. The dark shape receded beneath the surface.

He switched on the shortwave radio, tuning it to the Albanian station.

eight

HAHNVILLE, 1912

*T*HEY HAD LABORED UNTIL dawn, when sluggish gray light had finally illuminated their efforts. Along the wooden basket weave of the levee's edge, Rémi had found conical mud chimneys. Crawfish holes. Like a termite infestation in an old house, they weakened the framework. He had checked the water level again and saw that it had risen two inches. Despite their frantic efforts, the sandbags could only go so far. The higher the makeshift wall had risen, the more stout the base had had to be, and it had seemed as if they were trying to build a mountain from a bag of marbles.

Francois had appeared with a cartload of laborers. Clad in galoshes with their bellies full from cold cornbread and hot coffee that Tatie Bernadette had hastily sent along, the Terrefleurs workers had set upon the levee with fresh vigor. Soon after, the sheriff and deputy had arrived with more men from other plantations. At that point Rémi had actually felt hope.

However, as the hours had slipped by, the river had continued to rise and push against the thin structure with mounting force. Morning had now worn into noon, and Rémi decided to send Francois back to Terrefleurs for more supplies. They needed sandbags, food, and tents. They would remain there through the night.

But before releasing Francois, Rémi leaned over and spoke to him in a low voice, "While you are there, check the levee at Terrefleurs. I want to know how it's holding up."

❧

IN THE AFTERNOON, THE rain stopped, and everyone breathed sighs of relief. Their bodies ached from long hours of exertion and lack of sleep. The workers slackened, resting in wet grass on higher ground, discussing past floods. Rémi heard horse hooves, and was relieved to see Francois returning with the supplies.

"*Ici,*" he called, gesturing toward the least soggy stretch of grass.

Francois eased the cart into place, and Rémi started pulling out crates before Francois had even dismounted. The smell of steaming beans and biscuits caused Rémi's belly to cramp with sudden, almost savage urgency. It occurred to him that Glory Plantation was not sending provisions, and he wondered whether Francois's load would accommodate everyone present. But as he peered into the back of the cart, he saw several more of the same crates. Tatie Bernadette had guessed the situation and sent enough for the entire lot.

The workers formed a food line and all chatter ceased. Rémi looked across the faces of hungry men to Francois, who nodded in acknowledgment. Terrefleurs was safe.

As much as Rémi longed to fill his plate, he waited while the men dished up first. He watched as one by one, they began to consume their meals, and he waited for the line to dwindle. He thought of his wife's servant, Chloe, and how he would have preferred that she might have joined them. Not for labor nor skill in the kitchen, but she had about her a command that rallied others to toil, and her skill in healing could go far in situations such as these, where injuries and ailments prevailed.

He lifted his face toward the heavens, wondering whether the deluge had stopped for good this time. One of the laborers had finished his meal and was already back at work. Rémi joined him. Might as well work—it might take his mind off the smell of food until he would take his turn. But although the rain had indeed stopped, the water continued to rise. The sheriff lingered along the great sandbag berm, speaking in low tones with Elrod Chapman, who then saddled his mare and disappeared into the mist. Rémi did not pause to ask where his father-in-law had gone.

The deputy set off on foot in the direction of Vacherie, most likely to advise evacuation. Finally, the last man had filled his plate, and Rémi took from what was left. Cold and thin now, but enough. He told Francois to go home for the night and return with more supplies in the morning. Soon the sky would grow dark, and they'd have to pitch tents and build fires.

THE RAIN HAD STARTED again during the night.

At daybreak, the workers ate their breakfast, toted in again by Francois and his cart. He discreetly informed Rémi that the Terrefleurs levee was still in no danger, and that all was well at home. Rémi nodded, but silently cursed the Chapmans for not having reinforced the Crow's Landing levee. The water level had risen seven inches during the night as the rain continued to fall.

A few of the workers trudged back to the heap and resumed filling and hauling sandbags. Rémi joined them, working with verve, trying to appear confident. And yet he was on the verge of admitting defeat: With the water continuing to rise, they had little chance of laying enough sandbags to maintain the levee. Already, water streamed from leaks in the weaker joints. Should the levee burst while they were toiling, men could drown. Some of the workers were casting around with anxious eyes, and men from Terrefleurs whispered to each other with wary faces as they stacked the leaden bags.

Jacob Chapman glowered at them and strode to his horse, withdrawing his shotgun. He cocked the weapon, circling the workers.

"You boys better not be thinking about runnin off," Jacob said, and focused a hard stare at the men who had been whispering. "You just keep layin those sandbags and do as you're told."

Rémi stalked to where Jacob stood and gripped the shotgun. He leaned his face in close.

"Put that away!"

Jacob's harsh expression flashed in a burst of lightning, purple veins bulging at his neck. Rémi glared at him. They stared nose to nose while the thunder crackled and the rain streamed over their faces. Jacob's lips were curled in what was surely a precursor to a fight, and Rémi was ready for—even looking forward to—whatever might come.

But suddenly Jacob relented. He slumped, returning the shotgun to his pack, and leaned against his mount with his head lowered.

Rémi regarded the workers. He breathed heavily against his own fury in the wet air, sorry that Jacob had backed down even though he knew a fight would cause more woe than it was worth. He joined his brother-in-law beside the horse.

"I'm sorry, Rémi," Jacob said. "It's just that in Kentucky . . ."

"This is not Kentucky! Where is your father?"

Jacob sighed and squinted in the direction of the river. The sound of moving water was all around them.

"He's with my mother and little sister, down at the train station. They're gonna try to get to higher ground."

Rémi flushed. "At the train station! While his friends and neighbors are trying to save his homestead!"

Jacob lowered his head to a sulk. Rémi's fist was balled, longing to connect with Jacob's cheekbone. But he held steady and instead released a rueful laugh, and put his hand on his brother-in-law's shoulder.

"It does not really matter, *mon frère,* because this levee will not hold. We must get these men away from here."

Jacob closed his mouth and opened it again, but did not speak. Rain dripped from his hat and thickened to drowsy beads at his nose. He drew in a breath and dipped his chin once. Rémi squeezed his shoulder, then returned to the group.

"Allons, c'est fini." Rémi told his men.

Many of the workers from Glory and the other plantations did not speak French, but they recognized the content of Rémi's words, and responded by whisking blankets, tools, and other supplies into the cart. Francois loaded it with the Terrefleurs workers, and they headed back down the sodden road toward home. The sheriff set out on horseback to evacuate people from nearby plantations, and Jacob turned in the direction of the Glory main house. Men from other plantations dispersed, too, moving rapidly along the high ground.

And then the levee broke.

Rémi and four of the Glory men were still standing by. A small gush of water burst from the lower weave of earth and board, and the men erupted with shouts of alarm. Rémi grabbed the reins of his horse and pulled her up the hill as the workers scrabbled to high ground.

From above, the five men watched the wall of sandbags bow outward like a giant bubble, with a groan like a ship that had topsided. And then it gave way in a crumbling outpour.

The lead wave tore into the land. The muddy river followed in a steady crush, flowing in all directions over flat land like a drop of oil spreading in a pot of water. The men huddled on the crest, surprised to have escaped being swept away.

Rémi turned to them. "Get everyone out!"

They scattered over the hillside in the direction of the Glory workers' housing. Rémi mounted his horse and sped toward Terrefleurs. He was going to need his bateau.

nine

NEW ORLEANS, 2009

*I*N THE FOYER OF a grand mansion on St. Charles Avenue, Madeleine handed her wrap to an attendant and smoothed her white satin strapless gown. This kind of gala, hosted by the New Orleans Historic Preservation Society, wasn't usually her thing, and she wondered how Samantha had managed to convince her to come.

"Drop Jasmine off at my place," Sam had said. "She can play with Moose and Napoleon. There's bound to be someone at the gala who knows where Daddy Blank is."

Daddy was indeed an ardent preservationist. That was the thing: He was just as comfortable among New Orleans's elite as he was among the winos. Much in the same way he was just as likely to sleep on the finest pillow-top mattress as he was to spend the night stretched out in a damp alley, whichever way the breeze carried him.

Madeleine allowed Sam to steer her to the main ballroom. "You're going to be glad you came. You might just take an interest in preservation."

Madeleine rolled her eyes.

Samantha accepted a champagne flute from a passing tray and

jumped right into the business of sipping and mingling with her friends. She withdrew a pack of Capris and turned to Madeleine. "Going out to the courtyard for a puff. Wanna come?"

Madeleine waved her off. "No thanks, I want to take a look around. Let me know if you hear anything about you-know-who."

Sam nodded, and then said, "I know you're here on a mission, but try to relax a little, OK? This is supposed to be fun."

She strode away, disappearing into the laughter beyond the French doors. The crowd stuttered along, flowing from reception to the ballroom with the rhythm of blood through an artery. No sign of Daddy. Madeleine felt a prickling at the back of her neck. That sense of being watched. She turned, and blinked in surprise.

"Hello, Madeleine."

"Oh. Hello, Zenon."

❧

HE WAS STANDING ONLY a few feet away, one shoulder dropped and a hand in his pocket, the other hand holding a mixed drink—what looked like a scotch and soda.

"You looking fine tonight Maddy." Zenon's manner of speech assumed a kind of intimacy that caused the hair to rise on her skin, his stare traveling the length of her as if taking liberties. "Mighty fine, yeah."

She didn't reply. She felt an odd vibration in her blood. A rise in temperature that triggered a sheen at her neck. She looked away.

But he took a step forward, and the sensation intensified. His gaze invaded her with a long, thin trail of heat along her skin, blazing a wake of sweat over each curve.

"Zenon, I . . ."

She thought of the conversation at the flower shop, and how Anita had spoken of him. Madeleine had never thought of Zenon in that way before, but now . . . No, it wasn't attraction. It seemed more like a strange kind of intrusion. She'd felt this way once before when her home was burglarized. And as Zenon stood opposite her now she sensed the nearness of his abdomen, his lean build, a teenage memory of his plate armor muscles that tensed as he'd once labored in his yard in Bayou Black. She'd seen him that way, skin glistening in the sun as he'd bent his back to overgrown shrubs, or leaned over the open hood of a throwaway car he'd salvaged.

She tried to shake away the sensation. "Zenon . . ."

His gray eyes held steady.

She scraped her teeth together. "I didn't . . . I . . . I didn't know you . . . you cared anything about historic preservation."

He said nothing at first, but the affront in his eyes hinted that he knew she was trying to escape the moment.

Mercifully, he played along. His words came slow and deep. "People nowadays, they wanna do everything lackadaisical. It's only in the older buildings that you find a true sense of craftsmanship. Besides." He turned to the side, and Madeleine followed his gaze to the ballroom, where a wheelchair held the glowering form of Chloe LeBlanc. "Miss Chloe convinced me to come here tonight."

"Chloe?" Madeleine gave a start.

He returned her gaze. "I've been helping her out in a few matters."

Madeleine was puzzled. But the longer she stood in silence, the deeper she slid back into the quicksand of his gaze, and she wrestled to free herself from it. He had her on a thread and he knew it. And he seemed to want to keep her there.

Her senses burned. A strangely familiar cobweb settled over her mind, a betrayal, and her hands lifted almost of their own volition. They settled over her belly and felt the sleek satin fabric, a delicate overlay that heated when layered between the skin of her torso and that of her hands. And those hands wanted to move higher, up above her ribs.

Her heart raced. She felt exposed, unclean. It was as if she couldn't control her own movements. She turned away from him abruptly, hands shaking. Her eyes focused beyond the corridor, to the cool white marble of the entrance hall.

She blurted, "Have you seen my father?"

She heard blood throbbing at her ears and was unwilling to meet his gaze. But Zenon did not reply. He fell silent, and remained that way until she dared to look upon him again. And when she did she saw that his eyes had changed. The intensity had dimmed to frustration. He looked away, seeming to cast his thoughts elsewhere.

"Daddy Blank. I don't know." He snorted and looked down, and then up at her again. "Look, I'm sorry about Marc. Been meaning to tell you."

She swallowed.

"We were real close when we were kids, remember?" he said. "You and me and Marc? Things changed over the years and that's a damn shame. Marc was one of the good ones, yeah. I think he might've done something that he weren't proud of."

This left a bad taste in her mouth. Marc's sense of guilt over the electrocution had been plain to everyone. And the usual arguments reared in her head: an accident; in the electrical field this was a common tragedy.

Zenon watched her face as he spoke. "Wish I could have talked to Marc before he shot hisself."

Madeleine wavered. Tears emerged and she shook her head. "It's all right Zenon. We all have regrets."

He stepped toward her. "Do we?"

She straightened her back.

The intensity returned to his stare. "Is that how it goes then, Madeleine? We just keep fighting our instincts and leave it at having regrets?"

And at once the tide of heat washed over her again. Fierce and ringing, saturating every cell. So sudden it stole the breath from her lungs. And somehow she knew that he was doing something to her. The scientist disconnected from her body and observed that these compulsions were not her own. And yet that didn't make any sense. She took a step backward. He caught her wrist.

"How long you gonna fight it?" His eyes, stark and blue, forced their unsanctioned gaze into her.

She shook her head. "Stop. Zenon, don't."

And she yanked away, but he held her firm. His stare gripped her with the same intensity that he gripped her wrist.

"Don't what? Stir up some primitive urge? I think you'd like that, yeah. I think you'd like that a whole lot. Don't struggle with me, *chère*, you might just stir it up in me."

And she felt him sweep her in. A whirlpool devoid of oxygen or emotion or anything but the most basic, instinctual causations. And her mind did struggle.

"Stop it!" She wrenched herself from him.

His eyes lit, and his lips parted to a gleam of teeth. A look that sent fear charging through her.

But someone stepped between them, the height of his shoulders forming a barrier between Madeleine and Zenon.

"Excuse me. I'm a friend of Miss Madeleine. Have we met?"

She saw the clean, strong neck stretching below cropped brown hair, and realized it was Ethan Manderleigh. His words conveyed spotless polite, but the posture was that of a rooster ready to sharpen his talons.

Beyond his shoulder, she saw that Zenon's jaw was set. He gave Madeleine one last hard stare and then cut his eyes to Ethan. Zenon's face showed abject fury, and he clenched his fist. For a moment Madeleine thought a full-blown fight might erupt.

Instead, Zenon turned without a word and walked away, his houndlike gait threading the crowd.

Madeleine exhaled.

◈

ETHAN TURNED TO LOOK at Madeleine. The parallel lines of his brow, eyes, and jaw formed clean planes. And, Madeleine noted, those parallels seemed vastly serene in comparison to the pointed angles of Zenon's face.

"You all right, Madeleine?"

Her breathing slowed. "Yes, thank you Ethan."

"I didn't want to interrupt, but when I saw you across the room it looked like he was being disrespectful. You want me to go after him?"

She laughed, embarrassed. "No, that's not necessary. Zenon's an old acquaintance from way back when."

Ethan shook his head, gaze narrowing toward the foyer where Zenon was now leaving the gala. "As you say, ma'am. We'll let him off this time."

Madeleine felt so relieved to see Zenon go that she had to fight a new impulse: to clutch Ethan's arm and take counted breaths until her pulse returned to normal. She noticed he was holding a shiny black cane with a ball handle. It seemed an eccentric way to round out his black tie ensemble.

He looked at her. "You sure you're all right? I was so sorry to hear about your brother."

Madeleine nodded, and felt the ache return to her chest. "Daddy and I received the flowers you sent. Thank you. Ethan, I don't suppose you've seen my father lately?"

He considered this. "Haven't seen Daddy Blank since the day he introduced me to you. Is he here tonight?"

"I don't know. We had a . . . mishap. I came here hoping I'd find him."

Ethan nodded. "Well I'm sure he'll show. I remember him talking about this thing. Says it's liable to raise all kinda funding."

"I'm glad to hear that."

Ethan gave her a wink. "Don't worry. We'll wring out this here tuxedo rag and see if Daddy Blank don't shake out."

She smiled, and he offered his arm to her. "Shall we hit it together?"

And though her hands wanted to close around that proffered arm, wanted so much to absorb his warm invincibility, she felt a gate slam shut.

"Let's divide and conquer." The words came out sharp, sharper than she'd intended. She swallowed, trying to soften her tone, and added, "We're more likely to find him that way."

He blinked in surprise. Then he nodded and looked away, his gaze traveling to the foyer where Zenon had exited a few moments ago.

"You know, Dr. LeBlanc," he said, and the return of formality seemed not so much distancing as disarming. "Old acquaintances can be replaced by new ones."

Despite herself, she smiled at him. "An interesting notion, Dr. Manderleigh."

And then his expression became impish. "But first dance says I find Daddy Blank before you do."

And then he was gone.

She watched him shoulder into the crowd. To her surprise, he leaned on the cane as he walked. So the cane wasn't a prop after all. She hadn't noticed his limp when he'd come to her house with Daddy, but then again she hadn't been looking.

His flirtation was charming, though he was a very dubious match for her.

Quintessential old money New Orleans. That man lives in a different world.

An idiotic thought because technically Madeleine herself was old money New Orleans. But she grew up in poverty; hadn't been to charm school or gone sailing with the krewes. She had known nothing of her inheritance until college and had always found it hard to relate among the secretive inner circles.

Who was she kidding? She found it hard to relate in any circles.

❧

ACROSS THE ROOM, MADELEINE saw Chloe's houseboy moving toward her. His albinism made him look fragile, almost small and slender despite the truth of his average build. His coarse hair was yellow in contradiction to his African roots, and his broad nose and lips were also pale. But his eyes were not the trademark red or blue of an albino; they were brown.

He gave a nod. "*Bonsoir, Mademoiselle.*"

"Hello."

"*S'il vous plaît*, Miss Chloe would like to see you."

"I'm sorry, I don't remember your name." And then Madeleine realized that like his mistress, he'd never offered it.

"Oran," he said, and then turned, leading her through the crowd.

Madeleine shrugged and followed Oran to where Chloe sat in her wheelchair. "Hello Miss Chloe. I didn't know you were going to be here tonight."

"You see Zenon?" Chloe said.

Never much for chit-chat, that one.

The old woman coughed, a contraction of shoulders, then fixed her gaze on Madeleine again. "He told me about Marc Gilbert."

"Oh?" Madeleine said.

"That Marc Gilbert had a young lady. You did not tell me this."

"What? Marc had a girlfriend?"

Chloe nodded.

"Well if Zenon told you that he's wrong. Marc wasn't dating anyone when he passed away."

The old woman stared at Madeleine for a long moment. "He is good for you to know, yanh?"

"Who, Zenon?"

Chloe nodded, lifting her clawlike hand toward the crowd. "These people, they are rabbits. You should talk to that boy Zenon. He is strong."

A flash in her mind of the strange interlude only moments ago, and Madeleine shivered. "Yeah, I know him. We grew up together. He still has a fishing cabin on Bayou Black. Look, since you seem to know so much, perhaps you can tell me where my father is."

Chloe shook her head.

Madeleine said, "Then if you'll excuse me."

Chloe grunted.

As Madeleine meandered back through the crowd, it seemed folks were indeed talking about her father. Little snippets of conversation trickled through—whispers that ceased when people realized

Madeleine was standing nearby—and it sounded like all of New Orleans had heard about what happened in D.C. She tried not to seethe.

But Daddy Blank was not the only name on people's lips. Madeleine also overheard buzz about Joe Whitney, a prominent criminal defense attorney and member of the Historic Preservation Society. He was also a longtime family acquaintance, though not always a welcome one.

The gossip centered around a sprawling mega-mart slated for construction in one of New Orleans's historic districts. Apparently Whitney had helped the mega-mart get the municipal zoning it needed to start construction, and people were furious.

Madeleine spotted Ethan standing near the buffet surrounded by a group of sparkling young ladies. They all smiled and laughed, and Madeleine thought he seemed to belong there among them. A polished pendant in a string of pearls. Ethan Manderleigh was suited to *them,* she thought. Not to her and her crazy world.

But as if in defiance to her thoughts, Ethan looked up and caught her eye. He smiled and shook his head. No sign of Daddy.

One of the ladies followed his gaze, a green-eyed beauty who looked inquisitively toward Madeleine. Maddy nodded and smiled, and then she found Sam and strode for the safety of her company.

Samantha was standing among a small group of preservationists who were elegantly coiffed and gilded in their finest. They were ranting about Joe Whitney as if he were the Antichrist, a tirade all-too-familiar to Madeleine's ears. (*Joe Goddamn Whitney!* Daddy would say. *Can you believe he calls himself a preservationist?*) Madeleine had never thought much of Joe either, but when his wife died about a year ago she'd felt sorry for him.

"Joe Whitney's got some nerve helping that monster get built," Sam railed.

"Tchoupitoulas is overrun with strip centers as it is," a woman in blue chiffon said. "They can put that thing *outside* the historic areas, not here. We'll lose all the little Mom-and-Pops on Magazine."

Madeleine stepped into the circle.

"Hey there, Maddy," Sam said.

She took Madeleine's elbow and looked as though she was about to introduce her around, but there came the sound of silverware tapping on crystal, and the conversation halted. Madeleine looked over to where someone was beginning to make a toast.

Beside her, Samantha gasped.

At the center of the ballroom, raising his glass to engage the crowd, stood Daddy Blank.

ten

NEW ORLEANS, 2009

CROSS THE STREET, THE house stood quiet, orange light glowing at the windows. Madeleine's friend Samantha lived there. The little dog, Jasmine, was there now. Zenon took a long, slow drag on his cigarette. Dr. Madeleine Le-Blanc. All puffed up but still just some little black girl with Creole blue eyes. A little discipline would straighten her right out.

He'd been watching even before the gala, so he knew Madeleine had dropped Jasmine off here to play with Samantha's dogs, an Airedale mix and an Akita. That little terrier was the smallest of the bunch but she seemed to rule the pack.

Now, as he watched, Samantha's house suddenly rang with the sound of barking.

He craned his neck to see what had caused the fuss and saw a raccoon lumbering across the driveway. It hesitated when it heard the commotion.

Zenon grinned, focusing his mind to encourage the coon forward. It waddled up the steps and began rummaging for food among the potted plants.

The tiny shotgun-style house reverberated with the dogs' protests, and they raged at the window. Even from his hiding place across the street Zenon could see the mammoth one, Moose, hurl himself at the miniblinds. This made a terrific crash, and the coon darted off the porch. The dogs howled in victory.

The Akita leapt forward and slammed the blinds again, filling the air with another screech of metal on metal. Jasmine and the Airedale then took their own turns, and the Airedale caught some in his teeth as he sailed through the air, wrenching long sheaths free from the network of blinds.

Zenon smiled. The dogs were clearly having fun. Time to have a little fun of his own.

A glance at his watch confirmed Madeleine and Samantha wouldn't return for a good while. He stubbed out his cigarette and emerged from his hiding place. He was still wearing fancy party clothes, but what the hell.

❧

DADDY BLANK ADDRESSED THE forest of gowns and tuxedos, calling focus upon himself as he rang his spoon against his glass. His tux shone sleek like the plumage of a blackbird, the chain of his pocket watch gleaming in a dip of gold from his cummerbund to his pocket. Madeleine moved through the crowd with Sam in tow.

"My friends," he said. "The good folks on the board of advisors have done a tremendous job organizing our efforts in rebuilding New Orleans, this beautiful city, I dare say the pride of the South. Not to mention they know how to throw one hell of a party."

Laughter rippled through the crowd as Maddy and Sam found their way to an opening near the front of the circle. Madeleine was so focused on her father's words that at first she didn't realize she had planted herself next to Joe Whitney, her father's counterpart on the gossip hot seat.

Daddy continued, "We have all striven to preserve the historic buildings of our city, big and small, through our diligent labor, our financial contributions, and our time."

As if nothing at all had happened. As if he hadn't gone missing.

His voice was robust, accented in a combination of southern Louisiana and a hint of New Orleans. He looked youthful beyond his years.

As if he hadn't left her in Washington, D.C., standing in front of those politicians like a peeled housefly.

"And so I ask you to join me in a toast." Daddy raised his glass.

Madeleine became aware of Joe Whitney's gaze upon her. She turned sharply. Whitney's eyes were trained on her face, but she suspected they'd been lingering somewhere below her neck. Just once she wanted to catch him in the act.

Whitney smiled and whispered, "Why Miss Madeleine, or should I say Dr. LeBlanc, so nice to see you here this evening."

She nodded and returned her focus to the toast.

Daddy's glass was still raised, and she realized he was looking her way. "But I do not ask that we toast those members of the board, or even your hardworking selves." He paused and scanned the room. "For there are those among us, pretending to be our allies, who are in fact our enemies."

Whitney's gaze snapped to attention. Daddy was now staring directly at him.

"Devils who have come to sabotage the very cause they profess to defend. It is to them, our enemies, I would like to propose this toast. Because without them we would become complacent, and would not be motivated in our duties. They are the fuel to our fire."

Eyes began to flicker toward Whitney. Some guests pursed their lips to repress smiles; others openly chuckled.

And Daddy said, "Ladies and gentleman, please join me in a toast: To our enemies!"

The crowd chorused in return, "To our enemies!"

Almost everyone in the entire room nodded at Joe Whitney as they raised their flutes to him.

Almost everyone.

Whitney turned from white to scarlet, and then purple. His back stood rigid, and he did *not* raise his glass.

Nor did Madeleine.

⁂

ZENON COULD TELL THAT Jasmine caught his scent before she even saw him.

He was standing in the alley outside the bedroom. Samantha's dogs had been silent, probably dozing among the remnants of what had once been miniblinds. A breeze curled around Zenon and drifted through swelling curtains at the rear of the house.

With it, he heard the distant rumble of Jasmine's growl.

The sound of paws clicking across the wood floor, coming to a stop just opposite the wall near where he stood. The curtains swelled again.

From the alley, Zenon could see the tiny dog's illuminated form reflected in the mirror opposite the window. She sniffed the air, rising on hind legs with her front paws pressed against the dresser. She gave a low woof. Zenon remained still.

After a few minutes, he creaked atop the chain link fence and pulled himself up into a tree so that he could peer down inside. Jasmine worried by the dresser several feet below.

He revealed himself, curling his fingers under the window frame, and lifted.

Jasmine flew into a rage of wild barking.

⁂

MADELEINE DIDN'T KNOW WHETHER to throw her arms around her father in relief that he seemed clearheaded and safe, or march up there and throttle him.

Beside her, Whitney slumped. He grit his teeth under the scrutiny of the crowd and raised his flute with resignation, then drained the champagne in a single swallow.

"Miss Madeleine," he laughed with forced humor. "I am sorry to see that your father is having another one of his episodes."

Sam couldn't resist getting in her own dig as Whitney turned away. "I don't know, Joe, Daddy Blank seemed pretty lucid to me!"

Joe stalked off. Sam was grinning so hard it looked like the corners of her mouth might get hooked behind her ears.

She turned to Maddy. "Well! Guess that shows where you get your wit. Your father is an absolute hero. Called ol' Whitney out in front of everyone."

"Our exalted champion," Madeleine said in a flat voice as Sam started toward the crowd haloing Daddy Blank.

Madeleine watched Sam lean forward and kiss him on the cheek while others shook his hand or patted his back. Daddy had them absolutely charmed. He said something to the circle of folks who'd gathered around them, and they roared with delight. In a few weeks he may not even know their names, and they'll cross the street just to avoid passing him on the sidewalk.

She stepped back; no desire to join in with the worshipers. She saw Chloe across the way in the ballroom.

"Hello again."

Ethan Manderleigh.

She smiled at him. "Hello. Guess we found Daddy."

He shook his head with a laugh. "Guess we did. Trouble was I was supposed to find him first."

He leaned toward her with an enticing grin. Madeleine remembered the "first dance" bargain he'd laid and pressed away her own smile, averting her gaze. Suddenly music surged in the ballroom, and people flowed into it as if drifting on a wave.

"Anyway I know I didn't hold up my end of the deal," Ethan said as he offered his arm. "But perhaps you'll—"

"There you are!"

One of the debutantes linked her arm through Ethan's. She beamed up at him, that green-eyed pearl of a beauty Madeleine had seen before. "Music's started. First dance?"

Madeleine took a step back.

Ethan looked annoyed. "Miss Madeleine and I were just going to—"

"Go ahead," Madeleine interjected. "You two have fun."

The green-eyed girl tugged on his arm but he remained rigid, eyes fixed on Madeleine. She lifted her face and smiled. The young woman looked from Ethan to Madeleine and gave another tug. This time Ethan sighed and leaned his cane against the wall. He escorted her to the dance floor.

Madeleine watched them go, wondering what was wrong with her. One dance with a handsome brain doctor couldn't possibly hurt a thing, and yet she'd all but thrown him at the other woman. It occurred to her that she'd dodged him twice now. It wouldn't happen a third time.

And then to Madeleine's complete surprise, Joe Whitney approached carrying two champagne flutes.

Oh, joy.

"My dear." He placed a flute in her hand.

A comeuppance for having ditched Ethan. My, but don't karma move fast?

She accepted the glass with a raised brow. "Thanks, Joe. I'm surprised you came back. Anyone else would have slipped out of the building after Daddy's speech."

Joe took a sip. "Actually, Miss Madeleine, contrary to what it may seem, I did not come here for the sole purpose of losing verbal battles to LeBlancs. And I apologize if I was rude earlier."

She shrugged. "Apology accepted."

She made a point of raising her glass to him, since it seemed to be the fashionable way to address him that evening.

He cocked his head toward the orchestra. "Shall we dance?"

She paused. It seemed blasphemous to have scorned Ethan in favor of Joe. And she wondered why Joe would want to dance with her in the first place. It carried a whiff of scheming to it. But Daddy's burbling had gotten under her skin, and so Madeleine set down the champagne flute, straightened her back, and strode into the ballroom with none other than Joe Goddamn Whitney.

JASMINE'S SNARL ERUPTED WITH such ferocity that Samantha's dogs leapt from sleep, barking before they had even fully awakened. Zenon chuckled.

The window, which had been open only slightly, would neither rise nor lower more than an inch in either direction. He removed his fingers from the frame and rested back in the tree.

The Akita and the Airedale padded into the bedroom. Still unaware of his presence, they watched in alarm as Jazz continued screaming and bouncing toward the opening, her paws scrabbling at the dresser. Finally, she caught the lip and vaulted herself up, scurrying across the top and sending bottles of perfume and makeup flying in all directions.

Come get me, Jazz. Come on up through this window and kick my ass.

Seeing Jasmine atop the dresser snapped the other two dogs into action. The Akita rose to hind legs, stretching his massive head and clamping his jaws onto a bag of SunChips. He dragged it to the floor so that he and the Airedale could ransack its contents.

Jazz remained atop the dresser, raging at the open window.

Keep trying. I'll bet you can wiggle your little rat body right through the crack.

Though she jumped and scraped at the sill, the height of the dresser prevented her from gaining enough leverage to make it through the narrow opening, and she managed only to catch swatches of curtain in her teeth. Her paws dispatched a hand mirror that flew crashing to the floorboards, causing Samantha's dogs to pause in their gobbling, but only for a moment.

Zenon snorted. He couldn't get in and she couldn't get out. Enough of this.

He jumped from the tree and strolled to the front porch, dusting off his fancy slacks.

Jasmine pursued, sailing through the living room and slamming the fractured blinds. This time the other dogs saw him too. They leapt to the little terrier's side, frenzied and snarling, separated from Zenon by only a pane of glass and a rapidly diminishing set of blinds.

He paused, watching, then tapped the pane and said, "Be quiet." And from his mind: *Be quiet.*

The Akita and the Airedale trailed off. They licked their muzzles, panting, and rested back on their hindquarters. Jasmine was the last to settle down. She barked and peeled back her lips, her tongue darting over fangs. Then she, too, quieted.

Zenon smiled. *Stubborn like your owner, Jazz. Now then, altogether: Step forward.*

The dogs stood, a little uncertain, but they took their step in a disconnected gaggle. All three of them. The sense of power was intoxicating.

Zenon turned his focus to Samantha's dogs, speaking to them through the glass. "How about we have a little fun with Miss Jasmine?"

He visualized what he meant, and let that image transfer to the larger dogs.

The Akita bared his teeth, gleaming white in the darkness. He uttered a low, rolling growl.

"You ready, Jasmine? Cuz we're gonna see what you're made of."

AS JOE WHITNEY ESCORTED Madeleine to the dance floor, she felt eyes from every corner of the room. Indeed, they were an unlikely duo: He, twice her age and white as an egg; and she, a blue-eyed black Creole whose father had just scalded him in public.

But then Madeleine realized his angle. Waltzing with her, the daughter of his accuser, was Joe's way of winning back the crowd.

Madeleine felt Ethan's eyes on her as she danced. And when she met his gaze he looked bemused, as if laughing at her for dancing with Joe. His limp didn't seem to affect him much. He moved less than other folks, but that was about it. She gave him a broad smile. She and Joe danced through the song and then retreated to the outer rim of the ballroom. Sam appeared with Daddy in escort.

The men greeted each other coolly.

"Joseph."

"Sirrhh."

Daddy turned to his daughter and offered his arm as the quartet began to play a foxtrot. "Madeleine, honey, let's dance."

She gritted her teeth, having lost her heart for dancing, but took his arm. Behind her, to everyone's surprise, Whitney asked the same of Samantha.

"Well all right, fine," Sam said rolling her eyes.

Daddy was smiling with the carefree abandon of someone content to be right where he was rather than anywhere else on earth. And yet . . .

"So. Been taking your meds, Daddy?"

His smile vanished and he looked away. "Aw, who wants a chemical lobotomy? Those things make me sick."

She frowned. "Better than the alternative."

"Come on, don't be that way, kitten. I'll be fine."

He smiled and squeezed her hand as they waltzed, and then his face changed. He lowered his chin and said, "Listen honey, I'm sorry I left you in Washington like that. Cold feet, I guess."

He was struggling for words, an unusual phenomenon for him. "And then I was too ashamed to face you. I can see that things have hit you harder now that Marc's gone. Can you forgive me, honey?"

She felt tension in her eyes, and was disgusted to find a threat of tears. She breathed in deeply.

"I never should have put you in that position." And it was true; she knew better.

The waltz ended and as she released his hand, he pulled her in and wrapped her in a strong hug.

"I love you, baby girl," he whispered, patting her hair.

This time the dreaded tears found their way to her eyes, and she quickly blinked them away before he could see them.

They returned to the spot by the commode where Sam and Whitney were already waiting.

Sam looked at the two men and raised her brows. "So. Joe? Daddy Blank? Will you two be dancing the next one together?"

They both laughed. Joe grabbed two long-stem red roses from a table and presented one to Madeleine and one to Sam. For once, Sam was at a loss for words, and Daddy rolled his eyes elaborately as he turned to leave. Then Joe left abruptly too, and Madeleine saw he was making a beeline for Buddy Caldwell, attorney general by day and country music singer by night. Madeleine watched as both Joe and her father worked the room, each one shaking hands and demonstrating his own brand of wit.

"You're wearing those shoulder earrings again," Sam said.

Madeleine frowned. "Guess I got a lot on my mind."

"We can leave. I've had enough of all this pomp and circumstance. Wanna go to a titty bar instead?"

Madeleine looked at her, shocked, then burst out laughing. Sam gave her a sly grin. They turned and started toward the coat check.

"I know I'm a wet blanket," Madeleine said. "This whole thing with Daddy—Trying to keep him on his meds and off the street is like trying to bottle smoke."

Sam shrugged. "Maybe you should just let smoke be smoke."

"Sounds great, but the reality is that smoking can be dangerous."

Sam arched a brow and pointedly took out a pack of Capris. "You can't always do what's good for you, you know."

Madeleine tightened her lips.

Sam said, "Hey, at least you know he's all right now, Maddy. I'm just saying sometimes it's worth putting a little faith in miracles. He was brilliant and charming tonight. Talk of the town."

"Yeah. After he left me twisting in the wind in D.C."

"So that's what this is really about?" Sam tapped a cigarette from the pack. "Hey listen. It's understandable that you'd be mad at him."

Madeleine tried to slow her breathing, but her fury was on the rise. "Yeah, well, it's that and it's not. I'm just so . . ." She shook her hands. "Frustrated. That testimony in D.C. was for *his* benefit. To treat *his* condition. He's charming now because he doesn't feel sick and rummy, which means he's off his meds. It's just the first stage of the cycle. The next step is that he winds up on the street, wandering around muttering or shouting, or worse. You've seen it—he can get violent, Sam. And I sit around and worry that he's going to end up in jail, or dead, or God knows what."

She tossed her head, and then spoke the most frustrating truth of all: "And in the end, there's really not a damn thing I can do about any of it."

At this, her temper began to lag.

"I can't *make* him take his meds. But just now, I barely even tried . . ." She let the words fall away, and stopped.

Sam stepped closer and touched her arm. "I'm sorry Maddy. I didn't mean—I'm sorry." She knit her brows. "Forgive me?"

Madeleine took a deep breath, reassembling a state of calm. "No, don't. Of course I forgive you. But *I'm* the one who should apologize. Things got real weird tonight in a lot of ways and it put me in a funk."

Madeleine linked her arm into Sam's and squeezed, "Thanks for putting up with me."

Sam responded by touching her head to Madeleine's. "Guess we'd better get the truck."

Madeleine nodded, but an unsettling feeling stole over her: They were being watched.

She looked right and left, suddenly worried that Zenon might have come back. But no sign of him. And then she saw her. In the cloakroom a few feet away, the little girl stood partially concealed behind fabric. Though one single eye and a tousle of hair were the only visible features, Madeleine recognized her as the child who lived with Chloe.

She handed her valet stub to Sam. "Do you mind seeing to the truck? I need to check on someone."

"Sure," Sam said with a shrug.

She took the ticket and turned, pausing to light the cigarette as she stepped through the front doors.

Madeleine approached the small chamber. She couldn't imagine why this girl was allowed to wander unattended so frequently. It was about time Madeleine met her face-to-face.

JASMINE STOPPED BARKING. SHE took a step backward, a question emitting from her throat. The other dogs growled. The Akita's eyes held savagery. Jasmine lowered her ears and bent her legs in a cringe. A soft breeze gusted and crickets chirped from the drainage passages.

Zenon smiled. In his mind, he turned the screw another half step.

The Airedale lashed out, teeth striking Jasmine's haunches. She yelped.

The Akita stepped forward and snarled over her, his tongue gaping through fangs, his head almost as large as Jasmine's entire body. She gave a singing whimper, crouching wide-eyed with her tail curled beneath her.

The Akita snapped. Jasmine screamed and leapt to her feet, tail now erect and hackles raised. She peeled back her lips at the two larger dogs. The Airedale's teeth gnashed forward. Jasmine scooted backward.

Zenon watched, relishing how the little female bared her teeth while the larger males swayed at her flanks.

She'll put up a fight, yeah.

Jasmine backed up, sidling along the furniture. Cornered now between the couch and the wall.

Steady boys. Close the gap.

The larger dogs advanced with tails bristling.

Get her!

THE CLOAKROOM STRETCHED BACK far enough so a person might move freely among the hangers. A split door gaped wide at the top while barring entry at the bottom, with a valet bell resting on its ledge. No attendant.

The little girl was watching Madeleine, the only visible features being her clumped dirty blond hair draped over a single eye. The rest of her remained hidden between a hanging white sequined cape and a flowing golden chiffon wrap. Smudges were visible on the cape where it had come into contact with her.

Madeleine offered a smile. "Hello there."

The little girl said nothing. She pressed herself further back into the crush of fabric.

Madeleine leaned over the ledge. "It's all right. I'm not going to hurt you."

She looked down and saw the child's bare feet just below the hanging garments. Her ankle was streaked with ashen smears, and the ragged tips of her toenails bore black half-moons as if she'd neither washed nor worn shoes in ages.

"My name is Madeleine. Can you come out where I can see you, please?"

A hesitation, and then the child began to move. The cape folded in as she pressed forward out of the rack. Her face emerged, and Madeleine caught her breath. Not because the face was filthy; she'd expected that. It was the expression on that face—not that of a timid, shrinking little girl at all. This child wore no look of fear. She was smiling. In fact, she was grimacing.

"That's better," Madeleine said, though a bit unnerved. "You live with Miss Chloe, don't you? Chloe LeBlanc?"

The child did not move. She continued to show her teeth in that strange, bellicose grin.

Madeleine tried another tack. "Chloe LeBlanc, *elle est ta grand-mère?*"

Or maybe this girl's arrière grand-mère. The child was so young and Chloe so old, if the two were related there would have to be several "*arrière's*" before the "*grand-mère.*"

But nothing. The child just grimaced and stared through brown, horse-lashed eyes.

"What's your name, honey?"

"They say I'm Severin," she whispered.

The voice sounded normal, angelic even. As if dusted in gold from the fabric that draped over her.

"Ah, Severin." Madeleine reached out a hand. "You should probably come out of there, sweetie."

The child's eyes lit, and she moved forward, leaning out of the rack with the chiffon sliding over her. She pressed her tiny fingers into Madeleine's hand. But she did not step out. She continued to lean forward. Her mouth opened, and her eyes closed. And Madeleine realized she was about to bite her.

She withdrew her hand. "No biting!"

Severin blinked. Her grimace widened between spills of grimy hair.

A rusting voice came from behind. "Is it the child?"

Madeleine whirled around. Chloe sat in her wheelchair, Oran hovering at her shoulder.

"Yes," Madeleine said, and was startled to find her breath coming in sluggish exhales.

She looked over her shoulder and back toward the coat closet, but the little girl had withdrawn at the sound of Chloe's voice. "Severin's hiding in there."

Chloe sat very still in her wheelchair. "Yes."

She cast a look toward Oran, who moved to the closet, opening the lower section of door. Madeleine half-expected to see Severin dart out when he did so. But no. He pulled at the hanging garments, though he kept his eyes on Madeleine.

"You know, Chloe," Madeleine said, "Severin looks like she needs to see a doctor."

Chloe lifted a whiskered chin toward the closet. "A difficult one to handle."

Madeleine nodded. "Is she, is she a relation of yours?"

The girl's skin was stark pale with no hint of African in her blood, but that could be explained in any number of ways.

But Chloe said, "Never you mind about that."

"But I do mind, Chloe. I'm concerned for her welfare."

"You shall have a chance to talk to her more, Madeleine, if you're so concerned."

"When?"

"Not now. In a while."

"Do I have your word?"

Chloe looked annoyed. "Yes, you will talk to her!"

The windows flashed twice; headlights in the drive below. Sam was signaling from the truck with a host of vehicles in the valet's queue. Madeleine looked toward the cloakroom where Oran nodded at her.

"Well, good night," Madeleine said.

⁂

THEY LUNGED. JASMINE GAVE a single shriek and then fell silent.

The two male dogs were barking, frenzied, snarling and scraping at the corner where the couch met the wall.

Zenon strained to see through the darkness. Hard to tell if there was any blood. He wasn't sure whether they had her.

A scrolling beam of light panned the neighbors' houses. Zenon looked up. He saw a truck turning the corner onto the block. Madeleine.

He turned back to the window, beyond which the male dogs still drove at the couch in a fury. A flash of white caught Zenon's eye. Jasmine skulked out from the back end of the couch. Sneaking in a rush toward the back of the living room, low on her haunches, while on the opposite end, the larger dogs continued to rail at the space between the couch and the wall. She appeared to be wholly untouched.

Zenon had to laugh.

He shot a glance back toward the end of the block and knew he had but a handful of seconds before the headlights would catch him. He shook his head, regarded the snarling dogs again, and released. The barking stopped.

He ducked back into the shadows.

It's your damned good luck, dog.

He moved quickly, slipping back into his car as the headlights drew nearer. He closed the door to the Duster with barely a sound.

"What's with the dogs?" Josh asked from within the darkness.

Zenon jumped in his seat. "Shit man, you scared me!"

"Boo!" Josh laughed. "Who we lookin at over there, anyways?"

Zenon shook his head. "Man, what are you doing here?"

"Well hell, I ain't seen you in a while."

Zenon lit a cigarette and exhaled smoke into the car. He kept an eye on the house where Samantha and Madeleine stood in the doorway. As he watched, Madeleine covered her mouth, and even through the darkness Zenon could see the look of shock on Sam's face.

"What's wrong," he said to the figures. "Dogs been doing some housekeeping while you were gone?"

They both had a pleasant laugh.

Josh put a stick to his mouth and chewed. "You practicing on'm?"

"Yeah. Didn't get to finish what I started though."

A black car lumbered by. As it passed, they caught a glimpse of Chloe LeBlanc through the back passenger window.

"Shit," Josh said. "It's her."

"Miss Chloe? Was she looking at us?"

Josh twitched. "What do you think? She didn't come here by coincidence."

"We better watch it. That woman can see straight into our heads."

"No she can't. She might be able to do the mind thing a little, but she still has to rely on others to do her spying. Anyway you're getting better than her."

Zenon suspected this already, and he liked the way it tasted. "The student surpasses the master."

"Don't get too cocky. Just remember she's the one who evolved us. And she's the one who can tip the balance in our favor."

"I'd say we're doing our fair share."

"Shit, brother, we're just soldiers. She's the general."

"Man, it's unnerving," Zenon said.

The Akita broke from the house and tore across the street like a

racehorse, galloping in the opposite direction of the Duster. Samantha followed after him, evening gown flying.

Zenon smiled.

The Akita stopped abruptly near a cluster of crepe myrtle. He
stared down the street, black jowls shining blue under the street
lamp. He parted those jowls and gave a single, reverberating woof.
A warning. It sounded like the old boy was indignant. Didn't like
being on the string. And then, in a gesture akin to giving the finger,
the Akita raised his rear leg and peed on the shrubs.

Josh and Zenon guffawed.

"What's with all the dogs, anyway?" Josh said.

"Two of'm are Samantha's and the little one's Madeleine's."

"Oh I get it now." Josh frowned. "Madeleine again. What business you got with her?"

"Just checkin in on an old friend."

"Uh, checkin in is when you pick up the phone and say 'How's
things?' What you're doing, that's called stalking."

"Oh yeah? Well she just happened to show up at the gala tonight.
I tried the trick on her and I think I had her there for a minute."

"Tried how?"

"You know. Move this way or that way."

Josh looked at him for a long moment. "Man, you better play it
straight. And I promise you, it won't be cool if you wind up crossing
the old woman."

"To hell with her. Anyway she *wants* me to get with Madeleine."

"Well that dudn't mean kill her little ole dog!"

"Wudn't gonna kill it. And I don't sit around waiting for old
Chloe's blessing on everything I do. *'Kushtrimi del për të ligshtin, pse
trimi kujtohet vet.'*"

Josh sighed. "The hell is that, Albanian?"

"Matter of fact it is. Means the tolling bell is for the weak, the
strong initiates on his own. The thing with Madeleine is complicated. *She's* complicated. She don't even know her own head."

Josh snorted.

Zenon took a long pull on his cigarette and watched the sky. No lightning yet, but a hint of something was brewing up there.

He exhaled in a tempered stream. "She's a sensual woman, Madeleine. But she won't cool her brain. I haven't figured out what I'm going to do about her yet. On the one hand, there's the whole thing with Miss Chloe. But then me and Madeleine got a history, and she's running out of people. Some guidance is what she needs."

Josh huffed with a wave of his chewed-up stick. "Oh is that right? Listen, we've been over this. You need to cool it, bro. You starting to get a little weird on me."

"*I'm* weird?" Zenon laughed with a curl to his lip. "That's pretty bad, comin from you. And speaking of which, please tell me you didn't get that stick from somewhere here on the streets. I don't even want to know what variety of bacterial spores are on that thing."

"Shut up."

"Just plain nasty."

Josh said, "Man, *you* oughtta get a dog. Do you some good."

"What for?"

"I don't know. You could take it huntin. Hell, if you ever need to take down a set of blinds or somethin, seems like they'd come in real handy."

Zenon grinned. Lightning fluttered across the sky.

"Everything go all right with that last one?" Josh said.

"Just fine. She's out in the Gulf by Bayou Black." Zenon turned the key and the car wheezed to life. He fiddled with the shortwave. Enough with the Albanian station—time to try something new. He tuned the dial until he came across a language he didn't recognize at all.

Josh leaned back and tugged on his porkpie hat, settling the stick between his teeth.

eleven

NEW ORLEANS, 2009

ADELEINE RETURNED TO HER home on Esplanade just after 11 P.M. Her ballroom gown and elegant hairstyle made her feel as though, for once, she actually belonged in the Creole Victorian mansion with its double galleries. She usually felt dwarfed by the sixteen-foot windows with their carved wood trim. Tonight she wore black and white, just like her bloodline, and she imagined she really should feel as though she fit.

Until a few years ago, she didn't even know this house existed; and then one day Daddy Blank handed his son and daughter an envelope containing the keys and the deed. For a while, Madeleine had insisted he stay there with her, but he came and went with the carelessness of a dragonfly. And Marc, from the very beginning, had refused to leave the cottage on Bayou Black.

Tonight, Madeleine at least had the appearance of belonging, but she still wondered if she would ever feel truly entitled to this house.

Jasmine—always entitled—trotted ahead. Madeleine winced at the memory of poor Sam's place, which looked like a life-sized game of pick-up sticks after the dogs had had their way with it. She and

Sam had cleaned up as best they could and would face the rest tomorrow. Of all the times those dogs had been left alone to entertain each other, they had never gotten into such trouble. And Jasmine had been trembling when Maddy clipped her leash. Strange.

She fixed a steaming cup of tea and carried it up the curved staircase, Whitney's rose in hand. She set the tea down on her vanity, breathing in the rose's scent.

Men's voices rippled behind her.

She whirled, but found no one there. The bedroom lay empty. She cocked her head and listened, holding her breath, standing absolutely still. Had she imagined it? And then, faintly—it almost seemed like a thought—she heard humming.

She flung open the French doors to the balcony, and doo-wop harmonies soared up to her from the street.

> *Oh little bitty pretty one*
> *Come on and talk to me.*

Her father stood in the flickering glow of gaslight, still clad in his tux with his hand on another man's shoulder, their fingers snapping in time to the vocals. The song looped from a hum to the same harmonies in an Ohhh!, and then finally to lyrics and back again. Behind them, leaning against a silver Lexus hybrid with hand tapping along, stood Ethan Manderleigh.

Daddy opened his arms to his daughter above as he swayed and sang.

> *I'll tell you a story*
> *Happened long time ago*
> *A-little bitty pretty one*
> *I've been watching you grow.*

Ethan wasn't singing but he was keeping time. The twosome sang it through and ended with an abrupt silence that held for a heartbeat, and then all three burst into laughter. Madeleine leaned forward and tossed Whitney's rose over the balcony. Daddy caught it but recognized it as having come from Whitney and he pinched it upside-down like he was holding a dead mouse. The other singer took it instead, and the two clapped their arms around each other's shoulders, hooting in triumph.

Madeleine flowed down the interior stairs with Jasmine at her heels. She crossed the hall and threw open the front door. The other singer must have been Ethan's chauffeur because he was getting behind the wheel of the hybrid while Daddy and Ethan strolled into the foyer.

"Hiya kitten," Daddy said as he kissed her. "Guess I'm staying here tonight."

"Sounds good. Want some tea?"

"Yeah, in a minute. Lemme change out of this monkey suit." He headed for the stairs.

Madeleine looked at Ethan. "How about you? Tea?"

"Naw, just wanted to see that Daddy Blank made it home safe. Streets are crawling with Whitneys, you know."

"Mm. Indeed."

"And," Ethan added, "I wanted to ask you to have dinner with me."

"Dinner?" She smiled.

"Yeah, dinner. It's a manner of providing food-energy to the human body. Only it's done all leisurely and social-like."

He leaned against the door. His eyes held an easiness that swept her with warmth. It made her want to reach up and stroke the square line of his jaw.

"Tomorrow night?" Ethan asked.

"Hmm . . ." But she thought of her father and how she would be loath to let him out of her sight until she was certain he'd been stabilized on his medications.

Ethan seemed to sense her turmoil and stepped toward her. "I know you like good food because I've had your couche-couche and boudin. So this is a little intimidating for me. Hmm. I'll have to take you to the best place in town."

She arched a brow at him.

He said, "I know. Monkey Hill."

Madeleine laughed. "Monkey Hill? At Audubon Zoo?"

"Sure. You're a psychologist, so what better way to spend an evening than studying primates in their natural habitat?"

"I didn't realize New Orleans was a natural habitat for monkeys."

"All right, *unnatural* habitat. You know why they built Monkey Hill in the 1930s, don't you?"

Madeleine considered this. "So that the people of New Orleans could see what a monkey looks like?"

"Wrong. So that the people of New Orleans could see what a *hill* looks like."

She had to laugh.

He grinned at her. "Well, maybe we'll just *start* at Monkey Hill, then I'll take you somewhere with better food. Pick you up at seven?"

She bit her lip. She'd sworn to herself that she wouldn't refuse him a third time. "OK, but not tomorrow night. Why don't you call me later in the week?"

He narrowed his eyes. "Fair enough. I'll call you Tuesday."

She'd meant later in the week than that, but she relented. "That'll be fine."

"Hmm. 'Fine,' she says. Lord have mercy, woman. You're tricky."

She laughed. "I don't mean to be tricky. I am very much looking forward to seeing Monkey Hill with you. And your, um, driver."

He looked out the window, then cocked his brow at her. "Not a chance. I only hired him for the night 'cause I knew I'd be drinkin."

He took her hands in his and placed a chaste kiss on her cheek, sweet and cool. And then he released her and pivoted toward the door and grasped the handle.

But he paused there, back to her, shoulders broad and dark in the dim light of the foyer.

He turned around. "Hold up a minute, Madeleine."

He reached for her again. This time his warm hand went to the small of her back, and he kissed her fully, a firm, slow indulgence. And while this kiss was not entirely unexpected, the lusciousness of it did surprise her. The way he leaned into her; the way he tasted. His lips were soft and firm and confident and downright delicious. It felt as though currents of electricity had joined between them.

Her left hand slid up the wall of his chest and curled around his neck. He smelled like sandalwood and sun-drenched granite. Warmth radiated out to her limbs.

He released her, his fingertips just below her ear.

"Call you Tuesday," Ethan whispered, and then he turned and left.

MADELEINE WATCHED THROUGH THE glass inlay as Ethan strode to the hybrid. Her body held on to the feeling of sparks flowing through her. She still thought they made an unlikely pair, she and Ethan, but one dinner wouldn't hurt. And maybe one more taste of those sparks. She turned toward the kitchen and switched on the light.

"Nice boy, that Ethan."

Madeleine jumped. "Daddy! How long have you been standing there?"

He stepped toward his daughter. "Not too long. Long enough."

"Shame on you!"

"Well it didn't look like y'all wanted to be interrupted."

She shooed him into the kitchen and huffed, checking the kettle. The water was still hot. She steeped two mugs with tea and settled down with her father.

Daddy dunked the tea bag a couple of times. "Thank you, hon. I don't suppose you have a little nip of something for this?"

She rolled her eyes. "You're lucky you don't get a spoonful of cod liver oil."

"Or Chloe LeBlanc's voodoo brew."

Madeleine raised her brows. "I take it you saw her at the gala tonight?"

He nodded. "God help me."

"You know when this whole thing started, I was surprised to find out that Mémée's mother was even alive. You never talked about her."

"Well, honey, your grandmother never thought much of Miss Chloe, even though she was her own mother. Wasn't till after your grandmother died that I ever even met her. My mother kept her well away from us kids."

"And you kept her well away from us, apparently."

Daddy shrugged.

"Why did you?" Madeleine said.

"I don't know. It's complicated. Felt like I was being disloyal to my mother as it was. And anyway . . ." He sighed and rubbed the back of his neck. "Miss Chloe's an odd one. Old school river folk, you know? She has a funny way of showing you things. You wind up following her somewhere dark and weird. Don't get me wrong. She's smart, and she knows things. Next thing you know she's led you into the attic of a burning house, and she's guarding the escape ladder. Know what I mean?"

"No. As a matter of fact I have no idea what you mean."

He sighed. "Like I say, it's complicated. You kids were young, you had enough troubles. Didn't need to be bringin some crazy woman around to make things worse."

"She said she'd kept an eye on Marc and me from a distance anyway."

Daddy gave a rueful laugh. "Lotta good that didja."

And then he sobered, running his hand along his jaw and gazing into his cup. "I can't imagine why I wouldn't have just done right by you kids. You didn't have a mother, and I was no use as a father."

Madeleine's lips parted, surprised by the suddenness and vulnerability in his change of tone. "You loved us, Daddy, and you were there for us when you were well. We made it through OK."

"Did you?" His blue eyes held hers. "And where is Marc now that he made it through OK?"

Madeleine swallowed and said, "It's not your fault."

She averted her eyes, running her hand across the worn kitchen wall to that same scar, the place where paper bubbled up, and let her fingers explore the loose corner where it pulled back.

"Don't know why, but after all this remodeling, I can't seem to bring myself to tackle the kitchen." She looked at her father. "Tell me what else you know about Chloe."

He sighed. "Not much to tell, other than folks were afraid of her. My mama wanted nothing to do with the woman. Said Chloe's about as huggable as a frog in formaldehyde."

Madeleine grinned, not realizing she was still tugging at the bit of wallpaper until it pulled free an inch. "Oops."

The opening revealed several layers of paint and some crumbled plaster. To peel back two or three more inches would be to reveal the blemish where the wallpaper bubbled out.

Daddy nodded at the scarred wall. "Better leave that alone."

"I know. Can't seem to let it be. Like peeling a sunburn. And I'm convinced there's a mouse or something living in there. I've caught movement going on."

"What, you heard?"

"Not so much heard, but I could just tell . . ." Madeleine swallowed, unable to finish the thought, as she recalled that last phone conversation she'd had with her brother.

Daddy watched her face. "You're just fiddling because of worn nerves. Guess I been putting you through the paces lately."

She shook her head. "All I ask is that you keep up with your meds, Daddy. That's it. The rest of it . . ." she waved a hand.

He retreated within himself a half step. "Sure kitten. Sure I'll take'm."

His sincerity was underwhelming. Maddy felt her ears at her shoulders again. *Let smoke be smoke.*

He said, "I'm telling you darlin. You pull that off, you might find a whole lotta mess under there."

"What? Oh." She'd unconsciously resumed fiddling with the wallpaper, and it lifted another inch even as she saw what she was doing. She smoothed the loosened corner back against the wall but as soon as she removed her hand, the paper floated backward again. It looked as though once uncovered, it would never go back.

Daddy leaned forward and flicked a bit of material that dangled from within the layers. "Look at that. They plastered right over the original wallpaper. In fact it wudn't even paper—looks like they used fabric. The same pattern from the center hall. My mama said that was specially commissioned from Paris a long time ago."

"How long?"

"Four generations at least. Maybe more."

Madeleine swept her gaze over the kitchen and the foyer beyond, taking in the tray ceiling and other details that made the house unique. "Really? Paris?"

"Yeah. All these old Victorians put the best materials into the grand old center halls. Make a fine impression when you first walk in. Never mind that the rest of the house is shadows and dust."

"And beauty."

He smiled at her, miles of blue in his eyes. "You're right, kitten. Endurable beauty. You've kept the house up real well, too. Way better than I would have. Kitchen aside."

She laughed.

He pointed out the mahogany and cypress millwork. "See that? That's my favorite part. Cypress wood straight from the bayou. Local craftsmen right here in New Orleans carved those panels when they built this place. See that sugarcane motif on the frieze? Same as the one outside on the verandah? Cane's what led to the family fortune."

"Yeah. Funny. I didn't even recognize that was a sugarcane motif. Always thought it was just grass or something—some generic pattern like acanthus leaf." She paused, thinking about her grandmother and Chloe, and all the documents Marc had left spread out all over the little Creole cottage in Houma. "What else do you know about our family?"

"Not a hell of a lot, really. My mama didn't like to talk about'm. All kinda rumors about . . ." He paused with a laugh. "You know, family gossip."

twelve

HAHNVILLE, 1912

WHEN THE RIVER HAD burst through the sandbags and spread across the land, the initial wave had mellowed to a broad, shallow, creeping body. The rural folk, alerted to the situation by the sheriff and deputy, had watched the stealing tide as it crossed fields and swirled upon their shanties. The thin sheet of water hadn't seemed threatening at first. Its approach had been slow enough to allow people to grab belongings and move to higher ground. But its lean, sluggish movement had also deceived them into thinking they were not in danger. When the ankle-deep body of water had raised itself to waist level and then higher, the quiet tide carried relentless force. People who hadn't made it to the high ground had found themselves shooed up onto their rooftops, waiting powerlessly in the cool intermittent drizzle. People, dogs, mice, cats, and rats all shared the same rooftops and trees. Stranded cattle had waded through the swamped pastures with wild eyes, heads tilted above the surface, lowing, and then drowning.

Rémi and Francois had taken two vessels down the main artery of the Mississippi River to Glory Plantation—Rémi's bateau which was powered by a two-cycle gasoline engine, and the simple plantation pirogue trailing behind it in tow—where they'd found Jacob fishing from his balcony. They'd also collected several plantationers strewn along corrugated metal rooftops, the same Glory workers who had been sandbagging the levee the day before. A dry stretch of high ground outside Vacherie had served as a good location for a makeshift tent town that provided some shelter against the elements. Rémi and Francois had continued to gather those who were stranded, ferrying them to the high ground. They'd all been through this many times before.

By the second day, a nagging itch on Rémi's feet evolved into fiery boils. Helen's servant Chloe had made him a salve which soothed the fungus, and he'd continued the rescue efforts barefoot.

Now, on the third day, the rain ceased altogether and the weather was warm. Helen wanted to see about her mother who was suffering frail health in the wake of the flood. The rescuers had already found and relocated most of the people stranded by the floodwaters, and the Red Cross had managed to provide emergency shelter and food to the displaced evacuees, and so Rémi agreed to take her to the train station.

He perused the gallery, looking out over the expanse of his property while Helen, bags packed, gathered sweet peas to take to her mother. Terrefleurs' broad avenue teemed with the refugees who'd been rerouted as overflow from the tent city. The Mississippi sparkled innocently in the morning light, swollen but otherwise revealing none of the past week's treachery. But something else was wrong. Rémi couldn't say what. A quiet fiend, like termites in the foundation.

"*Tant de gens,*" came a woman's voice.

Rémi wheeled. Helen's servant Chloe was standing near the rear stairwell, a basket over her wrist.

"I've told you to use English," Rémi said.

She did not reply, only stood watching him. She turned and started down the stairs.

Rémi said, "But you're right, Terrefleurs is full. The workers are two and three to a bed."

She paused and turned back toward him. "Is dangerous. There will be fights."

"You know of some trouble?"

"Nothing in plain sight. Not yet."

"It'll only be for another day or two. The water's already receding. We'll keep them working—idle hands are the devil's playthings."

Chloe turned and continued her descent down the stairs.

Rémi saw Helen below in the kitchen garden, and watched as Chloe moved to the gate and across the whistler's walk to join her. Nearby, the gardener's six-year-old son, a harelip named Laramie who'd just recently begun plantation school, was picking debris out of the garden and loading it onto a wheelbarrow. He could barely reach the top but his deformity and his disposition made him look as though he wore a permanent smile.

Ironic that the little Laramie should be assigned to the whistler's walk; he was incapable of whistling. In the early days of Terrefleurs, servants were made to whistle as they carried trays from the kitchen to the main house—a way to keep them from sneaking food from the plates. A strange tradition of recent past, and an attitude that had long since faded. Nowadays, Tatie Bernadette's strategy for keeping servants from stealing food was to make sure their bellies were full.

Helen's long dark hair was woven into an elegant twist and neatly pinned under her bonnet, and she stood with her hand at the slender curve of her waist. She and Chloe commiserated in the shadow of the white-painted brick *pigeonnier* while the birds watched and cooed from their apartment perches. Chloe snipped stems of sweet marjoram and showed them to Helen who in turn examined them closely, smelling the leaves and tucking them into the basket. Rémi thought of the salve that Chloe had made for his foot, and wondered about Chloe's background, and where she might have acquired her medicinal knowledge.

The sensation returned to him, that an invader had come. He panned the area. His vision straining, he closed his eyes in frustration, and then opened them again.

Movement from the path below caught his eye. A tall black man clad in worker's overalls entered the garden. The man's gaze was fixed on Rémi with a striking expression—the lack of respect in the eyes; rotted teeth in an unsavory grin. He was not a field worker at Terrefleurs. Must have been an evacuee. As Rémi watched, he leaned over and whispered to little Laramie. Laramie looked different. A golden shimmer seemed to dance across his skin. Actually, to Rémi's tired eyes, that shimmer seemed to be coming from deeper within the child.

"*Hey, garçon!*" Rémi called to the stranger.

But the worker turned away from the harelip child and started toward the garden exit.

Rémi leaned forward and called again. "*Hey, garçon! Arrêtez!*"

The worker slowed. Helen, Chloe, and the child looked askance at Rémi for a moment, and then looked toward the far hedges where the worker was striding away.

"*Arrêtez!*" Rémi called again.

The worker halted. And then he turned around slowly, wearing an expression that registered somewhere between surprise and delight.

But that delight had aggression in it, the look of a coyote challenged by a housecat, and Rémi had to bolster himself to maintain an authoritative voice. "*Viens ici. Qui es-tu?*"

The worker gaped back with that same grin, only this time, the grin widened. And Rémi was certain he saw viciousness in it. The man's African skin lacked any sheen of sweat. His eyes were dark as though the pupil swallowed the whole of the iris. The man stepped toward Helen.

"*Arretez!*" Rémi said, jabbing out his hand and pointing at him.

He just continued, very slowly, each step in blatant defiance of Rémi's order. Chloe was wary and alert, her eyes trained on Rémi. The worker reached Helen and then leaned and whispered something into her ear. Helen seemed barely to notice; she gaped at her husband, bewildered.

Rémi darted for the stairs.

The worker turned and walked away, leaving through the garden gate, striding past the kitchen house.

"*Ho!*" Rémi called after him.

But by the time Rémi made it to the bottom of the staircase, he was gone. Rémi trotted in the direction the worker had been moving. Nothing.

He circled back to the garden where Helen and Chloe had resumed collecting legumes for Helen's mother.

Rémi called over to his wife, "*Chérie*, who was that? What did he say to you?"

She turned and looked back at Rémi with a hand to her bonnet, straining to see him over the hedge wall.

"What did you say, dear?"

"Who was that? That man! He just spoke to you!"

"I can't hear you." Helen shook her head. "Is it time to leave for the station? We're ready."

"What?"

Rémi cursed. He looked out toward the woods, then back at his wife. He nodded. He would talk to Francois about this man.

thirteen

NEW ORLEANS, 2009

A LITTLE BOY SPREAD his arms like airplane wings as he ran around the great oak tree near the Audubon gates. There were other children playing, too, but Madeleine was drawn to this one, perhaps because he was a mulatto like herself. He looked striking with bronze-colored hair and light brown skin and freckles on his nose. Nearby stood a couple that must have been the child's parents, a black man and a white woman carrying plastic cups filled with something cool. All three of them—from the little boy to the parents—seemed happy.

Watching them, Madeleine felt she could identify the weft and warp each parent had individually contributed in giving life to the little creature.

Creating a creature. A creature is a creation.

The little boy's golden hair color came from the mother, but the curly texture was from the father; as were the big brown eyes and soft wide lips. Cheekbones from mom. Madeleine wondered about the hidden traits: the pieces of his personality, the likes and dislikes, the medical conditions, the mental disorders.

And then she saw Ethan walking toward her.

"There you are, watching the children play. Cute, aren't they?" He kissed her cheek.

"Hi. Oh, yeah."

He looked at her face. "Wait, you weren't thinking about how cute they are."

"Well they *are* cute. But no, I was thinking about the traits."

"Traits?"

She shrugged.

He looked back up toward the great tree, where the children climbed and shrieked and scrambled around trying to catch each other. "Very observant, Dr. LeBlanc. And have you ever considered splicing your own traits with another humanoid? Purely in the interest of scientific investigation, of course."

"I—I . . ." her shoulders ratcheted toward her ears, a thing she would never have been conscious of until Sam had pointed it out.

He grinned. "Come on. You know you want to try your hand at creating creatures."

She gave a start at his choice of words. "Create creatures?"

"Why you lookin at me like you seen a ghost?"

She blinked, trying to think of a clever response, but he'd already taken her elbow and was pulling her toward the entrance.

"Come on, missy. We gotta lotta ground to cover. Besides, I have news."

"What?"

"Hang on. I'll tell you when we get through the gate."

He'd already bought their tickets so they didn't have to wait in line. Coming out the other side, the walkway spread broad before them, and she felt relieved to stretch out her legs and get moving.

They looped the path and he took her hand, leading her toward the exotic birds.

Madeleine looked over her shoulder. "Isn't Monkey Hill that way?"

"We're taking the scenic route." He strode at a fast pace despite his limp.

Madeleine said, "Doesn't it bother you, all this walking?"

He shook his head. "I try to get as much exercise as I can. Somewhere along the way I figured out the key was to listen to the body. I do shokotai to keep in tune."

"What's that?"

"It's a karate technique."

She asked, "Is the limp from an injury, or an illness?"

"Old football injury. Bumped my spine when I was in high school. Doctor said I'd never walk again."

"You're kidding!"

"Took me years, but I proved him wrong."

"Is this why you got into neuroscience?"

He grinned at her. "That's exactly why. Turns out I was lucky in the way my spine was broken. A lot of physical therapy and stubbornness, but I got around it."

She smiled at him, realizing that she liked his voice. In a way, he'd gotten into neuroscience and she'd gotten into psychology for similar reasons. Both of them had been affected by circumstances in their respective areas of study.

She said, "So what's this news you're being so mysterious about?"

"Kinda funny coincidence. We're gonna be working in the same department."

"Psych?"

"Yeah."

"You're kidding. Any study in particular?"

"A new program—Perceptual and Noetic Science."

Madeleine slowed her pace as she processed this, wondering when the department started throwing money at pseudosciences.

Ethan said, "Something wrong?"

"No, it's just kind of surprising. They're cutting programs left and right. This is the first time I heard anything about adding new ones."

Ethan nodded. "Well, it's got private sponsorship, and they're keeping it pretty quiet. Given the subject matter—you know, psi and all that, it can be pretty controversial."

"Wait, when you say psi, I assume you're talking about things like extrasensory perception."

"Well, yeah. Psi-gamma covers things like ESP. Psi-kappa relates to actions, like psychokinesis. We're exploring all of it."

"So as a neurologist, what exactly are you going to be doing with them?"

"Actually, in this sense I'm more of a neuroscientist than a neurologist. Anyway I'm looking at brain activity in cases of proven psi."

She cut him a sideways look and said, "*Proven* psi? Forgive my saying, but isn't that an oxymoron? Hate to be cynical, but . . ."

"It's all right. Wasn't so sure myself at first. But yes, there are quite a few instances of proven psi. Usually it comes up in the case of unique subjects—people with special abilities. But it's also reproducible and traceable in a lab with random subjects."

"Really."

"Really."

Her voice took an edge. "So you're saying that we're all a bunch of psychics."

He looked at her with tolerance, and she felt a twinge of reproach.

He said, "As a matter of fact, if you want to put it that way, yes. We are all psychics."

"Sorry Ethan. Not trying to be cavalier. I just have a hard time believing in something I can't study with hard evidence."

"I don't mind. A long time ago people didn't believe in invisible fairies that made you sick. Then Louis Pasteur took hold of a microscope and told us about germs."

She considered this. "Touché."

Ethan pointed toward the swamp exhibit. "Hey look. Albo gator."

She looked. A bright white alligator was lying on the banks a fair distance away. Albino like Chloe's attendant Oran. The contrast of the alligator's skin made it stand out like a starfish on a black piling.

Beneath their feet, the path changed to boardwalk, and Madeleine realized that up until now she'd been so focused on her own thoughts that she'd barely taken in the zoo itself. Screw pines crowded close around them, dense with foliage, and then they opened to strategically placed vignettes of lily pads, turtles, and cypress. A replication of a trapper's shanty floated on wood planks, and it reminded her of Zenon's tiny fishing cottage in Bayou Black. She remembered some controversy after the hurricane, when the zoo had outfitted the swamp shack so that it looked like other post-Katrina houses, with a tarp over the roof and a taped-up refrigerator. They'd even made it look like search-and-rescue teams had been there and found human casualties, complete with the grim painted X and the words, "gators fed."

Madeleine looked at the trees' roots rising out of the water, and thought of the wavy-lined patterns from her college parapsychology experiments.

"I remember those old flash cards with the squiggly lines and shapes—the 'guess which one I'm looking at' game. Is your team using those?"

"Zener cards. Haven't been on board long enough to know everything they're doing in the department, but I don't think they're using those."

"I imagine you're doing more sophisticated tests."

"Oh yeah. Real elaborate and complex."

"Really? Like what?"

He took her hand, and her cynicism felt suddenly unimportant under the spark of his touch. She looked up at his face and saw that he was watching her with a strong, quiet kind of depth. He withdrew his hand, and when she looked down, she saw he'd left a penny in her palm.

He said, "That's our complex, sophisticated testing equipment."

"A penny?"

He nodded.

"No wonder y'all found it easy to get funding." She handed it back to him.

He smiled and slipped the penny in his pocket. "The experiments go a little something like this."

He took her by the shoulders and turned her around so that she faced the railing. The replica swamp lay ahead, and two green dragonflies were joined in flight over a spray of ferns. Ethan stood behind her with his arms encircling hers, and he placed each of her hands on the railing and then backed away. She started to look over her shoulder at him.

"Don't turn around," he said, and so she looked straight ahead toward the pond.

A pelican sat dozing on a log, its head nestled back, its bill almost as long as its wings. She waited for Ethan to act or at least speak to her. But he remained silent and whatever he was doing back there, she felt certain he had his eyes on her. It made her skin prickle.

Finally she could stand it no longer. "What are you doing back there, just staring at me?"

"That's exactly what I'm doing."

She turned around and saw his amusement.

"Don't tell me you're conducting scientific experiments on staring," she said.

"Pretty much."

"And this is neuroscience?"

He stepped toward her and put a hand to her temple, smoothing a strand of hair. "It's all about your brain, Dr. LeBlanc. That feeling you get when you're being watched. It's not just coincidence. The brain emits waves—gamma waves, beta waves—and it's possible the brain knows how to intercept those waves too. When someone's brain is focused on you, you can literally feel it."

Her lips parted in surprise.

He said, "The brain picks up the waves, but it might not immediately register as a conscious thought. So it sends signals to the rest of your body to create other physiological warnings. Tension in the hair follicles, causing your hair to stand on end, and surge in blood flow to the upper extremities."

She was stunned. "So that feeling that you're being watched—you're saying it's real, not just a coincidence?"

"It's real all right. And it's a good habit to get into, paying attention to that. The more you tune in, the stronger it gets because you're forming neurons specifically for tuning in. Neuroplasticity. I'd be willing to bet a whole lot of crimes can be avoided if people just learned to trust their instincts."

"And the penny?"

"A randomization generator."

She thought for a minute. "You flip a coin."

"That's right."

"And what does that do for you?"

"Put two people in a room. The subject faces a wall, the researcher sits directly behind the subject. The researcher flips a coin and if it's heads, he'll stare at the subject. If it's tails, he won't. The subject has to guess whether or not he's staring."

"I see. And how often does the subject get it right?"

He shrugged. "On average, about fifty-four percent of the time."

"Fifty-four? Come on, that's hardly even noticeable. Chance is fifty-fifty."

"Yes, except that extra four percent above an even fifty-fifty makes all the difference in the world. It's repeatable, consistently, time and time again. You know what the odds are for that kind of result?"

"Tell me."

"202 octodecillion to one."

She grinned at him, aware that she had resolved to suppress her own mad scientist for the evening, and yet here he was relating on her own terms. Odd how all his talk about brain waves seemed to bring out the highlights in those brown eyes of his.

She said, "I have no idea how much an octodecillion is."

"I had to look it up myself. Lotta zeroes."

She tore her gaze away from his eyes, feeling lighthearted, and he slipped his hand in hers as they stepped off the boardwalk onto the path toward Monkey Hill.

She said, "I never thought of neuroplasticity in terms of psi before."

"Most people haven't. I know how you usually think of it, because I read about it in your paper on cognitive schizophrenia."

She laughed. "Sure. Part of the treatment is to assist the patient with creating healthy mental habits. Which is, essentially, neuroplasticity."

"I'd be curious to see the fMRIs of those patients, before and after."

She looked at him. "Does this mean you're going to pursue this for the rest of your career?"

He shrugged. "It fascinates me. Not something that originally attracted me to brain science, but the deeper I get into it the more exciting it becomes. But I'm not obsessive about it. There are other things that are important."

"Oh? Like what?"

"Oh, you know. Home life. Getting married someday. Creating some creatures." He grinned at her. "How about you?"

"I don't know. Haven't thought much beyond my career."

BATON ROUGE, 2009

ANITA RAN HER HAND along the smooth, brushed steel as they stood amid parallel shooting alleys. Zenon took the weapon from her grasp.

"Always assume it's loaded. And always point the muzzle downrange. If you're pointing at something, be prepared to shoot it."

She nodded, fiddling with her headphones and plastic safety glasses that converged in an awkward spot just behind her ear. In the next booth, the shooter fired several rounds in rapid succession. As the shooter's paper target swung into motion, she could see the shots grouped near the center circle.

"Wow," she said, raising her brows.

"Anita, this is important. Pay attention. You keep your finger *off* the trigger, and off the trigger guard until you are ready to shoot."

She shifted her weight, resisting the urge to point out that they had already gone over this. Many times.

"Got it." She smiled.

He nodded. "Load and make ready."

She held the gun with her right hand and loaded a magazine.

"Downrange," Zenon said. "Keep it pointed downrange at all times."

She sighed and swung the muzzle to point directly downrange. It hadn't been that far off, she thought. If it had discharged, the bullet would have just hit someone else's target. No biggie.

"Never thought I'd shoot a gun before. It's kind of sexy." She cut her gaze back toward Zenon, or at least toward the broad moguls under his black t-shirt, and wished she was wearing something sexier than these birth control goggles. She pulled the slide, chambering the round, and applied the safety.

"Magazine," Zenon said.

She let the empty drop to the floor. "My dad wanted me to learn to shoot. For protection. Did you hear about that girl, Angel Frey?"

He said nothing.

"They still haven't found her. I wonder if she's alive."

She inserted a fully charged magazine. As she did this, her pinky grazed the trigger guard.

"Finger off the trigger!" Zenon barked.

This startled her. She lifted the offending pinky finger and crooked it in the air so that it resembled the formal manner of sipping tea. Zenon's face clouded. Anita holstered the pistol.

"Gun clear, hammer down," he said.

The command sent a surge through her body. She pinched the slide and extended her arms, and finally—finally!—squeezed the trigger.

The gun jerked in her hands, and she couldn't see whether the bullet even hit the target, though she suspected it hadn't.

"Breathe, relax, aim, and squeeze," he said, stepping behind her and lifting her arms so that they were level. He held them with one hand and used the other to shift her hips to a centered position, pushing his knee between her legs. She felt his breath at her ear.

"Feet shoulder-width apart." He stepped back and folded his arms.

The hair stirred on the back of her neck. Though she couldn't see him, the knowledge that he was staring at her back gave her a thrill. She spread her feet and strengthened her stance, taking care to tighten her butt, then fired again.

"Better," he said. "Relax."

She fired a few more rounds and bit her lip, deliberately letting her arms sag a little. He reached out and lifted them again.

She smiled.

fourteen

HAHNVILLE, 1912

*A*S THEY TRAVELED DOWNRIVER into the floodplain, the scent of stagnant water and rot clung heavily in the air. Rémi had sent Francois out to continue rescue efforts in the motorized bateau, which meant that he, Helen, and Chloe had to huddle together in the little pirogue, powered only by Rémi's sweat. The floodwaters were brown and thick with the lifeless bodies of cattle and other livestock that had been swept away. Helen held her handkerchief to her mouth and clutched Chloe's arm as they glided along.

Raised post-and-beam plantation houses hovered over the water like genteel ladies lifting their hems to avoid puddles. Smaller outbuildings were submerged to the roofs. A rowboat sat tethered at the Locoul house, and servants bustled about controlling the damage as best they could.

The bayou had crept from the woods and mingled with the waters of the river, and the otherwise-familiar land was unrecognizable. Rémi navigated in the stifling humidity by following reeds growing from the earthen levee that ran along River Road. The sound of cicadas buzzed in the trees, along with the gentle lapping of water against the boat. Off in the distance, ever so faintly, came the unnatural sound of a bell ringing.

Rémi stopped. The faint ringing continued, not like church bells, but more like the sound of a cow bell, tolling rhythmically from the direction of the bayou.

Helen needed to get to the train station soon, but Rémi suspected the ringing came from someone in need of help in the flood waters. And so much time had now passed since the flood began, anyone who was still surviving out there would be in a desperate condition.

Helen followed his gaze to the cypress forest in the distance. "Go see who it is, Rémi."

He dipped the oar into the water and turned the boat in the direction of the ringing. They moved silently away from the main channel of the river, across a broad, watery plain to where a thicket of trees marked the borders to the swamp. The bell grew steadily louder. They pressed forward until they reached the heart of the *ciprière*. Because the towering cypress trees are naturally aquatic, the *ciprière* seemed unperturbed by flooding. The only hint came from the fact that the trees wore giant nests of Spanish moss at their bases as well as on their boughs. The ringing echoed all around them.

Rémi cupped his hand around his mouth and called out across thick waters: "Hallo?"

The ringing stopped, and the trio listened intently. Nothing but the sizzling noises of insects in the trees. A trickle ran down Rémi's temple, and it felt as though he was perspiring swamp water.

Then from beyond the cypress, they heard a woman's voice: *"Hallo! Ici! Au secours!"*

The bell rang out again, this time with fervor.

Rémi thrust the oar into the beery swamp, turning the boat back to the north by a thicket. They came upon a black woman cradling a child in a cypress.

She wept when she saw them, sobbing pleas of help and gushing relief in muddled English and Creole. In her arms lay a child of about six or seven, and he neither lifted his arm or raised his hand. She handed the limp boy down to Rémi, who passed him to Chloe and then helped the woman into the boat. The child's eyes were open but dull and rimmed red. His breathing came in ragged, wheezing efforts, and his body burned with fever.

Helen's pale eyes grew wide. "Rémi, the doctor!"

Rémi nodded. "Vacherie."

❧

HE NAVIGATED THE PIROGUE back to the main waterway. As they traveled, the woman babbled in her Creole-English mix, describing the events of the past several days.

Her name was Fatima. She told them how she had heard the warning that the water was coming, and had been evacuating when her son Ferrar disappeared. She'd gone looking for him and had found him trying to salvage his crawfish traps at the rim of the bayou. There the initial wave had hit, and though it had been a low, creeping wave, it had grown turbulent when it collided with the swamp. They had tried to wade and then swim back to Locoul Plantation. But, disoriented and exhausted by the tumultuous water, they'd taken refuge in a tree. They'd stayed there through the night, and the next morning they'd again tried to swim, but once again failed to find their way. By then, the wet chill had taken its toll on the boy, and he was succumbing to exposure.

The following day had passed with Ferrar growing weaker and more ill. Fatima was afraid to try swimming again, exposing her son to the cold water which by then had become foul. Finally, this morning, she'd noticed the bloated carcass of a cow drifting nearby. She'd slipped back into the fetid water to retrieve a bell from around its neck, and had been ringing it ever since.

Her hands were clasped around her son's, with tears streaming down her face as she spoke. Helen and Chloe patted and cooed, dipping Helen's handkerchief into the thick waters and trying to cool the boy's fevered brow. Helen stole furtive glances at Rémi as if to urge him faster with her eyes.

Fatima's gaze darted past Chloe, and then returned and fixed upon her as if noticing her for the first time. She addressed her in rural French.

I know who you are. You're from Elderberry Plantation.

Chloe shook her head.

The boy's ragged breathing grew louder. The four adults ceased conversation and stared at him. His rasping became a gurgle, and he writhed in his mother's arms. And then he clawed at his throat. Fatima gasped and grabbed his hands, but his small fingernails had already left bleeding tracks on his neck. Rémi pressed forth with all his might at the oars, frantically heaving for Vacherie, still a good distance away. Too far away. Rémi thought the child's shredded gasps were the most terrible sounds he'd ever heard.

But then the sounds stopped altogether, and the desperate silence that followed was far more horrible.

The child gaped, his tongue protruding to its farthest extent and his eyes wide with panic. Fatima grabbed his shoulders and shouted his name. His eyes rolled with abject fear, but his lungs did not fill.

Fatima screamed. "For God, my baby's not breathing! Ferrar!"

A burst of red appeared in his left eye. A blood vessel overstrained. He flailed.

Fatima clamped Chloe's wrist. "Help him!"

Rémi dropped the oar in the boat, seizing the boy and shaking him. Ferrar thrashed but did not catch a breath. Chloe reached past Rémi and thrust her fingers into the boy's mouth, but he responded with not so much as a gurgle.

Chloe touched Rémi's arm. "I must to have a reed."

He looked back at her in confusion.

She repeated herself, switching to French, and pointed to the clump rising out of the river several feet away. *"Tout de suite!"*

Realization dawned and Rémi started paddling for the reeds. He cursed and tossed aside the paddle and threw himself over the side of the boat. With a glint of his pocket knife, he severed a fistful and splashed back to Chloe.

She grabbed the reeds and also the pocket knife. Rémi climbed back in.

"Hold the head!" she said.

Rémi positioned himself behind Ferrar so that his knees were on either side of the boy's ears, his hands gently cradling the skull. Ferrar was no longer thrashing.

Chloe made quick cuts on the reed until she had a short, stiff tube, then blew through the center of it. The child's dark skin had grown ashen. She straddled his limp body and cupped her hands behind his neck, lifting so that his head lolled backward. She grabbed Rémi's hand and directed him to hold the child firmly so that he maintained this posture.

Chloe probed the V in the center of the child's collarbone. And then her fingers moved from the V up toward the chin, until she found the sensitive, boneless indentation just below the Adam's apple. Her knife flashed, slicing into tissue. Fatima cried out.

Chloe pressed her finger inside the boy's throat as blood began to flow. She sank the reed into the incision and blew a short breath through the tube. The child's lungs expanded, then lay still. She blew again, paused, then repeated the action. Each time the child's chest rose, then lay motionless. Blood flowed down the boy's neck and onto Rémi's clothing.

Chloe blew again, and then again, and again.

Finally, there came a strangled gurgle from the boy's throat. He gagged, a silent gesture at the mouth, but audible at the point of incision. His lungs filled and released on their own, each breath causing a hollow whistle through the reed.

Fatima sobbed and pressed her forehead to her son's hand. Helen, ghost-white and unsteady, trembled as she mopped the child's blood with her dampened lace handkerchief.

Rémi crawled back into position with the oar, and resumed haste for Vacherie.

f i f t e e n

BAYOU BLACK, 2009

THE CITY OF NEW ORLEANS faded to haze in the rearview mirror as they drove south, and Jasmine's tiny wet nose bounced along the window, leaving wispy patterns on the glass. Ethan sat at the wheel. Madeleine sat in the passenger seat with Jasmine in her lap. And wedged between them, chattering like a squirrel in November, sat Daddy Blank.

"So y'all had a good time at the zoo?" Daddy said.

"Yup," Madeleine said, and switched on the Cajun music station. Daddy patted his leg in time to the jaunty rhythms, and Madeleine smiled. When his schizophrenia was escalating he had a hard time tolerating things like radio and TV. His enjoying the music was a good sign.

"You went on over to Monkey Hill, did you?" Daddy pressed.

Madeleine said, "Yup."

"That's it? That's all?"

Ethan cocked an eye at him and then returned his gaze to the road.

Daddy said, "Oh, that's right. Y'all went out to dinner after, didn't you?"

Madeleine rolled her eyes and gave him a look. Daddy only knew about Monkey Hill because he'd been eavesdropping when they'd made plans. He'd been staying in the Quarter, so he wasn't aware that not only had they indeed gone to dinner, but they'd gone again the next night. And every few days since.

She stole a glance at Ethan's forearm, muscular and patterned with downy hairs, and she remembered that sandalwood-and-granite scent of him. An unbidden grin came to her lips, and she turned her face toward the window.

Daddy took another stab. "Crêpe Nanou was it? That where y'all went to eat?"

Ethan cleared his throat. "Sir, just so you know, I've been very respectful with your daughter."

"Not that it's any of your business, Daddy," Madeleine said.

"How do ya like that," Daddy said.

Ethan added, "Anyway, Miss Madeleine here barely gives me the time of day. Pert near had to set an appointment through her secretary just to trick her into goin out."

"That so?" And before Daddy even turned his head, Ethan had managed to sneak in a look toward Madeleine, which she in turn absorbed with only the slightest flash of the eyes.

Ethan replied, "Yessir. Kinda humbling too, considering her secretary's also my secretary now."

"Ethan's come on board as a liaison to Tulane's psych department," Madeleine said.

"So you're working together," Daddy said. "Isn't that nice. Guess it makes sense to have a neuroscientist hangin around a bunch of headshrinkers."

"Not exactly working together. We're both in the psych department, but his program is very closed and hush-hush."

The truck hummed beneath them, and the swampland crept in closer around the highway. Daddy's interest in the subject seemed to have evaporated. The song on the radio changed to a sleepy, sensual blues hybrid by Buckwheat Zydeco.

Ethan glanced toward Madeleine. "Tell me again what we're gonna be doing out on that swamp, darlin?"

"Collecting flowers for Sam to use at the flower shop. She wants to do an All Souls Day display on the second, with water hyacinths, or whatever pretty thing we can pull out of the bayou for her."

"Sounds relaxing."

Daddy said, "Y'all can sit around and blow bubbles in the lily pads. Me, I'm goin fishin."

Madeleine smiled at her father, then looked out as they sped through the swamplands and could already see drifts of water irises in bloom. Easy and nice out there on the water. She couldn't wait.

Out of nowhere Daddy muttered, "Can't take it no more"; he reached over and switched off the radio.

The truck fell to white silence. Madeleine looked at the now-vacant digital display and then eyed her father, wondering if the music had stirred the old confusions in him.

"You all right, Daddy?"

"Just like some peace and quiet every now and then, that's all. Can't a man just enjoy a little silence?"

ON THE OUTSKIRTS OF Houma, Bayou Black formed a glittering arrow that shot from the Mississippi feeders out to the Gulf. As if the mighty river had gotten antsy during her run and sent forth a projectile just so she could reach her destination that much sooner. Over time, she and her feeders had taken over forests and cane fields and saw to it that like the water, the landscape never grew stagnant. Otters were almost as common out here as feral cats, and so were coon or skunk or possum. Down the bayou, at the end of the little clamshell road, stood the old LeBlanc cottage, like Charon watching over the River Styx. Neither Madeleine nor her father mentioned to Ethan how they'd pointedly avoided setting foot inside the house.

Another day, thought Madeleine. *We'll tend to Marc's things later.*

Looking at it now, the most basic, raw Creole construction, it seemed both sweet and horrific to her, her childhood home was simple and loyal, unable to protect, and ultimately abandoned. Madeleine looked away from this place where she and her brother had spent their first days in the world, and where he had spent his last.

Jasmine bounded around the rear of it and came shooting back from beneath the structure, cobwebs and a dried elderberry leaf spiked to her hair. Madeleine brushed her off, glad to fuss a little and divert her focus.

As Daddy and Ethan loaded her brother's skiff into the water, Madeleine took out her cell phone and tried calling Chloe. The image of that girl, Severin, had been haunting her, and Madeleine wanted to make sure she was being tended to properly.

"LeBlanc residence."

"Hello, Oran? This is Madeleine LeBlanc. Is Miss Chloe there?"

"She's not at home."

"I see. Did she get the messages I left for her?"

"Yes ma'am."

"Because I wanted to ask her some questions about Severin."

"Mm hmm."

Madeleine sighed. "Will you pass along the message to call me?"

"I . . . Well, yes ma'am."

"Thanks Oran. Bye-bye."

The boat was in the water and Ethan pulled forward to park the truck over by the cottage. Jasmine skipped past Ethan down the dock and hopped over the seats to her favorite perch.

"You done making social calls?" Daddy hollered over the motor.

Madeleine tucked the cell phone into her pack and Ethan offered his hand to help her step off the dock. She thanked him, absently, while inwardly resolving that she was going to find out what was going on with the little girl Severin whether Chloe cooperated or not.

Shoeless and unwashed; too ragged, too wild, serious neglect was going on, and Madeleine wasn't about to just let it go.

The boat was suddenly in motion, the old Creole cottage disappearing behind them as they sped forth. The movement freshened her lungs with cool oxygen, and they passed forests of tall pine and oak until the trees became shorter: alder, elderberry, and scrub. Chinese tallow were turning ruby with the change of season, and the purple aster bloomed with wide red eyes in the centers of the flower heads. Bayou Black seemed to have the spirit of Halloween about it, with a bite of ionic charge that relayed echoes from another world.

The bayou broke free from the developed neighborhoods. They passed through the concrete-and-steel saltwater intrusion lock that acted as a valve, blocking the brackish water from mingling with the fresh, and then they entered the wilds. Here, the trees stretched once again higher and even higher toward heaven, grand water cypress with their priestly robes of Spanish moss.

Jasmine darted back and forth along the bottom of the skiff, peering over the side at her reflection as it zoomed across the surface of the water. Finally the bayou and cypress trees fell back, too, and they entered open fields of water hyacinths that spread like a royal carpet laying the way to the Gulf. All of it—the swamp and the marsh, and all the flora and creatures that lived there—was Bayou Black.

Here in the salty marsh, in the field of saline-tolerant flowers, Daddy cut the motor and secured the skiff.

Madeleine shrugged off her button-down shirt, leaving just her bathing suit top and cutoffs, and slipped into the water. Ethan followed in his swimming trunks. Daddy had his fishing hook baited and cast on the opposite side of the boat before they'd even dampened their hair.

"How's the water?" he called.

Madeleine wiggled her toes as the cool liquid permeated her sneakers. "Feels like heaven."

"I'll second that," Ethan said.

The flower collection baskets, fashioned out of old crab pots, floated on a towline. The water level hit at about chest height so they walked easily as they collected specimens.

"Gators ever come out this far?" Ethan said, looking around.

Madeleine laughed. "No, city slicker. They like the freshwater better, over yonder in the cypress forest. Not so big on the salt marshes. But it's best to keep an eye out anyway because you never know. Everything that lives out here is just plain tough. Animals, bugs, plants."

"I guess they'd have to be."

They bent their bodies so that only their heads were above the surface, and they moved forward in slow-motion giant steps through the water, no sound but the occasional splash and Daddy's spin cast. Ethan took a breath and disappeared beneath the surface. Madeleine parted a path through the flowers, avoiding an area of stagnant water where brown foam floated in drifts. She wrinkled her nose. Scum like that tended to breed unfriendly organisms, and this particular slick emitted especially vile odors. She moved on to fresher patches.

Ethan surfaced again. "Can't see a damn thing under there."

"What were you looking for?"

He shrugged. "I don't know. Fish. Critters. Pretty pair of legs."

She smiled, looking down at the water. She could see about an inch below the surface before everything faded to black.

"Any rules as to which of these flowers we should get?" Ethan said.

Madeleine untangled one of the irises and put it in the basket. "Go for the ones with full buds that haven't bloomed yet."

Ethan gave a grunt and rose from the water.

"What's the matter?" Madeleine said.

They were higher on a sandbar now, and the shimmering, silken plane rested at his rib cage.

Ethan shook his head. "Nothin. Somethin slimy just tickled my leg."

"You really are a city slicker. Haven't you ever come out to the bayou?"

"Been to it. Just not *in* it."

"Well, you never really know what's brushing up against your leg down there. Could be fallen branches or fish, or maybe something you'd just as soon not know about."

"Damn, woman. You're not putting my mind at ease here."

She smiled. "When Marc and I were kids we never gave it a second thought. We went swimming in the bayou all the time. And then one day we went free-diving with friends. Looks a whole lot different when you're using a mask."

She remembered being surprised at just how forbidding the water had looked beneath the surface, even with the aid of a mask. The bottom had been dense with trees and charcoal swamp litter, and swamp gas had bubbled up in a promenade of sparkling columns. Everything was black, including the water, and visibility stretched only a few feet.

Ethan said, "Well?"

"Well what?"

"What did you see down there with the swimming mask?"

"Still hard to see anything, really, even with the mask. Lots of shadows down below. In fact, I was straining so hard to see this one big lump that I got right up to it before I realized I was nose-to-nose with an alligator."

"What!"

"Oh, he wasn't gonna hurt anybody. They're not usually aggressive with people."

"Usually."

"Well, yeah. He was just lying on the bottom with these alien-looking eyes encased in these great big waterproof bubbles. I swear he looked like he was smiling."

She recalled the dim outline of him, the corners of his lips curved up at the ends and sharp triangle teeth in a jack-o'-lantern grin. Ever since then she'd wondered how many times she and Marc had gone swimming, not realizing *what* they might be swimming *with*.

"You mean to tell me you were down there pettin a smiley alligator like he was an ole pussy cat?"

"Good lord, no. I hopped out of that water like it'd begun to boil."

Ethan stared at her for a stark, suspended moment, arms folded across his chest. About twenty yards behind him, the boat rocked as Daddy cast his line back into the water.

Madeleine rose to a full stance. "Don't worry, whatever slimed your leg just now, it probably wasn't an alligator."

Ethan said, "You gonna get that one?"

"What one?"

"That." He unfolded his arms and stepped toward her. "Perfect one . . ." He reached for her and she straightened in surprise, and then he continued just beyond and grasped a robust iris with fat buds that were barely shy of bloom; all the while his eyes never strayed from hers. ". . . right there."

She felt his leg brush her knee, and she instinctively smoothed her hand over his arm, leaving a trail of pearl droplets. Skin at once fiery and cool from the sun and water. His head remained bent over hers as he passed the iris to the collection basket.

"Your old man lookin at us?" Ethan said.

Madeleine's gaze flicked to the skiff and back. "Can't see through that drift of flowers if we're down low in the water."

They simultaneously sank to chin level. He touched her waist underwater, fingers on bare skin.

She grinned. "I hope you both realize he has no business being nosy or playing chaperone. I happen to be a grown woman."

"Oh, yes ma'am. I realize you're a grown woman all right. I got that message loud and clear."

Then, in those shadowed waters of Bayou Black, their legs intertwined, their arms tangled, their frames loosened and became weightless. He pulled her close. She felt his chest press against hers, and then felt his lips press against hers. Water lapping softly, with garlands of irises lacing around them. Their bodies bobbed in gentle unison with the current.

"Your hair looks real pretty when it's wet, Madeleine."

"I like the way your skin smells in the sun."

And then he kissed her a second time, his legs fitting with hers. She let her eyes close and the world fall away, with no care to creatures beneath the surface or whether smoke was smoke. He held the small of her back and it seemed that her spine unwound in an arch toward him, her muscles forming a magnet to his, their bodies suspended outside of gravity so that they were two coiled strands winding around one another, twisting to become a single unit. Fitting together with perfection as though they could zip into place. She ran the tip of her fingernail gently up his neck.

"Kissing you in this bayou was a baaaad idea, Madeleine," he whispered.

"Mm?" And then she felt his erection press against her. The sensation sent an immediate wave of heat that caused her to draw in her breath. An internal flash of openness, a mental image—no; her body's imagined *kinesthesia* of completing the fit. Her mouth and her eyes widened.

"Time to cool down." She turned and swam away from him, reaching for the collection basket and moving on to another clump of flowers.

He gave a bearish growl and shook his head. "Alligator ain't the only thing that can make this old bayou boil."

THREE COLLECTION BASKETS STUFFED with water hyacinths and irises rested in the skiff. Ethan eased on his sunglasses. Daddy Blank had caught nothing.

"*Yet,*" he qualified. "I know a secret place."

He started the motor and Jasmine licked the swamp water from Madeleine's legs. Madeleine did not bother to towel off because she knew the water would soon turn to sweat, and she would never really be dry in between. Her cutoffs flapped wet in the breeze. The boat eased into the shipping channel, the wide, flat stretch of blue nestled between the swamp and the marsh.

Ethan pressed an ice cold beer against her knee. "Want one?"

Madeleine kept her voice low, knowing her father couldn't hear them over the roar of the boat. "No thanks. I've long since cooled off."

He smiled back. "Guess we're doomed to keep it that way for now."

She laughed. Her hair blew wild and she felt like a teenager the way she and Ethan were sneaking around right under Daddy's nose.

Ethan popped the top of the beer and took a sip, looking back toward the heart of Bayou Black. "Scads of flowers on both sides, but this stretch here doesn't have a one. It's like the boating equivalent to a freeway."

Madeleine said, "It is. We're in the Intracoastal Waterway—runs from Texas to New Jersey."

"They keep it clear for the ships then, I guess."

She nodded. "The smaller channels around here in Houma get overrun with water plants. It'd be the same in the Intracoastal if it weren't for good old government intervention."

"Suppose that's all right. But I always wonder when you try to mess with Mother Nature."

"I know. We've got this clear path for our boat but it also means we have a problem with saltwater intrusion in Bayou Black. The plants are a natural barrier against the Gulf—it's already the perfect pattern of saltwater to brackish to fresh."

"Is that why I saw a lock back there?"

She nodded, and realized that Ethan probably knew as much about the wetland balances as she did if he recognized the saltwater intrusion lock.

"Doesn't lock out often. Just when there's a good storm surge blowing in from the Gulf."

A barge loomed toward them. Daddy Blank turned the skiff off the Intracoastal and down another, slightly hidden waterway formed by *cheniers,* long fingers of high ground that ran from the mainland to the coast. The bayou seeped between the *cheniers* to create a labyrinth of aquatic arteries that seemed to change shape each time Madeleine traversed them.

She felt a quiet stab of unease. Looking into the vast shaded coves, trying to keep her memories locked away, she told herself that Daddy was just taking them on an aimless journey. True enough, a tropical storm might cause whole stretches of land to disappear permanently, and sometimes fields of aquatic plants multiplied so rapidly they choked off entire byways. These changes often happened in a matter of days, even overnight. And yet this particular byway had remained the same since Marc and Madeleine were kids.

"Wait. Where are you taking us, Daddy?"

He looked over his shoulder and winked at her.

The waterway narrowed as the boat drifted in. The forest loomed overhead, with trees reaching up twenty and thirty feet, their boughs draped in long, graceful ribbons of Spanish moss. Cypress knees, the roots of the tree, rose up out of the water to form a gnarled miniature mountain range. Daddy cut the speed of the boat, and the wind gave way to heat.

"Daddy," Madeleine said. "Let's not go in there."

"Don't worry, kitten, I know this place."

"Something wrong?" Ethan said, looking into her face.

"No. It's fine." And even as she said those words, she realized she was keeping the LeBlanc family legacy alive by telling their heirloom lie: "It's fine."

Ethan took her hand. It felt cool and damp from the bottle.

Daddy Blank carefully navigated past a spider city, and turned to the right, down a narrow, hidden opening in the cypress trees. Madeleine wrapped her free hand around her waist. Although the trees crowded around tightly, the skiff was still able to squeeze into the passage, and they pressed forward until they could go no further.

Daddy Blank grinned. "Best fishin in Bayou Black is right here in this slough."

"I know," Madeleine murmured, but she did not say, *Marc and I were the ones who showed it to you about fifteen years ago.*

"Man, this is something. Maybe I'll throw a line in the water too," Ethan said.

Sparse pearls of sunshine filtered through shrouds of Spanish moss. When they were children, Madeleine, Marc, and Zenon used to come here. The perfect place to play, catch bass, and check crawfish traps. They'd named it Crawfish Cove. To most folks, the bayou seemed like a feral maze. To her, its haunts and nooks were just as familiar as a town center, with Crawfish Cove being the favored saloon. It had been a place of comfort. A refuge. Though Daddy didn't know it, it had been where Marc had come to die.

Daddy baited and cast his fishing line with shrimp and Ethan joined him. A whir and a splash. Their faces shone with certainty that they'd catch something. And they would, Madeleine knew. They would in *this* fishing hole.

As children, Marc and Madeline had vowed that if the Child Protective Services officer ever came for them—which he never did—they would come and hide out here. Madeleine envisioned her strong, freckle-faced brother as a boy. Those angled blue eyes, the skinny arms. She was surprised to realize she felt warm with his memory. Surprised she could think about him without the familiar chokehold of grief.

A bright green carpet of duckweed stretched across the narrow waterway in front of them. It looked like she could hop out of the boat and stride across it like grass on dry land. She leaned over the side and picked up a clump. White, succulent roots tumbled below spongy, dime-sized green pads. She scooped up several clumps of duckweed and added them to the collection basket.

Suddenly, the green plane broke and something splashed at the end of Daddy's fishing line.

"Son of a gun," said Ethan.

"It's a good one!" Daddy said, his rod bending toward the water like a dowser. The line flashed and Daddy pulled, then let it run out again. The three of them strained their eyes but could see nothing but green. The air was hot and thick.

Daddy pulled again. "It's puttin up a good fight."

"Don't let it snap the line."

Daddy said, "Wouldn't it be something if there was an alligator hangin onto that fish when I pulled it in?"

Ethan and Madeleine blinked at him for a moment, then looked back at the duckweed turf, still and placid and innocent. As though nothing was happening down there.

"He still on the line?" Ethan asked.

Daddy said, "Hell yeah he's on the line!"

He pulled back and reeled, then pulled back and reeled again until the first charcoal flash of fish scales broke the surface and then disappeared. Daddy whooped and reeled like mad. Madeleine stretched the net out. And as she waited, she recalled hundreds of these same moments spent in this very cove. She felt grateful to realize that she didn't have to dread this place or her brother's memory. She could recall the good without staring at the awful.

Daddy gave one good lusty pull and the creature came flapping out of the water. Madeleine scooped it with the net. A good-sized bass.

"Looks like a ten-pounder!" Ethan cried.

Madeleine grinned. "It's about time."

THEY STOWED THE LILIES and hyacinths and duckweed in tubs filled with water, then dropped Jazz off with the Thibodaux kids next door.

Ethan slipped his hand into Madeleine's as they crossed the parking lot to Thibby's. "Those flowers'll keep fresh in the tubs?"

Madeleine nodded. "Sure. They'll easily last to tomorrow just the way they are. Samantha can take it from there."

"Well give me a call before you run them over to the flower shop in the morning. I'll help you load them up."

Ethan opened the glass café door and gestured Madeleine and Daddy inside. They were greeted with warm hugs from Nida Thibodaux and a welcome blast of cool air conditioning. Nida ran the café but kept a second part-time job selling real estate. Thibby sauntered out from the kitchen to see what Daddy and Ethan had caught: a catfish, a redfish, and two bass.

"Might as well serve'm all up, don't you think, Ethan?" Daddy said, handing them over to Thibby.

"Sure."

"All of it?" Madeleine said. "Don't you want to hold some of it back for later? I could fry it for you tomorrow."

"Nah."

She shook her head. In Daddy's world, tomorrow didn't exist.

The bus boys were stripping the red-and-white checkered vinyl cloths from the folding tables and pushing them to the perimeter so they could clear the dance floor for later that night. Cotton cobwebs and rows of crawfish string lights stretched across the wood paneling. A zydeco band was already setting up for the Halloween dance, and soon couples would be shuffling around the scarred laminate tile floor that was sprinkled with sand. Nida brought out frosty glasses of sweet tea and beers, along with a plate of sandwich bread and butter. Sheriff Cavanaugh appeared and sat down with them, happy to share a taste of fish, though he declined the beer.

"Gotta keep an eye out tonight," he said. "People get a little funny on Halloween sometimes."

"Spirits are restless," Nida said.

Cavanaugh shrugged. "Maybe. I know people are restless."

Ethan leaned over and whispered to Madeleine, "I like you this way."

"Which way?"

"Here in your element. Never seen you so relaxed."

"Is that so?" Madeleine was surprised to realize that she was indeed relaxed to her toes.

"Mm hmm. You always look like you're about to bolt. Had to run you all over the zoo just to keep you calm on our first date."

"What!"

He was grinning at her with pure, devilish delight.

She said, "So that's why you dragged me all through Audubon Park before we made it to Monkey Hill!"

Nida brought out biscuits and fried green tomatoes with herbed mustard for dipping. They ate lustily and swilled sweet tea—except for Daddy, who was downing beer as if it were tea—and as the band revved up Daddy explained to Ethan the nuances between Cajun music and zydeco.

Sheriff Cavanaugh turned to Madeleine. "I seen that Zenon round here th'other day."

"Well, he does have a fishing cabin out on the bayou."

Cavanaugh looked doubtful. "He live in Plaquemine and he work in Baton Rouge. There plenty a water in either one of those places. Why you think he come alla way the hell out here to do his fishin?"

She shrugged. "He's from here. Maybe he just wants to come home sometimes."

The sheriff shook his head. "That boy ain't thinkin bout no home sweet home. He come from mean stock and he mean hisself."

The band burst forth with music, guitar, and drums, a spoon sliding over washboard, vocals wailing.

Well, the little mosquito fly high
And the little mosquito fly low
If that little mosquito gonna light on me
Be the last damn thing he do!

Madeleine eyed the empty beer bottles that had collected in front of her father. His hand was slung over Ethan's shoulder, and Ethan, who'd only had the one beer out on the bayou, seemed to be taking it in stride.

"All right then," Ethan was saying. "If that's so, which one uses a washboard?"

"They both use washboard," Daddy replied.

Ethan chuckled. "Oh, and the washboard is such a common instrument. Come on now, there idn't any difference between Cajun music and zydeco."

"Sure there is! Cajun music was influenced by Scotch. Irish. German. French." He counted each on his fingers. ". . . American Indian. French."

"You said French already," Ethan pointed out.

"I know I said it, son, you ain't listenin. French. Anglo-American. Afro-Caribbean. And French. That's Cajun music. Now zydeco, that's black Creole music, plain and simple. It's bluuuesy." Daddy waggled his fingers.

Ethan looked skeptical. "Bluesy. With a washboard. Because the washboard is such a sad, soulful instrument."

Sheriff Cavanaugh winked at Madeleine.

Madeleine bent her head toward the sheriff. "Has Zenon done something wrong?"

He shrugged. "I don't know he do somethin wrong, particularly, but he have a whole lifetime of not doin right. I got a call from some detectives in Baton Rouge, got their eye on him. He always gettin in trouble, baby."

He took a sip of beer. "That Zenon is bad news. I knew his mama, mean as hell. She beat that boy all growin up. Then his daddy just disappear one day. His mama say he run off, but the gossip says otherwise." Sheriff spread his fingers and smoothed them over the table.

Madeleine shifted in her seat. She'd heard all this before.

Nida refilled Madeleine's tea and addressed the sheriff. "He just out there fishin, Keith. He may have had it rough growin up, but he got his own shop out there in Baton Rouge, got a nice normal life now."

"Yeah, he got a shop," Cavanaugh said. "Got a *gun* shop."

"What're y'all talkin about over here?" Daddy said.

"Zenon Lansky," Sheriff answered with a dip of his head.

"Zenon Lansky. That kid used to live next door? Aw, now why don't you leave that poor boy alone."

Cavanaugh shook his head. "I have not harassed Zenon Lansky, I was just cautioning your daughter here to look out for him."

"Maddy, why?" Daddy looked at her. "You see him lately, baby?"

She shrugged. "He was at the gala."

"He was? I didn't see him."

She nodded, shifting uneasily. She recalled the intensity of the conversation, how quickly it had spun out of control.

Her father pursed his lips. "That young man's had it rough, now honey. You probably better off making a wide circle when you see him. I know y'all was good friends growin up, it's too bad."

They sat quietly for a moment, and then Daddy turned abruptly to Ethan. "You know, zydeco means 'green bean.'"

"Green bean!" Ethan said. "What language?"

"Creole."

"That ain't the French word for green bean. Green bean is . . .

it's . . ." He sighed. "Aw hell, Maddy, what's French Creole for green bean?"

The entire table answered in unison: *"Haricot vert."*

"See?" Daddy said.

Ethan rolled his eyes. "Oh, sure, now it all makes sense to me. Come on now, Daddy Blank, how in the hell you get 'zydeco' out of 'haricot vert'?"

"Zydeco, 'aricot, they sound the same when you pronounce'm like you s'posed to. Put a 'les' in front of it and there ya go. Zy-de-co, *les har-i-cots.*"

Cavanaugh gestured to Madeleine and lowered his voice. "Anyway you be careful. Glad you brought them with you today but I know sometimes you go out in that swamp alone."

"I've been doing that forever. But I hardly ever go anymore."

Cavanaugh grimaced and wiped the back of his neck. "Well if you do go out there and you see Zenon Lansky in that fishin cabin, I'd appreciate it you let me know. And it wouldn't hurt you to keep that phone of yours close to you when you out in that swamp."

She shrugged. "My cell phone doesn't work too good out there. But I will tell you if I see him, if you think it's that important."

sixteen

HAHNVILLE, 1912

HELEN KNELT IN THE spongy soil and used her shears to snip a sprig of sage. Her fingers shook and her mouth was parched, and her wide-brimmed hat did little to combat the sun. The sage dropped through her fingers and fell soundlessly to the earth.

Chloe's rich molasses voice floated from behind a curtain of sweet pea vines, and mingled with a soft, warm wind that rustled the leaves. The flowers' scents infused the sultry air, perfuming the entire garden. Chloe bustled among the green bean topiaries and pretended not to notice Helen's struggle, but instead practiced aloud the nursery rhymes Helen had taught her. She formed her lips around the words, "Ring around the Rosie," working to improve her English pronunciation. She seemed to relish the pattern of rhymes.

Helen smiled as she listened to her chanting. Chloe's accent embraced the Rs with soft whispers, carrying an "H" sound before the "R" in "hRing" and "hRosie." Suddenly Helen hoped that Chloe's English pronunciation would not improve. She wanted Chloe to stay just as she was, and to speak English in that whispery accent forever.

"Chloe," Helen called, and the girl was at once by her side, lifting her off the ground and helping her to the stone garden bench.

"Sit there, Dearie Missus," Chloe said. "I finish with the herbs."

Helen obeyed and watched Chloe fuss over the small harvests in the garden, continuing where Helen had left off at the sage and spring onions. Helen raised her eyes to the privy beyond the path, estimating how long it would take her to get from the garden to the tiny building. She had no need to go at the moment, but when the urge did come it would be sudden and demanding, the same way the sickness itself had overtaken her.

She had awoken one morning with abdominal cramps and the need to rush to the water closet. Fortunately, Rémi had outfitted the Terrefleurs main house with full indoor plumbing, and the bathroom lay just opposite the ladies' parlor. The sickness that had gripped her that morning had prevented her from returning to the tent city to help with the relief effort, a routine she had begun after missing the train to join her mother. She had helped administer inoculations in the tent cities, but had never actually inoculated herself. Foolish in retrospect. At the time, she'd thought she was naturally protected from any flood sickness—workers' sickness. Now, a week later, she was still confined to Terrefleurs, and growing weaker by the day.

The privy outside the garden was a holdover from the time before Terrefleurs had indoor plumbing, only a few years ago. Helen was now ever so grateful that it had not been torn down, otherwise she would not have dared venture outside at all.

A wave of nausea hit her, dampening her brow and causing her to sway on the bench. The garden dimmed, and she had a sensation of falling but could not stretch out her arms to steady herself. Suddenly, strong, gentle hands hooked under her elbow and she realized that Chloe was at her side again.

"Dearie Missus. Enough, it is too hot. Time we go inside now, eh?"

"You're right Chloe. It's just too hot."

She tried to look directly at the girl, but the broiling sun injured her vision, and the garden looked silvery-gray and full of ghosts. "Give me just a minute, though, all right?"

Chloe dipped a handkerchief into a watering can and knelt before Helen, dabbing at her face with the cool, damp cloth.

"Do not to worry, Dearie Missus. The oak gall I give you, it make you feel good health soon."

Her face was smooth and confident, but Helen wondered if her voice belied a twinge of deep concern. Helen had been taking the oak gall all week, but the sickness only worsened.

"Chloe," she said, pondering the pasty substance the girl had been administering as medicine. "What exactly is an oak gall?"

"It come from the oak tree," Chloe said. "It hang on the oak sticks, in little balls."

She curled her fingers to demonstrate, her back straight and her chin lifted.

"Oh," Helen said, somewhat relieved. "Sap?"

Chloe shook her head. "No, not the sap. Not the blood of the tree."

She bit her lip. "It hang on the oak tree, but it do not come from the oak tree. The insect make it. How you say? It make the sting?"

Chloe made a buzzing sound, and fluttered her fingers like wings.

"A bee?" Helen said.

Chloe pursed her lips. "Mmm, bee? I think."

"It comes from bees? So oak gall is a kind of honey." Helen smiled at the pleasant remedy.

But Chloe pinched her brows. "No. Not honey. Not the bee. What is insect like a bee? It is long, and bigger?"

"A wasp?" Helen offered, puzzled.

"Yes, that is it. The wasp. She make the oak gall. The oak gall is her baby, inside the case, before the baby is born. It is like the egg."

Helen blinked. *"Larvae?"* She stretched out the word in alarm. "You've been giving me the larvae of a wasp?"

Chloe cocked her head. "Hmm, I do not know this, *larvae.* That is the wasp baby before she is born?"

Helen answered dully, "Yes."

Chloe brightened. "OK, so that is it!"

Helen frowned, and the wave of nausea returned. She tried not to think of the paste of wasp's larvae working its way through her digestive tract. She had complete confidence in Chloe's healing abilities, and she had seen the girl tend the sick with more efficacy than the doctor in the area. Nevertheless, Helen wished she hadn't asked the origin of this particular remedy.

Suddenly, Helen burst out laughing. "Chloe, you are a dear."

Chloe smiled, clasping her dark hands around Helen's frail white ones.

The gardener's son, the harelip boy named Laramie, turned at the sound of Helen's laughter. He was grinning with his split smile, an innocent dove with enormous eyes. Too young and sweet to be aware yet of his deformity.

Helen closed her eyes as a breeze lifted black wisps of hair that had escaped from the knot beneath her hat. The wind rustled the garden vines, and further beyond, it played among the magnolia and acacia and oak.

When Helen opened her eyes, she could see that Chloe's head was bowed, and that the garden still looked silvery-gray, as if it lay under moonlight and not full sun. And she knew.

"Chloe," she said, stroking her face, and feeling wetness on the girl's cheek. "You'll look after Rémi for me, won't you?"

Chloe sank to her knees and buried her face in Helen's lap, sobbing. Helen stroked Chloe's thick, rough hair, tied in large florets on either side of her head like beautiful, exotic flowers.

"Promise me, Chloe."

She could see the welt that crept from the girl's back and along her neck. She was so young and bright and beautiful and strong. Had endured so much. Helen could only wish to be that strong. What made her think she could help those shocked, desperate people at the tent city, and then walk away unharmed?

Chloe's weeping subsided. She raised her head. Helen gave a start at the girl's expression: flat, dead.

Chloe said, "I promise. I will look after him."

Helen closed her eyes. She felt herself recede under a tide, a beautiful, exhilarating drift. A sensation like she was on a barge on the Mississippi River, only the motion of it was freer, flying on a channel of air, not water. She could hear Chloe shouting at someone but she sounded very distant. And then Helen felt hands encircle her. She forced her eyes open again and saw Rémi. He was lifting her. She reached up and curled her arms around his neck. He carried her through the garden, to the stairs, into the house.

seventeen

NEW ORLEANS, 2009

ADELEINE HEAVED HER FATHER onto the bed when she heard the phone ringing. The alarm clock registered 9:08 P.M. in red LED digits.

"Thank you honey," Daddy said with a sway as he tugged at his shoes. "Guess I had one too many."

"More like four too many," she said as she ran for the hall phone.

She hoped it wasn't Ethan on the line. She'd let him believe she was going to run the flowers over tomorrow. In truth, she wanted to get it over with now. She hadn't actually said one way or another, but she didn't correct him when he'd voiced the assumption that she was going to do it in the morning. She didn't really need any help. Didn't want to put him out.

She managed to press Send while the phone was still ringing. "Yes?"

"Madeleine. You did not tell me you were going." That rusty voice.

"Chloe?"

A pause. "I would have come with you and your father."

"I'd been leaving messages for you to call me back, Chloe. How did you know I'd gone out there?"

"You did not leave messages for this."

"Well, I did call you because I want talk about Sev—"

"We are agreed to find out about Marc Gilbert together, yanh? If you said you were going to Houma I would have gone."

Oh yeah? I'll tell you where you can go!

The nerve! As if Madeleine had to check in with the old crank every time she wanted to—

But the thought was suddenly stillborn in her mind. As if Chloe had somehow reached through the phone line and killed it. And Madeleine would have bet one of Ethan's laboratory pennies that from somewhere on Toulouse Street in the Vieux Carré, Madame Chloe LeBlanc was staring in her direction at this moment.

Madeleine said, "Look. We didn't even set foot in the old house. I just took Daddy out to Bayou Black to collect some pretty aquatic flowers for a florist I know."

"Samantha."

"Yes, Samantha. And I have to go because it's late, and I have to take the flowers to the shop." Madeleine reached down and hoisted Jasmine up into her arms.

"I will send someone to assist you."

Madeleine paused. "What? No, I'll be fine."

"I send someone to assist you. It is not safe on Magazine this late."

"No. Seriously, Chloe, that won't be—"

But the line went dead. Madeleine snorted, slamming the cordless back onto the charging cradle. Jasmine struggled to be let down again, and hopped out of her arms.

eighteen

AGAZINE STREET LAY IN shadows as Maddy pulled into the alley. She hoisted herself out of the truck and eyed the oleanders near the rear entrance. A time or two, she'd found someone sleeping back there. In fact the last time it had been one of Daddy's street buddies, and she'd let him sleep in the upper level of the warehouse in the empty office space above the flower shop.

No one in the oleanders tonight. The evening swelled with a fresh breeze, Magazine Street was vacant, and the damp air formed swirling halos around the streetlights.

She let down the tailgate and tugged on one of the collection bins, and found it heavy. Miserably heavy. If Oran really was coming to help, she was ready to lay down her pride and let him, by God.

She abandoned the bin, setting it on the open tailgate, and walked to the front entrance, unlocking it.

The street lamp spilled amber light through the open door, and in its faint illumination the inside of the shop reminded her of the bayou. Plants dipped and played in the wind, rustling and casting long shadows. She groped for the light switch and didn't find it. But as her eyes adjusted, there seemed enough light to get around.

In a pool of illumination from the south window, Samantha's rustic wooden farmhouse table stood near the wicker chairs. The mere sight of it invoked a phantom smell of coffee. Likely Samantha would create the water display there. Madeleine cleared the table of potted ferns so that its surface lay clean and empty, and she ran her hand along the smooth, buttery wood. Its worn surface spoke of offerings that spanned a lifetime. She looked around for something to protect the surface from the flower bins, and found one of Samantha's canvas tarps. She snapped it open, drifting the fabric over the table.

Something warm and alive brushed her leg.

She jumped. "Esmeralda?"

The cat darted around a corner. Mazes of light stole through the windows and front door. The cat moved with a foxy way about her, as if she was getting away with something. As she slipped behind a shelf of plants, Madeleine saw a flash of white in her mouth.

"Esmeralda, what do you have there?" It looked like a little white mouse, like the kind the scientists use in lab experiments, or that the pet stores sell as "feeders." But most mice running around the city were gray.

Esmeralda lighted upon the plant shelf, turning her face away from Madeleine as if to both show off her prize and hoard it to herself.

"Drop it!" Madeleine said, repulsed. "You can't have that thing in here."

She stepped toward the cat, hand outstretched. Esmeralda let out an ill-tempered growl and tucked it down deeper into her fur.

"Esmeralda, drop that poor thing, or take it outside!"

She clamped a firm hand on the back of the cat's neck. Esmeralda spun around and hissed, dropping it on the shelf.

Madeleine stared, blinking, as her vision adjusted to the darkness. It dawned on her that she was not looking at a mouse at all. Realization snaked through her belly before her mind even registered what it was. It was a human finger.

A scream erupted from within her, and she jumped back, tangling with Esmeralda. The cat escaped and slinked to the corner of the shop, watching from under the plant shelves with a twitching tail.

The finger was slender with pink polish on the torn acrylic nail, and around it a gold ring glinted in the darkness. Black streaks and a white bone jutted from the ragged end where it had been severed just below the knuckle.

Madeleine screamed again, shock rippling through her body. She turned her back to the horrible thing and slapped at the walls for the light switch. Instinct told her to turn and run, because she also felt the sensation that someone was behind her, and for some absurd reason she was certain that it was the girl Severin. Filthy, grimacing Severin, watching from between dark shelves of potted plants, possessing the knowledge of how a severed human finger might have found its way into a flower shop.

Someone was there. Not Severin. She couldn't catch a breath. Her mouth turned to sand, and she was unable to speak his name.

Zenon stood broad-shouldered, arms tensed with the exertion of carrying a water-filled bin of bayou hyacinths.

"Madeleine?"

He set the collection bin down onto the painted concrete floor. She shook her head, trying to breathe.

Zenon said, "I heard you screaming, *chére*. What's going on?"

Did Zenon have something to do with that finger?

He took a step toward her, and she stumbled backward.

He lifted his hand. "It's all right, *chére*. It's all right, *'tite*."

His calming tone of voice sounded wrong, so wrong; and inside her head alarm bells were buzzing.

"What're you doing here?"

Hands still raised, he took another step forward. "Miss Chloe sent me here baby. Sent me to help y'all out. Did something happen? Is there someone in here?"

He panned the brick walls.

She backed away a few more steps, and her hip brushed the plant shelf where that horrible thing lay. She looked down.

But what she saw now was in complete disconnect from what

she had seen before. On the plant shelf lay a bit of white and pink felt fabric with a plastic eye and a string tail—a catnip mouse; a cat toy.

No finger.

And no Severin in the shadows.

Madeleine was shaking. She had seen a finger. A human digit. She was certain she had seen it. Saw it right down to the detail of nail color and jewelry.

She considered the possibility that perhaps with all the shadows, and Sheriff Cavanaugh's spook tales ringing in her head . . .

But no, she saw what she saw. She released her breath in a spasm.

Zenon took another step toward her. "What made you scream?"

"It's just that . . ." She swallowed. "Esmeralda startled me. And my eyes, I think they were playing tricks in the darkness."

She hugged herself, turning her back, and stepped further away from him.

"What you think, *chére*? You walking away from me like I'm gonna come after you?"

She turned to glare at him, steadying herself with the farmhouse table, and swallowed. "Look. I'm nervous and tired. It's nothing."

He came closer, his voice low and soft. "What made you scream? You tell me."

There was no way she was going to do that. How could she explain it? At once so foolish and unnerving. A tear fell down her cheek. But then a sensation stole over her.

Answer the question, chére.

She lifted her chin toward the stamped tin ceiling, and though it made no sense, though she had no idea why she was doing it, she heard herself telling him: "I thought I saw a human finger."

His head drew back in surprise, but his face also seemed wary. "What? Are you messing with me?"

"I told you it was probably nothing. Trick of light, or something."

His eyes narrowed, his posture aggressive. "A trick."

"It's just that it looked so real. The nail polish, and there was this braided gold ring. Why are you looking at me like that?"

His eyes searched her face and he seemed to be considering what she'd just told him. Finally, he said, "It's OK. I'm here."

He stood now only a foot away from her. And it actually gave her relief, his being so close. To know that he was strong, and even cocky, and that if someone tried to attack her right now, Zenon Lansky would prevent it.

She shook her head. "Ridiculous. It was only a cat toy. I'm embarrassed even to admit it and it's hardly worth mentioning."

She slid her finger under her eye in a quick gesture that she hoped would look like she had removed a speck of dust.

He caught her wrist, and ever so slowly, with a gentleness she wouldn't have imagined him capable of, he used his free hand to brush a tear from her other eye. He was standing far too close—so close she felt the heat that radiated from him. She wanted to jerk away from him but her body remained rigid.

His voice came softly, and yet at its core she still heard the aggression. "Don't you say it ain't worth mentioning. Don't you say that, no."

The way he gripped her wrist, it held a hint of dare. The same way he'd gripped her at the gala before Ethan Manderleigh stepped in. And also she felt that same eerie lock as though something else was taking control of her. The thought caused a tightening in her stomach. She couldn't step away. Instead she turned her face from him.

Zenon leaned forward. "Was a time I looked out for you. Now all you do is fight me. And you fight your daddy and Miss Chloe. Where does that get you, baby?"

She felt his breath at her neck. It sent a feathering ripple down the length of her throat, to her collarbone, to the stretch of skin at the opening of her blouse.

"You fight the people that belong to you and then go looking for a beau like that trust fund fool."

Madeleine stiffened and jerked her arm, returning her gaze to him.

He held her. "Yeah I know all about him. Tell you what else. You don't mean nothing to him because he can't begin to understand you. You think that mooncalf have any idea what a hard life is like? Me, I know. I had to fight just to survive. Just like you."

"Let go of me, Zenon."

To her surprise, he did. He let her go. Released her wrist and raised both hands, fingers open.

He said, "There you go. See how that works? You asked me to let go and I did. You're free."

But no, she wasn't free. That horrible something now clamped into place. Every bit as strong and fierce as the physical grip had been. Her body, all at once, did not belong to her. Her mind burned to release from the lock. She felt the impulse to reach out to Zenon, an impulse that seemed to come from somewhere outside of her. She fought against it. Her hands lifted and then balled into fists. He watched her intently, saw her hands. She felt like a sugar ant who'd traversed a sand trap, and any effort to climb out served only to call the ant lion.

"Madeleine. Fightin, fightin. I'd say you look like you want to kiss me. Go on ahead."

Eyes wide, she felt the first sickening wave of desperation. Her body had become her cage. She managed to prevent it from acting on these foreign impulses, but she still could not make it do what she asked: to push him away. To *get herself* away, far away, and to reclaim herself.

"Come on then," he said, and he leaned forward to kiss her.

Her stomach rolled. She managed to turn her face away again. She at least could do that. Her fists were still jammed at her sides, her eyes wide with panic. His lips brushed her neck, and then his hands lowered to her blouse.

No.

Her skin bristled at his touch. She lifted her arm to knock his hands away, but her arm moved only a few inches. He paused, eyes watching her with a darkened intensity. But he seemed to be watching with much more than his eyes. An electromagnetic web that entangled her, drawing her forward.

His fingers released the top button of her blouse. She flinched.

"Oh, you want me to stop? Just say the word, Madeleine."

And his demeanor darkened so profoundly it made her catch her breath. No longer any pretense of benevolence.

"Stop me Maddy. Go ahead."

But that word, that one single syllable, refused to form on her lips. She tried then to say something, anything.

She finally managed, "What are you doing, Zenon?"

His eyes gleamed, his voice soft and rough. "Don't you know?"

And then he released the second button, and she felt the evening breeze whisper across the tops of her breasts.

Knock his hands away and tell him to stop! Tell him to leave!

Why couldn't she do this? He wasn't going to stop on his own. She was trembling, not from fear but from rage and the effort of trying to make her arms move. But they had stopped obeying her. They were listening to that other thing that was not of her. The same thing that moments ago had caused her to tell him about the severed finger even though she didn't want to. The paralysis was horrifying. She felt sweat aspirating into her hair.

She said. "I don't understand what's happening. Are you doing this?"

He said nothing, but his smile caused her heartbeat to accelerate.

She tried again to tell him to stop, but she could not do that. She couldn't even say "wait." She could speak only of things that didn't matter. She said, "What are you doing, Zenon? Tell me!"

He put a finger to her lips, and whispered, "Evolving."

She caught her breath. She tried to shake her head. Panic engulfed her.

And then he said, "Shh," and she was no longer able to utter another word. She gasped, that horrible bramble sprouting in her throat, but she couldn't make a sound. She shook her head, wildly.

"What's that, Madeleine?" he whispered. "You shakin your head? You have something to say to me?"

His fingers grazed the skin above her bra, and moved down between them to the third button. She shifted, twisting her torso as if to escape. She sensed the foreign ideas, to beckon his hands to her, all over her. The wrongness of it. The shattering alarms in her head. She closed her eyes and retreated a step within herself.

He freed another button.

Something broke through in her. She managed to grip his forearms.

Their eyes locked. He was watching her. She struggled to maintain whatever part of her mind had managed to recapture this control. But it was already slipping away. . . .

He smiled. He gently disengaged her grip on his forearms, and he moved his hands lower. And then he yanked the top of her jeans and hoisted her off her feet. Her hips slid backward onto the table. The cloth tarp slid with her. A sandal fell from her foot and clattered to the floor.

She shook her head furiously, but the word still refused to form at her lips.

Both of his hands pulling at her blouse. "Go ahead and tell me to stop. That's all you gotta do, *chère*. You're a fighter, yeah."

And she was, at her core: fighting, clawing, raging. At her core she was breaking free from him and running for the door. If only her physical self could carry out the orders her mind had issued. It had disengaged from her, mutinous.

Her breath ripped from her in gasps. Her lips formed on the word "stop," but she managed only an "s" sound that fell backward and drowned inside her lungs.

She needed to make him stop. Had to make her body belong to her again.

A heavy breeze rushed from the magnolia outside to the ficus near the wicker chair. A hissing, swelling wind that sought each leaf and stem, shaking them.

She realized her struggle was futile. Her panic engulfed her more deeply into this awful sand trap. And so she sent her mind away, escaping, traveling with that wind that stirred the ficus, bringing that wind back to herself, flowing through her lungs. She closed her eyes. Accepted. She saw herself with a scientific eye, observed the situation, the subject's behavior. Her eyes opened again.

She said, "Stop."

Zenon's hand froze at the top button of her jeans.

And at once her body belonged to her again. She felt strangely calm, and her mind created no thought. She held onto this vast blank, the sense of self-abandonment. No emotion—not even revulsion or hatred for Zenon. He stared at her.

Madeleine pulled her blouse together. "Take yourself off of me Zenon. And leave."

The wind fell, not so much retreating as settling, and the ficus leaves grew still. Madeleine felt equally as connected with the wind and those leaves as with her own reclaimed body. She even felt aware of all the plants and the clay pots and the cat and the soil, as if every element in the flower shop, living and innate, played a role in diffusing the grotesque hold Zenon had had on her.

He said, "It would have been the right thing, Madeleine."

She stared at him, still and quiet as stone, holding strong to her senses.

Zenon backed away. And then he turned away. And left.

nineteen

RÉMI'S FAMILY ONLY HAD seen Helen twice. First at the wedding, and now at Helen's funeral. Rémi's mother and his brothers Didier and Henri lingered at Terrefleurs for three days of polite. Then, as though overcome with collective agoraphobia, they retreated to their more plush, gay homes in the city where they could enjoy the LeBlanc fortune without having to smell the burning cane fields that fed it. Rémi was once again alone with Terrefleurs. He leaned on the gallery, smoking tobacco and gazing at the row of workers' cottages.

He couldn't accept that Helen was truly gone. That she would not step out onto the gallery and slip her arm into his, and ask him to walk with her in the garden.

He blamed himself. She had been too fragile for plantation life. So naïve that while she assisted the physician at the tent city, herding evacuees into queues to receive vaccinations, she didn't see fit to receive those vaccinations herself. And when the flood brought its disease, Helen had no defense whatsoever.

The voice of a lone soprano drifted from the cottages, rising above the chirping of crickets and frogs. Her song rang with such loneliness that it caused Rémi's skin to tingle. Other voices joined her, not in the usual blend of folk song that filtered through the plantation in the evenings; these sounds combined to become many facets of a single voice. Rémi realized, then, that he was listening to a prayer.

He wondered whether they were praying for Helen's soul, and felt a small comfort despite the heaviness in his chest. But then, as a single thread to the chorus, he heard someone crying.

Rémi walked to the gallery and looked. He saw the workers gathered around one of the cottages. The song rose and fell and the weeping rose and fell, each in its own course of waves. He listened intently. He picked out the lyrics, a plea to the Lord to accept their son into heaven, and Rémi's palms grew slick under his grip on the railing.

He descended the steps, making his way toward the cottages even as the workers were forming into a procession, their bodies huddled around someone who'd emerged from the little cottage at the end of the row. They were moving in the direction of the chapel.

Francois appeared and put his hand to Rémi's elbow. "I didn't want to tell you yet because of Miss Helen's passing. There was another sickness."

Rémi looked at him in a daze. Standing at Francois's side was Tatie Bernadette.

She said, "I told him to stay close when the water rises. He goes off to play with his sling shot and only the good Lord knows what he gets into."

Rémi saw the procession approaching the chapel. He strode toward it. Leading the mourners was the gardener, and he was carrying his son Laramie in his arms. The child with the permanent harelip smile.

Rémi stepped forward, and the procession stopped in front of him. The gardener's eyes were rimmed red. Rémi put his hand to Laramie's forehead, and found it still damp from the fever that had killed him. Rémi let out a gasp of shock.

Even in death, the boy's face looked delighted. Cheeks plump and mouth wide, as though he'd discovered the angels and tossed his head back in joy. Laramie's mother, weeping and keening, leaned against her husband and kept shaking her head as the women huddled close to her.

Rémi slipped his arm around the mother's waist, and she turned and leaned on him. The father resumed his grim walk to the chapel while Rémi supported Laramie's mother. He watched the gardener's back, and saw Laramie's lifeless hand dangling below his father's powerful arm. The workers' voices continued their lamentations, musical ointment for the grief-stricken.

They stepped inside the chapel, stark, wooden, and damp-smelling. Too small to accommodate much more than the immediate family. Rémi released Laramie's mother to the care of her sister and cousin and stepped outside where the plantationers formed a halo around the tiny structure. He kept swallowing, but his throat felt crowded with something that refused to go down.

Rémi remembered that stranger who not long ago, had walked through the garden and had whispered to Laramie, and then to Helen. And now both were dead.

twenty

NEW ORLEANS, 2009

OUTSIDE THE DEPARTMENT OF Psychology, Madeleine stood in the dark near a cluster of smokers. The days were getting shorter but the moon was bright, a blood moon, the first full moon after the autumnal equinox. Ordinarily Madeleine wouldn't even notice the moon phase or any of those sorts of things, but her senses had somehow become razor sharp. Now she noticed everything. The misty halo around the street lamp even though there seemed no tangible moisture in the air; the sawflies in the loblolly pine. The loblolly itself. She was loath to give in to her usual mind chatter, lest she miss some detail of the vitality that surrounded her.

That strange fascination had continued ever since her encounter with Zenon. Though she'd gone over it time and again, she still couldn't make sense of what had happened. Wasn't even sure how she'd stopped it. Or whether she could again.

"Hey baby blue." Ethan strode through the glass doors and walked over to her. He leaned over and kissed her. "Something's wrong."

She gaped, caught off guard that he could key in to her distress so quickly, and suddenly couldn't think of a single word to say to him.

He took a step back and eyed her. "Hmm. Something really is bothering you. Don't worry, ma'am, I know how to handle this. We just march you around until you settle down. Come on, you're in good hands."

She shook her head, feeling like a complete idiot, but mutely walked with him along Freret. He prattled about work. Gas lamps flickered on the porches, and streetlights cast sepia tones across the neighborhood, making the houses look like giant decorated graham crackers. Most had double galleries, stacked one atop the other.

Ethan was saying, "I wanted to show you my lab, but it's not really set up yet. Just an office. Nothing woo-woo. I'm still working on the woo-woo."

Madeleine tossed her head, giving up a half laugh, half sigh as they turned in the direction of St. Charles.

"You met with the director today?" he asked.

She nodded. "Yes. I start again next week."

"That's good."

She said, "Yeah, but he wasn't exactly enthusiastic about it. Between lack of funding and the debacle in D.C. . . . Anyway, are you still looking at neuroplasticity, in terms of boosting intuition?"

He nodded. "Of course. It's an ongoing study."

"Tell me again how that works."

He shrugged. "It's pretty straightforward. What is neuroplasticity? A brain change. You build neurons. How do you change your brain? By repeating an exercise, over and over, same way you would if you were trying to build a muscle."

"But what's the exercise? If you want to bolster your intuition, what is it that you have to repeat over and over again?"

Ethan looked at her, his face quizzical. "Well first you just pay attention. So say you have a moment when you feel like you're being watched, you don't dismiss it. You turn your focus inward to strengthen your sensitivity. Or when something happens like you suddenly know your father is about to call, and then the phone rings. You just kind of savor the feeling."

They were striding quickly through the neighborhoods, and the movement of her body did indeed seem to tame her anxiety. The neutral subject matter helped, too.

And though he clearly knew something was on her mind, Ethan continued to play along. "The more you do it, the easier it gets. Meanwhile, you're taking a thin little back-road neuron and turning it into a major highway in your head. Neuroplasticity for your intuition."

She sighed. "I don't even know if it's intuition I'm going for here. Are there other factors, other ways you can heighten the effect? Grooming basic psi skills?"

"You mean aside from neuroplasticity?"

She nodded.

He said, "Well, there's the genetic factor. Gene plasticity, if you want to call it that."

"Change your genes?"

"Sure. Same way that what you eat or the kind of exercise you do can stimulate gene receptors, you can stimulate the receptors for your sixth sense."

She thought about this. "Funny. It wasn't so long ago that we thought our brains and our genes were unchangeable. Now we know better. But I imagine there's a heredity factor, too."

Ethan nodded. "That's something my team is looking at really closely—how much genetics plays a role in psi."

"Psi. It's such a strange little word for all this."

"I know. But there's no other word that sums it up."

Madeleine tried to sound casual. "You know what's funny about that? The letter itself, the Greek character, Psi ψ, they call it the devil's pitchfork because of its shape."

"Why is that funny?"

"Because they used to associate psi phenomena with the devil. Insanity, too. You know, Chloe actually said my father is haunted by a devil. I just think it's funny that to this day, the two are linked by that one Greek letter."

Ethan shook his head. His eyes were soft and inviting. She kept a measured distance. The incident in the flower shop still left her feeling like she'd been disloyal, even though she'd done all she could to fend Zenon off.

Ethan looked like he was about to reach for her, and she turned away.

"Oh, look!" Madeleine pointed to the cemetery. It spanned the block ahead, but already they could see the candles flickering. "November second. All Soul's Day," she said.

They crossed the street and gazed at the raised stone crypts, whitewashed for the occasion and adorned with yellow chrysanthemums and red cockscombs. On one of the farther graves, someone had draped an angel's outstretched hands with strings of black immortelles.

Ethan put an arm around Maddy and urged her forward. "Neighborhood's on the rough side. We should keep moving."

She stiffened. "Sometimes I feel more at home in the rough neighborhoods than anywhere else. It's where most of my patients are from. And it reminds me of where I grew up."

He gave her a sideways look. "All right. We'll stay here."

They both frowned at the cemetery. *You think that mooncalf have any idea what a hard life is like?* Zenon had said. Madeleine wished she could shake the words out of her head. Zenon was wrong. Zenon was an animal. Zenon had said he was evolving. He'd said . . .

Ethan looked at her. "You ready to tell me what's really bothering you?"

She turned her back to the headstones and eyed the crooked shotguns across the street, old, hurricane-worn, and yet still hanging on.

She said, "Yes. But first, what about . . . what about things like telepathy. Or even . . ."

"Or even what?"

She cleared her throat. "Implanted suggestion."

He looked at her. She kept her gaze on the leaning porch of the house ahead.

He said, "I gotta say, Maddy, your level of interest is a little surprising."

She said nothing.

He sighed. "All right. You know I'm approaching this from a position of neuroscience, and parapsychology is new to me. But yeah, the general opinion of telepathy is that it's just an extension of intuition." He waved at his head. "The same highways in the brain, only more of them. Same is true with implanted suggestion. If telepathy is two-way, then implanted suggestion is a one-way version of that, where the subject isn't necessarily aware."

"Not necessarily?"

Ethan shrugged. "No. Awareness tends to weaken the effect. But you're getting a little beyond me here. I study patterns in fMRIs for a living. What you're talking about, I mean, implanted suggestion, that's pretty much mind control. My team's not looking at that. There've been experiments along those lines in the past, but we're talking grim wartime stuff. Or underground. Usually involving narcotics and electroconvulsive therapy."

She said, "What about legitimate experimentation?"

He shook his head. "I have no idea."

"What about generally accepted means of manipulating the brain? We can use brain implants to block or stimulate certain sectors of the brain, right?"

"Come on Maddy, this isn't—"

"We can target single neurons or groups of them. We can even assist patients who are unable to move or speak by using brain implants to communicate with us through computers."

He sighed. That tolerant patience he'd shown was still there, but it was wearing thin. "True. And? . . ."

"So if it's possible to do that, and if telepathy does exist, we could make certain leaps. On one end of the spectrum, you have telepathic abilities like the feeling of being watched. Something just about everyone's experienced. And on the other end, the ability to reliably, *reliably*, transmute thoughts."

"Madeleine."

"So if the basic fact of telepathy is scientifically proven, the question is, to what extent are we truly capable?"

She stopped and turned to him, daring to look him full in the face, her hands open. "And if we can implant mechanisms into the human brain that can communicate with a computer, isn't it possible for a telepathic impulse to accomplish the same sort of thing? And by the way, *what other sorts of things are we capable of?*"

"Madeleine?"

"What?"

"Please tell me what's really on your mind."

❧

THEY RETRACED THEIR STEPS, walking back toward where their cars waited in the so-called "Jurassic parking lot" on campus. Madeleine told Ethan what had happened in the flower shop. She told him everything. He listened with a grim expression. When she finished, she waited for him to say something, but he just walked alongside her in silence, the only sound coming from his limping footfalls on the battered sidewalk.

Finally, he said, "Tell me this. Did you kiss him?"

"No. He kissed me and I turned away. I didn't want him to."

"But you didn't tell him not to."

She opened her hands. "It's hard to explain. I just couldn't. It wasn't until I stopped fighting inside. It was weird, I just—I just thought about the wind. The wind was blowing. I heard it in the leaves of the potted ficus and . . . and then I told him to leave."

"Are you attracted to him?"

"No."

"Were you ever attracted to him?"

"Never."

He stopped walking and turned to her, hands in his jacket pockets, face tense. "So how is it that at the time, you'd let me believe we were gonna take those collection baskets to the flower shop in the morning? Together. And yet you wind up going there in the middle of the night with Zenon?"

"I didn't go with him. He just . . . Chloe . . ." She sighed.

"Tell me why you didn't let me help you to carry them to the shop. Let's start with that!"

She swallowed, her gaze at her feet. "I honestly don't know why I did that."

"You've never once let me help you. With anything. You tense up if I so much as open a door for you."

"I guess with the flowers, I didn't want to put you out. It seems so stupid now."

He gestured back toward the cemetery. "And all this talk about belonging in the rough neighborhoods. You wear it like a badge of honor. I wonder if it's another way to alienate me."

Her mouth opened.

He said, "This thing with Zenon, I don't even know what to make of that. In fact you and I should take a step back. And you should figure out what you really want. Me, I've laid out exactly what I want. I'm done with casual dating. I want someone who's gonna be part of my future. Someone who wants to create some creatures, and I don't mean splicing genes in a damn Petri dish. I'm talking about rug rats and Little League and pigtails and snotty noses. Do you even want any of that?"

She stared at him. "I don't know, it's just . . . I've always had my mind on my family and career. . . . Never really thought—"

"Well maybe it's time to think. I'm gonna do a little thinking of my own."

twenty-one

HAHNVILLE, 1912

RÉMI COULD STILL HEAR Laramie's mother sobbing and whispering from within the chapel, even though the plantationers were still singing. Their voices, which Rémi had found soothing at first, now buzzed sideways in his head. He backed away from them, putting his hands to his ears, feeling a sudden need to get away. He turned from the cottages and made for the brush, and the voices weaved and entangled with the dissonance of night creatures.

Daylight was fading, the chatter from the bayou reaching crescendo. All about were sounds to bewilder and frustrate him. He came upon the eastern well and sat down on packed dirt, leaning against the hard, cool stones.

In a clump of grass by the base of the well lay an assemblage of pebbles. He recognized them as a slingshot collection. A burning in his throat. It occurred to him that he was thirsty and he thought about what Tatie Bernadette had said, that Laramie might have drunk water from this well. He looked, and saw the drawing pail hanging from a nail in the railroad tie beam, and wondered if the water was indeed tainted. He pulled back the wooden lid and peered into it. The well reflected his silhouette, framed on the glassy surface by pastels of late sunset.

He sensed that he was not alone.

Rémi scanned the thicket but saw no one. The sensation persisted, and with it, a hatch of dread. He conjured the day the stranger had come to the garden, whispering to Helen and Laramie. He'd had this same feeling then. He closed his eyes, imagined a light switching on, and then opened them.

Slowly, he became aware of movement nearby, and heard a groan from the thicket.

He spun about. The sound seemed to be coming from an expanse of rotting wood. It had been a main branch of an oak tree that was hundreds of years old, wide as three men side by side. The intonation rose once more, deep and inhuman, like the sound of a hurricane tearing the roof from a house.

Rémi pushed the palms of his hands into his temples and squeezed. The outline of the log was a crooked ramp in the fading light. He sensed movement on it.

Cold dread cleaved Rémi's chest, but he stepped toward the log, straining his eyes and ears.

Something *was* moving. The log was swarming with termites. One of the insects fluttered onto his knuckles, and he jumped back and shook it. He wiped his hand repeatedly and pressed it under his armpit, a tremor pulsing his spine. The log crackled as a smaller branch fell under the fervor of the insects. He had never before known an infestation to work so ravenously.

Then the entire log creaked, and as Rémi stood transfixed, it split and fell open. He stumbled backward in horror, gasping. A black man's hand protruded from the hollow center. The stench of carrion was overwhelming. Rémi gagged and reached for his hunting knife, thinking he must hack away the crumbling log to expose the body, and release the poor devil who had become entombed there.

But the hand moved. Fingers flexed and closed around a branch.

Rémi backed away from the thing, his knees failing him when his feet touched the well, and he slid to the ground, eyes rooted to the log. Another hand emerged from the wood and pulled, and then the log crumbled open.

A hulking form climbed from the rotting wood and rose to his full height over Rémi. He had ebony skin that flurried with the occasional panicking termite, wings flashing indigo mirrors of sunset. His overalls were dusted with moss and rotting wood. He stood, heaving, eyes trained on Rémi. He was the same man that Rémi had seen whispering to Helen and Laramie.

Rémi grappled to find his voice. It came strained and croaking. "Who are you?"

The stranger stared, the whites of his eyes the only discernible feature in the growing darkness.

He answered, "Ulysses."

Rémi found his strength and struggled to his feet. He searched for words to challenge this man and demand an explanation, but his voice failed him. He could not think how a living person could emerge from that log.

Instead, Rémi managed to say, "What do you want?"

Ulysses pulled back his lips, revealing black gaps between his teeth. He stretched forth his massive hand and before Rémi could stop him, forced his fingers inside Rémi's mouth. He wrenched one of Rémi's teeth free from its socket.

Rémi sank to the ground, bleating in surprise. Ulysses rolled the tooth between thumb and forefinger and then tasted it as one might sample the freshness of milk. He turned and thrust it back inside the log, burying it under crumbling wood and insects. Rémi coughed, lurched, and gagged, spitting mesocarpic blood like pomegranate pulp.

Ulysses laughed, a deep runble. Teeth flashed in the evening light, the canine points tapering at the ends. Rémi could smell the rot of his breath.

Ulysses turned and faced the well. His back muscles flexed visibly through the thin, filthy shirt as he moved. Rémi heard the sound of water meeting water, and realized that the brute was urinating into the well.

"*Merde!*" Rémi cried and jumped to his feet.

Ulysses emptied himself and turned back.

"What . . . what are you?" Rémi whispered.

The brute leaned toward him so that his face was inches from Rémi's, the stench of decay nearly overwhelming. *"Je suis votre damnation."*

Then he turned, striding toward the woods, and disappeared.

Rémi stared after him. He dared not move nor even breathe. His mouth tasted bitter with blood, the defiled tooth lying somewhere within the rotten log.

RÉMI APPROACHED THE GARDEN in a daze. Francois was standing outside the kitchen house tapping tobacco into a paper wedge, and he called out to him. Rémi kept pace. His mind was tumbling over the taste in his mouth, and the strangeness and dread. Not a thing he could fluidly describe. He was barely aware as Francois strode over, cigarette still unrolled in his hands.

"Rémi, what's ailing?"

Rémi continued toward the house.

He stopped and turned around. "Francois. Condemn the eastern well. The water is foul."

twenty-two

NEW ORLEANS, 2009

A HEADACHE CLUNG LIKE a crab behind her eyes. Jasmine fussed to be let outside and so Madeleine heaved herself out of bed and slumped down the stairs in her cotton sleeping shorts and tee. She felt nauseated, even wondered if she was going to throw up. She had barely slept at all.

She turned the handle to the French doors and stepped barefoot onto the pavers, and almost immediately, the fresh air lifted her spirits. The sunlight turned to gold in the fine hairs on her thighs. Jasmine bounded over to the ivy and watered them. The courtyard was small, a hidden garden, and the focal points were the climbers—honeysuckle, ivy, Carolina jasmine. Madeleine's favorite was the honeysuckle. She and Marc used to play hide-and-seek among them in Houma, tasting the nectar. She stepped over and plucked a flower, pulling the stamen through the petals, and touched her tongue to the sweet jewel at the base.

A pinprick on her forearm. She slapped, and pulled her hand away to a bloodied ink blot. Jasmine trotted over at the sound of the slap.

"That's the problem with honeysuckle, Jazz. You gotta be ready for mosquitoes if you want a little sweetness."

She ushered the little dog back inside and up the stairs, and then tapped on her father's door.

"Go away."

"Come on, Daddy, get up."

"Nobody home."

She turned the handle and poked her head through. "Rise and shine."

"Come on, baby girl, I got a headache."

"I have a headache too. All the more reason to get up and shake it out."

Jasmine vaulted onto the bed and tongued Daddy's face.

"Gyadh!" he cried, and dove for cover.

"Come on Daddy. We're going back to Bayou Black today."

He sat up and blinked at her, face puffy. "What? We was just there coupla days ago."

"We need to deal with that house. We can't put it off any longer. Anyway, I'm ending my sabbatical and won't have the time later."

"I can't do it today. I have to . . ."

She waited. Daddy frowned as if searching for words.

Madeleine said, "Well?"

"Good God, baby, you know it's too early for me to think up a good excuse. Why don't you be an angel and leave your poor papa alone?"

"Breakfast in ten minutes. We're having sandwiches. Wear your grubbies."

She patted her leg twice. Jasmine released Daddy and bounded through the door.

Daddy whimpered with saintly resignation. "You're a hard woman, Maddy."

BY THE TIME THEY reached Bayou Black, the pain in her temples had lifted. Ironic, because the task at hand would itself be one giant headache.

They stood armed with every possible weapon of cleaning artillery Madeleine could round up, along with boxes, tools, and industrial strength trash bags. But the moment they opened the door, the cleaning arsenal seemed paltry. The old Creole house reflected how Marc's state of mind had turned. And the place had only festered since he was gone, succumbing to mold, rodents, and bugs. At the sight of it, Daddy Blank looked like he was about to swing his right foot behind his left, snap an about-face, and march back to the truck. Madeleine grabbed his arm.

Jasmine galloped inside and dove for the moldering laundry, then took off like a remote-control race car, zooming through the house, eyes wild and tongue streaming. Her glee induced Madeleine and her father to take those first shaky steps across the threshold.

Daddy said, "We oughtta pay somebody to come do this."

Maddy shook her head. "Wouldn't do us much good. We have to sort through everything anyway. Look at this." She picked up a stack of papers. "Here's a farm ledger from sixty years ago, and here's a flyer for a *fais do-do*." She lifted her shoulders. "And this one's an old tax lien. What do we keep and what do we throw away? It's not really something we can hire out."

Daddy looked at the ledger in her hand, then stared past it toward a stack on the coffee table below. "Terrefleurs. My God, look."

He picked up a folded, yellowing document from the coffee table. She scanned it over his shoulder.

The heading, PLAT MAP and TERREFLEURS PLANTATION stretched across the top in scripted block letters. Beneath that, LEBLANC. The delicate paper had worn through at the folds. It showed a single oblong plot of land bordered by the Mississippi River at one end and a stretch of bayou at the other. Though Madeleine could not discern the size of the plot, from the scale she guessed it covered hundreds of acres, if not a thousand.

Madeleine said, "Wow. That was our family's plantation? Who owns it now?"

He eyed her and set the paper back down on the coffee table.

"We ought to go see it," she said. "After we've cleaned everything up."

He frowned. "It's a long ways away. Probably all boarded up and fenced off."

"But it looks like it's near Hahnville. Two hours, tops. It'd be fun, even just to drive by."

He grimaced, rubbing the back of his neck. "Where did Marc get all this stuff, anyway?"

Daddy unearthed Marc's old radio and switched it on, and they both jumped at the booming volume. Madeleine remembered how it had been blaring when she arrived the day Marc died. She and her father glanced at each other, and he turned it down.

She opened the curtains. Roaches and silverfish of all shapes and sizes, having taken over like a pack of squatters, darted for cover as light flooded the room. Absolutely every article of clothing Marc owned was strewn about the floor.

"I wonder how long he was like this," Daddy said.

Madeleine shook her head. She had been so caught up in research and preparation for the House Ways and Means Committee that she had failed to visit her brother in the weeks before he died.

She checked her father's face, thinking about the battles he had fought with his own mental state. As hard as she tried, she just couldn't rule out the correlation with Marc.

Daddy's deterioration had begun long before she could remember, intensifying just before her mother walked out and never looked back when Maddy and her brother were about nine and ten years old. Not long after, Daddy started disappearing and reappearing at odd intervals, and when he came home Marc and Madeleine clung to him for some sense of stability. But he was often out of his mind, and sometimes prone to violence, and his children began to regard his visits with both longing and dread.

So many things needed to be discarded: Marc's reading glasses; his favorite baseball cap; his cell phone. Madeleine wondered if it even worked. She found the charger and plugged it in.

When they'd come of age, Maddy and her brother had learned of the living trust their father had formed. After growing up in poverty in Houma, they could barely comprehend what seemed like unlimited wealth, not to mention ownership of the grand old house in the Quarter and the warehouse on Magazine. Madeleine had moved into the mansion and enrolled at the university, and had taken to city life like a bee to clover. Marc, however, had been suspicious. He was comfortable with the safe life they'd built out on the bayou. He took an apprenticeship as an electrician, not wanting to touch the family money. Soon he became a journeyman, and then a master, and finally had started his own modest electrical contracting business. He'd led a simple life; a satisfied life. Until the accident.

He had been on a commercial job with a journeyman who worked for him. A miscommunication, a careless error; a small explosion. His employee had been electrocuted—burned so badly that his cell phone had fused to his hip—and he was no longer able to father children. Marc blamed himself.

But Madeleine sensed that it wasn't just guilt that had led to Marc's suicide, that she was still missing something important about her brother. She and Chloe had both resolved to find out what had gone wrong with Marc, and Madeleine felt the strange occurrences of late had something to do with it. How, though, she wasn't sure. Everything seemed murky and oblique, like having glimpsed movement just below the surface of the bayou, and straining to see whether it was a fish or a turtle or even the tip of something larger, like an alligator. The only way to tell for certain was to wait quietly and see what it would do. Or dive in after it. It was the possibility of the alligator that kept her from diving.

❧

THEY'D BEEN CLEANING FOR hours. Madeleine watched her father as he discarded relics from a lifetime, setting Marc's things in sacks or boxes depending on whether each item should be dumped or salvaged. They had decided to hold off going through any paperwork until tomorrow. Madeleine wondered why and how Marc had unearthed all these documents.

She dragged another Santa sack of garbage to the living room, then opened the front door, and gave a start. At the bottom of the steps, hand on cane and elbow supported by the pale, yellow-haired Oran, stood Chloe LeBlanc. Her black Mercedes sat next to Madeleine's truck in the driveway.

Madeleine stepped out onto the porch. "Chloe. Hi."

"Have you found something in there? Something to know about Marc Gilbert?"

Madeleine sighed, hand to hip. She looked back at her father who was peering at Chloe through the window. He made a wave of disgust and shook his head, then shrank back toward the hall.

Madeleine turned back to face them. "Hello, Oran."

He nodded.

Madeleine said, "Won't you both please come inside?"

"You found something?" Chloe asked.

"No, Chloe. Heaven's sake. A lot of old documents. But from the looks of things, Marc was just plain depressed. That's why he killed himself. End of story."

The old woman frowned and turned away from the door. "Then I have no need to go back in there. I found nothing of substance either."

Madeleine glanced over her shoulder again, and then returned her gaze to Chloe. "Go back? You . . . you've been inside the house?"

Chloe gripped the cane and looked toward the great oak tree near the bayou, where the family had always hidden the key.

Madeleine felt invaded. She hadn't lived in the little house in years, but she didn't like the idea of Chloe breaking in and rummaging through Marc's things.

"Chloe, you need to tell me when you want to come to the house. Otherwise it's trespassing."

Chloe harrumphed, her voice creaking as she took a step down from the porch. "Banned from it, am I? Your grandmother wouldn't let me in either! And what for? Nothing in there I haven't seen already! Nothing new to know!"

Oran still held Chloe by the elbow, and Madeleine stepped down and took the free one. The last thing she needed was for Chloe LeBlanc to pitch a fit on her doorstep and break her hip.

"Nobody's banning you, Chloe. There's no need for dramatics. All I ask is that you notify me when you want to come. And before I forget, is Severin with you?"

Chloe's eyes pinched into a dour sulk, and Oran watched Madeleine's face as if he feared what she might say next.

"Never you mind about that now, Madeleine. Never you mind."

"I want to help that poor girl, Chloe. It's important."

Chloe puffed an expulsion of breath, and if Madeleine could believe the old woman capable of laughter, this might have been it. "You can see it any time you like!"

It? A sour ripple shifted inside Madeleine's stomach at Chloe's choice of words. She thought quickly. "Tuesday then?"

Chloe flicked her gaze from Madeleine to the porch swing, and gave the slightest nod.

"Is that a yes, Chloe? I'll see her on Tuesday?"

Annoyance on Chloe's face. "As you like."

Chloe panned the lawn and gestured her cane toward the dock. "Take me to the water now. Just Madeleine."

Maddy gritted her teeth. Oran immediately fled to the car, sliding behind the driver's seat before Madeleine could even answer, leaving Chloe swaying under Madeleine's grip. It almost seemed as though Oran feared Madeleine. Skittish thing.

"All right then, Chloe," Madeleine said. "Let's go."

Chloe shuffled, her cane pounding dimples into the delta soil between patches of St. Augustine. Madeleine was surprised at the strength in the old woman's arm. Her bone density and balance might require her to use a cane or a wheelchair, but other than that Chloe was healthy as a spring grackle.

"If you don't want to come inside the house, Chloe, why are you in Houma?"

"Oran said you left a message that you were coming. I thought I might check in on my great-granddaughter face-to-face."

Madeleine raised a brow at the old woman's companionable demeanor.

Chloe scowled. "You look at me with sass."

"Just seems like a sudden change. I didn't know you were looking for that kind of connection with me."

"I am a human, eh?"

Chloe coughed, working her cane with measured steps. "A very long time ago when I was still a girl, almost grown, I was all alone. I had nothing. There was a woman who took me in. She was good to me. But there was a flood and she was persuaded to drink poisoned water, and she died."

Madeleine frowned. "That's terrible. Who would persuade someone to do a thing like that?

"Her choice to listen. When she died, I knew I had to be harsh to survive."

Madeleine was trying to follow, unsure what Chloe was driving at or why she was telling her these things. But she wondered if perhaps a softer person lived underneath that hardwood exterior after all.

Chloe said, "You are going back to the university?"

"Yes," Madeleine replied.

"What is this, cognitive schizophrenia you talk of?"

"It's not really widely recognized in the scientific community yet."

"Tell me," Chloe said. "This is like your father's devil, yanh?"

Madeleine sighed. "It's not a devil, Chloe. It's a form of schizophrenia where the subjects don't exhibit the rambling, disordered thought patterns of typical schizophrenics. They can clearly describe their hallucinations. And they're not as nervous. More to it than that, but that's it in a nutshell."

"You are leading this research, then?"

Madeleine nodded. "As long as I can. Funding is tough to get. I've only seen a handful of patients who were affected this way. I suspect there are lots of others out there who are undiagnosed. I want to see that they all get the treatment they need."

Chloe sneered. "Is that so? What is it that they need?"

Madeleine was taken aback. "They need special therapy and medications."

"You look through a microscope glass, you see creatures. I look around and I see no creatures, so I say you are crazy. But with your microscope, you know they're there. You know they will still be there even if you pretend not to look. Senses don't need treatment, Madeleine." The old woman crooked her finger as she shuffled toward the banks. "You hear, and if you don't like what you hear, do you choose to go through life with stoppers in your ears? The madness comes because the river devils are jealous and they demand attention. To see them is not sickness. It is a gift."

Madeleine regarded her from the corner of her eye. "You use the word 'devils' and then you call it a gift."

"If you could see the unwelcome guests that live in your house, the termites, ants, toads, mice. Would you pretend not to see them? Does that make them go away? Listen to me, *p'tite*. Maybe you take notice and you learn what you can do with them. A clever person can take the venom from the throat of a poison toad and use it for other purposes."

Madeleine said, "You mean like making medicines?"

"That is one small way."

"I hear you, Chloe. But sometimes people see things that just aren't there. It's confusing and upsetting for them. Those are the people I'm trying to comfort."

Jasmine trotted out to the end of the dock and stretched in the sun. The thin banks were aflutter with dragonflies and a single blue heron.

"Chloe, did you and my great-grandfather live outside Hahnville? Because Daddy and I came across a plat map for a plantation called Terrefleurs."

"Stay away from that place." Chloe's words were firm, but they came in a drift as if she were merely thinking aloud. "Dangerous to you, in that place."

"What do you mean?"

Chloe's nostrils flared as she panned the bayou, almost as though she was sniffing the air like a bloodhound. Her gaze rested back on the old house.

"You have much work. I will send someone to assist you."

"What?" The proclamation startled Madeleine in more ways than one. "No, Chloe, do *not* send anyone over to help. It's late and we're done for today anyway. And certainly don't ever send Zenon Lansky over again."

Chloe eyed Madeleine. "He is able. A better match for you than you might think."

Madeleine gaped. For one nerve-sparking moment, the memory of being ensnared by Zenon flashed through her mind.

"Out of the question, Chloe. If you deliberately sent him to the flower shop in some kind of matchmaker attempt the other night, that was a mistake. I don't want him near me. So don't send him my way, not now and not ever."

twenty-three

BAYOU BLACK, 2009

FTER EVERYONE LEFT, MADELEINE and her father continued to work until the daylight hours faded to night. Marc, Chloe, Zenon, Ethan, Daddy—they all haunted Madeleine's heart with their own sweetness or sting, or both. But the physical labor helped scrub her thoughts. Madeleine let herself go to what she now thought of as the fascinations; everything around her beamed with a strange kind of life force. The wood floor seemed to respond to her care the way resurrection moss blooms to life after a rainstorm. Even the house seemed kinder, tidy and comfortable and clean, the way she'd remembered it growing up.

Madeleine retrieved Marc's cell phone, now fully charged, and powered it up. She looked into the "recent call" log and found her own phone number. The last person he'd called before he died. She scrolled through the menu options and opened the photo app. Two pictures in there: One of Daddy and Madeleine on the porch swing, and the other, to her surprise, was a picture of Marc smiling, his arm around an old friend from school. Madeleine tried to recall her name. Millie? Lily? She peered at the image, the girl's sharp chin and bright eyes smiling next to Marc. About ten years older than the last time Madeleine had seen her, and a few pounds plumper. Emily. Emily Hammond. Madeleine remembered now. And she even remembered Marc mentioning her. But Emily had moved to Nova Scotia. She probably came back to visit family from time to time—her parents lived not too far away in Houma. Madeleine wondered if she and Marc had gone on a date or something.

She turned off Marc's cell phone and slipped it into her bag. She thought about checking in on the Hammonds, and then thought of Chloe, of how she'd said she'd been in the old house and had found nothing new. Chloe would have been wading through all those papers and photographs. She probably never powered up Marc's cell phone, nor did she likely know anything about Emily Hammond.

"Look at this," Daddy said.

He was standing at the closet by the front door. Inside, one of the walls was gaping, with very old lengths of wire running along the studs.

"Marc was going to update the wiring," Madeleine said.

"It'd have been the first time since the old place was built. Look, it's the old knob and tube."

Madeleine knew nothing about knob and tube wiring. Marc was the electrician of the family. She looked at the black, rubbery-looking ropes that crumbled out when Daddy brushed them with his thumb.

She grabbed his arm. "Don't do that! You could get shocked."

"If we wind up selling this place, we'll have to disclose that it's got old wiring. Funny Marc never got around to updating it."

"I guess it's like the cobbler with no shoes. He was the electrician with ancient wiring."

Madeleine looked around the little house with satisfaction. They'd completed most of the sorting, and tomorrow's tasks would demand less emotional energy and more of the physical, things like cleaning and moving. *Praise be!*

She and her father rewarded themselves by sitting out on the porch swing eating buttermilk biscuits and fried chicken from Thibby's, though Madeleine could do little more than pick. Now that her physical labor had subsided, she had Ethan on her mind. The more time that passed since their conversation, the more empty she felt. He'd become a significant part of her life without her truly realizing. And his talk of future and children—Madeleine rarely dared to think of such things. Pretty little family units in pretty little houses were the stuff of dreamscapes. Something for normal, privileged people.

The sky was flooded with stars, the scent of elderberry greens enriched the humid night air, and the nocturnal beasts of the bayou sang lullabies.

"You doin all right, kitten?" Daddy said.

"Sure. I'm fine."

He sighed, listening to the night sounds. "Got everything under control, don't you." He regarded her. "Sometimes I wonder what you'd do with yourself if you didn't have us driving you crazy." He paused. "Well, me driving you crazy."

She shook her head. "Stop it. You know I love you."

"Ever put a star to sleep?"

"To sleep? What do you mean?"

"You turn'm off, like turning out the lights."

"I remember this game when we were really little." She recalled Marc mentioning this to her on the phone.

He pointed a chicken bone toward the sky, then wiped his hands. "Pick a star. Any one of them up there."

She smiled up at the heavens and selected a single pinpoint of light.

"Now." He leaned back, chin tilted upward. "Focus on just that one. Keep your eyes on it. Now tell it to go to sleep."

She gazed at her star, speaking to it in her mind, telling it that it was time to rest.

Sleep for now, little star. You've done your job.

The pinpoint burned a moment longer, and as Madeleine watched, it glimmered and winked, then disappeared.

Immediately, Madeleine's mind churned out explanations: an at-mospheric waver, heat gas, a distant cloud.

But then she decided to let it go, and let her mental log state that she did indeed put a star to sleep.

She laid her head on her father's shoulder, glad that she had taken that sabbatical, and not just because of the research. A cool breeze stirred from the bayou, and Daddy closed his warm hand over hers.

Despite what had happened, despite the circumstances and a lingering thread of sadness, Madeleine knew of no better place at this moment than sitting on the porch swing of Bayou Black with her father. After all, this was her childhood home.

⁘

DADDY GOT HIS WAY. And Madeleine got her way. After spending the morning sorting and packing things that had survived yesterday's culling, Madeleine mollified her father by hiring someone to do the rest of the cleaning. But in exchange, she talked him into driving out to Hahnville with her so they could find the old plantation house. He'd been reluctant, but when Madeleine mentioned that Chloe had warned her to stay away from the place, Daddy grew indignant and suddenly insisted they go.

A continuous earthen levee ran high along the north side of the road, blocking any view of the Mississippi River. Most of the houses they passed were old and modest. Natural gas companies owned a good share of the land here, and sprawling industrial plants replaced the plantations that once stood along River Road. They drove under bundles of large pipes that stretched overhead, connecting to the great river beyond.

Though the old plat map hailed from the 1850s, she was confident it would provide enough clues to help them find the Terrefleurs site. The curves of River Road and the Mississippi were the same now as they had been a hundred and fifty years ago. Madeleine kept an eye out for a distinct stretch of high ground above a bend in the river.

Daddy pointed out Esperanza Plantation as they passed, still intact though not open to the public. Some, like Oak Alley and Evergreen Plantations, had been fully restored to their original grandeur. The chances of Terrefleurs having survived the years were slim, and even if it had, it would be in someone else's possession. But she couldn't wait to see it.

The river turned, and the road along with it, and Madeleine's gaze swept toward a swelling of land just beyond the bend. A flash of an old rooftop between thick branches covered with kudzu. The building was almost completely obscured by thick screens of bramble and oaks and magnolia and the climbing vines. But she did see that flash of roof on the high ground, and she was certain she'd found Terrefleurs.

twenty-four

HAHNVILLE, 1912

THE WHISKEY HAD SPUN cobwebs through Rémi's head, but he found himself unable to sleep. A pervasive sensation that the fiend Ulysses was in his room. That he'd settled into the fibers of Terrefleurs, tainting the very bousillage of clay and moss that insulated the cypress walls. Or even deeper. Deeper than that. Ulysses had invaded more than Terrefleurs; he'd somehow invaded Rémi. He'd continued to appear at random since that first moment by the well. Rémi sat up and looked around, but he was alone.

When he rolled over on his belly, something crackled beneath him in the bed. He lit the lamp and pulled back the bedding. There, tucked within the Spanish moss stuffing of his mattress, lay a bundle of bone, feathers, and herbs tied with twine. A gris-gris.

He grabbed the dubious magical charm, cursing as he pulled on his dungarees, slipping the straps of suspenders over his bare chest. Earlier that night he had discovered that his evening meal had been tainted with some foreign substance—it looked like a mashed root. Apparently one of the workers had slipped something in his food in order to calm his nerves.

He opened the door to the gallery and threw out the gris-gris. The moon-drenched evening was filled with the scent of warm, wet moss. He uncorked his whiskey and sat on the porch, taking a deep pull directly from the bottle.

Even in the darkness, he could see the river flowing beyond, glints of moonlight shimmering on her surface. The Mississippi provided transportation, sustenance, and the·very life force that fed this land. And when she turned violent, the river took life away.

A cigarette butt was lying under the railing. He retrieved it and struck a match against it, drawing in deeply. It tasted like a moth-eaten shawl.

Somehow, the river made him think of Helen's servant, Chloe. He thought about how she had saved that child from suffocation by slicing into his throat and breathing her own life into his lungs. He pondered how little he knew about this person whom he had taken into his home.

Rémi suddenly felt the hairs rise on his arms, and he turned to see Ulysses sitting in the chair next to him.

Rémi glared at him. "You leave here!"

Ulysses continued to grin, then reached over and took the whiskey bottle, drank from it, and set it on the table. Rémi's shoulders slumped. He wondered whether the gris-gris and the tainted food had anything to do with Ulysses's presence. His mother was one to respect river magic, and even sought guidance from a voodoo priestess in New Orleans on occasion.

The fiend spoke in French. "Your wife was no good, a remnant of your past. It is better that she is gone. You should kill her brother, too. He will take what you have and sleep in your bed."

Rémi said nothing, refusing to acknowledge Ulysses. Smoke blew from his lips in a long, slow trail. He lifted the bottle from the table and sipped, resigning himself to a night spent in the company of this river devil.

❧

IN THE STILLNESS THAT settled on the plantation just before midnight, Chloe emerged from a tiny cottage along the row of field workers' housing. She checked her moon markings to make sure the time was right. Over her thin gingham dress, she wore a sling that knotted behind her long neck and formed a large pouch just below her breasts. The high, bright summer moon was suspended in the perfect position. She headed toward the dark chambers within the woods.

She wove her way through the dense foliage until the tall, draping trees parted to reveal a damp meadow. The sound of frogs grew louder, and she knew that she was nearing the swamp. She paused and collected long stalks of thimbleweed, gently pulling the hairy stems from the ground, taking care to keep the shallow rhizomes and root system intact. She made a small bundle of the plants and tucked them into her sling.

A snapping noise broke from the direction in which she had entered the woods. Chloe dropped to the ground. She crouched low amid the tall grass and reached into her sling, fingering the knife inside. No light in the nearby woods.

She sat motionless for a long while, straining eyes and ears against the emptiness. The night brought forth only the usual sighs that came from the wind and creatures along the water. She withdrew her knife and turned it over in her hand, keeping an eye to the woods. When she was sure she was alone, she rose and strode in the direction of the swamp.

She paused over a mound of Indian pinks, the flower lobes shaped oblong like pinking shears whose name they bore. Chloe checked over her shoulder once, then bent and grasped a stalk and handful of leaves, digging the knife into the ground to free the tangle of roots. She tucked three stalks into her sling and then continued south.

Soon the shimmer of moonlight on water shone through the openings of dense woodland. Chloe wound her way through logs and thick, sharp roots until she was standing in the shallows. Her knife slashed through long tendrils of climbing hemp weed that spiraled up the trunk of a cypress. She tucked this, her final quarry, into her sling.

Moving out until she was waist-deep in the bayou, she stirred the water and poured it over her face and body. Eyes closed, lips moving, although she did not give full voice to the chant. She opened her eyes, then lowered her body deeper into the water. She washed her hair.

She sensed an atmosphere of danger in the bayou. Dipping her hands, she poured black shimmering droplets over her head, trying to release herself from anxiety, but dread formed in her chest. She stood and turned toward the bank, aborting the ritual.

She was not alone.

Chloe felt a hand clamp over her mouth. She tried to scream, but the sound came muffled. An arm curled around and gripped her elbows. She groped for her knife as someone pushed her body downward into the water. A strong grip pinned her arms, but she found the tip of the blade inside her sling. She managed only to slice her fingertips.

She was suddenly beneath the surface, and the knife slipped away. Liquid closed in on her face and pried into her mouth. Her lungs squeezed and her stomach lurched. She thrashed from the iron grip and spun around, drawing in a single desperate gulp of air before being forced under again.

She tried to focus. Tried to force her thoughts to converge and loosen the hands that gripped her. But her mind was too wild. Fluttering now, edging into a seductive, peaceful darkness. She knew she was on the verge of death.

She strove for one last attempt to save her life. She managed to free her hands, raising them above, and found a face. She dug her fingernails into the flesh of eye sockets.

⚜

RÉMI JERKED HIS HEAD back as he felt the skin tear under his eyes. He knocked her arms away from his face, gripping her two wrists with one hand, while his free hand clamped over her neck and held her down. He heard the sound of laughter and looked up to see Ulysses on the opposite bank. The fiend was sitting with elbows on knees, his lips pulled back.

The strength waned from the arms that fought him. Rémi looked into the water and tried to see her face, but saw only blackness and fragments of moonlight. Disembodied flowers and stems danced atop the surface. He tried to blink his vision clear as droplets of sweat and blood and water stung the gashes around his eyes.

He looked up again at Ulysses, who was watching, open-mouthed, with a look of hunger. Rémi released his grip on Chloe's arms and then raised her head above the surface. She lolled drunkenly, water bubbling from her mouth.

Ulysses sprang to his feet on the opposite bank and thundered at Rémi. *"Finissez-la!"*

Chloe's body convulsed, and froth spewed from her lips.

Rémi wound his arms around her waist and dragged her to the bank, then draped her belly-down over a log that jutted above the water. She continued to retch as he seated himself next to her, his feet dangling in the bayou, hands pulling nervously at his hair. From the opposite bank, Ulysses was glowering at him, pacing like an animal.

Finally she stopped gagging, and her shuddering breaths slowed in rhythm. She raised her head over the log and turned wide eyes toward Rémi.

"Your demon has turned on you," Rémi said, waving at the opposite bank. "Now he wants you dead."

Chloe looked over her shoulder in the direction where Rémi gestured, but Ulysses was gone.

Rémi gave a futile laugh and shook his head. "You killed my wife with that fiend, and then you killed a helpless child. I want to know why."

Chloe could only shake her head, unable to speak.

"Don't lie!" He slammed a fist on the log, and Chloe recoiled weakly. "You've been conjuring that devil!"

Chloe made gurgling sounds, and once again shook her head.

"Non, monsieur, non," she managed, just above a whisper. "The ritual is for to help . . ."

Her words trailed off, and Rémi glared at the water.

"It began just after you came." He reached into the water and pulled out a stem of Indian pink that had been in Chloe's pouch. "What is this?"

"It kills the worms," she said. "The children have swollen bellies."

He frowned at her, then pulled another stem from the water. "This?"

"Thimbleweed." She looked full into his face. "It treats . . ." She took a breath. "Bewitchment."

He ran his fingers along the limp stems and repeated the word, "Bewitchment." He let the plants slip through his fingers and into the bayou, where they bobbed among the litter of the other contents of Chloe's sling.

They sat quietly for a time, Chloe struggling to catch her breath. Finally, Rémi offered his hand, and helped her off the log and onto solid ground. Together they walked back through the woods until they came to the main house. Rémi brought her up the steps to the gallery and into the men's parlor, where he lit a lamp and a cigarette. He sat opposite her, and regarded her soft features in the amber glow.

"You tell me now," he said. "Where do you come from?"

Chloe watched him for a long moment. She let her gaze travel the dimly lit room, her nostrils flaring. She seemed to arrive at a decision, and began to speak in broken English and Creole.

※

CHLOE TOLD RÉMI SHE had been raised by her grandmother, who schooled her in native Houma medicine and the ways of the river. Chloe knew nothing of her parents, only that she was half black, half Houma Indian. Her grandmother died when Chloe was twelve years old, leaving her orphaned and homeless. Not knowing what else to do, Chloe sought work at nearby Elderberry Plantation.

But at Elderberry, the workers shunned her as an outcast, and the plantation overseer often beat her. She managed as best she could, using her medicinal abilities to gain acceptance, and she learned the art of voodoo practiced by so many plantation dwellers. As she grew older, however, the overseer began to fixate on her, and she feared for her life. She decided to leave Elderberry.

The overseer pursued her, and she traveled with stealth in order to avoid being caught. For although the government had long since abolished slavery, the lawmen did not frequently act on behalf of the black workers. She wandered north, seeking work at plantations along the river. Her reputation as a practitioner of medicine and river magic preceded her, and the black populations treated her with reverence and fear. They provided her with food in exchange for spells and treatments, but they did not allow her to live among them. She became widely known as both a voodoo priestess and Houma medicine woman, a combination that earned her a great deal of respect, but no home.

Finally, she came to work for Helen. Because most of the Glory Plantation workers had come from Kentucky, they were unfamiliar with the legends that surrounded Chloe. Her appearance indicated nothing more than that she was of African descent, and so she was finally able to blend in. By the time she came to Terrefleurs, her position was already secure.

Rémi listened to the words with both fascination and skepticism. He questioned her on details, probing for any motive she might have to bring ill will to him and Terrefleurs. However, the story sounded truthful. It proved obvious that Chloe genuinely grieved for losing Helen.

Satisfied that Chloe had not used black magic against him, Rémi began to tell her what he knew of Ulysses. He explained how he had glimpsed Ulysses just before Helen's death.

Chloe fingered the damp sling that still lay limp around her neck and then removed it, casting it to the floor. "Why did you try to drown me in that swamp? Was it because Ulysses told you to?"

"No," Rémi answered. "Well, maybe. He speaks to me, but he

has a stronger way of communicating than that. Just by being there, I know what he wants of me. And sometimes I cannot tell the difference between a thing that he wants and a thing that I want. When I found you collecting your plants for charms I thought you had conjured Ulysses to torment me and kill my wife. But after I had you in the water I saw him there, goading me on."

Rémi paused, remembering Ulysses's grimace in the swamp. "Why do you think he wanted me to kill you?"

The lamplight flickered on Chloe's coffee-colored skin, and she sat silently for a long while. Then she said, "Maybe he thinks I can drive him away."

"Can you?"

"No way to know. He seems very powerful."

Rémi nodded. "Powerful enough to kill."

Chloe shook her head. "No, he cannot do that. Missus Helen and Laramie did that to themselves. Think of what you saw. What did he do to them? Only whisper. He makes suggestions, and they believe it comes from within their own thoughts."

"I saw him sully the well."

"That was only his wishful play. His way of whispering to the sickness in the water. This world to him is no more than a picture. He can't really touch it, only whisper. It is different now for you because you can see him."

"I don't want to see him."

"But he would still be there. He has always been there. You can try to drive him away, or I can bottle him. We could use his power to your advantage."

"I just want him to go away! Can you drive him away?"

Chloe said nothing. Rémi felt exhausted and desperate.

"Please help," he said, and his voice caught on the words.

She reached out and stroked his shoulder. He was touched by the kindness, and tears spilled from his eyes. She rose to her feet and laid both arms around him, letting him weep into her wet dress as she stroked his hair.

They stayed that way for some time, clinging to each other in the lamplight of the men's parlor. And then, as dawn began to glow purple over the Mississippi, Chloe loosened her wet dress and let it fall to the floor. She unwound her under wrappings, revealing breasts that were full and firm, capped with soft circles the color of coffee. She reached for Rémi.

He grabbed her wrists and pushed her back. Chloe was barely more than a child, a servant. A stark betrayal to Helen. And yet . . .

He stared at her, riveted, unable to think clearly. The air in the parlor felt heady and chilled.

She took his hand and pulled him to the bed, and he allowed it. They peeled off the rest of their clothing. She smelled like cut tupelo gum, and the fresh bayou water was still shining in her hair. He put his face to it, taking the droplets on his lips. He lowered his hand between her legs. Already she was slick and open. He pressed his nose to her neck and drank in the scent, letting his fingers explore the feel of her.

She pushed him aside and then rolled onto him, taking him in her hands, pressing her velvet center just at the tip. He pushed forward but she did not let him enter; she held onto him with both hands curled along his length, and she moved him against her opening in repeated up and down circles as she rocked her hips. He didn't understand what she was doing. He gripped her buttocks but she straightened her back and held. Helen used to lie beneath him like a nesting dove, soft and warm, a gentle smile. Chloe was moving against him with a sense of demand. He felt he might shatter if he didn't enter her soon. Sweat pearled at her collarbone and ran down her breasts as she moved. It made him want to taste it, taste her, devour her. She gasped twice and stopped, mouth open, sustaining her pressure against him, eyes on his. He didn't dare move.

She leaned forward, and spread her legs wide. She pushed him inside. He shuddered at the streak of sensation that shot through his body. Chloe reached back to support herself with his thighs. She felt damp and scalding against him. She started moving again, arching her body in time with his breathing. They advanced in quicker gasps as their momentum intensified. He rocked with her, sweat curling from his neck to his back. Inside, he felt suspended, silent.

The sky flowed from violet to indigo to gray, and then finally, to a gold-touched white. And as the first direct rays of sun touched leaves of cane, Rémi finally found sleep, lying intertwined with the woman who, only hours before, he had sought to murder.

twenty-five

NEW ORLEANS, 2009

ADELEINE'S GAZE SWEPT OVER a chain-link fence with hoop barbed wire that ran along the perimeter of Terrefleurs. She slowed the truck and leaned down to get a good look. A thick tangle of bramble obscured any view beyond a depth of five feet.

"I don't see anything." She chewed her lip, brow furrowed.

Daddy Blank shrugged. "Not much to see."

Drainage ditches running along either side of the road prevented her from pulling over. Instead, she drove on and parked at a mechanic shop about a half mile beyond the site. A deadbolt secured the aluminum roll-up doors; no one around. She got out of the truck.

"Where you goin now?" her father said.

She spread her hands. "I want to see it! Don't you?"

"I thought we was just gonna drive by! You wastin your time, baby."

Madeleine's exasperation arced. "What's gotten into you? If you don't want to come then just stay here. I won't be long."

She got out and strode in the direction of the old plantation. After a half a minute she heard the truck door slam, then Daddy's foot-falls.

"Hard-headed."

They slipped through a torn section of the old chain-link fence. Daddy grumbled at the NO TRESPASSING signs, but Madeleine ignored them.

The bramble, however, was a much more formidable barrier than the fence. Coils of blackberry bushes towered above their heads, and they had to plod through a labyrinth of tunnels that seemed to dead-end at every turn.

Eventually, though a little scratched, they emerged on the other side at an overgrown dirt road, and beyond it they could clearly see the remains of an old Creole house. The west end had crumbled and the roof splintered, revealing black gaping holes. Nevertheless, the massive size and the fact that it sat high on piers gave it an imposing presence. A porch wrapped around the entire perimeter, and a stair-case sagged like an accordion at its center. But the bottom steps were a pile of rubble with no visible way to get to the top.

Madeleine's forehead glistened with sweat, but not just from the heat and exertion. Her mind raced with the possibilities of who had once inhabited the place.

"What do you think," she said. "Distinguished old gentlemen and gracious southern belles?"

Daddy finally began to warm to her enthusiasm and smiled. "Probably."

"Our ancestors," she said. "I wish I could have known them. All we got is Chloe."

"You met your grandparents too. And your great auntie. You were just too young to remember."

A sea of vines and branches seemed to blanket every inch of space beyond the house. Madeleine and her father picked their way around the side, peering under the great porch where through broken windows they could see remnants of black and white marble tiles in the basement.

Madeleine was dying to get in there.

"What time is it, Daddy?"

He took out his pocket watch and regarded it. "Five to six."

She believed him. Daddy had a knack for telling the time of day, and it had nothing to do with his engraved golden pocket watch, which was just a ruse. That thing hadn't ticked in years. But for whatever reason, he consulted it when asked, and reported the time of day based on his much more accurate internal clock.

She figured they had about forty-five minutes before sundown. At the rear of the house, the side facing away from River Road, a smaller staircase wound to the top. It, too, was in disrepair, though not nearly as hopeless as the one in the front. Several lower steps were missing, leaving about a five-foot drop. In that space, a twisted ladder bridged the remaining gap, the wood so old and warped that it spiraled upward as if it were some hybrid strain of the bramble that surrounded it.

Madeleine took hold.

"Careful. This thing's got dry rot," Daddy said, then muttered, "Guess that proves it's from the LeBlanc family."

He followed her, carefully maneuvering up and onto the stairs, avoiding broken steps. At the top, they could look out over the rear of the property from the broad veranda.

Over the wall of vines, outbuildings emerged, most of which were either overgrown or caving in. Two neat rows of what must have been housing were divided by a thin dirt road that had been so compacted from use at one time that the foliage still could barely penetrate the soil.

To the east, the pointed roof of a small building rose from a choking nest of vines. Remnants of white paint curled from the old brick of the top. They could see a row of perfectly spaced round holes, and under each hole, a peg.

Madeleine asked, "What is that?"

Her father squinted at the structure. "Dove cote. Or I guess a pigeon house, not that I know the difference between the two."

"One's for doves and the other's for pigeons, I suppose," she said.

"Dunno the difference between those either."

"I read somewhere that they used to use the bird droppings to help fertilize gardens."

But as they surveyed the savage tangles of brush around the pigeon house, she found it difficult to imagine someone might have once had a cultivated garden there. Beyond the scattered outbuildings, the ancient trees obscured all but a sliver of the great bayou, already singing with frogs and insects beginning their early evening banter. Madeleine and her father walked along the porch to the front where the swell of the earthen levee came into view. Beyond it would be the Mississippi.

"I guess before the modern levee had been built up, they had a clear view of the river," Madeleine said.

She tried to imagine her ancestors looking out over the great Mississippi from this porch. A thick breeze suddenly chilled the damp of her neck, and with it, something changed. The air, to be sure; but something else, too. She shivered.

And as she looked at her father, that cold air seemed to have affected him, too, clearing away the warmth. His face changed, a tension at the brow, and his shoulders rose and held.

"Let's take a look inside before it gets too late," she said, turning back toward the rear door.

"I don't know why you're hell-bent on seeing these devils," her father muttered under his breath.

She halted, startled, and turned to him. "What?"

She watched him closely. His jaw clenched and he looked away, but said nothing more.

A cold tremor crept down her back. Daddy had made a slip. Was he changing? But something else was happening, too. Something indefinable. She felt as if she had stumbled into a great spider's web.

"Come on, Daddy. Let's go inside."

"I ain't goin' in there!"

Her brow furrowed. She knew better than to push him when he was agitated. She kept her voice gentle, and even managed part of a smile.

"Alright then. Why don't you wait here in the fresh air where it's nice and cool. I just want to take a quick look around."

❦

MADELEINE RETURNED TO THE open door near the back stairs. When she stepped through, darkness engulfed her. Plywood covered the windows, and sparse patches of light spilled through the doorway and gaps in the roof. Her nostrils flared against a barrage of odors—the faintest hint of herbs and flowers, though musty and laced with mold, animal hair, and rotting wood and fabric. But beneath it all she found the odor of something far more sinister. Something had died in the house.

Again, she felt the wave of dread, as though a cold drop of oil was spiraling down her vertebrae. Her senses grew taut. It seemed natural that the condemned house would smell like dead animals. Probably possum, raccoons, and all kinds of creatures had nested there.

A few steps deeper inside the house, and shapes began to take form in the darkness. She was standing inside some sort of pantry just opposite a dining room. The interior did not have any of the grand woodwork or moldings of the mansion in the Quarter, though a carved mantel framed the tiled fireplace. Layers of torn wallpaper covered the plaster walls, much of which had chunked away, revealing slats of wood beneath.

Beyond the dining room, light flooded in from where the roof had smashed through on what must have been a living area. The east walls were still standing, covered in black and white toile, but the entire west section was rubble. A credenza, a secretary, and odd pieces of furniture stood amid the debris. She opened the door to the secretary, found it empty, and closed it again. Madeleine shook her head at the notion that the beautiful antique should fall to rot.

A sudden movement caught in her periphery, and she thought she saw a male figure hulking just a few feet away. She gasped and stepped backward, but realized that it was a trick of shadows. The wind had stirred the limbs of the oak and magnolia, eclipsing the splashes of sunlight in an erratic shadow dance. But the movement drew her attention toward a dim corner where a rolltop desk stood.

A fine old piece, made from the same bayou cypress wood as many of the furnishings in the mansion on Esplanade. Not ornate, but sturdily constructed and obviously crafted by someone who took pride in the work.

Madeleine raised the rolltop, made from a single piece of wood that had mellowed over time to a honey and cinnamon color. Inside, she found small drawers and cubby holes for sorting. One by one, she opened each drawer and closed it, admiring the hand-crafted dovetails that formed the joints. The desk appeared empty, and she was about to turn away when she realized something was out of place.

Inside the center cubby hole, a wooden peg protruded slightly. She reached in and removed it, and then felt around until she found a piece of loose molding. When she tugged at it, it pulled, revealing a small hidden compartment.

Inside were a blank-faced wooden doll and a small metal flask leaning against the panel. The doll was not painted and had no dressing, but its face had distinct cheekbones and recessed eyes. The wood was smooth and dark.

She unscrewed the cap to the flask and smelled lingering fumes of old whiskey that disappeared after a single whiff. Behind where the flask had been sitting, she saw a small leather-bound book. She opened it and tried to read, but found only handwritten French filling the pages, and she was not exactly proficient. She gingerly scanned through, spotting words she recognized: *voudrais, fenêtre, LeBlanc.*

Madeleine felt a jump of excitement to see her family name. She flipped to the first page. A single line in French:

"Le Livre de Marie-Rose LeBlanc"

"Mémée," Madeleine exclaimed aloud.

Her grandmother's name, her grandmother's diary. Madeleine scanned through pages again. If she had a little time, she could probably translate it. Mémée might even have written about her own father, whom Chloe'd referred to as having a "river devil" just like Daddy.

She bit her lip. She had no idea who might be the current owner of Terrefleurs, but obviously someone had cared enough to leave a ladder outside. She had no claim on the property, was indeed trespassing, and certainly had no right to rummage through its contents.

Nevertheless, she took the book.

She reasoned that once she got a good peek and translated it properly, she would contact the current owners to return it. She arranged the desk back to the condition in which she found it, leaving the flask and the doll in place.

She followed a hallway to her right, where an unusually narrow door opened to another room. The stench of the house grew much stronger here and she covered her mouth. She could also hear insects buzzing. Obviously, this room was the source of the worst smells.

She pushed the door open wider. A gaping hole in the ceiling and roof illuminated the room. A chifforobe, the only item of furniture, stood on the west wall, and in the east corner she saw a large, sticky-looking black stain on the floor. It was crawling with flies.

Madeleine recoiled, gagging.

The desire to take flight gripped her. But she clamped the fabric of her t-shirt over her mouth and forced herself to breathe evenly until the room stopped tilting. No dead animal nearby. No hint at what had shed this slick of rotting blood. The flies were fat and sluggish; their sick humming almost as intolerable as the smell.

In the shadows opposite the blood lay a pile of objects. She could see a glint of glass and some sort of dark canvas material. She took a shaky step deeper inside the room.

She saw a camping lantern and a dark blue knapsack and some folded newspaper lying amid cigarette butts. Flies hovered like zeppelins. The newspaper had not begun to yellow, so she guessed that it was fairly current, though she could not bring herself to examine it more closely with all the drunken flies waiting in her path.

She'd seen enough.

"Termites."

She jumped, and turned to see her father standing in the doorway.
"What, Daddy?"

He didn't reply.

"Let's get out of here, Daddy. This room is awful. There was a hunter here or something."

She gestured at the stain that swirled with flies each time she moved. "Someone must have butchered an animal. A deer maybe." She could think of no other explanation. "We should go."

But her father remained framed by the door, blocking her way.

"Rats and termites," he said.

"What?" She swallowed, trying not to allow the fetid air into her lungs. "The house is rotting away. Termites are the least of its problems."

"Right there." He pointed at the wall beneath the window. "You see?"

She kept her eyes on him for a long moment, then turned to look where he was pointing. Nothing there. She grimaced; he had changed so swiftly.

"Honestly Daddy, it's time to—"

"You wanna come here to raise Cain, had to stir it all up, now, you take a look." He grabbed her arm and turned her toward the wall. Flies ballooned up from the black stain and bounced against her skin.

"Daddy, please!"

He held her with force. The sound of her own heartbeat drummed in her ears.

"You look," he seethed, gripping her arm. "Like putting stars to sleep, only backwards. They've been there. Right there! The whole time. You tell'm to *show themselves to you!*"

His words grew louder, mounting to a near-shout at the end, and Madeleine could not tell whether he was addressing her or the wall.

She stood, eyes wide, staring where her father pointed.

Despite dread and worry, despite all sense of reason, she let the thought come into focus:

Let me see.

In the darkness . . . movement.

A tuft of hair. A glint of wing. Ripples in the shadows.

Madeleine broke free from her father's grasp. A heavy fly spiraled from the dark mass and buzzed her face. She fled the room, fled outside to the porch. She was coughing and spitting, filling her lungs with fresh air, leaning over the railing to catch her breath.

Her father emerged from the doorway and stood beside her.

The breeze sighed from the river, and the crickets chirped in unison among the stretching shadows. Madeleine's lungs caught with intermittent shudders.

"I'm sorry, kitten," he whispered.

She regarded him warily, her hand at her stomach. Given the intensity of his manner only moments ago, it seemed impossible that this fugue could be so short-lived. Cognitive, yes, but too cognitive. Almost as if he had not slipped at all, but had acted with clarity.

"We should go," she said.

The creature sounds from the nearby swamp reminded her of Bayou Black, and offered some comfort, however slight. She descended the rear steps and realized they had just enough daylight to make it back to River Road.

She took one last glance toward the bayou at the far end of the property, and stopped. A shape moved through a clearing in the distance and disappeared into the foliage. It looked like a man, a black man clad in overalls.

"Somebody's here," Madeleine said.

They scanned the clearing and caught another glimpse of the shape.

It *was* a man. He was not wearing overalls, however, but instead wore jeans and a t-shirt with a baseball cap. And he was coming toward the house.

❧

MADELEINE FROZE ON THE rear stair of the Terrefleurs main house, then realized that the man had not seen them yet. He entered another large clump of brush and disappeared.

"Come on," Daddy whispered.

They quickly and quietly finished their descent down the stairs and the ladder, and padded through the compact dirt around to the front of the house.

"Keep quiet," Daddy said.

They ducked into the thicket of trees, pressing forward to the mouth of the blackberry bushes. The old house was still visible beyond the dirt road. They paused, hidden among the thorny tendrils, and watched. Madeleine felt a rivulet of sweat slide from her temple.

They heard footsteps and the groan of rotten wood at the rear stairs. A shadowed figure appeared at the back of the wraparound porch and moved toward the front of the house. He lit a cigarette, illuminating cupped hands in a flare of light, then he leaned forward on the railing. His face emerged from shadow.

Zenon.

Madeleine gasped. But as her surprise dissipated, anger swelled to replace it. Zenon had attacked her that night in the flower shop, she was convinced of it. He had discovered a way to transmute thought. A sense of fury hatched inside her, so dark and savage that she felt her lips peel back in a grimace. She began to rise from her hiding place but Daddy caught her arm, clamping his hand over her mouth. He frowned and shook his head, releasing her, tapping a finger to his lips in a hushing gesture.

Madeleine glared at him. He was right though; this was not the time or place for a confrontation. They waited, motionless in their hiding place. Zenon seemed unaware of their presence, taking slow drags from his cigarette and looking out in the direction of the Mississippi. He looked comfortable, completely at ease, and yet he was a trespasser same as they. Sheriff Cavanaugh's warning percolated in her mind. She would have wondered if perhaps Zenon had been the hunter responsible for the bloodstain in the bedroom, except that she suspected that Chloe had sent him here. Sent him to come looking for Madeleine.

But if that were true, why hadn't he approached the house from the road, as she had? Zenon had come up from the bayou.

The mosquitoes, waiting amid the berries, began to sting. She resisted the urge to slap them, and instead regarded Zenon as he smoked. As children, she, Marc, and Zenon had in common that antisocial quality that made them outcasts. For Marc and Madeleine, it had stemmed from their mother abandoning them and their father fading in and out. Zenon's parents had both been drunks, and he would often come to school with bruises and broken bones.

Madeleine remembered a day when she and Marc had been catching crawfish over by Zenon's house and overheard his mother screaming at him. The door had swung open and Zenon had come running out, but not before his mother had struck him on the skull with a cast-iron skillet. He'd staggered and swayed. From where Marc and Madeleine had been sitting in their skiff, they could see blood flowing from Zenon's ear as he ran into the woods. Both his parents beat him, but his mother—she was the worst.

Madeleine stole a glance at her father. He was watching the house. She began to feel foolish standing there, getting perforated by insects, spying.

Zenon dropped his cigarette over the railing to the damp foliage below. He stood and rubbed his head, and walked back around to the rear of the house.

Madeleine and her father both exhaled, deep and silent. They turned together and stepped through the tangle of sticker bushes, quickly at first, then slowed when full darkness enveloped them.

"I wonder why he came from the back of the house, not the front where River Road is," Madeleine whispered. "Is there a road back there too?"

She saw her father shrug as he moved ahead through the tunnels. "Nothing but swamp back there, far as I know. Must have come in by boat."

"I don't know why we're hiding from him."

"Best to lay low."

The maze of thorny tendrils seemed to have grown more dense in the small time they were at the house, but eventually they did emerge onto the road. Madeleine looked back. The old house was no longer visible through the veil of foliage and darkness.

They walked along the open road in silence, heading back to the truck. Madeleine thought about Zenon in the flower shop, remembered the feel of him against her, and the invasion of his touch. And she remembered how he'd insinuated that she was better off with a man like him, not someone with the reserved, gentle strength of Ethan Manderleigh.

twenty-six

HAHNVILLE, 1916

DEBT SAGGED ON TERREFLEURS like weeds on a fishing line. Before Helen died, Rémi had leveraged much of his farming equipment and the next season's harvest to assist his in-laws' start in sugarcane. He'd also expected that the Chapmans would actively pursue a successful crop from the land they had intended to sow. However, one season had passed, and then another, but nary a sprig of sugarcane had graced the soils of Glory.

True, Rémi knew Jacob had been preoccupied with other things. It had taken a long time for Glory to recover from the flood, considering her landowners knew nothing about farming or Delta life in general. In the meantime, Rémi had been schooling Jacob in the benefits of modern conveniences, such as electricity and plumbing. He had helped him wire his New Orleans row house with a system of electrical knobs and tubes. And at Glory, Rémi had showed Jacob how to run a pipe from the Mississippi River to his house. Farmers could lawfully draw from the river in order to irrigate their crops, and so, too, could a farmer irrigate his home.

But by far, the most valuable thing Rémi taught Jacob was how to execute the current massive project: erecting a durable levee. Under Rémi's supervision, Jacob had managed workers in constructing a sturdy wooden skeleton that served as a backbone for the structure. Now, Jacob's hired steam-powered dredge was trawling out the river, grunting and wheezing like a great steel beast of burden. Even the workers looked as though they were made of metal. Their dark skin shone like plate armor from the sheen of their own sweat, bodies taut and patterned as though forged from stamped metal molds. They were hauling the dredged sediment in wagons, depositing it along the stretch of the Mississippi that bordered Glory, creating a stout berm.

"This levee, *mon frère*, it will be higher and stronger than any built by the Army Corps of Engineers," Rémi told Jacob.

"You think it'll hold up if the water rises again?"

"Not *if*. The water will rise again, that is to be certain. A matter of time, *alors*. Whether it holds depends on you. Will you maintain it this time?"

Jacob shook his head with a laugh as he squinted at the shimmering river that stretched white as the sky it reflected. "Oh, I'll maintain it all right. I may be hard-headed but I learnt my lesson this time."

"We'll see if you do. But you keep your word and this levee will reward you. Other plantations might fall, but Glory will remain dry. This structure is already strong as any."

"Strong as the Terrefleurs levee?"

Rémi nodded reflexively, and then thought for a moment. "Maybe even stronger. My levee was built a long time ago; it's held well enough because my family has always maintained it. But your new Crow's Landing levee is getting attention from both man and modern machine, and it is much bigger."

"Glad to hear it. Because if there's a weak spot along the river, I don't want it to be at my place next time."

Rémi's gaze narrowed at his brother-in-law.

Jacob added quickly, "I ain't wishin bad lack on the Terrefleurs levee, neither. I know yours is strong. Let's all just try to stay dry."

Rémi said, "Hmm. Well maybe your dry land will inspire you to dress her with a few seeds, eh?"

Jacob laughed, as did Rémi, but Rémi continued to chew on the notion that the Crow's Landing levee could outperform the one at Terrefleurs. He told himself this was not a competition; that one needn't gain over the other. And yet what was it that Ulysses had said of Jacob? It seemed ill-advised to heed the ravings of a river fiend, and yet the words echoed from his mind:

He will take what you have and sleep in your bed.

twenty-seven

ADELEINE GAZED AT THE digital display on the cell phone, the picture of Marc with his arm around Emily Hammond. Madeleine wondered about the day that picture had been taken. Probably nothing—an accidental encounter. Wasn't as if any of the Hammonds had come to the funeral or sent notes of sympathy. How close could Marc and Emily have possibly been? Perhaps he'd bumped into her at Thibby's, chatted and snapped the picture as a farewell before she left for Nova Scotia. Perhaps. She doubted it. If Marc was seeing Emily before he died, Madeleine wanted to know.

Madeleine figured out how to navigate to Marc's contact list on the cell phone. Emily Hammond was listed in there, but the number was a 985 area code, not Nova Scotia, so it was likely for her parents in Houma. Madeleine pressed Send and put the phone to her ear.

A woman's voice answered. "Hello?"

"Yes, hello, this is Madeleine LeBlanc."

Silence.

Madeleine cleared her throat. "I used to go to school with Emily, and I wanted to get in touch with her. I don't suppose she's there in Houma?"

Several seconds ticked by. Nothing.

Madeleine looked at the screen to see if the call had dropped. The timer was still counting. "Hello?"

"I'm here," the woman said, and her voice sounded stiff.

"Is, uh, is this Mrs. Hammond?"

"Yes it is."

"I'm sorry to trouble you. I just wondered—"

"You stay away from us, you hear?"

The words froze on Madeleine's lips. She'd only met Mrs. Hammond a few times in passing, and she'd always seemed congenial.

"I don't understand," Madeleine said.

Mrs. Hammond spoke, her words coming slowly. "Emily ain't here. Lives in Canada now. And even if she was home I wouldn't let any a you people come within a hundred feet of her."

"Mrs. Hammond, I don't—"

She heard the airy connection go silent as Mrs. Hammond hung up.

twenty-eight

HAHNVILLE, 1916

*U*PON COMPLETION OF THE new levee, Rémi taught him how to maintain it, pointing out how crawfish made mud chimneys in the structure's walls. Jacob appointed one of his workers to regularly check for and remove them, and he himself watched for erosion or other signs of weakness. Rémi was glad Jacob was finally taking genuine interest in these matters.

Still, when it came to plowing the fields, his interest waned. "Late in the season, and anyway what's the hurry? We'll maybe plant next year."

But to Rémi, money left fallow was money in waste. And although the Chapmans were diligent with payments toward their loans, Rémi was nervous over the extent Terrefleurs was now tied to Glory. Better to have no loans at all. And should there come a year of disease or drought, or infestation of some sort, Rémi's credit would already be at full stretch, and he would not be able to secure a loan to wait out a crisis.

Rémi hefted the broom as he stood with Jacob under the eaves of the carriage barn at Terrefleurs. Nearby, from the limbs of a bay tree, bottles and jars hung like suspended soap bubbles, catching bends of light and casting them in stars to the earth below. Jacob waved the Spanish moss torch under the wasp's nest until the insects fell, smoke-drunk, and veered off toward the wood.

Chloe's voice drifted from among linens snapping on the clothesline. "Patrice!"

Rémi looked over his shoulder, and saw the tiny Creole girl watching with round eyes.

He said, "Dangerous here, *petite*, you might get stung. Go see your maman."

Jacob eyed the three-year-old as she turned toward flags of sheets, and then his gaze lifted to Rémi. Rémi was still smiling. His brother-in-law's face dawned with realization as he looked again between Rémi's blue eyes and those of the Creole girl. Rémi met Jacob's stare, daring him to speak.

Jacob said nothing.

Rémi looked back at her. She raised the new tupelo doll he'd carved for her and waved it at him. When Patrice had been a newborn babe in arms, he'd put his nose to her tiny head and drunk in the fontanel, recognized the scent like tupelo gum, so much like that of her mother. He vowed that Patrice would have a new doll carved from this wood every year as long as he lived.

"*Allons Patrice*," Chloe called to her daughter.

Chloe's face appeared from between two sheets, and little Patrice trotted toward her. Chloe looked up and saw the men watching. Her gaze lingered on Rémi for a long moment before she disappeared behind the washing again, and Rémi saw that Jacob took note of that too.

So be it.

Jacob cleared his throat. Rémi could see that he was going to ask him about Chloe and the little one. But Jacob did not express what was on his mind. Instead, he gestured the torch at the trees that stood between the house and the river.

"What're all them glasses hanging in the trees?"

Rémi smiled at his brother-in-law's avoidance of the subject. "They're spirit jars. The people believe they capture evil spirits."

The laundry snapped in the breeze, and all else seemed quiet from the woodland to the gardens. Nothing out of place. How long this small reprieve might last, he did not know, but he would not question why Ulysses was leaving him alone for the present. Perhaps the spirit jars had caught the river devil after all.

Jacob chewed his lip. "You're real indulgent with'm. I heard you took Miss Chloe into New Orleans to visit the grave of Marie Laveau."

Rémi's eyes narrowed. "I see the gossip parlors are in full swing. Do you have a specific question for me, *mon frère?*"

Jacob colored. "No. I mean . . ." he cleared his throat again. "Reason I wanted to talk to you, we're just wondering—my dad and I— whether it even makes sense for us to raise cane on over at Glory."

"You don't want to grow sugar?" Rémi's attention sharpened.

Jacob raised the torch again. "We're just giving it some second thoughts. We'll probably grow it, I just wanted to get your take."

The last of the mud daubers vacated the nest, and Rémi knocked it off, using the end of the broom to smash the cells into a rain of clumped mud.

"*Mon frère*, I think you are ill-suited to farming in general, not just of sugarcane. Plantation life is tremendous work."

Jacob sniffed and said nothing. Rémi knew he was not a man who cared to dirty his hands. Certainly he counted himself among the rugged, chesty men of the country, but in reality he was more likely to share their song and drink than their physical toil. In this way, Jacob reminded Rémi of his brothers, Henri and Didier, who'd moved to New Orleans in order to lead a more fashionable city life.

Rémi asked him, "Why would you grow sugarcane to begin with? What do you hope to get out of it? Money?"

Jacob shrugged. They continued to the next mud dauber's nest and flooded it with smoke.

Rémi said, "*Ecoutez*. In olden days, it was enough for a sugar farmer to produce raw cane and sell it. But now with modern technology, we have refineries all over the Delta. We used to just grow the sugar, but now we must refine it too, either in a Sugar Trust refinery or on the plantation."

Rémi gestured with his chin toward the pecan allée. "At Terre-fleurs, we used to refine our own sugar, but the process is no longer cost-worthy. This industry is eroding. We have had price wars and political problems."

Jacob said, "It don't sound like the Sugar Trust is doing its job."

"The Sugar Trust was formed many years ago to save us, keep monopolies like Spreckels and C&H from squashing us. But now the Trust holds too much power."

"Y'all seem to be doing fine," Jacob said.

"Right now we are lucky. The beet sugar crops in Europe were destroyed by disease, so there is good demand for the cane sugar this year, but it will not last. Eventually the beet crop will recuperate."

"You refine your cane through the Sugar Trust now?"

"Yes, *bien sûr*. The refinery here on River Road is owned by the Trust." Rémi paused, watching the wasps fall and hover, then sidle away from the wooden structure. "They are having some trouble now with the government."

"Our Trust refinery?"

"Yes, well, the Sugar Trust is having trouble. The government investigated them because now they are the monopoly. A politician from Puerto Rico runs it and they play games to get around import tariffs from the islands. Those tariffs were supposed to make things easier for us growing here. But the Trust sneaks around all that and makes their profits bigger."

"I guess the government will put a stop to that," Jacob said with a dip of his chin.

Rémi gave him a wan smile. "No, I do not think so, *mon ami*. Yes, the government investigated the Sugar Trust, but now the entire world is at war. And where did the investigation go? They stopped investigating. The government needs the Sugar Trust to keep things stable. Keep the money flowing and the sugar growing."

Jacob frowned.

Rémi continued, "The smaller plantations in Louisiana, we try to hold on against all the price fluctuation. But it is hard to keep up. That is why so many sugar planters stop growing cane. Maybe they grow pecans, maybe they don't grow at all, like at Glory." Rémi nodded toward Jacob's land downriver. "Before you bought it, the former owners stopped growing sugar there for a good reason: losing money. And for what? To grow sugar, because that is what they have always done? That would be *stupide*."

Rémi cast a glance at Jacob over the cypress and Spanish moss torch, and could see lines creasing his brow as he squinted toward the fields.

"Why do *you* still grow?" Jacob asked.

Rémi sighed. "I have all the workers. Where would they go if I shut down? Sometimes I make a good profit, sometimes I lose money. But a plantation is not just a business. It is a living thing. You don't just stop her. You must kill her. But I know one day it will all end." He waved a hand toward the Mississippi. "Big companies will own all the sugar. I do not know what is going to happen to the workers when it is all over."

Rémi shook his head. "I try to turn the new ones away when they come, but they all need work and they need a place to live. Some get on the train and go north to New York City or Chicago, but most of these people only know how to work the fields."

Rémi suspected Jacob's family had never paid much heed to the private lives of the workers. At Terrefleurs, the workers were weary and poor, but their lives were very much interwoven with those in the main house.

They heard a child's laughter, and saw that Patrice and Chloe had moved to the kitchen garden. No longer obscured by the hanging linens, Chloe stood in full view, and also in full view was her belly, swollen in late term pregnancy. Jacob's jaw went slack.

Rémi smiled at his scandalized expression, but at the same time, he knew the world would react in the same way. Even worse. A white man taking a black woman as a mistress was not so uncommon, but that didn't mean it was accepted.

Rémi walked inside the carriage barn, clouds forming in the dirt floor behind his footfalls, and rested the broom on a hook. Jacob still refrained from asking about Chloe. Rémi supposed his brother-in-law felt it wasn't his business, and he was right.

"Come, *mon frère*, time for a little cherry bounce on the gallery."

"Should we get them other ones?" Jacob said with a nod toward the wasp nests among the trees.

"Leave them. They will keep the black widows down."

Jacob nodded, and then stood in thought for a moment, the torch crackling. "I appreciate your advice, Rémi. About the sugarcane I mean. All the same, just so you know, we're gonna probably stick to our plans. Everything's set up for growin cane." He shrugged. "I know that ain't what you want to hear—you're riskin your own hide for us, and we're much obliged. So, I do promise to talk it over with my father. We might change our minds, but I gotta say, I doubt it. My father thinks since we got everything in order, we might as well plant the damn sugarcane, and quite frankly I agree with him."

twenty-nine

NEW ORLEANS, 2009

ANOTHER HEADACHE. IT HAD played at Madeleine's temples when she'd awoken that morning and it lingered on as she and Sam spent the day sorting through Marc's documents at the Special Collections Division of Tulane's Howard-Tilton Library. Listening to Sam, Madeleine sat and ran her fingers back and forth across her mémée's diary.

Sam was on her feet, leaning against the table. "Madeleine."

"Mm?" Madeleine blinked at her.

"Did you even hear a single word I said?"

"Yes. You said . . . well, no. I guess my mind was somewhere else."

Sam pointed at her legal pad on the broad wooden table. "I was saying, I've gone back as far as 1846, and Terrefleurs was still listed with LeBlanc ownership. Can't figure out when the family bought it, exactly, but it definitely pre-dates 1846."

"Wow, I had no idea."

Sam said, "Your eyes are bloodshot. You OK?"

Madeleine shrugged.

"Worried about your father?"

Madeleine looked toward the rows of books and didn't answer. Daddy, yes, for starters, but in truth she couldn't get Ethan out of her mind. Her gaze slipped to her grandmother's diary, which she had pushed aside, and the screen saver on her laptop had long since kicked in to a starfield tunnel.

"Well, I found out a lot about my great-grandfather, so that's good. Sounds like he, too, suffered from cognitive schizophrenia. Kind of blows a hole in my theory about street drugs causing the condition in Daddy. But aside from that, I can't make much sense of what Mémée wrote."

She nudged the diary toward Sam. "You've made far better progress than I have."

"Don't look at me, I don't speak Creole."

Madeleine sighed. "I thought I did, but it's different from what I'm used to."

"You figured out enough to find out about your great-grandfather's condition."

"Yeah. I do get some other stuff too. Mémée mentions *Compère Lapin,* which is Briar Rabbit. She used to tell us those stories when Marc and I were little, so *that* I understand. And she writes about her father carving dolls to keep the bad spirits away. But there's this whole other part. Something about pigeons."

Sam said, "Well, you mentioned there was a pigeon house at Terre-fleurs."

Madeleine said, "Yeah, but I just don't get what she was trying to say. Best I can figure out, she was writing about pigeon games. Her mother—Chloe—made her do some kind of exercise, but she and her sister didn't like it. Something about stacking pigeons. Whatever that means. Probably just my shoddy translation skills."

Sam thought about this. "Were they cooking?"

"Pigeons?"

Sam shrugged. "You know, squab. I hear pigeons is good eatin. Stack em up and eat em up."

Madeleine smiled, and then chuckled. And then suddenly she was quaking with laughter to the point that tears were blurring her vision. One of the students at another table frowned.

Sam grinned and whispered, "Was it really that funny?"

Madeleine shook her head. "I guess I just needed to laugh."

Sam settled into the chair next to her. "Tell me what's on your mind. Is it your father?"

"He is slipping. Definitely slipping. And I haven't seen him in a few days. Not since we went to Bayou Black."

Sam eyed her. "But that's not it. It's Ethan, isn't it?"

Suddenly, Madeleine's eyes filled again and tears spilled over to her cheeks.

"Hey," Sam whispered, slipping an arm around her shoulders. "Oh, sweetie. It's all right."

Madeleine shook her head and dashed the tears away. "No, ignore me. It's just tension. I have a headache and it's getting to me."

Sam lifted a brow and gave a humorless laugh. "What? Who in God's green Earth do you think you're kidding, Maddy? Tension?"

Madeleine looked at her.

Sam said, "You're in love with him. It's OK to say it."

"No I—I can't be in . . . We've taken a step back, just as things were starting to get serious. But I think it's over."

"It doesn't change the fact that you're in love with him."

"Why do you keep saying that?"

"Aren't you?"

The tears came again. Madeleine shook her head, not sure if the gesture was meant to answer Sam's question, or to deny her own idiotic blubbering.

Sam held her arm in place, rubbing Madeleine's shoulders. "Tell me again what happened."

Madeleine took a shaky breath. "We just had a disagreement over a misunderstanding, and his sense of trust was—"

Sam thumped her shoulder. "Yeah, you said all that the first time. Now tell me what really happened."

Madeleine looked at her friend. Sam's eyes were glassy as her own, and Madeleine felt touched by her empathy, and so she took a deep breath and told her the deeper truth about what happened. She kept her voice in a low whisper, perpetuating the somber air of the library with her hushed tone. Such a stern partition of space. What Marc must have meant as an illusion of space, Madeleine thought, even as she was telling Sam about what happened with Zenon at the flower shop. She even told her of the incident before that, where she'd felt the same sense of invasion at the gala.

Sam listened carefully. "Tell me again how you stopped it in the flower shop."

Madeleine shrugged. "It's hard to explain. Didn't feel like some heroic breakthrough or anything. It was subtle. I quit fighting inside."

She recalled her rage and then the sudden absence of emotion. "And it's like I projected myself into the wind, just a last ditch effort to escape, and I thought of him and me in there as though we were mice in a laboratory. I just observed."

"And then you were all right?"

Madeleine nodded. "Suddenly I was me again, only I'd changed who I was. Or became more of who I'm supposed to be. As if by letting go of control I somehow gained something."

"You should practice that."

"Practice what?"

"What you just described. Because what if it happens again?"

Madeleine thought about this. "That's what bothers me. I've been avoiding Zenon, but you're right. It could happen again. I'll be damned if I'm going to let him toy around with me."

She looked at Sam. "I tried to explain it to Ethan, but I must have sounded ridiculous. I don't think he knows what to make of it. *I* wouldn't have believed it myself if I hadn't been there."

"Did Zenon acknowledge the . . . the what did you call it, implanted suggestion?"

"When I asked him what he was doing, he said, 'evolving.'"

Sam's expression took on a new depth of gravity. "My God."

They were silent for a moment, then Sam said, "Your grand-mother's pigeon game."

"What?"

"Didn't you say that Zenon and Chloe have some sort of weird connection?"

"Yeah, he said something about having done some work for her. And she keeps trying to fix me up with him." Madeleine suppressed a shudder.

"You said you'd felt the same sensation when you were around Chloe before."

Madeleine nodded. "She has a trick of getting her way. In retrospect, it felt similar, though not as strong with her. It happened on that first meeting, when she wanted me to report on what I learned about Marc's suicide."

"And it worked."

"Not really. It seemed artificial, even then. I haven't told her about this." She reached into the box from the Houma house and pulled out Marc's cell phone, navigating to the picture of Marc with Emily Hammond.

Sam looked at it. "Marc had a girlfriend?"

"It would appear that way. Chloe had actually told me as much at the gala and I didn't believe her. But now that I found this, my gut tells me to keep quiet about it. If she knew I found something I'm sure she'd try to use the trick."

Sam was frowning. "But *why?* Is she just that nosy?"

"I have no idea," Madeleine said, rubbing her eyes.

"Well, if Chloe knows the suggestion trick, maybe Zenon learned it from her."

Madeleine thought it over, but it seemed doubtful. "Maybe. I guess. But what's it got to do with pigeons?"

"If you wanted to learn how to control someone's mind, wouldn't it be easier to start with a simpler mind?"

Madeleine gazed at Sam, thoughtful; troubled. "Like the mind of a pigeon?"

❧

MADELEINE SWITCHED OFF THE radio. It couldn't possibly compete with the turmoil inside her head. She and Sam pulled up in front of her house, standing elbow-to-elbow among the other mansions, all with scrolling wrought iron and wood trim piping, all glowing violet in the sleepy Gulf sunset. Madeleine thought about what Ethan had said about wanting to find someone with whom he might share a future, have kids. She looked at her house and wondered if she could truly indulge in it that way. Let it be a home. Fill it with her heart.

Esplanade was bustling with the usual French Quarter activity: tourists, buskers, hustlers, locals. Madeleine pulled the keys from the ignition and opened the door. She heard her father's voice. He sounded angry.

Sam pulled her door handle, and Madeleine grabbed her wrist. "Hang on. It's Daddy."

He stood two doors down, shouting and pointing. Sam and Madeleine watched and listened. Sam's brow creased in a frown.

Madeleine groped for her cell phone inside her bag. "He's in a rant."

"What should we do?"

But before Madeleine could answer, Daddy focused his shouts on a passerby, a teenager wearing a dark blue backpack. Daddy lunged at him.

"Jesus!" Sam gasped.

Books and papers tumbled to the sidewalk.

"Stay in the truck! And call Vinny!" Madeleine threw open the door and ran for her father. Daddy had grabbed the teenager by both arms and was shaking him, eyes wild. The kid thrashed with his fists balled.

"Daddy! Let go!"

At the sound of his daughter's voice, Daddy released the boy and spun around. The teen turned and gaped at Daddy and Madeleine. His cheeks were flushed and his eyebrows had come together in an angry V. Other passersby had stopped to watch from a safe distance.

"It's all right," Madeleine said to the boy as she stepped toward her father, hands open and voice more calm than she felt. "My father's sick. We've called the police. You should go home."

The kid glanced at the onlookers and then pointed his finger directly in Daddy's face. "Hey, fuck you, old man."

Daddy's eyes were wide, his jaw tense. Mercifully, he ignored the teen and stared at his daughter. The boy stooped to gather his books and papers.

"Daddy, it's me. Come on, let's go on inside."

He took a step toward her and then stopped, pointing toward the house. "There's poison in the very walls. River devils nesting there."

"All right—"

But then he shouted, so loud that she took an involuntary step backward. "It's a vehicle of death!"

She shouldn't have shrank back like that. Just as bad as aggressing toward him. Madeleine tried to remain calm and steady, but she was too familiar with the violence in her father's eyes.

"I hear you, Daddy. Let's just walk a little."

"The air in that house is poisoned!"

The teenager had stuffed his things back into his backpack. He leaned his face directly in front of Daddy's. "Asshole! You're fucking crazy!"

He spat. Daddy darted forward with his lips pulled back to reveal his teeth. The boy jumped back.

Madeleine put her hand to her father's arm. "Forget it. Come on Dad—"

But he jerked away from her as though he'd been stung by a wasp. "Get away from me! What are you? You brought them here!"

Madeleine kept her voice soothing. "I want them out, too. It's me, Madeleine."

"You ain't no little girl. I know who you are. You brought them here."

Daddy's fist whipped out and punched her in the cheek. The boy turned and ran.

Madeleine staggered to her left, struggling to catch her balance. A second blow. The sky funneled away and concrete skinned her palms. She pushed against it, trying to use that plane of sidewalk to get her bearings. She felt as though she were on her back with the pavement looming over her like the lid of a coffin. Crushing her knees. But that couldn't be right. She must have been face-down, lying prone. . . .

Is he going to kill me?

The seams between each concrete square opened to sprouts of black thorns that spiraled upward in lazy, trembling spurts of growth.

"You're one of them, aren't you!"

A kick to her middle. The muscle beneath her rib cage responded with a single spasm followed by paralysis. Her mouth opened. Her lungs did not fill.

He wouldn't. He won't. He'll stop himself before it's too late.

"I know what you are!"

Hands at her throat. Her lungs couldn't fill. Above, sweeps of lavender clouds disappeared to bramble. It stretched up and folded over her, hid her inside its tunnels. Laughter in there. A child's giggles.

Severin?

The little girl was right. The bramble was safe. Predator and prey on equal footing. Madeleine let herself seep into the black hollows. A cocoon of silence and darkness.

thirty

ON A COOL FALL morning, Jacob and Rémi set out to catch an alligator. Time had passed at Terrefleurs with the usual fluctuation in seasons: hot and less hot, with the occasional surprise of actual cold. Chloe's waist had returned to its narrow form, and she'd been walking the plantation in the company of infant twin boys. Rémi had noticed the shock on Jacob's face when he'd realized the black twins had blue eyes. Still, Jacob had said nothing.

Now, as the first glow of sunrise was breaking over rows of sugarcane, Rémi dressed and then greeted Jacob, leading him to the chicken coop. Ulysses could appear at any moment, and this knowledge caused anxiety for Rémi. Though Chloe seemed to have done her best to free him of the demon, Ulysses had been showing his face with increased frequency. Other than Chloe, Rémi had told no one about him.

Jacob seemed far too energetic. Rémi thought it odd that Jacob had never seen an alligator in the wild. After all, he had lived in Louisiana for years now. A milksop who had not properly adjusted to plantation life, as yet regarding it with an adventurous and romantic eye, Jacob still could not seem to foster an interest in the actual *work.*

"I'm gonna have to get at least three alligators," Jacob prattled as Rémi selected an aging cock. "If we get a real big one I'm gonna have it stuffed and put in the huntin lodge. The other one I'll get made into boots, and the last one y'all can cook. I know you Creoles like to eat'm. I never tried it but then again you don't see many alligators in the Kentucky mountains. I don't really want to cook it for myself but y'all can cook it up and maybe I'll try some."

Rémi severed the cock's head. Blood snaked across Jacob's shirt and shocked him into silence. This gave Rémi some satisfaction. He cleaved the fowl into smaller pieces and then stuffed them into a rice sack. Packed with the carcass and a modest amount of provisions for a day on the river, they loaded the rowboat and launched it into the bayou behind Terrefleurs.

Rémi handed Jacob the oar and then settled himself comfortably with a flask of whiskey.

"You row, *mon frère.* Perhaps you will actually sprout a real callous on your hand."

Jacob seemed to take this new duty in stride, and let Rémi direct him through the labyrinth of bayou. The sound of winged insects buzzing in the trees filled the air, distracting Rémi from his frustrations and easing his mind. Of course, the whiskey helped, too.

Rémi expected to see the river devil at every turn, but did not. Instead, he heard Ulysses's whispers in the hissing snakes that wove themselves into Spanish moss, and he smelled his sour breath in the cattle-piss pastures as they warmed in the morning sun. Ulysses was all around the *ciprière,* but not immediately before him. Finally, they reached a shaded slough.

Rémi tossed Jacob a ball of twine. "Hang a bit of meat from one of those boughs."

Jacob reached into the sack and selected a wing, plucking some of the feathers, and suspended it from a branch of water cypress. It dangled alongside robes of Spanish moss, shifting gently with the breeze over the water's surface. Jacob looked down at his blood-stained shirt.

"You are getting good and dirty today," Rémi said, his Creole accent thickening with whiskey. "Are you sure this is for you? I can tell Tatie Bernadette to show you how to tat lace instead. That is a much cleaner hobby."

"Very funny," Jacob said.

The two men pushed the rowboat onto the shore, then out of the way. They settled amid the tangled brush on a clearing of packed soil along the bank where they could observe the bait. Jacob cocked his shotgun and held it crossed over his chest, pointing away from Rémi.

They waited.

THE MORNING WARMED. RÉMI was dozing in the sultry swamp air. He heard Jacob slapping at mosquitoes who laughed at the pungent oil he had smeared over his skin to keep them at bay. In Rémi's mind, the cypress and pine stretched taller, slowly, wavering, the way a lone seed from a milkweed parachutes away on a gentle breeze. The bramble too, stretched its thorny branches, coiling and winding until it enveloped Rémi, forming mazes of sunlight and blackness.

A hand at his shoulder. "How long do we have to wait?"

Rémi opened his eyes, then closed them again.

Jacob shook him. "I said how long do we have to wait?"

The trees and bramble receded back to their original dimensions, leaving Rémi feeling exposed and slightly agoraphobic. He snorted and sat upright, glaring at Jacob as he took a healthy pull from his flask.

"Isn't it a little early to be drinking that?" Jacob asked. "How long do you s'pose before we see an alligator!"

Rémi wiped his face. "How do I know? Sometimes only a little while, sometimes you sit all day and never see one."

Jacob cursed. Rémi scanned the water, the thicket, and up above. All seemed quiet. He sighed and offered Jacob the flask. Jacob hesitated, then took a swig. He gestured toward the placid water.

"You catch a lot of gators round here?"

Rémi nodded. "Some. Easiest way is to shine them. You hunt them at night, and bring a lantern. You see the eyes shine in the dark, then you shoot them."

He withdrew a rolled cigarette from his pocket and lit it, blowing fragrant smoke toward the water. "But it is better sport in the daytime. I used to catch them with my bare hands!" He spread out his fingers.

Jacob looked impressed. "Really? How'd you do that?"

Rémi reached over and retrieved the flask. "Well, first you find an alligator."

Jacob chuckled.

"You find an alligator, and you walk up to him very slowly. If he is near the water, and you move suddenly, he will swim away. You should leave him alone while he is in the water because there he will always win. But if he is on the bank, and you move slowly, you can walk up to him and grab him behind his head."

Jacob's eyes swelled. "You ain't serious." He took the flask again from Rémi and helped himself. "You really do that?"

Rémi nodded with pursed lips. "You can't be gentle, like a . . ." he groped for the English word. "Like a sissy."

He tilted his head at Jacob with a sidelong smirk. Jacob straightened with mild indignation, but let the comment pass.

"You must be strong," Rémi added. "Once you have him, he will fight and thrash. But if you have him behind the head, you hold on tight, and he cannot hurt you. Then you may do with him what you like."

Jacob snorted and waved. "Aw, you just funnin."

Rémi narrowed his eyes. He pulled up his shirt and moved a suspender to the side, revealing a long scar running from just above his navel to the outline of his rib cage.

"This is not *funning*."

Jacob was awestruck. "How did that happen?"

"I did not have such a good hold on him. I held him and he thrashed." Rémi moved his shoulders. "He knocked me off him. Used his teeth. Then he ran away to the water."

"I guess you were lucky. He could have killed you."

Rémi shrugged. "The alligator, he is not so anxious to get you. He would rather be left alone. Get away. But this was bad enough. I nearly died from infection."

Jacob spat into the brush. He sighed and shifted in the tall grass, and seemed to be struggling for words.

"Look here, Rémi. I want to thank you. You've been real good to my family, even though my parents haven't really been able to show their appreciation." He chewed his lip. "Fact is, they don't understand your ways out here. Maybe it was a mistake for us to come out to Louisiana like this. Anyway, you've been real decent. I know things didn't work out the way you'd planned. . . ."

At this, Jacob's voice trailed off, and Rémi felt a burning in his throat. Jacob reached into his satchel and pulled out a long thick wand of linen rags.

"Well, I brought you this." He thrust the parcel into Rémi's hands.

Rémi unwound the rags. As they fell away, they revealed an embossed leather sheath cradling the blade of a bowie knife. Rémi pulled it out, holding it so that it gleamed in the sun. From handle to blade, it ran the length of his entire forearm. He gave a long, low whistle.

"This is beautiful, my friend. Almost too beautiful to use. In the swamplands, things do not stay beautiful long."

Helen's face flickered in Rémi's mind.

Jacob laughed. "It ain't meant to sit around makin pretty. Go on ahead, beat the hell out of it. That's what it's for. Besides, I have another gift for you. Something I think you'll like even better."

Rémi lifted his brows. "Oh?"

"Yep. My gift is this. We're not getting into the sugarcane business. I'm gonna go ahead and get into banking with my father. We've closed out with the co-op, so your name's no longer on anything we have."

"No sugarcane?" Rémi said. "What will you do with Glory? All that land?"

Jacob shrugged. "We're looking at cotton, maybe. I got cousins in cotton. But even if we do that we'll lease it out. Truth is, I'm no farmer!"

Jacob gave a hearty laugh. Rémi laughed too, a release of surprise and pleasure. It occurred to him how much he truly liked his brother-in-law. All entanglements and politics aside, Jacob was an affable fellow. And generous, too; the bowie knife was a magnificent thing. Perhaps Jacob was a little lazy, yes, and not terribly manly, but at least he chose to be a banker, a profession where those qualities did not matter.

"You are a good man, Jacob. Thank you for the knife, and for the news. I admit that I am relieved to hear it."

Jacob laughed and slapped Rémi's shoulder, raising the whiskey. But then he frowned, shaking the flask.

"Aw hell, it's empty!"

Rémi stood. "Do not fear. As your guide, I have come prepared."

He reached into a moldering blanket under a seat in the rowboat, and extracted a full demijohn. Jacob laughed. Rémi heaved it over his forearm, hooking the loop with his thumb, and took a swig that leaked down his chin. He passed it to Jacob and rested a hand on his shoulder.

"Jacob, *mon frère*. You might be a good fellow after all. I always thought you were just a fancy pants."

"What? Who you calling *fency pents?*" Jacob said, mocking Rémi's accent.

Rémi put his other hand on Jacob's shoulder. ". . . but I misjudged you. You are like my brother, even though you are an American."

They roared and slapped each other on the back.

"Well, '*mawn frair,*'" Jacob returned. "You're my brother too, even though you are a Frenchy frog-eating Creole savage." He belched. "From the backwater."

The two bugled their laughter out over the water, and Rémi felt as though his mind tilted with the ricocheting sound; up through the treetops into the wildest reaches of the swamp. The demijohn traveled back and forth.

Morning wore toward noon. Jacob taught Rémi the words to his favorite mountain song, "Keep My Skillet Good and Greasy."

Well I's walking down the street
Stoled a ham of meat
Keep my skillet good and greasy
All the time, time, time,
Keep my skillet good and greasy all the time

Jacob spoke the words and Rémi repeated them, and together they sang only slightly off-key in the simple melody.

I's a-goin to the hills
For to buy me a jug of brandy
Goin give it all to Mandy
Keep her good and drunk and woozy
All the time, time, time
Keep her good and drunk and woozy all the time.

The boom of the duo's voices echoed through the swamp, melting with the call of the herons and sawing insect wings. The demijohn's contents dwindled, and they continued to sing with gusto as they lay on their backs across the packed soil, singing at the sky, singing with their eyes closed. And then once again, the trees and the bramble were stretching, encroaching, protecting, concealing. Rémi sang into the bramble, then laughed. His voice no longer echoed. Swallowed up in the thorns. He heard birds and Ulysses whispering to the snakes. Rémi nestled deeper into the sun-dappled passages, away from the sound of the river devil's voice. But he fretted that Ulysses must be high in the boughs, looking down and seeing all, so Rémi turned down one of the black tunnels. He heard faint splashing sounds amid the chirping of birds. He sensed someone stirring nearby. Jacob.

"Hey the chicken's gone," Jacob said.

And for a second time, the bramble withdrew, and Rémi was no longer hidden. The return to a wakeful state dragged on him as though his blood had filled with lead. His head and stomach were on fire, and his lips felt pasted with hoof glue. He wondered if Jacob felt the same, because he heard his footsteps fade to splashes, as if his brother-in-law were drinking soupy water from the bayou.

"Damn it, Rémi, I said the chicken's gone."

Splashing again. Then Rémi felt Jacob's boot nudge his leg. He rolled over with a groan, shirt plastered with sweat in the stifling air.

He ventured to open one eye. Jacob was rummaging in the boat for the sack that contained the rooster parts, which was apparently covered in ants, because he cursed as their sting perforated his skin.

Rémi blinked a smile, and sat up.

Jacob took out the largest hunk of the carcass and rinsed the ants in the swamp. "Damn it!"

He waded back to the lure, attempting to tie the chicken onto the broken length of twine still dangling from the branch.

Rémi cast a groggy glance toward the woods, and then back to the water, squinting out the shape of a drifting log, and the fuzzy outline of two people. Something about them set off alarms inside his dim mind, and he tried to shake off the fog.

It felt as if the cicadas must have left the trees and crawled inside his ears; their grinding seemed to emanate from his very brain, vibrating wings fluttering behind his eyes. He saw Jacob struggling to tie the hacked rooster to the limb, but the broken twine was now too short.

Behind Jacob in the water, Ulysses came into focus. Rémi sat up.

Ulysses's eyes were fixed on Jacob. A silvery gleam caught Rémi's attention, and he saw that Ulysses was carrying a machete.

"Ulysses, no!"

Jacob lowered the carcass with his left hand, still holding the twine with his right. "What?"

Rémi struggled to his feet. "Get out of there!"

Ulysses raised the machete.

Rémi staggered toward his brother-in-law, splashing into the bayou. With both hands on the machete, Ulysses gave one fluid swing, cleaving the bone above Jacob's hand. Jacob shrieked.

The cicadas returned to Rémi's vision, fluttering against his sight. Branches stretching. Rémi tried to call out, strained to see; he caught a glimpse of Jacob slipping below the water's surface before the bramble and the cicadas blotted everything out. Slumber beckoned. Escapist slumber. Safely hidden. He sighed, yielded.

thirty-one

NEW ORLEANS, 2009

ADELEINE OPENED HER EYES. The bramble retreated. The sky opened wide. Darker now. Sam hovered above.

Madeleine rolled, gagging, her lips grazing the pavement. She saw and heard through a haze, felt skipping flashes of reality and dream. Her esophagus convulsed, and her brain zeroed in on the single task of opening that air passage.

Slowly, her throat relented, and oxygen filled her lungs.

"Maddy, oh my God!" she heard Sam say.

Madeleine struggled for breath. She blinked, trying to say something, trying to tell Sam she was fine, but her throat was sluggish.

Sam was frantic. "Here, don't get up! Can you speak?"

Madeleine tried, but nothing came out.

"We need to get you to a hospital!"

Madeleine shook her head. She pushed herself up from the pavement and looked around, but no sign of Daddy.

"Try to lie still," Sam pleaded.

Madeleine finally managed to whisper, "No, just need to catch my breath. Where did Daddy go?"

Sam shook her head. "I don't know. I was calling Vinny and saw through the window. God, Maddy, I thought he was going to kill you. By the time I got out of the truck he'd run off."

Madeleine whispered, "Let's just get inside."

Sam helped Madeleine to her feet, and they took shaky steps toward the house.

"Honey, you need to go to the hospital."

Madeleine shook her head. "No, I'll be fine. I want to be here in case he comes back. He's dangerous. Is Vinny coming?"

"Two patrol officers are on the way. Friends of Vinny's who understand the situation."

Madeleine nodded. She had no qualms about locking her father up when he was in a violent state. She hoped they could find him before he did something even more dreadful.

thirty-two

HAHNVILLE, 1916

BAYOU WATER FILLED RÉMI'S mouth, shocking him from his swoon. He spat. The swamp roiled and frothed in a struggle that he did not at first comprehend. He saw Jacob's hat floating on the surface like a wood-sprite's boat amid sticks and leaves. Then he realized that Jacob was in the bayou, twisting and shrieking, bobbing in the direction of deeper water. A great leathery tail lashed the surface.

Rémi lurched back to the bank and grabbed his shotgun. The alligator was dragging Jacob away from shore, tiring him out. It likely intended to pull him under water to pickle him before feeding. Jacob was screaming.

Rémi aimed the shotgun, peering down the barrel through the V until the beast was in his sights. He saw the tail roll over, exposing a cotton belly. Rémi fired. He pumped and fired again, and then once more, until it stopped moving. Jacob's legs continued to thrash at the surface, and Rémi vaulted into the water after him.

The hunk of fowl and Jacob's mangled hand, canted at an unnatural angle, were still clenched inside the animal's jaws. Rémi grabbed

Jacob's hair and yanked his head above the surface. Jacob gobbled for oxygen, then in a single desperate motion, wrenched his arm free of the beast, gouging his own skin and severing his index finger as he did so.

Jacob lifted the hand out of the water. Blood flowed in rhythmic waves from his wounds. Rémi dragged Jacob back to shore and tore off his own shirt, splitting it into shreds, and wound Jacob's hand while Jacob looked on in rapture. Rémi twisted a stick into the bindings and tightened. Jacob yelped but allowed Rémi to secure it. The pulsing blood eased to a trickle. They paused in stunned exhaustion, blinking and heaving.

"Did you get him?" Jacob asked.

"What? Ulysses?"

"Did you get the alligator?"

Rémi stared at him, his chest rising and falling as he caught his breath. "He is dead. We must now get you to a doctor."

"Get'm and bring'm back for me."

"Are you crazy? He's full of buckshot. We are going back now!"

"I want that gator!" Jacob rose and stalked back into the water.

"Merde!"

Rémi grabbed Jacob's good arm and shoved him back toward shore, and then clumsily attempted to divine the alligator's body from the shallows.

❧❀❧

AFTER SOME TRIAL, RÉMI had managed to lasso the alligator to the boat, and he'd towed it back toward home. The return journey had transpired in fewer than forty-five minutes, but in that time Jacob's skin had turned porcelain, and he'd begun to shiver. Rémi had covered him with a moldy blanket.

When they finally reached Terrefleurs, Rémi barked orders at two plantation children who were catching frogs along the banks. They ran toward the main house for help, returning with Chloe.

Rémi heaved Jacob out of the boat, then swung Jacob's good arm around his shoulder while Chloe supported him under the maimed one. Together they half-walked, half-dragged Jacob up to the main house. They took him to the sick room, where Rémi left Chloe alone with her patient. He walked out to the gallery and leaned his hands on the rail, looking out over the kitchen garden past the birds perched along the *pigeonnier*, scanning the landscape for any sign of Ulysses.

A group of plantationers had gathered where the alligator still floated alongside the boat like a fender, the children daring each other to touch it. Francois shooed them away and dispatched instructions to prepare the alligator for supper and to alert Glory Plantation of the accident.

The people of Terrefleurs scurried into action, loading the great beast onto a cart and parading it to the kitchen house. The cook would butcher it, pounding tenderloin steaks and frying them in lard, and she'd set them aside for Rémi, Chloe, Jacob, and the higher-ranking workers of Terrefleurs. She would cut the rest of the tail meat into strips and mix it with sausage and gravy for alligator étouffée. Rémi thought of Jacob's wish for a pair of boots, and told Francois to set the hide aside for him.

Rémi returned to Jacob's sick room. Chloe had given Jacob something to ease the pain, and he seemed removed from his wits as she tended the mangled hand.

Rémi pointed at Jacob. "You see? Ulysses did that. He cut him with a machete!"

"*Non,*" Chloe said in a hushed tone. "It was an alligator! You brought it home yourself."

"I saw him use a machete!"

"The river devil uses these tricks to show what he wants. Jacob listened, and the animal listened. They did this themselves!"

Jacob shivered and rolled on the mattress. Chloe moved him back to his original position. He roused, saw Chloe, and laughed to the point of emptying his lungs. Gray sputum freckled the sheets. Jacob waved his maimed arm at Chloe.

"What do you think, old gal? Gonna save my hand, or start calling me Stumpy?"

Chloe's expression was grave.

Jacob's grimace froze on his face. "I was jokin about that."

He looked from Rémi to Chloe. "Good thing I wasn't holding that damned chicken with my right hand." He laughed nervously. "Hey, you ain't really gonna saw it off, are you old gal?"

Chloe asked Rémi to bring her some hard alcohol. By the time he returned with a bottle of bourbon, Chloe had removed the dressing except for the band of tourniquet and was washing the wound from a pitcher. Below Jacob's arm, the water inside the basin turned pink. Chloe folded one end of a mangrove root into Rémi's hand, then held the opposite end on Jacob's tattered flesh. She recited something in a dialect Rémi only vaguely recognized as belonging to the lower native lands, and the few words he caught made very little sense. As she chanted she poured bourbon over the root connecting Jacob's hand to Rémi's. When the alcohol reached Jacob's hand, he screamed and tried to pull his arm away, but Rémi held him fast.

"You should trust her. You need river medicine for this."

Jacob groaned, and then slurred to a laugh. "You letting her work that voodoo on me? Does this mean I'm going to sprout me an itty bitty new hand?"

Rémi could not help but chuckle, and when Chloe finished, he took a swig of the bourbon. "You know, *mon frère*, you scream like a woman."

Jacob's laugh became a braying hee-haw, exaggerated by pain and liquor.

Chloe scowled. *"Tais-toi!"*

The men attempted to sober, but errant snickers burst their pursed lips. Chloe roughly bound Jacob's hand with clean bandages.

"Ow," Jacob protested. "Your little witch doctor got a mean bedside manner."

The door to the sickroom opened, and the physician, Doc Shaw, entered. His gaze lit on Jacob, then swept the room, resting on a pentagram that Chloe had drawn on the floor, topped with a cup of river water and a dish of salt. Jacob was howling with laughter, and he waved his bandaged hand in the air.

"Look, Doc, they gonna saw off my hand!"

The doctor blinked. "I heard you got in a fight with an alligator, son. Had a little something to drink, did ya now?"

Rémi steadied himself. "My brother-in-law is . . . not himself at this moment due to pain medicine."

Doc inspected Jacob's wound, and as he leaned forward Rémi realized that the doctor was himself in his cups. A miasma emitted from the doctor's sweat and breath, an evolved sourness that could only come from a days-long bender.

Doc Shaw sighed. "Yup. That girl cleaned him up real good, but he's lost a lot of blood and I'm afraid that injury's a little too far gone. Now son, you know that hand's gonna have to come off."

"Just call me Stumpy!"

Doc Shaw gave him a tired look and turned a slow eye to Rémi. "It's good that Miss Chloe gave him a little something to calm his nerves, being as the sedatives I carry are mild in comparison."

Rémi gripped his arm. "You sure you are clearheaded enough for this?"

Doc Shaw's expression remained placid. "It ain't exactly going to require a delicate touch, Mr. LeBlanc."

He nodded gravely toward Chloe. "This is not a difficult procedure, young lady, but it's a difficult one to watch. I suggest you run along now. See if they need some help downstairs and keep the children out of earshot."

But Chloe remained where she stood. "I will assist."

Rémi wrinkled his brow. "Should we not take him to the hospital in New Orleans?"

"No, that wouldn't be wise."

Doc Shaw made ready for the procedure. As he carried no sort of instruments for amputation in his black leather bag, Chloe went to see what Francois might have among his tools. She returned with a saw and a gun screw that Francois had modified to serve as a clamp. Rémi handed the physician the gift Jacob had given him, the new bowie knife, the sharpest and the truest blade on the plantation. Tatie Bernadette appeared with strips of old linen sheets.

Doc Shaw turned to Jacob. "You ready for this, son?"

Droplets of sweat sprang to Jacob's brow. It seemed that for the first time he absorbed the enormity of the situation, and he began with vehemence to protest the removal of his hand. The physician explained to him that the procedure was a necessity, and that Jacob's very life was at stake.

Jacob turned to Rémi. "You always givin me a hard time about bein a sissy. Well now you watch. I'm gonna go through with this and you can tell everyone I took it like a man."

Rémi stared at him. "You have my word, *mon frère.*"

Jacob looked at Doc Shaw. "Have it your way then, Doc, I'm ready."

Doc Shaw nodded, and he and Rémi bound Jacob to the bed lest he struggle during the procedure. Jacob began to sing "Keep My Skillet Good and Greasy," his eyes fixed on Rémi. Rémi put his hand on his brother-in-law's shoulder and sang with him.

Honey if you say so, I'll never work no more
I'll lay around yo shanty all the time, time, time
I'll lay around yo shanty all the time

The blade moved. The men sang.

Rémi marveled at Jacob's stoicism as he sang through clenched teeth. The odd groan of misery broke through, but Jacob kept returning to the song. It did seem unlikely that only a few hours before Rémi had considered his brother-in-law not the least bit manly. Now Rémi believed him manlier than any in Terrefleurs, and possibly even Louisiana.

Jacob's hair was slick with sweat, as were the bindings that held him steady on the mattress. They sang the song over, repeating it for the full length of the procedure. Jacob sang through each moment until it was finally finished, never missing a stave.

thirty-three

❦

AM INSISTED ON STAYING the night. Madeleine had declined, but Sam was having none of it. She lingered long after the policemen had left, putting off going home to feed her dogs and grab an overnight bag as long as she could.

"You sure you'll be OK for a couple of hours?"

"I'm fine. Go on ahead, I'm a big girl."

"Yeah, you're a big girl who can't stand to let anybody help her."

Madeleine chewed her lip. "Ethan said something like that to me."

"Well he's right. Letting people help you is a show of faith. You sure you don't want me to call him?"

"No, we'll talk again soon, but not like this."

"Tell you what else. I wish you would've let me take you to the hospital. Here." Sam grabbed a fresh ice pack from the freezer and exchanged it for Madeleine's limp one.

When Sam left, the house was cemetery-quiet. There had been no sign of Daddy. Madeleine turned on the TV in the bedroom to The Weather Channel, killing the silence. She started a bath and let the tub fill while she went down to the kitchen to fix a cup of tea.

At the little round kitchen table, while the kettle churned on the stove, the wallpaper hung loose near that same bubble that had been driving her mad. It reminded her of the day Daddy had introduced her to Ethan. So much had happened since then, and yet here she was, staring at the same damaged, fragile paper she had been unable to leave alone.

And despite herself, she still couldn't resist. She leaned forward and tugged at it again. Perhaps if she pulled it all the way off, it would be less of an eyesore. Or motivate her to undertake the kitchen remodel once and for all.

As she pulled back the top layer, Madeleine saw yet another pattern lying beneath. The same toile she'd seen in Terrefleurs. Not surprising that the family would use the same paper at two residences; it made her smile. Though old, the material proved thick and of good quality, and Madeleine realized it was fabric, not paper. The more she pulled, the more she saw of the original design beneath. The fabric halted just before the scar in the wall where it bubbled out, forcing Madeleine to give it a concentrated tug.

Suddenly, it gave way and came off the wall in a broad sheet, exposing a hole of lathe and crumbled plaster where the bubble had been. She coughed against the dust, turning her head and squinting. A tickling sensation shot up her arm. She looked down and saw an outpouring of black spill from the hole. Bramble. It snaked toward her in rolls. She gasped and took a step back, but even as she did, she saw the dark stems disperse into spiders. They flew up her arm and disappeared at her hair. She jerked her arm away, trying to shake them off her body. The sudden movement sent fresh courses of pain through her abdomen where her father had kicked her.

The room was spinning. She had to grip the chair even though the spiders were scattering across it. The tea kettle was shrieking now. Spiders were darting to every corner of the kitchen and disappearing into crevices. She brushed and slapped until she was certain they had vacated her body.

She turned off the fire beneath the kettle and the kitchen was once again silent.

Fabric gaped horrifically behind her. Fabric that had concealed a nest of spiders, not bramble. Simple everyday spiders.

A cup of tea no longer seemed appealing. She turned her back to all of it and headed for the stairs and her bath. The last thing she needed was for the tub to overflow on top of everything else.

She peeled off her clothes and caught a glimpse of her face in the mirror. A tomatoey knot on her right cheekbone. But most of the damage Daddy'd done was at her neck and torso, not her face. And yet she wore a haggardness that looked as though she'd been beaten daily for weeks. A sallow, poisoned look. She'd be returning to work sporting that look.

Sam's ice pack felt cool against the knot as Madeleine settled into the scented bathwater. She thought of the time when she was fifteen years old, when Daddy had gone on a rampage and beat her in an attempt to "exorcise her devils." Marc had come home from fishing in the bayou to find his sister crumpled on the floor with their father raging at her. That's when Marc had snapped. He'd ripped a loose board right from the siding of the house and whacked Daddy across the back. And then he heaved it and swung again, and the board connected with Daddy's shoulder. Daddy snatched the board from his son's hands, and then paused, looking as though he might finish them both off, but instead he just left. Was gone for several months after that. One of the many times Marc and Madeleine lived alone together.

Though bloodied and wracked with pain, Madeleine had been horrified at what her brother had done.

"Daddy can't help it," she'd told him. "He's sick. When he's sane, when he's his real self, he wouldn't harm a frog."

"Horseshit," Marc had said. "Daddy can take his medication and be normal. I'm tired of sitting here wondering if maybe one day he'll kill us or himself or all of the above. If he gave a damn about us at all, he'd be taking his pills like it was his religion."

Jasmine clicked across the mosaic tile floor and up to the claw-footed tub. She rested her paws and nose on the rim and peered in,

Kilroy-style. Madeleine smoothed her head with her wet hand, slicking her kewpie doll hair down flat.

"All right, Jazz, I'm done wallowing."

She sighed, unplugging the drain. Jasmine shook her hair back to its frizzy state.

But as Madeleine rose and stepped out of the tub, the room began to swim again, and her vision faded. She reached out to steady herself with the towel bar, but caught only a handful of cloth. She veered, crashing to the floor.

And then, black.

❧

MADELEINE OPENED HER EYES unsure whether an hour or just a few moments had passed. Her cheek was pressed to the mosaic tile and Jasmine's tongue was flicking her ear. A shard of pain throbbed at her forehead where her skull had cracked against the tile. She put her hand to her head and felt around, but found no blood. The cheerful voice of a meteorologist reporting the national forecast floated through the doorway of the bedroom.

Madeleine rolled over with a groan, and Jasmine pressed her nose to her skin.

"It's fine, Jazz."

She was doing it again. Telling that damned LeBlanc heirloom lie. She wasn't fine. She'd just fainted out of the bathtub. Sam had been right; she should get to a hospital.

With some effort, she hoisted herself to her knees, then lurched forward and vomited into the toilet. And then again. She climbed to a full stance with the pedestal sink for support and glared at herself in the mirror.

In addition to the swollen cheek Daddy had bestowed, she now also had a knot on her forehead and pearls of vomit on her lips, not to mention circles under her eyes from chronic headaches. She rinsed her face. When Sam returned, they'd go to the hospital.

I should call her to let her know. I should get dressed.

She tried to think where her cell phone was, but her head was pounding. She fell into bed naked, asleep within minutes.

❧

"WOOF."

Jazz was standing on the bed, nose pointed at the door. Again: "Woof."

"Shut up, Jazz."

Madeleine tried to coax her back down on the comforter, but the little dog jumped off the bed and trotted out the door. Madeleine looked around, aware that she should be doing something, though the pillow lured her like quicksand. She was supposed to be getting dressed, she remembered, but she couldn't recall why. She just wanted to sleep.

Jasmine was barking downstairs.

"Jasmine, shut UP!" Madeleine shoved her battered head under the pillow.

Samantha. Sam was coming back. She had a key though. She could let herself in.

Jazz continued to bark downstairs, her excitement escalating, and then she was whining and yipping. Madeleine listened for the sound of Samantha opening the door in the foyer below. Nothing. Then suddenly, Jasmine fell silent.

Madeleine sat up. "Jasmine?"

Nothing.

"Jazz!"

She heard her galloping up the stairway. Jasmine bounded through the door and leapt up on the bed and stuck her paw into Madeleine's eye.

"Shit!" Madeleine flailed as Jasmine dodged away and spun around, whining and growling.

"What is it!" But even as she groped for a bathrobe, Madeleine caught a whiff of something not quite right. Smoke.

"SHIT!"

The smoke detectors pierced all sounds in a sudden burst.

She jumped out of bed and ran to the stairs. An orange glow flickered at the front downstairs wall.

"Shit shit SHIT!"

She was pinto-bean naked, stumbling, looking for a bathrobe. Her hands seemed to have lost their dexterity and she could not form a coherent thought with the smoke detectors screaming. She managed only to stagger and curse.

"Closet!" she said aloud.

Her body followed the command and retrieved a terry cloth robe. A crashing sound downstairs. Madeleine wrapped herself in the robe and made it to the landing again when another sound caused her to pause.

Over the hysteria of the smoke detectors, she heard her father's voice calling her name from downstairs.

"Daddy?" she yelled back.

And then she clapped her hands over her mouth, because she realized what was happening. That *he* had set the fire.

She backed toward the bedroom again, but he was already coming up the stairs.

She felt completely vulnerable. An image of the shotgun flashed through her mind, locked in the cabinet downstairs. A terrible means of protection against her own father. She would have to get down to the living room to reach it.

Then he appeared at the top of the stairs, reaching toward her. "Baby girl!"

She raised her hand in a *stop* gesture. "Don't come any closer!"

His eyes were wide. "Honey, we got to get out of here. This house is a vehicle of death."

Madeleine's back stiffened. But he clearly recognized her.

Jasmine approached Daddy with her tail tucked under, and he scooped her up. "We have to go out the back to the courtyard. The front door's swallowed up."

"We can use the balcony off my room."

"No good. We could make it outside but we'd have to crawl over a wall of fire to make it to the ground. Back balcony, honey, follow me."

He headed toward the opposite direction of the corridor.

Below, flames ballooned up the drapery in the foyer and with sickening, coiling beauty, the middle floor became entangled. Flames rolled and tunneled. Black banshees of smoke swirled toward the center of the house. Even as she staggered forth, bright flames were disappearing under curtains of black. It had been only a minute or two ago that the smoke alarms had begun sounding.

She staggered after her father, who turned again and called to her.

"Come on, honey!"

They covered their mouths with their clothing and dropped, creeping along the passageway, moving as fast as they could on all fours. Madeleine's lungs cramped. She felt her way along the hall, winding, following her father until visibility shrank to sheer black and she could no longer see him. She realized the hall runner ended beneath her hands and knees, and she felt only floorboards. How could she have lost her way along the wide, straight hall runner? She flung out her arms but felt nothing, not even a wall, only the flooring and the sense of fire folding itself toward her.

She rose in panic, but the smoke immediately netted her. She collapsed back down on her belly.

"Honey! Madeleine!"

"I'm here!"

Their hands found each other. They touched faces. She could feel Jasmine's fuzzy head just below her father's chin. She saw nothing but senseless blurs that scorched her vision.

She moved alongside him, keeping her body close to his as she crawled on her elbows in a side-to-side scrabble like an alligator.

Glass panes in front of them. The rear balcony. Then all at once they were outside, gulping fresh air and stumbling down the fire escape.

Daddy set Jasmine down when he reached the courtyard below, and she vaulted up into Madeleine's arms. Madeleine clutched her tiny, trembling body.

"Baby girl," Daddy said, patting her hair. "Madeleine, you all right, honey?"

Madeleine felt a rush of comfort at the sound of him speaking her name, and realized she was shaking.

"Daddy, what happened?"

"I had to bust in to get you. Didn't have my key on me." And then other hands were on her, and the courtyard filled with firefighters.

"This way, ma'am," someone shouted. She allowed herself to be led out into the street. She and Jazz clung to each other as if they each held one end of a winning lottery ticket. Madeleine wobbled, and someone steadied her, and she vacantly registered that she was walking barefoot on filthy pavement as she climbed into the back of an ambulance.

Madeleine cleared her throat and voiced the ridiculous announcement that her house was on fire. An oxygen regulator clamped down over her face.

"Ow," she said into the mask and touched the plastic over the knot on her cheek.

But the air inside that apparatus tasted divine. She breathed in, tried to pull herself together.

Daddy sat with her at the rear of the ambulance, his hand on her knee and an oxygen mask over his own face. He watched the firefighters struggle against the raging house. An EMS worker took Madeleine's pulse, and spoke calming words like "you'll be all right" and "shallow breaths." Jasmine made herself disappear into the terry cloth. All around, flashing emergency lights competed with the shimmering glow of the burning. Madeleine's home. The same place she was supposed to fill with her heart.

She felt something condense inside her. Emotion and hope purifying to basic survival.

Madeleine lifted the oxygen mask from her face. "I'm all right, now, thank you."

The EMS guy began to protest, but then a policeman's uniform came into view, and Madeleine saw that it was Vinny.

"Daddy Blank! Madeleine! Lord Jesus." He looked into her ragged face, eyes wide with concern.

Daddy peeled his oxygen mask away. "I did it. You can haul me away."

They gaped at him.

"Daddy," Madeleine said carefully. "Shut up."

"I burned it. And y'all oughtta just let it burn. That house was gonna kill us. You can just go ahead and cart me off."

"He doesn't know what he's saying, Vinny, he's . . ."

Madeleine's words trailed off as she noticed the fire chief standing beyond the doors of the ambulance, staring at them. Dangling from his hand was a dented gasoline can.

"He's sick. He's schizophrenic." Madeleine's voice broke on the word. "He only sounds lucid now because he's a cognitive . . . a cognitive . . . and that's when . . ." She gulped. "Vinny, tell them, he can't help what he does."

Vinny's hand was on her arm. "Madeleine, it's all right. We'll sort this out." He and the chief looked at each other. "Samantha's on her way here now."

"He doesn't know . . ." she insisted.

Daddy kissed her good cheek. "Don't worry honey." He waved his hand in the general direction of the jail. "I been in that place a thousand times."

The fire chief took Daddy Blank's arm and said something to the EMS about taking a sample of Madeleine's blood. Then he, Daddy, and Vinny all disappeared into the insane disco lights and shadows. Madeleine was vaguely aware of a rubber tourniquet cinching her arm. She thought about the horde of spiders earlier that evening—it seemed like ages ago now—when she just couldn't keep from picking at the layers of paper to see what lay beneath.

At least I don't have to deal with that awful spider wall now.

She laughed aloud; a bursting, nervous, insane person's laugh. The paramedic regarded her with a tolerant smile and stabbed her with a needle.

thirty-four

ÉMI HELD THE GLEAMING hook between his teeth as he finished running the line through loops along the rod.

Little Ferrar watched with wide round eyes, one of which was still darkened with the bloodburst of years ago. His skin had welted into a permanent X at the base of his throat as if he had been marked with stigmata. Other than these scars, however, he showed no lingering effects from the day he nearly died. Chloe's incision had missed the voice box so he was able to speak like any other child. But as Rémi worked, he kept stealing glances at the strange shimmer that seemed to emit from deep within the boy. A golden shimmer Rémi could only see when he looked with the inner searching. The kind of searching that revealed Ulysses. Rémi had seen this phenomenon before—in young Laramie, the gardener's son.

Rémi tied the hook in place and handed it over to the boy, who whooped and made at once for the swamp.

He was followed by a gaggle of smaller Locoul children, all wanting to touch the rod and reel. Not a homemade fishing pole, but a real one purchased at a store, and none of the children had ever had one like it. The older boys looked on wistfully from where they stood painting the austere Creole house.

"*Merci encore, Monsieur LeBlanc*," Fatima said.

She explained how her son had made a quick recovery after they rescued him years ago, and the doctor had told her that Chloe had saved Ferrar's life.

Rémi listened politely, speaking to her in her own soft, sleepy Creole French. They walked along the banks while the Locoul house's many vibrant colors disappeared to a homogeneous white. Even the wooden shutters were painted white, and Rémi felt a bite of annoyance.

Fatima thanked him again and praised Chloe's medicinal abilities, which were widely recognized among the bayou farms and plantations. Rémi asked her how Chloe had come to be notorious among the people who worked the lands, and Fatima replied that everyone knew the story of how Chloe had cut her son's throat and given him life through a river reed.

Rémi smiled, and reminded Fatima that she had known of Chloe before that. In the boat, she had recognized her and begged her to save her son.

Fatima seemed nervous and was wringing her hands, but Rémi gently prodded her as they strolled away from the main house.

"She was starving when she came to us," Fatima finally said.

She went on to recount a story that at first paralleled the one Chloe had told him; that Chloe had escaped from Elderberry Plantation, far to the south. The plantation was notorious for its ill treatment of workers. When slavery had been abolished years ago, the plantation owners resisted the change, and kept the people working under fear of violence. Still, more and more workers drifted away, usually under cover of night, and sought work at other plantations or traveled to faraway cities such as Chicago.

"We have a field hand here named Jaime," Fatima explained in rough Creole. "He escaped from Elderberry and when he spied Chloe, he made the sign of the devil. Said she was born of an Indian woman and a black man. That she's a conjurer. She uses black magic to heal and to curse.

"Our folks weren't about to take her in. I think they were afraid of her power in the river ways. Thought she'd bring trouble. They sent her to the kitchen and filled her with supper, then sent her on her way."

Rémi nodded. This much he already knew. "And so? After she left?"

Fatima kept her gaze fixed at a row of alders. "She left. And so, she left."

"Come now, that was not the last you heard of her."

Fatima cut a nervous glance toward Rémi, eyes glassy.

"You have nothing to worry about, *chère*. What happened after Chloe left?"

When Fatima spoke again, her voice trembled. "After she left, the day after, the overseer came here."

"From Elderberry Plantation?"

Fatima nodded. "He came looking for her. He knew Jaime, and made Jaime tell him where Mademoiselle Chloe had gone. Jaime didn't know. But the overseer gave him a thrashing and Jaime told him that she'd been here, and he told him which way she was heading when she left. The overseer, he took off after her."

Rémi listened carefully as Fatima continued, "We all gave Jaime an earful on that. He shouldn't ought to have told that man. The overseer was on horseback and Chloe barely even had shoes on her feet. We thought that would be the last we would ever hear of her."

"And then?"

"Then, two or three days later, a Locoul hunter found him."

"Found who? The overseer?"

Fatima closed her eyes with a nod of affirmation. Rémi was surprised to see her face was streaming with tears.

She said, "He was in a pine grove."

She swallowed. "Forget what you think you know about voodoo. It's a peaceful religion. Our priestess at Locoul never once spilled a drop of blood! People always think voodoo is about zombies and blood sacrifices. It's not. It's about life."

She paused, considering, while tears continued to stream. "Well, it may be true that some have the power to invoke zombie slaves, and they say that Chloe has that power." Fatima stole a glance at Rémi. "But that isn't what voodoo stands for."

"Woman, are you trying to tell me that a man was murdered here in the pine groves?"

Fatima took a shuddering breath. "I shouldn't ought to tell you these things. But you saved my son's life. I tell you what you ask me. That man, they say he was torn from chin to belly. They say his blood marked symbols on the trees surrounding him in the stand of pine."

"Oh, come now, *chère*. What you say is too fantastic."

Fatima said, "None of us here begrudged her for killing the evil man. He had whipped Jaime and threatened to send our foreman to the courthouse for poaching. And we'd heard stories of Elderberry. Mademoiselle Chloe probably had no choice. But how can a little colored girl, half-starved and carrying nothing but the threads on her back, kill a man double her size? It was plain to see. Mademoiselle Chloe conspires with spirits of the river, and she knows how to cultivate their favors."

Rémi was shaking his head. "These things you say, if there had been a murder as you described, I would have heard about it at Terre-fleurs!"

Fatima closed her eyes, a wrinkle at her brow. "You understand, it's trouble for us. When the hunter found the body, he moved it to the swamp, away from the pine trees with the blood symbols. The hunter came back here to Locoul and told us what happened. But to the whites, he told them some crazy story about a mad boar who must have attacked the man. The workers agreed that this was probably true, and that so-and-so had seen the mad boar gore a deer, and someone else's dog had been attacked.

"Nobody spoke of Chloe, and the whites at the main house don't bother with workers' affairs, so they believed the hog story."

Rémi said, "The mad boar. This I remember. It killed a man at the swamp, and they buried him in a charity grave at Vacherie."

Fatima was nodding.

Rémi said, "You mean to tell me you all made that up? I was part of the hunting party who tracked down the hog!"

Fatima's tears had dried. "Yes. We had the feast at Locoul. No one here would ever speak of it because they're afraid of Chloe's curse. I tell you these things because I owe you my son's life. If Chloe should seek revenge on me, then I am at her mercy."

❧

SADDLED ON HIS MARE, Rémi held a chicken under his arm, a gift that Fatima had insisted he accept. He didn't know what to make of the woman's story.

Mademoiselle Chloe conspires with spirits of the river, and she knows how to cultivate their favors.

As the mare trotted in the direction of Terrefleurs, Rémi turned to look back at Locoul. The structures gleamed white amid the magnolia trees. A jarring sight, as he was so accustomed to seeing the Locoul main house in the contrasting mustard, vermillion, and moss colors it had always borne. Painted the single color of white, it looked unreal, like a serigraph.

He continued homeward, pondering Fatima's tale. She had seemed so fearful of Chloe's wrath. The story of the plantation overseer had unsettled Rémi, though he could understand why Chloe had not told him about it. Who could say how much of it was true? But innocent or not, had the Locoul workers not protected Chloe in the matter, she most likely would have been tried and convicted, and even hanged.

The mare's hoof-falls formed a rhythmic sound. The chicken clucked in nervous opposition, giving Rémi two quick kicks. He shifted it to the other arm.

Chloe was a strong girl who had survived a great ordeal, but Rémi wondered if she was truly capable of bringing harm to anyone.

She had saved the Locoul boy's life, and had probably saved Jacob from developing a severe infection, hand or no hand.

Jacob's recovery had been a quick one. Though the physician had amputated his hand below the left wrist, Jacob seemed not to be in poor spirits. Rémi had tried to visit him as he recuperated at Glory, but the Chapmans had refused him at the door. Jacob later came to see Rémi at Terrefleurs and in fact coerced Rémi into getting in his motorcar and going with him to a la-la in Vacherie.

Rémi had wondered how Jacob had gotten himself invited to a la-la, a celebration of music and dance enjoyed by the Creole poor, whom Jacob had previously seemed to regard as little better than livestock. Somehow, Jacob was thought of as a hero among the people now, though he spoke not a word of their language. Rémi had had to translate when folks at the la-la tried to talk to him. The musicians had played "Keep My Skillet Good and Greasy" over and over so many times that Rémi thought he might sever his own hand if he had to endure the song one more time. Apparently the news of Jacob's manly endurance during the amputation had spread throughout the parish and beyond.

At the la-la, Jacob, sporting a new pair of alligator boots, had sung along with the musicians. He'd even tried to play the accordion by using his stump to hold and squeeze the hissing instrument while the fingers of his right hand slapped at the keys. He'd had very little success, but the crowd roared with delight all the same.

As the mare trotted down River Road, Rémi passed Creole houses, one after another, that had each buried their brilliant colors under the same bland white paint. Just like the Greek Revival houses of the Americans.

A bitter taste formed at Rémi's lips. New laws made it illegal to speak French in Louisiana. A preposterous thing. Many Creole workers never left the plantations, and the children did not always go to school, so how could they even learn English? The Creole children who *did* attend school were now taking whippings if they spoke French. What was so terrible about French? Why should fine, hardworking people be ashamed of their ways? Somehow it had become stylish to treat the land and the people who honored it like quaint trinkets.

Suddenly Rémi was disgusted with himself for having painted his own home white, years ago at Helen's behest. How anxious he'd been to assimilate. Creoles were not native French and yet they were not quite Americans either, and so they were supposed to abandon their ways and conform. The music, the language, even the way houses were built, all the hallmarks of Creole life, had become a scourge in the eyes of the wider population. Rémi's anger grew, and he savored and nurtured it, until he was in a full rage.

The chicken squirmed under his tightening grip, and he wrung its neck.

"Easier to carry now," he heard Ulysses say in French.

Rémi looked down to see the fiend striding alongside his horse, keeping pace on the dirt road. Ulysses pointed at the dead hen. "The chicken. Easier to carry."

Rémi regarded the limp thing and tucked it into the folds of a saddle bag.

"Yes," he replied, also in French. "Easier now."

"You should have wrung that boy's neck instead of the chicken's, bah!"

For the first time, Rémi realized that Ulysses did not speak lay-man Creole like the impoverished workers, with poor grammar and a drowsy twang. Instead, he spoke cultivated French like Rémi, as if he too had known a classical education in Paris.

Ulysses glanced at a small newly white cottage and said, "The houses are changing to white because the Creoles want to be American."

Rémi shook his head. "That's not why. Creoles are painting their houses white to avoid persecution for speaking French, that's all. Creole colors make the houses easy targets when the authorities come down the river, looking for French speakers."

He gave a bitter laugh. "As long as the houses are white, the stupid officials cannot tell the difference between a Creole house and an American house."

"Ah, so they look the same," Ulysses said.

"But they look nothing the same! We have the trim, the shape of the galleries, the hip roofs. The Americans build their houses like the Greeks, with the tall columns. Fit for a white island in the Mediterranean, yes? Ridiculous for river life."

They rounded the bend, and Terrefleurs greeted them with a swelling breeze from the river. Even his own main house was whitewashed. Not because of the law—he had painted it himself years ago when Helen had wanted him to conform to the American ways.

The drive passed through the pecan allée to the carriage barn where Rémi dismounted, leading the nag into the shelter.

He looked at Ulysses. "Tell me, does Chloe commune with you?"

Ulysses sneered. "Ah! You ask me about the mother of your children?"

"In the beginning, you wanted me to kill her."

"Why are you concerned? You slide yourself between her legs and that is all you need to know."

Rémi frowned. "If you have some sort of arrangement—"

"I can arrange to crush your bones, mud farmer, if you bore me so."

"Then do it! You expect me to live in fear of you? Go ahead and kill me if that's what you want."

"Maybe it's not worth my time to take your bones. Smaller bones are sweeter, yes. Little teeth, like the ones in your daughter and sons. Three children now. Should I start with the oldest? The one with the wooden dolls."

Rémi clenched his jaw. "Stay away from her!"

"Bring me blood, caitiff. Kill that boy Ferrar, who should have been dead long ago."

A silhouette shifted by the door. One of the workers, making himself available while keeping a polite distance. The plantationers had grown accustomed to Rémi's mutterings.

Rémi thrust the hen into his hands as he strode from the carriage barn. "Here, take this to the kitchen house."

Ulysses was singing, a ghastly chant of children's teeth and bones, no doubt meant to torture Rémi's mind. He knew Ulysses's ways. Chloe was right; the fiend seemed capable of making illusions of what he wanted, but he could only execute through tricks and whispers.

Rémi circled the basement of the main house. Through the windows he could see the marble floor and fireplace, the double wine cellar. Inside, Creole. Outside, homogeny. One of the planks of siding had given to rot, and the layer of white had curled up to reveal a burst of color from beneath. He unsheathed his new bowie knife and scraped a long swatch of the cracked white paint.

Francois appeared at Rémi's side. "What is that you do?" he asked in English.

Rémi replied in French, giving the order to paint all the buildings of Terrefleurs in their original Creole colors: Orange, coral, red, and teal.

thirty-five

HERE WAS GOING TO be a cocktail mixer to raise funds for the search for Angel Frey. When word had gotten to Ethan about what had happened, he had asked Madeleine to go, if for nothing more than to get her out into the world. She'd been staying with Sam until she'd gathered enough necessities to move into the flat above the flower shop in the old warehouse. Already she'd cleared out a bedroom that had been used as an office, and would tackle the main living space. It had a modest kitchenette and a full bath, but it also had ugly industrial carpet, a stark suspended ceiling, and two work cubicles that Madeleine wanted to remove. A far cry from her mansion on Esplanade, but she was grateful to have a place to live.

Between starting back at Tulane and scrambling to put together a home space, she'd managed to stay busy. But in the quiet hours of the night, prickling and sleepless, she lay both anticipating and dreading the fire chief's investigation. The arson factor had complicated things.

Ironic, Madeleine thought, that she had just salvaged the precious things that belonged to her brother, had hauled them into the mansion on Esplanade, and now everything was burned. All of it gone. All except the documents, including her grandmother's diary, because they had been in the truck when the house caught fire.

Since the fire, she and Ethan had been talking regularly on the phone, but this was the first time they'd gotten together since the night of All Souls.

They walked side-by-side through the shadowed Vieux Carré, but they did not hold hands. Madeleine touched her face, still battered from her father's attack. It had made for quite the impression at her first day back on the psychiatric ward.

"Who's gonna be there tonight?" Madeleine asked.

"Usual crowd. Lotta politicians. Media folks. The Frey family's pretty well-connected."

"The social elite," Madeleine said, and instantly recognized the tone of snobbery in her own voice.

"Actually," Ethan replied, "they're hardly elite. Her daddy's a crewman on a Mississippi River rig, and her mama's a schoolteacher. They're both active in the outreaches and that's why they're well-known."

Piano jazz poured from one of the halls along the dark street, though Madeleine could not tell which, and it seemed as though the Quarter itself was breathing music. No one else around. Madeleine felt the sense that this one little block had cultivated its own kind of life force for hundreds of years, and it sprang from every stone, every shingle, and from alley cats and chrysanthemums and even the limestone. Another illusion of space, like the kitchen or the library, but one that coursed with life.

"Listen Ethan, the last time I saw you, you told me I used my affiliation with the poor social classes to alienate you."

A faint smile played at his lips. "Did I say it like that? Didn't know I could talk so purdy."

"All right, I'm paraphrasing. But the point is, I think you might have been right. I think I might have been dealing with some prejudice against the privileged classes."

"Me included."

"I'm afraid so."

"Do you feel that way now?"

Madeleine stretched out her fingers and touched his hand. He immediately folded his over hers.

She said, "No. People are just people, and of course it doesn't matter what class they belong to. It's just me trying to root for the underdog, but in doing that I turn it into a competition. Maybe my prejudice against old money New Orleans just stems from my own fear."

"What are you afraid of?"

"Hard to say. Forgetting my roots, I guess. Though now that I say it aloud, I realize I'll never forget who I am or where I come from. That's probably not what really scares me."

Ethan paused by an alley. "This is it. The Pelican Club."

The quiet, unassuming corridor would have been easy to miss but for a single light at an entry part-way down. The flanking walls were patterned in brick, crumbling and rounded at the edges, cobbled like the paving stones in the streets. A half-moon grate bloomed with wrought iron fleurs de lis. She turned to look at him. The clean lines of his face were illuminated in gaslight, his thick dark lashes and brows seeming to form a gentle current, drawing her in, sharing his kindness and calm. It made her feel suddenly shy.

She put a hand over the bruise on her cheek and looked away. "Should we go in?"

"Not just yet." He reached up and brushed her hair away, then took her hand, and she knew her bruises showed even in the dim light. "I want to know what it is that does scare you."

She said, "I think . . ." she lowered her eyes. "I think the real fear is . . . It must be that I'm afraid of going soft."

The gaslight made shadows dance across the brick. She watched them fold and tumble over one another.

Ethan stepped forward and raised his hand to the curvature at the back of her neck. "So what's so terrible about being soft?"

"When you're soft, that's when they sink their teeth in." The words sounded idiotic even as she said them.

Ethan had to have been looking at her though she couldn't meet his gaze. But with each fear and prejudice she voiced, she felt them weakening, like ice shavings that melted away under direct touch. It made her smile despite herself.

He said, "Tell you what, Madeleine. Anytime you feel like you're a soft, chewy center, I'll be your hard candy shell. We'll give'm something to sink their teeth into."

She crumpled in a laugh. He wrapped his arms around her, her forehead against his chest as she giggled, the old brick at her back. He pressed his face to the top of her head and chuckled.

What if we just stayed here, right here, leaning against this wall, for hours?

She raised her head and looked at him. "Ethan, I missed you."

"I missed you too, Maddy. More than missed you. I love you."

She nodded, feeling no fear in the truth of it. "I love you."

She lifted her chin and he lowered his, their lips meeting. Soft and warm. He was so still inside, and that stillness seemed to flow from him and wash through her. It formed a distance against the bramble.

Footsteps on the street, but she didn't care. She was in love with Ethan Manderleigh and it felt clean and right.

But then the footsteps slowed, and she heard Zenon's voice: "Well I'll be damned. The overlord and his little colored girl."

Madeleine's eyes flew open.

ZENON WAS STRIDING PAST, a nasty grin smeared across his face as he continued to the doors of the Pelican Club and went inside.

Madeleine felt sick. Ethan stared after him.

Madeleine said, "Should we skip it?"

"I'm not lookin to hide from him. But you've had it rough over the past few days. Maybe you don't wanna deal with this just yet."

"I don't want to hide from him either. But Ethan, I need to know, do you believe what I told you about the night in the flower shop?"

He frowned at her. "I don't know. I believe that you believe it. Beyond that, I accept it, that's all."

More footsteps, and a couple appeared. They passed arm-in-arm and continued into the Pelican Club. The sound of voices and laughter filled the alley as they entered. Cocktails in full swing. The doors closed behind them and the alley fell silent again.

Ethan said, "Assuming it's real. Assuming that guy really can play with your mind like that. You know what to do about it?"

Madeleine nodded. "It's a way of not fighting. The more I fought inside, the less control I had. So I just kind of blanked out my mind and observed it like a scientist. Completely objective. And then I was free."

He watched her face, listening. "OK then."

She took his hand and they turned toward the entrance.

thirty-six

NEW ORLEANS, 1920

HE NUPTIALS OF RÉMI and Chloe were, by environment, a strange affair.

Jacob had heard that Didier, Rémi's younger brother, had died while serving in the Great War. However, his death was not a result of battlefield heroics, as fighting had long since quieted on the front. Jacob hadn't given it much thought until he'd spent the evening in one of the new underground cat houses that cropped up after the Storyville sweeps, where gossip seemed to be the prime method of keeping roses in the girls' plump cheeks. There, he learned that Didier, who was stationed in Paris in the service of peace, had reportedly succumbed to delirium brought on by a longtime battle with syphilis, and died despite heroic treatments of mercury, iodine, and arsenic. A sobering tale in more ways than one. Jacob rarely put much stock in saloon gossip, but the account seemed convincing enough that he preferred to while away the evening with wine and good tobacco, and keep the lounging girls at a safe distance.

Jacob had attended Didier's funeral, consoling Rémi and his

family on Toulouse Street in New Orleans. That was when Madame LeBlanc, Rémi's mother, also perished.

Madame LeBlanc had been inconsolable, and Jacob knew that she'd imbibed medicinally prescribed bourbon when she'd taken those fateful steps from her upstairs room and lost her balance, tumbling over the banister, falling four floors to the marble foyer below. An improbable fate, as the stairwell was quite narrow. It spiraled downward in ovals, with no more than eighteen inches of shaft separating the handrails. On the way down Madame LeBlanc should have hit another banister, or possibly even have landed on another section of stair, an event that would have resulted in injury but could possibly have saved her life. However, she was a woman of slight frame, standing under five feet in height and of lean build. And when she tumbled over the railing she hit neither banister nor stair step, but instead fell straight down unobstructed through the eighteen-inch gap.

The guests looked on in horror as she lay on the marble. Jacob had rushed to her, taking her hand and patting it stupidly, impotently, though the old woman's face was already fixed in an unbecoming gape. She'd bled only daintily and Jacob had hoped she might survive. But the physician had been in attendance—the same one who'd prescribed bourbon for her nerves—and he'd confirmed that Madame was dead on impact.

Jacob attended a second funeral, this one held by Rémi for his mother. Henri, who must have been terribly distraught over these tragedies, was nowhere to be found. In fact, Jacob had noticed that there were markedly fewer mourners present in comparison to the previous sad occasion.

Though Madame LeBlanc had been a prominent member of society, the gentle classes were not above superstition, and Jacob suspected they were taking care to distance themselves from the seemingly accursed LeBlancs. However, Jacob noticed that there was one person present at Madame's funeral who had not been at Didier's: Chloe. Rémi had not only brought her, but had taken her to stand by his side for the committal.

Then, a week after his mother tumbled to her death, Rémi married Chloe. Jacob could not help but wonder about the timing and the soundness of his friend's judgment.

❦

RÉMI AND HENRI WERE now the sole heirs to the LeBlanc estates. Henri was no longer able to produce children because he had suffered his own wartime injury—one that actually occurred on the battlefield when a petard grenade took his leg and his virility. And so Rémi felt it was now his sole duty to continue the family legacy. Henri had retreated to his home on Esplanade in an alcoholic haze and remained unavailable throughout both his mother's funeral and the wedding.

Rémi had already considered marrying Chloe long before this, but loathed the public scrutiny that would surely erupt from the interracial union. His own mother would have objected, and might possibly even have stricken Rémi from her will. But there came to Rémi a sudden urging notion, that now-familiar pipe smoke in fog that he never chose to deny, and he'd decided to marry Chloe without further delay.

And now that his mother was gone, there would be no familial outcry.

A Justice of the Peace presided over the small ceremony, and witnesses included only Rémi's closest friends; among them, Jacob Chapman and the senior workers of Terrefleurs.

Chloe had been a grounding strength to Rémi since Helen's death. Already she had begun to oversee business transactions for the plantation, as Rémi had become complacent and let his accounts slip toward bankruptcy. But most importantly, Chloe had already produced three children, two of them boys.

The series of funerals, however, were not the only somber outlay to the couple's new life together. New Orleans had suffered much loss of citizenry due to the Great War, and for the two previous years, Carnival had been canceled.

And in strange coincidence, the day Rémi and Chloe were married was also the eve before the Volstead Act was to go into effect. Rémi was disgusted. First the government had outlawed French, then shut down the Storyville brothels, and now this. The new act prohibited the manufacture, sale, or distribution of alcoholic beverages within the United States. And in a city where alcohol had historically oiled the machinery of everyday life, the coming Prohibition caused a city-wide panic.

Rémi had taken Chloe to a honeymoon dinner at La Maison du Rêve, a quiet, bohemian eatery frequented by wealthy artists, outlaws, and in general, the fringe of society. A place where an interracial couple might enjoy an elegant dinner without molestation. But on this night the diners were whispering among themselves in speculation of how tomorrow's ban on alcohol would impact New Orleans. Because it was the last day one might legally purchase liquor, the guests had all ordered wine with their dinners.

The restaurateur, however, having anticipated the ban, had let his stock of wine and spirits dwindle. He apparently did not want to find himself the next day with a stout inventory of alcohol that the authorities would surely confiscate and destroy, along with his profits. And so, early in the evening, the wine cellar ran dry. The depleted stock ignited a fever of outrage among the diners.

"You'll not serve me drink?" one guest bellowed, rising from his seat. "The ban does not begin until tomorrow! You oughtn't force your morals upon me!"

"I wouldn't have come here had I known," declared another.

Rémi and Chloe finished their honeymoon dinner with haste, surprised that their fellow diners felt so passionately about a simple matter of drink. While annoying, the Volstead Act was little more than a nuisance to Rémi. Prohibition was not a concern at Terrefleurs because they rarely purchased alcohol; they either manufactured or traded for it. The plantationers could only vaguely grasp the concept of such a ban. How would the authorities enforce it? Surely they wouldn't bother to venture out to every farm and plantation.

Rémi and Chloe left La Maison and ventured into the dark winter streets of New Orleans. Already, people of every race, creed, and class were cramming the cobblestone roadways. The gas streetlamps illuminated their faces, shining with euphoria and desperation. They all sought that one last drink before the ban. It seemed every single person within the city limits had emerged to hail and bid farewell to drink.

Rémi took Chloe's hand and led her through the crowd to a small tavern he knew to be quiet and intimate. Standing in the doorway, however, they found it overflowing with people.

"We go back to the house," Chloe urged.

"This is our honeymoon. We won't let them spoil it."

Chloe seemed unconvinced. The crowd was boisterous, and she insisted upon returning to the house on Esplanade, which they had been occupying since Madame LeBlanc's death. The men inside the tavern were making lascivious advances toward the women, and they in turn abandoned their sense of propriety and were behaving flamboyantly. Most of the women had likely never before set foot inside a tavern, and would have considered it improper to do so. But somehow for this one night it became fashionable, and prostitutes and debutantes alike rollicked with abandon.

"I am your wife and you should honor me," Chloe said. "You are now the only one to inherit your family's fortune. That is because I cast spells for you and brought you good luck."

Rémi looked at her with amazement. "Good luck? Are you referring to the death of my mother and brother? Those tragedies had nothing to do with you. And I am not the sole heir, as my brother Henri still lives."

Rémi escorted Chloe inside the tavern with the promise to indulge only a single toast to their new union before returning home.

When the other patrons learned that they were newlyweds, however, they cheered afresh with jubilation. Everyone in the tavern bought Rémi and Chloe drinks, and then Rémi bought a round for the entire house. Women who otherwise would never have acknowledged Chloe's presence suddenly became her new chums. Rémi and Chloe were king and queen of the night.

Rémi felt euphoric. He reveled with a freedom that he had not known since Helen died and Ulysses had begun to appear. But now he had not seen Ulysses in over a week, and wondered if perhaps his period of darkness was over. His new wife was his salvation, and he wrapped himself in worship from strangers, knowing not a care in the world.

Chloe, however, was glowering. "I do not understand these women in their fine clothes and expensive jewelry. They allow themselves to be fondled. This is polite society?"

"They're celebrating," Rémi said. "And we should too. Look, someone just sent more champagne."

"They can take their champagne and go hang!" She stood and straightened her jacket. "Stay if you like. I go back to the house."

She strode toward the door, and Rémi, bewildered and heavy on his feet, made to follow her. He fumbled through the crowded tavern as hands pulled on his clothing and sirened one more drink, one *last* drink of ages for the lucky groom.

He finally broke free from the tavern, only to feel the slap of the winter wind. The crowd was almost as thick and raucous on the street as inside the tavern. Chloe had gotten far ahead of him by now, and he strained to keep her in sight as he lumbered after her. He could see the back of her soft white woolen hat and matching suit that bloomed out at her calves as she bobbed ahead in the throng, her erect posture and strident gait easily discernible against the slumped, ambling bodies of the inebriated crowd.

Rémi's shoes dragged as though filled with cement, and it took all the concentration he could muster to focus on her. He hadn't realized he was getting so drunk. As they moved toward the heart of the Carré, the crowd grew ever more dense, and Rémi had to turn his shoulders sideways to press through. He feared he would never catch up with her.

Angry howls erupted from the center of the street, and punches began flying. Rémi couldn't tell what had caused the brawl. He saw Chloe stop as she found herself in the midst of rabid shouts and lunging bodies. Next to her, one man flung himself at another, and she stepped backward just in time to avoid getting knocked to the ground in a tangle of belligerents. She turned to her left and disappeared into an alley.

"Wait!" Rémi called after her, but his voice was swallowed in the rabble.

He pressed forward with renewed vigor, but his progress was slow. He kept an eye on the gap between buildings where Chloe had disappeared, and noticed a tall black figure moving toward it. He paused and looked back at Rémi. It was Ulysses. He followed Chloe into the alley.

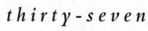

thirty-seven

NEW ORLEANS, 2009

THEY DID NOT IMMEDIATELY see Zenon inside the Pelican Club. Many familiar faces, including Vinny and Joe Whitney. She also saw Anita, Sam's intern at the flower shop. She was smiling and two-stepping her way from group to group. As Madeleine wandered through the dining hall with Ethan, it struck her how many people knew this missing girl, Angel Frey. She seemed to have had just as much presence in New Orleans as in her home of Baton Rouge. And although people tend to glorify those who are no longer with us, it seemed this girl had possessed a rare heart. She was an altruist, clearly, a regular in charity and volunteer work while still holding down a full-time job, just like her parents.

As Madeleine said her hellos, not a single person inquired about the bruises on her face. All offered sympathy about the fire, though. Likely the incident had been fodder for hot gossip.

Ethan turned and shook hands with a very tall man whom Madeleine didn't know. "Madeleine, this is my buddy Shawn."

"Pleased to meet you," she said as she took his hand.

"Ethan and I went to school together. I know your father."

"Oh?" Madeleine smiled.

Ethan clapped a hand on Shawn's shoulder. "Shawn here writes for the *Times-Picayune*. If you read it this morning you might have seen his exposé on Joe Whitney."

"That was you? I did read it. Congratulations."

Madeleine looked over to where Joe was engaged in conversation with some older gentlemen. Ironically, he was more likely to make appearances when in the midst of a scandal than when things were quiet. Joe looked up and caught her eye, then launched himself in her direction. She braced.

"Ethan and Miss Madeleine!" Joe cried as if they had been triplets separated at birth. "And my good friend the executioner! I gotta hand it to you, old man, you really gave me a tar-and-feathering in the paper today."

"You're certainly good-natured about it," Shawn said mildly, and then with just a teaspoon of acid: "Because it looks like there's going to be an official criminal investigation."

Joe snorted. "I'm not worried. Nothing illegal transpired, I can assure you."

"Least nothing they can *prove*. Yet."

"Of course you realize, I'm gonna have your head on a platter. *And* your ass. Both the paper and you will be named for libel."

Whitney was speaking loudly, much more so than was necessary for any normal conversation. Madeleine suspected he did this more for the benefit of the wider audience, the New Orleans socialites who were now looking over their shoulders at him. Zenon was looking too. He caught Madeleine's eye. She stared back, refusing to avert her gaze. Very slowly, his lips curved upward in a smile.

"You might want to start looking for another job," Joe Whitney was saying, and Madeleine tore her gaze back to them.

Shawn raised his voice to match. "Bring it on. Because I got the paper trail. Your board membership under an assumed name for the spin-off company, whose interests are currently under investigation. Your consulting fees, your approval for zoning—I even have a copy of a bonus guarantee for $268,000, plus ongoing fees that'll earn you millions. I'd be happy to share it all in a court of law. Especially during your run for city council, assuming those rumors are true."

Joe's face was made of stone. "I will neither confirm nor deny any intention to run for council." He looked around, then leaned in, lowering his voice. "Just tell me one thing. Just one thing. Where did you get these lies?" He threw his head toward Madeleine. "Was it her father?"

Madeleine laughed aloud. Daddy couldn't have gotten to the inner circle of this mega-center deal. He had been notoriously in opposition to it.

Shawn shook his head. "I see your temper is finally starting to crack, Joe, 'cause you're losing it. You *know* I wouldn't tell you."

"You just did." Joe spoke through clenched teeth. "I can read it on your face, plain as day." He turned to Madeleine. "If your father has been breaking into my home or illegally eavesdropping on my affairs, I swear to God I'll have him locked up so fast he won't know what hit him."

"You'd have to get in line," Madeleine said flatly.

Joe turned and made for the bar.

Ethan regarded Shawn. "Did Daddy Blank really tip you off?"

To Madeleine's surprise, Shawn shrugged. "Not like it's that big a secret. Daddy Blank already called Joe up to gloat from the cooler."

Madeleine gave a start. "What? What's Daddy got to do with it?"

Shawn looked at her in surprise. "He didn't tell you yet? A while back, Daddy Blank contacted me about Whitney's scheme. I would never have known where to look. He gave me names, told me what to look for, gave me every single detail. Guess he must have infiltrated the board meetings or something."

"No, that's not possible," Madeleine stammered.

"Well, he was vague about how he got it. What matters is that it checked out."

Shawn's eyes scanned her bruises. "I heard about your house. Let me know if there's anything I can do."

Madeleine made no reply. Someone else was already insinuating himself into the circle, shaking Shawn's hand. Madeleine looked over her shoulder. Zenon was talking to Anita Salazar. Actually, Anita was talking to him and he seemed indifferent.

I wish he'd go back to Baton Rouge and stay there.

She noticed Vinny was walking toward her, and she and Ethan turned to greet him.

"Howdy howdy," Vinny said, shaking Ethan's hand and then giving Madeleine a light hug. "I got some news about the arson investigation."

"Oh?" Madeleine clenched her fist.

"Yeah. It was Daddy Blank set that fire."

"Are you sure about that?" Madeleine asked. "Because you can't take anything he says into account. He's liable to say whatever . . ."

Vinny was shaking his head. "I know, I know it baby. Listen. The investigation showed that the fire was started by means of gasoline distributed along the front porch. A gas can was found nearby with Daddy Blank's fingerprints on it. And honey you know he confessed."

Madeleine's cheeks burned. Ethan put a hand to her back.

"There's more." Vinny's voice softened. "I know you don't want to press charges, but the city's going to. And your insurance company probably will too."

"Why would they press? . . ." But she already knew the answer.

"That's just the way the law works, Maddy," Vinny continued. "Two other houses got burned bad because of that fire. We're lucky no one was seriously hurt."

Madeleine had heard about her neighbors' homes, and had been horrified that they were caught up in this.

Vinny went on. "The fire chief talked to the DA's office, and they're gonna recommend that Daddy Blank get treatment in a state facility until he is no longer a danger to himself, or anyone else."

Madeleine let out her breath. "I didn't realize they would put him in a hospital. That's good, Vinny. Once he gets on that medication, he does really well."

Vinny smiled. "Now, there is something else. The fire chief asked about your blood results, and it appears that you had a very serious case of carbon monoxide poisoning."

Ethan and Madeleine both gaped.

"You had forty-six percent hemoglobins carryin carbon monoxide. That's real high. If it'd been much higher, it could've killed you."

Madeleine's hands went cold.

Vinny said, "You must have had symptoms: headache, nausea, fatigue. Sometimes dizziness and fainting."

Ethan turned to Madeleine. "You said you fainted coming out of the bathtub on the night of the fire. And all those headaches."

Madeleine shook her head. "I put brand new furnaces in that house just a couple of years ago."

Vinny nodded. "They said they found severely corroded and blocked flues. The high-efficiency furnaces ain't gonna help none when your flues are all gummed up. The gases just come in and circulate through your house. They say the chimney for the gas fireplace in your bedroom was the worst one. If your windows are open and the air circulates through, it's not so bad. But your house was sealed up tight."

Ethan said, "Should she see a doctor?"

Vinny shook his head. "They said once you get out of that environment your blood returns to normal."

Madeleine could hardly believe her ears. "All this time with those raging headaches, and all I had to do was open a dang window?"

Ethan said, "Funny they just hand the lab results to the fire chief, just like that. I thought there were laws against revealing your personal medical information."

Vinny's hands went up. "Don't look at me. I'm just reporting back to y'all."

"Well," Madeleine said. "They have their own way of doing things around here. But I'll tell you what *else* is odd," she paused to think it through a moment. "Really odd. Daddy said he burned the place down because the house was a vehicle of death."

ANITA WAS ALONE. MADELEINE looked around but didn't see where Zenon had gotten off to. She excused herself from Ethan and Vinny and joined Anita at the bar.

"Hi, Anita."

"Hey, Madeleine! How you doin?"

"Good, good. Are you all right?"

"Sure! Sam keeps me busy."

Madeleine bit at her lip. "You . . . still taking those shooting lessons?"

Anita rolled her eyes and then nodded toward the corridor where the restrooms were. "With him? Yes. It isn't getting me anywhere though."

"You came here with him, did you?"

"No, we just bumped into each other. Not like he knows I'm alive."

Madeleine touched Anita's wrist. "It's probably just as well. He's off, Anita. In a lot of ways."

"You mean he's got a dangerous side? I get that impression too." Anita smiled. "But that's what makes him sexy."

A door opened in the corridor and Zenon appeared. He started toward them. Madeleine's grip tightened on Anita's wrist.

"I'm serious, honey," Madeleine whispered. "Be careful."

Anita looked surprised. "OK."

Madeleine felt a slight jump inside as Zenon drew nearer—the dual urge to run for the door and sock him in the stomach.

Zenon shoved his hand in his pocket and appraised her. "Well Miss Madeleine. You've been avoiding me."

"Excuse me." Madeleine turned to leave.

Ethan looked up and caught her eye.

Zenon said, "It's a good place for pigeon games, ain't it?"

Madeleine stopped mid-stride. She turned toward Zenon. His eyes were dark but smiling.

Madeleine said, "Where?"

"The place where you went trespassing, yeah. Good place for pigeon games."

Madeleine took a step toward him. "What do you know about that?"

"Why don't you ask Miss Chloe, *chère?*"

Anita was looking from Madeleine to Zenon, bewildered.

Madeleine came closer and lowered her voice. "How did you do it, Zenon?"

His lips parted, and his tongue ran along the inside of his mouth. "You want another lesson? I'll be happy to show you baby."

Anita scowled. "Why don't you two get a room!"

She turned, grabbing her bag, and strode for the door.

Madeleine felt the tug. A wash of electricity. She went directly to an inner stance of observation, not so much as a conscious means of self-defense, but more of a scientist's riveted attention when on the verge of a breakthrough. Emotions aside, the experience itself was fascinating.

Zenon drew his knuckle up Madeleine's forearm. "You can be my apprentice."

Madeleine jerked away, his touch crossing a line that dissolved any desire to dissect this phenomenon. She turned and collided with Ethan. He looked livid.

"Let's get out of here," she said.

Ethan's face was tense. "What are you doing over here?"

Madeleine took his hand and tugged, trying to pull him toward the door.

From behind her, Zenon said, "Better keep a tighter leash on your little colored girl. She comes purrin every time you look away."

Madeleine paused to look. Ethan's eyes were wide. She could see the veins in his neck.

"He's just trying to push your buttons, Ethan."

Ethan tensed his jaw. He remained wooden, his teeth in a clench. Zenon stepped forward. For a flash, Madeleine recognized the delight on Zenon's face, the way he'd looked when he was a kid, pulling his traps up from the bayou knowing they would be filled with blue crab.

"Come with me," Madeleine murmured, pulling gently at Ethan's arm.

He stared Zenon down a moment longer, then turned. His expression was like stone. They strode away from Zenon, away from the bar, and all the while she felt Zenon's tug. Trying to possess her body. He wanted her to turn back around and . . .

The room was silent. She wasn't sure how long people had been staring. She kept perfectly still inside as she moved, Zenon's clamp just as impotent against that stillness as if it were trying to grip a field of steam. She and Ethan walked through the wood-and-glass doors and were outside. Zenon's tug disappeared.

Madeleine breathed in to full capacity and then released just as completely. Ethan kept stride with her down the alley. Madeleine stole a glance at his face, which was still gripped in fury. She wasn't sure what to say to him and suspected anything she did say would come out wrong.

She heard a swell of voices behind her and knew the doors to the Pelican Club were opening.

She and Ethan turned onto the street. Madeleine looked over her shoulder but couldn't see into the alley, couldn't tell who'd come out of the restaurant. Beside her, Ethan's face hardened.

She quickened her pace.

"I'm not going to run," Ethan growled, and he stopped short.

Madeleine paused. Ethan had pulled his hand from her grasp. She looked back toward the alley. If it was Zenon who'd followed them out of the Pelican Club, they'd know in a moment.

"We should just go," she whispered.

Ethan's eyes fixed on hers. Something ratcheted into place inside him. Something awful.

"Ethan, don't—"

His hand closed over her throat.

Madeleine managed a half gasp before the intake of air sealed off. Her pulse jumped. Ethan forced her backward and pinned her against the wall. And then his grasp relented just enough to allow her to breathe. He was holding her, frozen, not attacking and not withdrawing.

She looked to her left and saw Zenon watching at the mouth of the alley only a few feet away. His arms were folded across his chest. No delight on his face, only intense concentration.

Ethan's eyes were wide, almost dazed. She couldn't move under his grip, a sensation that made her want to claw at him. But she didn't. Nor did she scream. New instincts came forth, instincts that warned her not to give in to panic. She could see the turmoil in Ethan's face. He clearly didn't mean any aggression toward her; he was fighting inside. Fighting Zenon.

"Blank," she whispered. It was all she could manage.

Ethan's eyes registered understanding. Recognition of the phenomenon. But for a moment, his grip tightened around her throat and she felt her voice box press against her windpipe. Rasping. She closed her eyes and intensified the calm. Insisted that her shoulders loosen.

Ethan's hands released.

She opened her eyes again. Ethan had turned from her and was walking toward Zenon. His gait was limping but steady. No sign of anger. He looked like the firemen when her house was burning; not so much intending to fight the flames as neutralize them.

Zenon heaved his fist, and Ethan knocked it away, and then jabbed Zenon in the throat. Zenon doubled over. Ethan threw a second jab, this one knocking Zenon sideways and onto the pavement.

Madeleine saw Ethan in profile. No veins bulging at his throat. No fury. He was calm as the mist. Zenon crawled two steps away from him and then sank into the stones.

Ethan turned back to her. "Are you all right? I couldn't—"

"I know. I know exactly what happened." She touched her neck, faintly sore but uninjured. "I'm OK. You stopped it in time."

thirty-eight

NEW ORLEANS, 1920

*U*LYSSES TURNED AND ENTERED the alley behind Chloe. Rémi bent his shoulder and surged through the crowd. He cursed his own drunkenness, and for having brought Chloe to the tavern. Why had he done that? He would never have brought Helen to a place like that.

He reached the mouth of the alley and dashed in. He could see two silhouettes as they struggled. Chloe's white handbag lay open in a filthy gutter, and Rémi could hear the sound of tearing fabric as Ulysses ripped her clothes.

"Vile demon!" Rémi cried as he rushed Ulysses. "Let go of my wife!"

"Your wife, hey?" Ulysses replied with surprise, his words slurring, and he let go of Chloe.

As Rémi drew nearer, he realized he had been mistaken about Ulysses. The man attacking Chloe was white, a big, dirty brute in a worn jacket. Rémi slowed, and the man looked him over with one eye cocked.

"You're *married* to this little nigger whore?"

Rémi pulled back his fist and drove it into the man's jowls. The brute staggered backward, head pitched, but he recovered and hardened his gaze on Rémi. Growling, he bent his head and rushed Rémi like a bull, shoulder to Rémi's diaphragm, knocking him to the cobblestones.

He heard Chloe gasp, and marveled at the way it sounded very far away, like a puff of wind that stirs an oak tree on a distant hill.

The alley turned black.

CHLOE WATCHED AS THE brute straddled her husband, beating him bloody.

"You will not strike another blow!"

He stopped short, gaping at her. His eyes registered surprise at her audacity, and yet his jaw turned slack and his tongue protruded as he accepted the command.

Rémi was out cold. The brute seemed to take sudden notice of this, and chuckled. He reached down and slapped Rémi's face, but Rémi's head only wagged dully with the impact.

Chloe gritted her teeth. "Get away from him!"

The man picked himself up and turned back to Chloe. He reached for her in the darkness, his breath husky and sour with alcohol.

But she had already unsheathed the knife she kept in her garter belt, the knife she carried in a city she did not trust, and on a plantation where danger comes as frequently as the phases of the moon. And when the oaf put his greedy hands on her, she plunged the blade into his chest.

He gaped, his eyes wild and glinting in the darkness.

He sank to his knees, still grasping her arms. She wrenched the knife free from his chest. He moaned and collapsed to the ground, his head landing next to the soiled white evening bag in the gutter.

He rolled over and crawled a few paces, then slumped prostrate on the cobblestones.

"I'm dying," he whispered, spittle dropping to the filthy stones. He lifted his head and called out louder: "I'm dying!"

Chloe wiped the bloody knife on what was left of her white suit jacket and then lifted her hem, thumbed the band of her garter belt, and resheathed the blade.

"Help! Help me!" The brute put his hand to the wound and grimaced at the black blood. "She's killed me!"

She folded her arms and looked toward the crowd at the end of the alley, and could not tell whether they were brawling or celebrating. Worse than any Mardi Gras, this eve of Prohibition. She'd never seen such collective wildness.

"Nobody hear you." She crouched next to the fallen man. "Cry louder."

He looked up at her with hazy eyes.

She shoved him hard, causing him to roll. "Cry louder!"

"Help me!" His voice was high and shrill. "Help me! She's killed me! Help!"

He bawled and shuddered, and she could see he was growing weaker.

Chloe shook her head. "They do not hear you."

"I'm dying," he sobbed. "You've killed me."

She stood and regarded him. "You are not dead yet. You not dead until I say you are dead."

She stepped over his body and walked to where Rémi still lay unconscious, and nudged him with her foot. The man quieted for a moment. She felt his eyes on her in the shadows.

"Who are you?" he whispered, and in his voice she heard deference and a hint of awe.

When she did not answer, he said, "Help me. Lady, please help me."

She folded her arms and looked back over her shoulder at him, then down at Rémi again. Two useless men in the gutter. The marriage, at least, was legally sound. Should anything happen to Rémi, she and her children would have a home.

She considered this monstrosity of a man who'd felt her blade, and wondered whether she might put him into service.

She said to him, "No, I think I let you die here. You be dead by morning. You rot in the stinking gutter where you belong."

"No! Help me dear lady, please help me."

He wept, repeating the words. She grew nauseated with his puling. Finally she turned back to him, leaning over his trembling shape, speaking to him in a whisper.

"Better for you to die. If I help you, you belong to me. You do what I say. Better for you to die, for sure."

He whimpered, his voice high and thin. "No. I don't want to die. Help me. I'll do whatever you say."

"What you have to live for? Stealing money for liquor and molesting women? Be a man, once in your life. Die tonight."

"No! Please help me. I'll do whatever you say."

She stared at him. "What is your name?"

"Bruce." The word was a puff of air as he stifled a sob. "Bruce Dempsey."

She leaned over, hands on her knees. "Bruce. You stinking drunk. You will not even remember me tomorrow, if I let you live."

"No ma'am," he pleaded. "I'll remember. I promise. I . . . I belong to you."

She narrowed her eyes. He had spoken the right words. Perhaps he was not so dumb.

"Hmph. We will see."

She moved her hand under her skirt and once more removed her knife from its sheath. She crouched down next to Bruce and folded the blade into his hands.

Nearby, Rémi groaned and shifted, but did not rouse.

"Bruce Dempsey. Cut off your ear and give it to me."

His jaw dropped, and the cold air around him filled with his vinegary breath. "Mother of God. What sort of black magic is this?"

Chloe rose to her feet.

"Devil's whore! I should rip your throat out!" He lurched and slashed at her with the knife.

Chloe took a single step backward and watched him struggle. Dempsey swayed to a sitting position, and then ran out of fury. His hand went to the wound, which now coursed afresh with blood.

"Mother of God." He slumped backward and lolled flat on his back again. The knife clanked against the cobblestones as he released it.

"Dear lady. Please, have mercy on me."

She gathered her purse and its spilled contents, then turned and walked away.

"Have mercy," he cried after her. "Mercy! Mercy! I'm begging you! Oh my God!"

She left him there; left him to die and left her sot of a husband in the alley with him.

"You monster!" Dempsey screeched.

She joined the crowd in the street, a hand over her belly, letting herself fall in step with the flow. Another child would be coming, their fourth, though she hadn't told Rémi. A good thing to have these children. She could school them in her ways, groom them for a new era, and create new leaders. Four children were a good start, but Chloe knew she should bear more. The more children there were, the stronger the line. She looked back over her shoulder toward the dark alley. She should retrieve Rémi, then, lest he die of exposure during the night.

Chloe turned and pressed back toward the maw of the alleyway. It occurred to her that she knew at least one person in New Orleans. Jacob Chapman had attended the wedding, and would remain in town for a week. She detested the man, a lazy playboy, but could call on him for assistance. She paused outside the alley and looked around for street children. She could pay one of them to send word to Jacob Chapman.

From the alley came Bruce Dempsey's shrill voice: "Take it then! Take my ear!"

Chloe paused. Dempsey fell silent, and she listened for any sound from him. She waited.

Then suddenly, shrieking. The alley coursed with the sound. She knew that he had done her bidding. The crowd streamed around her.

Dempsey's screams hovered just above the volume of the horde, but no one took notice. Chloe watched the throng of people as they ambled by, too absorbed with the ecstasy of the moment to notice the shrieks of a dying man. She stepped into the alley.

A couple, arm in arm, stumbled in behind her. The man's bolo was untied, and the woman was giggling from under her cloche hat. They staggered, arms wrapped around each other. Bruce Dempsey let out a piteous wail. The couple stopped short and peered into the blank darkness, then spotted Chloe in her blood-smeared coat. They turned and stumbled back into the street.

Dempsey lapsed into sobs behind her. She turned and walked back to where he lay bleeding. He writhed and wept, his hands over his face, and she watched him for a time.

She folded her arms against the cold. "Bruce Dempsey."

He removed his hands from his face and looked up at her in wonder. "God in heaven. She's come back. I thought you'd left me here to die."

"Give it to me," she commanded.

Dempsey's face contorted. "It's here."

He shuddered, and his hand grasped a mottled piece of flesh and cartilage that lay next to him on the stones. He lifted it with a trembling hand.

Chloe wrapped the ear in her handkerchief and slipped it inside her purse. "You belong to me now."

"Yes," he whispered.

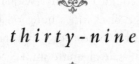

thirty-nine

ANITA LET THE TOP down on the Mustang, and Julie hopped into the passenger seat without opening the door. They were both dressed to kill, Anita's ruffled sleeves fluttering like angel wings in the sudden rush of air as she careened out of the driveway.

She drank in the warm, sumptuous Gulf South wind. Next to her, Julie's arms were stretched up into the air, fingers spread. The Mustang sped toward the freeway and away from Baton Rouge's city center.

"Hey, take it easy," Julie protested, cupping her hands over her golden hair, which was now slapping at her lipstick. "Maybe we should put the top up."

"Too late," Anita shouted over the wind with a smile. "We're halfway there."

Julie pouted as exit signs whizzed by. "I don't see why we have to go way out to the boondocks for this!"

Anita laughed but continued on, sunglasses shading the bright afternoon sun. She knew why. Same reason she'd taken the self-defense class, and the handgun training. She zoomed the Mustang right up to the front door of the gun shop.

"Hey, is this a real parking place?" Julie asked, but Anita was already entering the shop.

Julie followed a minute later, and made straight for a mirror hanging on a wall near the register. Anita lingered back by the crossbows.

From beyond, she heard someone drone through a crackling radio in a language she couldn't identify. Wasn't Spanish or anything normal like that. Large black rifles hung on the walls behind the counter, and handguns lay in neat rows in display cases. Anita's nose twitched at the odor of stale cigarette smoke. She pressed her finger to the pointed tip of an arrow on display. It looked like a miniature spacecraft, black with shiny steel blades. ASSASSIN, the display read.

Julie was making noises of disgust, and she took out a comb and hacked at her hair. "We are definitely putting the top up on the way back! Looks like I stuck my finger in a plug outlet."

"May I help you?"

Anita jumped at the sound of Zenon's voice. Julie looked startled when she recognized him, then her eyes narrowed. Anita trained her focus on the display case, pretending to be absorbed, though she continued to watch in her peripheral vision.

He was stepping out from the back room and wiping his hands with a rag. A dark blotch sagged under his left eye. He wore a simple gray t-shirt tucked into his jeans. It made him look tough.

"Why hello there," Julie said in her silkiest bedroom voice. "No, honey, I don't need any help."

In a mechanical motion, Julie pivoted on her foot to look at Anita, and Anita focused intently on the crossbows, heat burning her cheeks. Julie pivoted back again to face Zenon.

"It's my friend over there who *needs help*."

Anita turned around and lifted her brows as if she were just now noticing Zenon's presence.

"Well hello again!" She dazzled him with her brightest smile.

Zenon nodded back with a blank expression.

"What happened to your eye?"

He didn't answer; only stared at her until she dropped her gaze.

"Well," Anita said. "Uh, I came here because I wanna buy a gun, instead of having to use a loaner at the shooting range."

Zenon folded his arms over his chest. "You'll have to complete your training before you can get a handgun permit. The state also requires a $100 processing fee."

"Do I really gotta do all that? I'm going on a road trip next week. Gonna stay with Julie's family in Houston, then I'll head out to see my aunt in Florida. I'll be driving down all alone."

"You can't cross state lines with a handgun anyway," Zenon said, gesturing to a display rack. "Try a stun gun, or pepper spray."

Anita regarded the blister packs. Some looked like pens or flashlights.

"I heard pepper spray doesn't work on people who are on drugs."

"Products that use CN gas are not as effective on violent attackers under the influence of narcotics or alcohol. These here are pepper spray. They use a substance extracted from chili peppers. When sprayed directly into the eyes, it'll subdue an attacker for up to forty-five minutes."

"Well!" Julie turned to Anita. "I now understand your sudden fascination with self-defense. You have found the absolute living authority on the subject!"

Anita ignored Julie's comment and leaned over the glass where the stun guns lay.

She tapped her fingernail on the glass. "What's this one?"

"That's a Taser," Zenon replied, unlocking the cabinet. He placed it on the counter.

"Is that like a stun gun?"

"They're similar. A stun gun shoots out pure electricity, but you have to be in direct bodily contact with the assailant. When you shoot a Taser, you can be up to fifteen feet away. These hooks clamp into the assailant's skin, and the wires pulse electricity. The pulses interfere with communication between the brain and the muscular system, causing the assailant to lose control."

Anita pondered her slow progress at the shooting range. "What if I shoot and miss?"

"As a back-up, the unit will also work at close range, just like a stun gun."

"I'll take it!"

Julie chimed in, "Hey, maybe I could try it out at the university bookstore. See who tries to cut in front of me in line. Zzzzzzt!"

Anita and Zenon stared at her.

"That was a *joke*," Julie said.

Zenon closed the case and disappeared into the stockroom.

Julie whispered, "Now I get why we had to sail out to the far reaches of Baton Rouge to go to this particular gun shop."

Anita grinned. "Isn't he cute?"

"Well, yeah, but don't you think he's a little . . . I don't know," she waved her hand. "He's a little stern. Not exactly a comedian."

"I know. But it kind of turns me on."

Julie shook her head. "Anita, honey, look at you. You've got every jock, nerd, and scholar we know wanting to ask you out, and you get all moon-eyed over Bubba in there. I just don't get it."

Anita pinched her.

"It stinks like old cigarettes in here," Julie said. "I'm gonna wait out in the car. And I'm putting the top up."

Anita watched her go. She fidgeted, waiting for Zenon. The radio was still buzzing in that foreign language, and it didn't look like any radio she'd ever seen before. Zenon reappeared from the stock room.

"What's that language they're speaking on that radio?" Anita asked.

"Hungarian."

"Oh my God! You're Hungarian?"

"No."

"You speak Hungarian?"

"No." He switched off the radio.

She cleared her throat to hide her nerves. She'd intended to ask him out but he was so brusque.

Instead: "You and Madeleine seemed awfully friendly the other night."

He said nothing.

"Are you dating?"

"No."

"Good, because . . ."

He said, "That'll be $169.95."

She dug in her purse. "I'll put it on my Visa." She handed it to him.

As Zenon ran the card, Anita leaned over the counter and stuck her pinky into the crevice under the cash register.

"Who's the angel?" she asked, pulling the necklace out and dangling it on her little finger. The afternoon sun glinted on the gold handwritten name. She cocked her head, realizing the chain was a name necklace, and her heart sank.

"Is it your girlfriend?"

Zenon took the necklace from her and tossed it into a drawer without a word. The credit card machine churned out the sales slip.

"Guess it just ain't my business," she mumbled, and signed the receipt.

⚜

"WHAT THE HELL WERE you thinking?" Josh said. "You kept the *necklace*? The fucking *necklace*?"

"I thought you knew!" Zenon replied. "I've kept it right there the whole time." He turned and muttered, "Thought you knew everything."

"Jesus Christ almighty. It's got her name right on it! I'm serious, man, what were you thinking?"

"How the hell I know that was her name? I thought it meant angel as in angels and devils. Shit."

"What are you, stupid? You want to get caught?"

Zenon reddened. "Get *caught*? You said there was no way I *would* get caught. You said you'd take care of everything."

"Yeah, if you stick to the goddamn rules!" Josh pressed his fist to his forehead. "I mean it man, you better cut this shit out, right here and now. Don't be keeping no more goddamn souvenirs."

Zenon breathed out through his teeth and leaned on the display case. "All right. Didn't think it would hurt nothin. I'll get rid of the damn necklace." He jammed out a cigarette, and didn't mention the other memento he'd kept.

"Damn right you'll get rid of it. And now you're gonna have to get rid of her, too." Josh flung his arm at the door where Anita had left moments ago. "What a goddamn mess."

Zenon stared at him. "That girl has no way of knowing who that necklace belonged to."

"Oh no? It's been all over the news: Angel Frey missing. She could put two and two together. Do you really want to take that chance?"

"Jesus Christ, man, you said you had my back in all of this. You said nothing could happen to me."

Josh leaned forward. "I told you, you had to stick to the goddamn rules. You're keeping souvenirs. I told you to chill."

"You and your bullshit. You know what I think? I don't think these marks are any threat to me at all. I think they're a threat to *you*. You and that old woman."

"Dammit Zenon! You keep right on with this shit. Just go ahead. You're gonna find yourself in a prison cell."

The word *prison* gave Zenon pause, and his anger slipped a notch.

"I know. All right." He shook his head. "Look, I'm groping in the dark here. You tell me I'm s'posed to go get this mark but not that one. Makes me some kind of vigilante but I don't know why. What the hell am I doing this for, anyway?"

Josh snorted. "I've told you a thousand damn times."

"Tell me again."

Josh ran his fingers through his hair and leaned against the counter. "They're a different race of souls. We gotta get rid of them."

"Why?" Zenon crossed his arms. "What's so bad about them?"

"They're gonna take over, that's why. They'll *own* people like you. That what you want? Be somebody's pet?"

Zenon shifted, looking away, and brought a cigarette to his lips.

"It's so simple. But you gotta make it complicated. And now," Josh leaned his face in so that it was inches away from Zenon's. He pointed at the door again. "Now you're going to have to get rid of her, too."

Zenon blew out a long, slow stream of smoke.

forty

NEW ORLEANS, 1920

JACOB CHAPMAN HAD, ALONG with the rest of New Orleans, been celebrating the eve of Prohibition. It took some time before the street child found him, for Chapman was not at the hotel as expected, but at a saloon nearby. The boy told him that he had encountered Chloe on the street and she had given him a dime to track Jacob down. Jacob and his driver, following the boy's directions, found the alley just as freezing rain began to fall over New Orleans. The child led Jacob into the darkness. There, he saw Chloe, a prostrate Rémi, and a bleeding, shivering ruffian.

"Who is this man?" Jacob asked Chloe as he paid the child a second dime and sent him on his way.

"That is Bruce Dempsey," Chloe answered. "He belong to me."

Jacob frowned but did not press. Icy rain stunted any desire for conversation. When Chloe said that Bruce Dempsey belonged to her, Jacob assumed she meant that Dempsey was her friend. He attributed her strange choice of words to the fact that her English was a bit spotty.

Still, it seemed a strange turn of events for Chloe and Rémi's wedding night that they should end up tattered and helpless in an alley with a thuggish-looking stranger. The icy water penetrated Jacob's clothing and chilled him to the bone, causing the stump of his left arm to ache. No use questioning poor Chloe on a hoary night such as this.

Jacob asked whether Bruce Dempsey could walk. In reply, the hulking man blubbered and shivered. Jacob and his driver were able to get Rémi into the car fairly easily, but it took all three of them—Jacob, the driver, and Chloe—to move Dempsey.

Jacob regarded Chloe as they struggled with the man's bulk. Her clothing was torn and bloodied. But her face showed no sign of alarm or frustration, and she seemed not the least bit affected by the freezing rain.

It appeared that nothing fazed her; not now, and not even when Jacob had lost his hand on the hunting trip. He wondered what she might have done had the boy been unable to locate him at the saloon, and she was truly stranded with the two bedeviled men in the freezing rain. Somehow, Jacob knew, Chloe would have managed to get them all home. She was not a woman who knew how to be helpless.

The motorcar was too narrow to accommodate all of them, and so Jacob instructed the driver to take them back to the house while he ran the distance on foot in the cold rain. He had long since sobered under the inhospitable conditions.

The church bells tolled midnight, and with their ringing, Jacob knew a new age of temperance had begun. Alcohol was no longer a legal substance in the city of New Orleans, nor anywhere in the United States. As Jacob dashed through the streets, revelers emptied the saloons and taverns and drifted to their homes, and the saloons and taverns locked their doors for good. Jacob wondered whether, if the weather had been less severe, there might have been a riot at that final moment. Instead the midnight hour came as a whisper. Carousing New Orleanians were systematically doused with freezing rain and their first taste of widespread sobriety. Jacob suspected that they did their best to extend the moment on the sly, smuggling home bottles of bourbon and brandy purchased at cut-rate prices, stuffed in their winter coat pockets.

He bent his head against the wind and trotted toward Esplanade, trying to guess what might have occurred in the alley. Clearly both Rémi and the strange Bruce Dempsey had drunk themselves to the point of casualty. But why would Rémi do such a thing on his wedding night, saddling Chloe with the burden of escorting him home in such a state? She herself might have been accosted, or worse. Rémi was not the same man who had married Helen only a few years ago.

With reluctance, Jacob had gotten used to the idea of Rémi's fraternization with Chloe. They'd had three children together, and now, he had married her. The matter had been elevated to the public eye. No turning back. Jacob could only imagine the scrutiny the couple would endure.

But stranger still, more and more it appeared that Chloe bore the true burden of the relationship. She had begun to take responsibility for the plantation's financial state. She, an uneducated black woman, had learned the machinations of plantation economy and prevented Terrefleurs from falling to ruin.

And to be sure, Rémi himself had become a handful. So prodigious had become his thirst for alcohol that Jacob could not remember the last time he had seen him sober. Even without the odor of whiskey or bourbon on him, Rémi behaved in such a way that Jacob could tell he had been drinking. Hallucinations and frightful outbursts. And Chloe remained by his side to quiet him.

She was a strong, beautiful colored woman with an iron will. Rémi LeBlanc was not the first to fall under the bewitchment of alcohol, but he might be the luckiest, with a woman like Chloe to prop him up and preserve his lifestyle. Jacob could only imagine what it would be like to have such a woman to soothe him.

When Jacob arrived at the grand house on Esplanade, the servants were waiting at the door. He could tell by their pinched expressions that they did not approve of these strangers' presence at the house, and he wondered if Chloe was having difficulty managing them, on top of everything else.

The servants had already loaded Rémi and the hapless Bruce Dempsey into beds, and so there seemed little else for Jacob to do but return to the hotel.

"Thank you for coming to me, Monsieur Chapman," Chloe said.

Jacob took her hand. "Chloe, when will you learn to call me Jacob?" He gave her hand a squeeze. "It was my pleasure to be of assistance. Please call me if ever you need anything, anything at all. I am at your service."

She looked at him with wide liquid eyes set in broad cheekbones, and he thought her beautifully exotic.

THE LAST OF RÉMI'S surviving relatives had fallen dead. Jacob learned that the day after Rémi married Chloe, dock workers along the riverfront discovered the body of Rémi's oldest brother, Henri. Witnesses had seen him drunk and staggering in the Vieux Carré the night before, but such had been the state of nearly every other resident of New Orleans, and no one thought much of it until the next day.

When the workers retrieved Henri's brined body, they all agreed that the cause of death was drowning, probably hastened by his inebriated state. Jacob heard much gossip as to whether the poor devil's demise was accidental or deliberate. Some said that Rémi's brother committed suicide because he had lost his youngest sibling and mother in the space of one week, or because he no longer possessed the ability to have children.

But talk of murder did abound. With the last surviving brother gone, Rémi LeBlanc would become the sole heir to the LeBlanc fortune. Perhaps Rémi LeBlanc, said to have fallen on hard times, killed his brother for control of the family money. Or perhaps his new wife, rumored to be a voodoo priestess, arranged for the brother's death in order to satisfy a bargain with the devil. Still other rumors speculated that Chloe had him killed because she believed that bad luck came in threes, and when two LeBlancs fell dead in the space of a week, the voodoo priestess sacrificed the brother in order to save her new husband.

Jacob took staunch offense to these tales, and at least twice his outrage came to blows.

Of course, some folks believed that Henri's death was a simple drunken accident.

Whatever the cause, the bizarre events that had befallen the LeBlanc family made for riveting conversation in the salons and halls of New Orleans society, and also in the brothels and back rooms of its subculture. Though the fading war in Europe and the new Prohibition law provided New Orleanians with much fodder for discussion, it was Rémi and Chloe LeBlanc who'd become the talk of the town.

forty-one

ADELEINE WALKED PAST THE nurse's station to the visiting area. She wore her white lab coat, badge, and a still-battered face. Daddy had been admitted the previous afternoon, her day off, and was already stabilized on his meds from his time spent in jail. Madeleine looked forward to having a real conversation with him again—chemically altered or not.

She scanned the couches and tables in the visiting area. Several patients were reading, chatting, or watching TV. Daddy rose when they spotted each other.

"Hey, baby girl." Daddy kissed her cheek, but his gaze was fixed on the foil-covered paper plate she'd brought along. "Welcome to my humble temporary abode. You bake a chisel into a cake or something to bust me out?"

"Bust you *out?* You all but busted *in* this time. Here, I see you've zeroed in on your supper."

"Well, now, don't mind if I do." He laughed as he accepted the plate, but he looked hazy and tired.

They settled onto plastic chairs in front of a round laminate table. The medications that kept him clear were probably making him sick. That was the trade-off: He was either out of his mind, or he was lucid but suffering the side effects of the meds that had brought him back.

He peeled back the foil and peered inside. "Mmm-mm. Jambalaya and cornbread. Thank God. The food's so bad here I can't eat it. I do better scrounging in the Quarter."

He eyed a woman at the other end of the room. Her plastic ward bracelet dangled from the hand she used to hold a novel, and her hair was backlit by the sun as though she'd stepped out of heaven.

Daddy hoarded the plate close to his chest. "See that one over there? She's a klepto."

Madeleine looked again. "That angelic-looking thing? Did she take something of yours?"

"My pocket watch is missing."

"Oh no!" Madeleine looked over at the woman, doubtful. "Maybe you just lost it."

"Maybe. But just because she didn't take it, dudn't mean she's not a klepto. I've been in here enough times I can spot'm a mile away."

He regarded the patient—she was absorbed in her book and seemed to have no idea Daddy was talking about her—with a sideways nod. "Yeah, I got my eye on her. She's kinda pretty anyway."

Madeleine lifted a brow. Daddy smiled as he appraised the heavenly kleptomaniac.

He said, "But that shrink of mine. He's the craziest one of all of us. Narcoleptic."

"Narcoleptic?"

"Yeah! My own shrink! You don't believe me? He's in his office sleepin all the time. He even sleeps while we're havin our session. I got up and moved the furniture round while he was dozin off the other day, just to mess with him a little."

That got her giggling, and it felt good to laugh. But then Daddy was looking at her full in the face. His brow creased. The intensity of his concerned expression suddenly drained her laughter away.

He said, "How'd that bruise get there?"

Her hand went to her cheek.

"Ah, baby girl." He shook his head, aghast, tears springing to his eyes. "My baby girl. I'm so sorry." He swallowed hard. "You're my sunshine, honey, I don't know how I could ever hurt you. You're the best thing that ever happened to me."

Madeleine's eyes brimmed over. She took his hand and they sat in silence, gripping each other. Sunlight poured through the window and stretched their adjoined shadows across the laminate.

"Daddy, I know it's hard for you. I know the medications make you sick."

His voice was hoarse. "Yeah, they do make me sick. But it isn't just that. I—"

He worked his lips as though straining to formulate his thoughts into words.

He said, "Madeleine, I know you want to believe I can just take some medicine and get better. But there's more to it than that. And then the coming back, it's like, it's . . ." He sagged in his chair.

She watched him closely. "What's it like?"

"It's hard to explain, baby." He shook his head, quiet for a moment, and then said, "I have conversations with someone who supposedly isn't really there. It's funny, you always see in the movies how you can just ignore these things, but that just isn't so."

She nodded.

He said, "But this other person—or thing, I don't know—he tries to talk me into . . . Things I would never consciously do. But the way he phrases it, it makes sense. Especially if I follow him into that other place. That damned bramble."

Madeleine sat up straighter. "What? What do you mean?"

Daddy frowned. "I don't know, I guess it isn't even the way he phrases it. I'm doing a piss-poor job of explaining this."

He growled in frustration and looked toward the window. "I guess it's how he *wills* me. And later I'll remember what I heard, or what I saw on the other side, but I don't remember the *sense* of it. That's what's important. The sense. Words are words, but there's a whole feeling, like a . . . an understanding."

He looked at her, and his gaze landed on her bruises. "Of course, when I realize what I've done to you, I get to wondering if maybe I am just another crazy person."

She swallowed, but it did little to lighten the ache in her throat.

Daddy said, "You want to know what it's like taking those pills? You just wake up and find yourself in the real world again. You're still seeing things but you're here. You're sick, and everything moves slower, and harder, and dumber."

He shook his head, eyes red and damp. "It's misery. But you know that's what normal is. That's how it's s'posed to be. You look around, and you're . . ." He shrugged. "Embarrassed. You find out you're actually a monster."

The anguish in his voice turned a vise on her heart. She was weeping. Barely breathing.

His hand trembled when he spoke again. "And there you are, useless, a burden to your family. To your own children."

"Daddy, it isn't like that at all, you know that. We love you." She stopped. "*I* love you. Yes, I worry, and we have to figure out a way to get a handle on the violence. But it won't do either of us any good if you see yourself as a burden or a monster."

But as she spoke, she heard herself from the standpoint of the observing scientist, and the scientist noted the overwrought stoicism in her voice. While her words were a true reflection of how she felt, she knew there was more to it. More to say.

And so she said, "Truth is I need you, Daddy. I love you but I need you, too."

He squeezed her hand. Her mind buzzed like a radio picking up multiple broadcasts: fears, scenarios, hopes, frustrations, the bramble; and it suddenly exhausted her. She couldn't observe through the tangled inner noise. So she shut off her thoughts. Radio silence. Just like she'd done with Zenon, only this time she did it not as a means of self-defense, but to strengthen the twisting, complex connection with her father. She heard the murmurs of other patients and their visitors, the television bleating out some enticement to a car lot in

Metairie, and all of it passed through her as though she were the now-familiar field of steam. The life force jumped in that field. She felt it radiate from her and all around her, even in their oblong shadows on the laminate.

Thoughts pressed back in. She knew she couldn't keep them at bay for long. At the forefront of the returning flood of thoughts was a digital image of Marc, his arm slung around Emily Hammond's middle. But this time Madeleine recognized the life force dancing in that picture too. Fresh and sparkling.

"Daddy," she said.

"Yeah."

"Marc was dating a girl named Emily Hammond. I think they might have had a child."

"Yeah."

She swallowed. "So it's true?"

He looked at her, eyes full of sadness and love.

She said, "If you knew this, why didn't you tell me?"

"Marc's gone now honey, and that girl, she left. Moved up to Canada. She and the baby."

Madeleine shook her head. "But why? It's not that simple. This means you're a grandfather. And I'm an aunt."

"Honey, don't you know it's better this way? Let that girl have her life. That baby's gonna grow up safe and normal."

Madeleine stared at him. "Does this have anything to do with Chloe LeBlanc?"

Daddy shook his head very slowly to the side and back again. "Don't say anything to old Chloe, honey. Don't ever let her know."

"You'd better tell me why."

"She watches. Got her eye on everything we do."

"All right. I got that. But why?"

"I tried to tell you before."

"Tell me again. I may be listening with new ears."

Daddy said, "Your mémée, she thought if she kept Chloe away, we'd all be safe. But you see how it is. Chloe gets her way regardless.

Even if you never meet her face-to-face. It's like she's grooming us for something. I don't even know what. That's why she ought not know about that little baby up there in Canada. One thing peels away and then it just gets worse and worse."

"I'm not following you, please be specific. Is it about pigeon games?"

Daddy's eyes sharpened. "You didn't start in with her, did you? I always thought you were too practical to believe any of that."

"I—I am. But I read about it in Mémée's diary, and I witnessed . . . tell me, what exactly are pigeon games?"

Daddy eyed her, then let his gaze drift to the window. "Honey, I just don't know. It's something to do with manipulation, that's all I got. I told you, when Chloe comes around I just turn and walk the other way. Never got so far as the pigeon games."

"Well then tell me this."

"What?"

She folded her arms across her chest and looked into his eyes. "There was an article in the *Picayune* about Joe Whitney. The reporter says you gave him the information."

Daddy nodded, his face grave.

Madeleine said, "So when did you do all that?"

He raked his hand through his hair and blew out a long breath. "When I came back from D.C., honey. Can't you see? I couldn't stand up in front of all those congressmen and tell them I'm crazy, not if they don't know the bigger picture."

"What is the big picture then?"

"It's right in front of you! Girl, you've known me for close to thirty years but you made up your mind a long time ago. Got a degree as a headshrinker just so you could tell me I had delusions of grandeur."

"I'm just asking you, Daddy. That reporter, Shawn, said you were very specific about names and dates, told him exactly where to look. Please, just tell me where you got the information about Joe Whitney."

"Where do you think?" He reached up and took her face gently in both his hands, stroking her skin with his thumbs. "Same place I found out about Marc's baby child. Down in that damn briar."

HOUSTON, 2009

ANITA AWOKE TO WHAT sounded like emergency sirens blaring into the early Houston morning. She slapped at the largest button on the alarm clock until the wailing ceased. At first she couldn't remember where she was, then she realized she was in a guest bedroom at Julie's parents' house. The clock glared at her and refused to divulge the time. Or maybe she couldn't see it because her clumped mascara had glued her eyes shut. She fell back asleep.

Nine minutes later, she repeated the drill, and then again and again until she leapt out of bed with the awareness that she was now late. Her mouth was pasty and sour from the bottles of Shiner she and Julie had downed the night before, and Anita was grateful that she lacked the ability to smell her own breath. She patted her face and tried to shake out the grogginess.

She slipped on a filthy bra under the t-shirt she had slept in, and reached into her bag and retrieved a pair of jeans that were four sizes too big for her. Perfect for the road, Anita thought, and shoved her fists deep into the pockets.

As she grabbed the rest of her things, the Taser gun she bought from Zenon tumbled out of the wadded pair of clam diggers she had worn the night before. She smiled as she remembered how she and Julie, already lightheaded from the Shiners, had watched the training video that came with the weapon. Julie had instantly perfected her Bubba imitation, and recited parts of the video as if Zenon were the trainer, twirling the Taser on her thumb like a gunslinger. But the Taser didn't have a trigger so when she twirled it, it had gone flying. It sailed through the air and they both dove for cover, expecting the thing to send out random ropes of electricity.

Needless to say, the training video was probably wasted on them.

Anita shoved the Taser into one pocket of the baggy jeans and then put the can of pepper spray in the other. She patted the bulges and checked herself in the mirror.

Julie's mother had made coffee and was already in the shower, but other than that, the house was quiet. Anita finished getting ready and then dragged her heavy bag down the stairs and onto the Houston street. Still no chill in the early pre-dawn despite the fact that it was already well into fall, and as she locked the front door Anita was grateful that she did not need a jacket, because God knows she would have never thought to pack one. She heaved her luggage into the trunk of the Mustang. She was facing a sixteen-hour drive to St. Petersburg.

She pushed the hair away from her eyes and slipped the key into the driver's side door, suddenly struck with the sensation that she was being watched. She looked up.

She gasped. Zenon Lansky was standing right in front of her.

She relaxed a bit when she recognized the face, but the shock continued to pulse through her. He was standing so close. How did he get there without her noticing? And what was Zenon Lansky doing in Houston?

forty-two

HLOE ARRANGED FOR THE burial of Henri LeBlanc, but elected
not to hold a funeral. She also chose not to inform Rémi of
his brother's demise right away, as he was still suffering the
ill effects of the previous night's activities. Chloe aborted all further
nuptial celebrations and set off with her husband for Terrefleurs. One
night of honeymooning was as much as she cared to endure.

She packed a trunk with items that had belonged to Rémi's brother,
and instructed the house staff to load it into the motorcar bound for
Terrefleurs. In it were strange mementos: mostly battlefield relics from
the Great War. But Chloe found them to be fitting, lest Rémi roman-
ticize the memory of his brother and his ruined body.

The drive home was agonizingly long. Freezing rains from the
night before had transformed River Road into an endless rope of
pulled taffy. Rémi suffered a nervous stomach and spoke of the river
devil, crying out the name Ulysses in a near fever, attempting to leap
from the motorcar as it bounced along the sodden road.

Chloe pondered her new acquisition: Bruce Dempsey. She
thought it important to establish herself outside of Terrefleurs. She

hoped never again to have to rely on loathsome playboys such as Jacob Chapman, and those New Orleans servants were simply not trustworthy.

❧⚜❧

RÉMI AND CHLOE HAD borne little resemblance to newlyweds when they'd returned to the plantation. In the weeks following their wedding, they hadn't shared a bed; they'd barely spoken. Rémi had retired to the men's parlor where he'd slept fitfully for days, grappling with the ever-present visions and bilious words of Ulysses. Chloe had instructed Tatie Bernadette to remove all alcohol from Terrefleurs, and to cease production of it. They kept Rémi stone sober, but still his visions had continued to rage.

After several days, Rémi had emerged from the men's parlor and wandered the plantation. He had taken to disappearing for an afternoon or for a day, haunted all the while by his rogue spirit companion. He'd been coherent, but at the same time vacant. Women of the plantation had called him the *loup-garou*, a man-wolf of the bayou, and had told their children that he would carry them off to the swamp should they misbehave.

Chloe, meanwhile, had met with sudden and unexpected resistance from her business associates. They'd shut her out. She'd tried to arrange for an audience with them, knowing she could compel them to resume business with Terrefleurs. But they'd refused any dealings with her, and had insisted that Rémi personally supervise all further transactions. Impossible, of course, for Rémi's mind hadn't recovered since their wedding night. Any words from him were of the kinds of truths that most would deem nonsense. Parading him in front of the suppliers and buyers who fueled the sugarcane crop would prove disastrous. Chloe had no intention of exposing her vulnerabilities.

The January sugarcane crop had been the most prolific harvest they'd seen in years. The Terrefleurs mill was bursting with cane stalks, and Chloe had held a feast to celebrate the gifts of the spirit world. The people had exalted her as their heroine, a priestess whose influence with the spirits held tremendous power. But soon after, they had questioned whether she was lacking in the proper influence over mortals.

Later, when the sugar mill still remained full even though weeks had passed since the harvest and the celebratory feast, Chloe had noticed seeds of doubt sprouting among the workers. She overheard their questions: Why were they not carting the raw sugar to the refinery where they could sell it for processing? Why was the cane still in storage, falling to borers and rot? How could Terrefleurs survive if it was unable to sell its sugar?

The weeks had continued to roll by, and now the cane still remained in place, moldering in the sugar mill. Chloe knew the workers were talking. And she could think of nothing to remedy it, because the truth had become apparent to all: Chloe was unable to arrange for the sale of the sugar harvest.

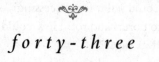

forty-three

A T THE TOP OF a ladder, Madeleine pulled at the framework of suspended ceiling, hands protected in rough leather work gloves. Ethan climbed up on the folding table and joined in. They'd already removed the ceiling tiles and stacked them by the door next to the disassembled cubicles. Ethan and Madeleine tugged until the metal skeleton gave a groan, and the entire grid unzipped and clattered to the canvas tarp below. A parachute of dust billowed into the flat. Madeleine teetered and Ethan jumped down and reached for her, steadying the ladder and her leg. She was coughing and laughing.

"Come here," Ethan said, and she let him pull her off the ladder.

"Thanks." She walked to the kitchenette and stepped over Jasmine's pet gate.

She opened the window, fanning the dust. "I'm thirsty. How about you?"

"Parched."

"Water or beer?"

"Both."

She retrieved them, including a glass of water for herself, while Ethan dragged the debris into the pile of rubble by the door. Jasmine yawned and stretched in her dog bed, having been sequestered in the kitchenette where she was safe from the renovation work. Madeleine gave her a treat and patted her fuzzy head, then stepped over the pet gate to join Ethan.

They sat on the empty canvas tarp with their drinks. Ethan wrapped his rough hand around hers. She felt grimy and sweaty but pleasantly exhausted, her body having flexed new muscles during the demolition. The breeze from the window was quickly banishing the stored-up heat in her bones. She pressed her fingers into the metacarpal ridge of his hand.

"Your hand's cold," he said, and rubbed it.

"Mmm, yours is warm."

She looked at his face, and saw a smudge of dirt running along his cheekbone. It made him look attractive in a rough-and-tumble way. She thought of the Audubon Zoo, when they'd talked about his escapades in neuroscience and she'd found him so deliciously irresistible. The very memory of it stirred her.

"Tell me again how the brain emits and intercepts wave patterns."

He looked at her, surprised and sweetly oblivious to her ulterior motive for asking the question. "Well, of course the interception part is just theory, not yet proven."

"Isn't it?"

"There's no way to demonstrate that in the lab other than through periphery indications—raised hair, pulse, sweat."

"Mmm. Raised hair. Pulse. And sweat. Little periphery indications."

He regarded her quizzically.

She said, her voice a little on the rough side, "I guess because of the way the brain is structured, technology hasn't figured out all the nooks and crannies."

"Exactly. Not yet. Most parts of the body function in a way that we can measure. But the brain is different."

She leaned in closer, angling her chest toward him. "How so?"

"Well, uh . . ." He looked her up and down. "Take memory. We used to believe that memory was stored in specific parts of the brain, now we understand memory is distributed. It's like a hologram."

"Is that so?"

He was watching her intently, and seemed to finally catch on to the tone in her voice, the languidness of her posture, and the way her own brain must have been emitting some intense gamma waves that conveyed a very specific, very good idea.

His eyes intensified. "Yes ma'am. That is so."

"Go on."

"Well, the uh, the way . . ." His gaze was fixed on hers, but he licked his lips and rallied. "Holographic film doesn't just record an image. The actual surface of the film is rippled. It's all . . . wavy."

Her fingers stroked his hand, and then traced a wavy pattern up between the bones of his forearm. "Wavy. Like the surface of the brain."

He laughed. Or maybe just shivered through his vocal cords, breaking into a wide smile. "Yeah, yeah, yeah. Like the surface of the brain."

She couldn't help but grin.

He said, "So when you have a laser. It shoots the light. I mean, you need two beams of light. To intersect. Or multiple beams. With mirrors."

"Mmm."

"And they intersect at the ripples that scatter the light waves. Creating . . . creating a 3-D image. And the brain . . . it's the same with memory. I'm having a hard time concentrating with the way you're looking at me, Madeleine."

"That's because the brain can't function as a multitasker." She reached up and touched the smudge on his cheek, and he caught her hand and kissed the underside of her wrist.

"Come here." He pulled until she was seated in his lap, his hand running up and along her back.

His lips pressed against hers—sweet and heated like cinnamon. She combed her fingers through the cropped hair at his temples, and then down, along his neck, reaching just below his collar where his skin was even warmer.

"You must be exhausted," she said.

"No ma'am. Not in the least. You?"

"I'm a ball of energy."

Their lips joined, arms encircled, bodies coiled. They were smiling, delighted for this very good idea. His hands were large and strong. They kneaded the muscles in her shoulder and down her back. She let her own fingers travel down the front of his shirt, curling under the short sleeve and over the ridge between his elbow and shoulder, her thumb stroking the hot underside where his arm rested at his upper rib cage. She could smell dust and sweat and plaster. She wanted to be closer to him. Smell his base scent beneath it all.

She rose to her knees and pressed herself into him. Her head was above his, her hip at his abdomen. She curled her right knee around his middle and lowered back down again as though on a wave. His hands slipped under the bottom of her tee to the small of her back. The sensation of skin on skin caused a shiver to radiate through her body.

It felt as though a powerful magnet inside her chest had locked with something inside his. That connection was blocked by the layers of cotton clothing that separated them. She tugged his t-shirt and pulled it over his head, then her own tee was coming off, both of them tugging to free it. And then it was gone.

She whispered, "Do you have protection?"

He fumbled about and pulled a thin packet from his wallet. "Should we go to the bedroom?"

"Too far."

Her skin pushed against his. Two layers of the same creature. His hand at her back, releasing her bra clasp. The straps dropped from her shoulders like feathers. It felt as though their hearts were sending electrical pulses to one another, joining in the same rhythm, and the chest cavity where her heart rested inside her own body seemed yet another illusion of space. A bundle of tissue that camouflaged something far more alive. The life force inside her had linked to the one inside Ethan. They were entangled beyond any hope of extrication.

Her limbs opened like the wings of a butterfly. He hooked his arm around the backs of her thighs and lifted, supporting her with his arms and legs, holding her back, laying her gently onto the canvas. He unfastened her jeans. She lifted her hips and he pulled, tugging them over and down. She kicked them off. Dust from the renovation work swirled around them and caught glints of light from the window. He was already unbuttoning his own jeans. She pulled on the fly, each button releasing in a downward succession. He was erect over the top of his briefs. He pulled off his jeans and they fit their bodies together, rib to rib, hip to hip. His erection pressed into her skin. The heat center moved from her heart, down lower, and the need to join with him felt both excruciating and exquisite.

She drew shallows breaths as they snaked around one another. Limbs locked with limbs, fingers exploring skin. She heard the clink of glass, and looked to see that her water had spilled onto the tarp. It looked gorgeous. Late morning sunlight bending to diamonds in glass and liquid. He raised his head and looked at her.

"We're both filthy dirty," she whispered.

She dipped her fingers into the water and brushed the smudge off his cheek. He smiled at her. He dipped his own fingers into the water and moved them down, under the fabric of her panties, between her legs. The cool liquid on his rough hands made her arch her back. His mouth covered hers, lips open. His fingers moved slowly, easily, and they found the ridge just above the opening. She gasped. A fresh, sparkling ripple unwound from her. It expanded through every nerve and then every cell in her body, escalating. She reached down and took him in her hands, mirroring his movements in broader strokes.

She pulled him toward her.

"Hang on, Madeleine," he whispered.

He pulled her panties off, moving them slowly down her body. And then he had the packet open and was pulling off his own underwear, putting the condom on. His face was sweet anticipant. His chest was white with curled black hair. She wriggled out from under him and pushed on his shoulder until he rolled onto his back, and she draped herself over him, pulling him to her. She felt the solid mass press at her opening. Heat ricocheted through her. She pushed forward, trying to take him inside, and then relented a little and pushed again. His hands moved from her rib cage down to her hips. She took his length with two hands and angled her spine, and pushed once more. He entered then, and a murmur escaped from her throat. A searing burn between her legs. His hands smoothed the wall of her abdomen, thumbs to her ribs, and then caressed her breasts.

She moved over him, slowly rocking. Quiet, warm, and sweet. Through the window, the branches of the magnolia tree dipped with the breeze and sunlight danced through the shadows. She leaned forward, stretching her body, stretching out her legs. She straightened her back with a curve to her tailbone so that her buttocks rose up and at the front, her soft, sensitive ridge now pressed against him. She paused at the shock of feeling. He slid his hand down her back and pushed his hips so that he was angled along that ridge. She clamped and pushed back. The heady sensations returned. She and Ethan started moving again, moving in rhythms.

The connection felt as though they were caught in the vibration of the earth itself, a core source that caused waves on the ocean and wind that left ripples in sand. A connection that repeated from earth to the elements to humans in one motif after the other. Waves coursed through their bodies and echoed in their movements.

And then the sensation crested and she threw back her head and cried out. Vibrant streaks channeled through her. She went still, though the sensation continued its course, and she could do little more than witness her own pleasure with a sense of awe. Ethan waited. Her lungs seemed to have forgotten to fill.

She melted against him and drew in a careful, staccato breath.

He cupped his hand behind her neck, rolling her over, and then he lifted her up and carried her to the bedroom. "That was a good start."

※

STEAM FILLED THE BATHROOM. Madeleine couldn't see her own reflection in the mirror. She had already bathed and dressed and was towel-drying her hair while Ethan finished his shower. She wandered out into the living area.

The main living space looked so much larger now. She looked up at the newly revealed stamped tin. A few ragged screws up there. Some repair and touch up to do, but she marveled at the immediate transformation. The flat had gone from eight-and-a-half-foot ceilings to a spacious ten-foot height. The desolate fluorescent tray lights were gone too. She went to the kitchenette and opened the pet gate so Jasmine could roam freely, and put some food in her dog dish.

Ethan appeared with wet hair, wearing just his jeans. "This place is incredible. It's starting to look more like Sam's flower shop down below."

She nodded. "Seeing it like this, it makes me wonder why anyone would ever cover it up. Look."

She pulled back a corner of the industrial carpet under the tarp, revealing the broad plank wood floor beneath. Like the stamped tin, the original flooring was rough and scarred but solid. Genuine. The suspended ceiling and flat loop carpet now seemed like they'd been part of an absurd costume, a straitjacket for the original warehouse space.

Ethan said, "Wasn't it your family who carpeted over it? I mean, you've owned it forever, right?"

Madeleine shrugged. "There was a tenant who used it as a machine shop for decades. They must have done all this. I actually didn't even know this warehouse was in the family until around the time I went to college, when Daddy deeded it over to me and Marc."

"Really?"

"Yeah. That was right around the time the machine shop closed down. I wound up renting out the lower space to Samantha. Found out about the house on Esplanade at about the same time, too."

"You mean to tell me you had no idea about all this?"

"None."

He said, "So you just figured that little house on Bayou Black was it."

"Yeah, that was it."

"Your father," Ethan said carefully. "Was he always like he is now? I mean, one minute he seems fine and then . . ."

Madeleine gave a rueful smile. "I remember him fading out when we were really young. But he would leave, I mean physically go off for a few weeks, so we didn't see it as much. But my mother left when Marc and I were nine and ten, and that's when we realized how serious it was with Daddy."

"Because then he was home all the time."

Madeleine shook her head. "No, he still went off and left."

"When y'all were nine and ten?"

"Yeah."

He looked puzzled. "Who looked after you?"

"We looked after each other."

"No adults at all?"

She shook her head.

"But what about, you know, food and shopping and all that?"

She shrugged. "We just made do. Whenever we ran out of food, we went fishing and caught more food. If the electricity was turned off, we burned candles and used the old hand pump for fresh water from the well. We'd cook on a little hibachi. Sounds bad, but at the time it felt like camping."

Ethan looked perplexed. "People had to have known there were two kids out there living alone."

"It only went on for a few weeks at a time at first. Longer when we were teenagers. If some adult asked about Daddy, we'd just say he was sick. We didn't want social services to get involved. There were neighbors and school teachers who'd send us home with loaves of bread or sacks of beans."

Ethan looked at her with warm, soft eyes. "No wonder you're so tough."

She felt embarrassed, and stepped toward the bedroom. "You want a clean t-shirt? The people from my church brought me a whole bunch of them after the fire."

"Yeah, thanks."

She found one that had a fleur de lis on the front and SAINTS written across the back.

He pulled it over his head and said, "What about the other thing. The way your father figured out Joe Whitney's scheme. He always been that way?"

Madeleine shook her head with a tired shrug. "I don't know. I don't even know what to make of that."

"I'd sure like to see an image of your old man's brain."

That got her laughing.

But then Ethan said, "Wouldn't mind seeing a picture of Zenon's brain, either."

She frowned, but the way he'd brought up Zenon had caused her to bypass any dread and anger and go straight to examination. "What do you think you'd find up in there?"

"I don't know, maybe an enlarged pineal gland. Hyper- or hypo-activity in the amygdala. Or maybe his brain just looks like everyone else's."

"I wonder if an fMRI would show signs of a criminal mind."

"Sociopathic?"

"Yes, or he might even be psychopathic. I haven't spent enough time around him since growing up to make that determination. He's manipulative. And seems to disregard any sense of right and wrong. So he could be either. The question is whether he's rash and disorganized like a sociopath, or calculating like a psycho-path."

"In that case I'd also be interested in seeing what his prefrontal lobes look like."

Madeleine smiled at him, smiled at how odd the statement sounded.

He said, "Come on, we'll walk Jazz and then I'll take you to a late lunch before I head into the lab."

"I can't. I'm supposed to head out to Bayou Black and meet with Nida about selling the old house."

"Ah, I forgot. Wish I could go with you."

"I know you've got patients to see."

She picked up Jasmine's red leather leash and pulled it through her fingers. Jasmine danced at the sight of it.

Madeleine said, "You know what's interesting?"

"What?"

"When you struck him in that alley, you weren't angry. You were angry before that, but not when it came to blows. Then you were cool as a cucumber."

She clipped the leash onto Jasmine's collar. "The second you reclaimed yourself you looked completely calm, even when you struck him down."

"That's because I wasn't angry. Not at that moment anyway. It was pure defense."

He frowned. "I'm glad you'd told me about clearing your mind. That made all the difference. A lot like Shokotai."

"You're supposed to clear your mind?"

"Yeah, that's how you stay always at the ready. Your reflexes are slow when you're daydreaming."

She considered this. "Odd. I never realized the mental game involved in martial arts."

"That's ninety percent of it. Part of the discipline is to lay down your fear of death, which in most cases is not even an issue, but you're supposed to act like it is. Like every physical confrontation is a life and death situation, and you choose not to fear death."

"I imagine that would keep you focused."

"That's the idea. Of course it's one thing to talk about it in theory, but it's a whole other thing to put it in practice, especially when it wasn't my own safety I was worried about."

He ran his hand up along her arm. "I don't ever want to worry about being used as a tool to hurt you again."

She looked into his eyes. "You've learned how to counteract Zenon's trick. So have I. It appears we're safe from whatever it is he's using."

"That guy ought to be locked up."

Madeleine thought back to Sheriff Cavanaugh's warning, and felt a new respect for his instincts.

forty-four

BAYOU BLACK, 2009

THE CABIN WAS SMALL. Smaller than Anita's own dorm room. No glass on the windows, just cutouts that had been shuttered closed. Newsprint covered the walls. Very dark. But she knew he was just outside.

When Zenon had first grabbed her, he'd made her get in his car and drive to an empty alley. There, he'd bound her wrists. He'd put her in the trunk of his car. At first she'd tried to kick her way out. But then she'd realized she had either broken or sprained her ankle, her fear so numbing that she never even felt the pain. Felt only a sudden realization that her foot no longer worked. She had no idea how long she'd been inside that trunk, but it had to have been several hours.

And in those hours, she'd had time to think, and she'd made some guesses. She believed that Zenon had brought her to some backwater corner of Louisiana. And she believed that he meant to kill her. No; worse than that.

She had seen his watchfulness, his delight in any form of action she took, like when she struggled or screamed, or the reasoning, and then pleading when he moved her from the trunk of the Duster to the hull of a boat. If he meant to kill her outright, he would have done so in Houston when he'd knocked the pepper spray from her hands and shocked her with her own Taser.

She was about to die, this she knew, but not before he'd played his games.

As she lay on the floorboards of this place, this horrible outhouse of a cabin, she knew she had to get out. He was waiting for her out there in the way a snake waits outside a mouse's burrow. But she didn't care. She had to move. Was damned if she was going to lie around until he decided to come in and start.

She would run. Busted foot or not. At least it would be over soon. She rolled to her feet and limped to the door.

And he was indeed waiting.

forty-five

ADELEINE THOUGHT THE BAYOU had seemed dark. Though mid-day, the overcast skies had thickened, and the Spanish moss swayed on the trees like the hair of mermaids swimming through the tides. Madeleine had taken the boat out for a quick jaunt before her real estate meeting with Nida. Her senses had never felt so awake. She wanted to touch everything, smell it, experience it. And she carried her luxury of sensations after making love to Ethan. That, too, she'd experienced with this new acuity.

She'd lingered too long out there and had to tether the boat at the dock instead of pulling it onto the little trailer. She'd do that later, after she met with Nida. She prided herself in her ability to do these things alone.

Her hair was blowing into her eyes as she stood on the porch of the little cottage, talking to Nida and Thibby, and she kept tucking errant locks behind her ear. That wind was heavy with the scent of water. Funny how you can barely smell clean water if you put a cup of it right up to your nose. The scent came through best when atomized. She couldn't get enough of that scent.

"As long as you ask a reasonable price," Nida was saying, "you can probably sell the old place within two or three months."

Madeleine said, "That's good news. I need to turn it over as fast as possible."

Nida and Thibby looked at each other.

"The insurance come through on the big house in the Quarter yet?" Thibby asked.

Madeleine shook her head. "Given the circumstances, they've decided not to pay out."

"Well can't you sue?"

"I could try, but it's kind of hard to look them in the eye and demand compensation. I mean, one of the deed holders deliberately burned the place down."

Nida clucked her tongue and seemed to be at a loss for words.

Madeleine didn't tell them the worst part, that the LeBlanc estate would be liable for the other two damaged houses, and the insurer wasn't going to pay for those either. Selling the Creole cottage on Bayou Black would bring in only a modest sum, but every bit helped.

"Don't worry baby," Nida said. "We'll find you a buyer."

Madeleine hugged them both and waved good-bye.

She opened the front door to take a final look around, telling herself that she needed to make sure all the windows were locked. She needed to do something, anyway, though she wasn't sure what.

She felt she'd collected all she could in trying to learn what had gone wrong with Marc—Mémée's diary, Chloe, Emily Hammond. But she hadn't quite held these facets up to the light yet, see what shines through . . .

The little cottage looked so different with all the furniture gone and the wood floors scrubbed to a gleam. No lingering scents of garlic and paprika; no clues that she or Marc or Daddy had ever been there. Clean and cold. And somehow the house already felt invaded, like a snake had slithered inside when she wasn't looking. Her sharpened senses knew this. The new window in her mind.

Her cell phone buzzed in her pocket. Sam's name on the caller ID. "Hello?"

"Maddy, it's Sam. Are you anywhere near the flower shop?" The tone in her voice was strained.

"I'm in Houma, honey. What's the matter?"

"It's Anita Salazar. My intern."

Madeleine's fingers gripped the cell phone. "Is she all right?"

"I don't know. She's gone missing. She was supposed to be driving down to Florida, but she never showed up and her family's worried."

Madeleine felt her stomach tighten. "Maybe she's out with friends. She could be anywhere."

"They found her car. She'd been staying with a friend in Houston. She'd gotten up early in the morning and left with her suitcases. The suitcases made it into the car, including her purse and her wallet."

"My God. Have they called the police?"

"Yes. They're saying they can't file a missing person's report until she's been gone for forty-eight hours."

Madeleine was silent for a moment, unsure what to say, and then: "Listen, honey. I'm wrapping up here and then I'll be heading home. Are you alone?"

"Yeah, but Vinny's on the way."

"Good. I may be a few hours but I'll call you as soon as I get back. OK?"

"OK."

They rang off. Madeleine covered her mouth and gazed through the front window. She barely knew Anita, but she hated to think anything could have happened to the bright, vibrant girl. And Sam, with her empathic nature, must be sick with worry. She'd grown close to Anita over the time they'd spent together in the flower shop. Madeleine wished she could be there right now to put her arms around Sam's shoulders and comfort her.

The lights went out.

Madeleine jumped. She could still see well enough from the daylight, even though it was cloudy out. Her hand went to the light switch and flipped it off and on, but nothing. She walked to the kitchen and tried the switch in there. It worked.

Must be a burned-out bulb.

But when she returned to the front area, she smelled burning hair. And she heard a thump. *Bom-bom.* A double thump. Rhythmic like a heartbeat, but very slow and hollow. Madeleine turned slowly in a circle, looking for . . . she didn't know what.

"Madeleine . . ."

A child's voice, coming from the closet. Severin's voice.

Madeleine's heart sped and then cramped. Chloe and Oran were both in New Orleans, so why would Severin be here? She felt suddenly overcome with dread. She opened the closet door.

Nothing. But no, not nothing. A rat was lying on the floor inside the closet. Limp, front teeth exposed in a grimace around a length of black wire, a brown stain on the baseboard. It was falling back slowly from the small ledge as though it had been on its feet and had only just gone limp. But Severin wasn't in there. And even as she looked, Madeleine wondered if she'd even heard Severin's voice at all, or whether she'd imagined it.

The rat moved. It jerked with a suddenness that made Madeleine jump. Its head smashed into the baseboard where the brown stain was, and then it fell limp against the floor again, making a double thump. Like a heartbeat. The head was wedged atop the base molding and was rolling back down slowly, teeth still clenched at the wire. When it reached the bottom, it would complete the circuit and jump again.

Madeleine recoiled. Her purse slipped from her arm and fell to the ground. The rat had chewed through the exposed wiring, clearly, but the horrific sequence was too bizarre. Almost staged. As if for her very benefit.

She wanted to run from the house. But she had to see. Had to see beyond that rat, because she knew there was something else in there. Marc had told her what to do, and her father had shown her how.

Like putting stars to sleep, only backward.

She closed her eyes, allowing it to come forth. She imagined that a layer was peeling away. And it did. Inside her mind, the veneer lifted. Much more easily than she would have guessed.

Something scratched her foot. She opened her eyes.

❧

BRAMBLE. IT CURLED ACROSS the floor. Coiling, wrapping, unfolding; moving easily, even gently. A thorn had scratched her ankle. It had come from the closet.

On the floor of the closet, with her hand on the rat, was Severin. She was naked and squatting. Her long, matted hair tumbling down the length of her spine, her body streaked with filth. She was looking at Madeleine. Her lips were pulled back, but it looked more like she was baring her teeth than smiling.

"Come play a little some with me." Severin's voice was childish and soft.

Madeleine screamed. It came from a strangle in her throat. She stumbled backward but her feet caught in the bramble. She turned, deliberately turned her back to Severin.

My God, I truly am losing my mind. Just like Daddy.

"I said, come play with me." Severin's voice, though still soft and childlike, grew harsh.

Madeleine turned a loathing glance toward her, her body shaking with fear and revulsion. The child lifted the rat by its tail. It stared with dead, glassy eyes and wooden-looking teeth. This time, when it fell, its teeth released the wire.

"You can play a little some with this beast. It listened to the whispers. I'll get another."

"No," Madeleine whispered. "Not real. Not real."

She stumbled across the bramble to the door, reeling, unable to endure the toxic air inside the house, and found her way to the porch. She was gulping for oxygen as the breeze washed over her.

I must be sensible. I need to act with presence of mind.

She walked, shaky at first, around the side of the house to the electrical panel and tried to pull the breaker. She had to shut off the electricity and disable that faulty wire. Her hand shook, and she had to pull twice, but she managed it.

I'll turn the other off too. I'll put the layer back. Hide the bramble.

She stepped back to the porch. She'd dropped her keys and purse inside. But as she put her hand on the door knob, she faltered.

From within the house, the floorboards creaked.

"Oh my God," Madeleine whispered. She had to think.

I am hallucinating.

No other explanation. Her mind tumbled with wild psychoanalysis. *Schizophrenia. Just like my father.*

She opened the door.

Severin was standing there, and her matted hair stretched to her bony legs. Her nude body was shadowed and gray despite the brilliant rays streaming through the cloud break. Madeleine stepped back, knowing that what she saw wasn't real, and yet that knowledge didn't help. She folded her arms and turned away. The bayou spread before her. The place where she and Marc used to escape.

She should get to a hospital. She was having an extreme episode, and needed treatment.

"I told you to come play." Severin moved toward Madeleine, her tiny feet shuffling.

Madeleine backed into the porch swing, sitting abruptly. Trying desperately to ignore this image of Severin.

It isn't real. It's just a figment of my imagination. It isn't real.

"It isn't real!" Madeleine said aloud, willing the hallucination away. "It isn't real!"

She realized then that she was sobbing, burying her face in her hands.

"Don't make tears," Severin said. "Here, I'll push you."

The porch swing began to rock gently back and forth, and Madeleine's body shook. Suddenly she could not bear to have the girl at her back anymore, and she leapt to her feet. She clutched at the porch rail, her legs threatening to give way. She had to get away from her. She had to think.

She stumbled down from the porch and made for her truck on unsteady feet.

"Where are you going?"

Madeleine stopped. The keys were still in the house. A cold wind stirred from the bayou and lifted a thick dirty tendril of hair into the child's face. She was staring at her from the porch, blocking the front door. Madeleine couldn't bring herself to brush past her to get inside. Inside, where the briar was still curling and unfolding. She looked out toward the water. The boat was rocking at the dock.

Severin stepped down from the porch and moved toward her.

"Oh God. Please just go away."

But Severin drew nearer, and Madeleine succumbed to the urge to escape, though she knew it was futile. Ridiculous to think she could outrun a hallucination.

She scrambled toward the dock. It was useless trying to be practical. She was driven by instinct now. And her instinct was to run.

forty-six

BAYOU BLACK, 2009

ANITA TWISTED SHARPLY TO her left, jerking, but he brought her down on her side. Sun-bleached driftwood snapped beneath her. She screamed and flailed. She saw a glint of metal in his hand, and she rolled over on her stomach and tried to claw away from him. A sudden pressure in her back, and she saw the knife streaked with blood. She kicked in desperation while the blade flashed over her. Her hand curled around a sharp stick and she plunged it into his shoulder.

Zenon went rigid. Anita scrabbled out from under him and tore into the woods. The foliage was so thick she had to hack at it with her arms, unable to run through the crush. The litter of rotten wood on the ground shifted under her feet. Had she killed him? Trees were twisting in the heavy breeze. She heard the sound of thrashing behind her, but she couldn't tell whether it came from the approaching storm, or him. She pushed forward with all her strength.

Where am I?

She racked her brain. She could not tell how long they'd been in the car, though she guessed it had to have been several hours.

Anita scrabbled over a fallen tree trunk that stood higher than she did.

She realized her strength was failing. Her hands and feet were going numb, and her legs threatened to buckle. He had wounded her. How could she not have known that the knife pierced her body?

Her steps were increasingly ragged. Her hands and clothing were soaked in blood. She could hear him somewhere behind her, and she cursed the sounds her own body made in the woods, giving her away. She realized:

I am going to die.

I am going to die.

And then she felt the strange inclination:

Come back. It's over.

Yes. She should turn back and go to Zenon. She felt the tug with absolute clarity. That is precisely what she should do.

Anita retraced her steps to find him. He was in there somewhere. She no longer had the strength to climb over the log, but she saw a thinner area of brush and stepped into it. It formed a rough path back to the place where she'd left him.

Come back.

She held her arms out, stepping calmly. Where was he? The pathway twisted, and now she wasn't certain whether it led back to him or in another direction.

The notion left her. Disconnected. She stopped moving, confused. Couldn't remember why she'd thought it logical and right to return to Zenon. In fact, the thought that she'd almost done that very thing sent her into a fresh panic. She turned again, though she had no idea which direction led toward or away from him. She ploughed through the brush. Ran.

The trees parted and she found herself at the edge of an expanse of black water. She backed away and whirled around. A tunnel ran through the brush, a much clearer trail that turned back into the woods. But the trail would leave her much more exposed. With her injured foot and her body becoming sluggish, he would eventually catch her.

She stretched her arms out before her and stepped into the water, opaque like a mirror. Like oil. She swam as quickly and silently as she could. Stinging in her back as the bayou stole her blood. The splashing water filled her ears when she raised her head, and when she sank beneath the surface to propel herself forward, the sound was deeper than silence. Thick and rushing like blood flow.

At the far bank, she stole a look around, but did not see him. She swam further to where the water T'ed off into a smaller passage hidden by a thick stand of trees. A little rest. Just for a moment. So difficult to move now. She hung suspended in the water, and the water pulled the heat from her so that she would match its temperature. She felt as though she was becoming part of it. The bayou wrapped around her, shielding her, claiming her.

She thought, "I would rather die than let Zenon catch me."

One more effort to lurch forward, and she reached the grove of water cypress. Her limbs would no longer stretch. Her body was curling into itself like a petrified spider. Something inside her was loosening, trying to escape that husk. An inner wobble like an egg yolk that wanted to break through the shell. She felt strangely elated, but yet she still fought.

She could only move in sluggish pulses now. Tried to disappear among the tangled root system. A refuge opened to her, a place where the giant cypress knees rose high and formed a cove large enough for her to slip inside. She huddled in, her colorless, shaking hands grasping at floating plants and waterlogged sticks, creating a nest among those roots. She braved another look across the water.

He was there, pacing along the bank, little more than a dark shadow. He turned to the trail behind him, then disappeared into it.

Anita let out her breath in a rush, even as her vision was blurring. She felt suddenly weightless, euphoric. A cool, brilliant nirvana. She should rest. She should . . . Her body detached. That inner wobble was so strong. A helium balloon contained by a cobweb. She broke through it.

forty-seven

HAHNVILLE, 1920

CHLOE SUPERVISED ROUNDING UP the cattle herself. The herd was small, and so with the exception of two milking cows and a bull, Terrefleurs would need every single one.

In the previous days, every man, woman, and child on the plantation had helped revive the old refinery that lay at the far end of the cane fields. The structure had gone to waste and was overgrown with brush and vines. The field workers had hacked away at the tangles until they unearthed the rotted building beneath. Inside, light poured through holes in the wall and ceiling, illuminating the rusted equipment that lay in dust.

Refining raw sugar had been a part of Terrefleurs' cycles before the days of the Sugar Trust. Now, with Chloe unable to sell the cane through the Trust, she decided Terrefleurs would once again refine its own sugar.

She was taking a considerable gamble, because decades had passed since they had done it, and only a few surviving old-timers had any vague memory of the process. Francois told Chloe the three basic steps: separating the crystals through a centrifuge, vacuum pan evaporation, and charcoal filtering. They would be relying on spotty knowledge and archaic, rusted equipment. If the attempt failed, they would ruin the crop in the process, and the plantation was in no position to lose an entire season's yield.

The workers had scrubbed the rust from the centrifuge and vacuum pan. They would use the pan to boil molasses, and it was imperative that it contain as few impurities as possible. Even the centrifuge, which separated the raw sugar juices from the cane, had to be sparkling clean so as not to introduce bitter flavors.

Francois had replaced corroded and missing parts as best he could through the makeshift machine shop that he'd used to repair farm equipment in the past. Chloe saw to it that the workers patched the refinery's roof to prevent rain from seeping in, but other than that, she did not spare them to completely repair the structure. Terrefleurs could afford to refine its own sugar once or maybe twice, and even then Chloe could only hope to break even in the process.

When the refinery was ready, it was time to focus on acquiring the charcoal that would filter impurities from the raw sugar. Traditionally, the process called for animal charcoal.

Chloe strode down the rear steps, intending to go to the corral where the cattle had been assembled, but she heard Patrice's voice shouting from somewhere nearby. It sounded like she was counting rapidly. Chloe looked to the *pigeonnier*. The twins were in the garden with Tatie Bernadette. She looked to the workers' allée and saw children running from the kitchen house in a pack while Patrice finished her count. The children hid themselves among the cottages. And then, down the center of the allée, Patrice came running. Her cheeks were plump and flushed, her legs long and gangly. She searched, the children melting into their hiding places as she approached and peeking around the sides of the buildings when she wasn't looking. Patrice found a little boy crouching behind the rain barrel. Both of them shrieked and Patrice tagged him.

"Patrice!" Chloe shouted.

Patrice jumped to a stance and faced her mother with her hands behind her back.

"Ici!" Chloe said.

Patrice ran to her and presented herself in the same stance. Her hair was pulled tight from her smooth dark face, and it fanned out behind her in a pony tail of spun sugar.

"Did I not tell you to stay away from the children?"

"Yes'm."

"Why do you disobey me?"

Patrice turned and looked toward the others. The children had retreated out of sight in the allée.

She looked back at her mother with her chin down and her blue eyes wide. "I don't know."

"You don't know! You think I have time for your bad behavior? You think I have nothing better to do?"

"Maman, why are the cows in the corral?"

Chloe put her hands to her hips. "They are in the corral because it is time for slaughter."

"Each and every?"

"Listen to me, eh? This place is dying. We will butcher the cattle to feed the people, and make charcoal from the bones. After that there will be no more food."

Chloe pointed down the allée. "And no more children. You see? Their parents will leave here. Good as dead. And their children go with them, good as dead. This is what happens when a plantation dies."

Patrice listened, eyes filling with tears.

Chloe leaned over, a hand to her belly. "Here now I have you and your brothers. And soon there will be another baby. What will we do on a dead plantation? We will have to leave too, and try not to starve. Your papa is lost in the spirit world. He can do nothing."

Patrice's eyes spilled over and her lip was trembling.

Chloe said, "I told you to work your pigeon cycles. That is the only power you have. You do not listen to me, you are as good as dead too."

Patrice covered her face with her hands and sobbed.

"You idle around and play with dolls." Chloe leaned in close. "I should throw those dolls into the well. You have too many. Six dolls!"

"Non Maman!" Patrice sagged to the ground, weeping. "Papa made those dolls for me."

Chloe took her arm and pulled her up to her feet, then shook her. "You practice your pigeon cycles with your brothers, or I will throw your dolls in the well. Go in the house now! You tell Bernadette to give you a thrashing!"

❦

ONE AFTER ANOTHER, THEY had cut each beast's throat. The plantationers had been nervous. Though butchering cattle and other animals was not uncommon at Terrefleurs, such widespread slaughter was shocking even to the most seasoned hunters. To calm the workers, Chloe had called for ceremonial drums, and bade the women dance at the bonfire. The ceremony had lasted all day long and into the early winter night. The people of Terrefleurs had given thanks to the beasts for laying down their lives, and had implored the spirits to accept their sacrifice and look upon them with favor. Chloe had noticed that not all the plantationers were willing to set their Christian faith aside to honor the river spirits.

The workers had butchered and processed the meat, making as much use as possible of each carcass. Some of the beef they had roasted for the feast, some they sold, and the rest they had smoked in a newly erected smokehouse, the old one being too small to accommodate the glut. The workers had crushed hoof and horn, boiling them along with the hide to make glue and waterproof oils.

And finally, the bones. First they had boiled them to remove the gelatin, to be used later for cooking. Next, they'd placed them in a large fire pit to burn. No one could remember how long it would take to burn the bones into animal charcoal, but they'd soon determined the heat had to be extremely high, and the burning process had taken over a week. The skies over Terrefleurs had blackened with smoke of the charcoal fires, and the cold humid air had been choked with vile odors of decomposing carcass and animal glue. Folks had gone about their work with handkerchiefs tied at the backs of their heads, covering their noses and mouths, and Terrefleurs looked like a plantation of bandits.

When they'd accomplished their task and the fires had cooled, all that was left of the bones had been brittle black lumps of charcoal. Chloe then ordered the processing of the sugar.

The odors produced by the slaughter and burning of the cattle had paled in comparison to the stench of the sugar refining process. For days, the overworked plantationers had endured the piquant sulfur-caramel smell of burning cane. Similar to the smells emitted by the nearby refineries on days when the wind carried the air pollutants south to Terrefleurs, only on their own land, there had been no escape.

The stench had been nearly unbearable, and the thick black smoke had crouched in a suffocating fog over the plantation. The workers had kept the handkerchiefs over their air passages, and in the mornings they'd coughed black spew. Chloe had tended those that were particularly frail, reminding them of the plantation workers of olden times, unpaid slaves who had to endure the foul air on a regular basis.

Everyone had been exhausted and demoralized, but the refining process had continued, and the juice did indeed separate from the cane. And in the pans, it had evaporated to hot molasses. The workers had purified it with the charcoal made from the bones of Terrefleurs' own cattle. The fires and the stench had finally subsided, and the bundles of cane in the millhouse had been replaced by mounds of near-white refined sugar. Chloe had ordered the workers to add molasses back into some of the granules to make a supply of brown sugar as well.

Now, a week later, she had finally sold both the white and brown sugar. She watched the barge carrying the yield as it drifted lazily down the Mississippi.

forty-eight

BAYOU BLACK, 2009

A STRONG WIND WAS blowing in from the Gulf, and the little boat pushed forward grudgingly. Madeleine leaned her head down and let the breeze force oxygen into her body.

Severin had not followed her. Madeleine was so very relieved to have escaped her that she was tempted to pretend that nothing at all had happened. Perhaps if she didn't think about it she could convince herself that she had not witnessed the horrible apparition. Perhaps the dirty child would never appear again.

But Madeleine knew better.

In fact, she knew that she had already played the pretend game too long. She had made light of seeing this child before, and had ignored other signs too, such as pretending that the severed finger in Sam's flower shop was just a trick of light. Such pretending had kept her from seeking treatment, and the condition had gotten much worse.

Ahead on the water, the byway narrowed to the saltwater intrusion lock, and the flood gauge looked high. The boat pressed through and on the other side, lightning flickered on the horizon. She knew it would rain but didn't care. She had to think, calm down, clear her head. Sort this out before Severin appeared again. Madeleine thought about her father and her great-grandfather. She figured she must be carrying that same tainted genetic trait as they did. Hidden within every cell of her body was a ticking bomb, waiting for the proper moment to ignite. Her entire life had been advancing toward this, when her genes would reveal their nasty little secret.

It's a treatable condition. I can take medications and function perfectly well.

Her father had always vacillated back and forth between lucidity and violent madness. Medications made him sick and rummy.

The bayou widened to the Intracoastal Waterway, and as it did the wind slapped wet salt across her face. A roll of thunder burbled from the far distance in the south. It began to rain.

Her father had pointed out how she thought it so easy to tell him to take his pills and everything would be all right. But now she was the one staring into the vortex of insanity, and it no longer seemed so simple. Thus far she had not seen a single schizophrenic who reliably took his meds. Not one. And in her father's case, he might be strolling in his undershorts on a street corner one day, or physically assaulting people he loved the next.

Oh, no.

No, no.

That's not for me.

For one brief, terrible moment, Madeleine wished she had the shotgun in the boat with her. She would have jammed it under her own chin and . . .

And as her mind curled around the fantasy of the shotgun, she understood.

Her brother Marc must have had these hallucinations too. He had tried to talk to her the day he shot himself. He knew what was happening to him; understood better than anyone what kind of future lay ahead, having been raised by a schizophrenic father. He had called Madeleine to tell her. To warn her? He had plenty of time to think about it, to look at Daddy Blank's life and determine whether he wanted to follow in those footsteps.

Was he planning to tell her that she was next?

Oh, Marc. My dear, sweet brother. Why didn't you shoot me too?

No. She had to get a grip. Though her father and brother shared this same affliction, she did not need to follow either of their paths.

She would seek treatment. Simple as that.

Unlike Daddy, she would be religious about taking the meds. A little numbness and nausea were a small price for maintaining the life she had built. With early treatment, the chances of success improved. She had found true happiness in her home and friendships. The blossoming love for Ethan.

The wind let up slightly as she turned off the larger waterway and down into a smaller passage of the bayou. She licked the spray from her lips, and for the first time grasped that she was tasting salt. The sea was pressing into the freshwater bayou. This was not to be a routine rainfall; a storm was surging in the Gulf. She had noticed earlier that the water had been creeping up the flood gauge in the saltwater intrusion station. Houma had had its share of storms already, and the shrubs that were ordinarily rooted above the surface on the banks were now partially submerged. She needed to get back.

But she could not yet face it.

She was certain Severin would be waiting for her when she got back. Madeleine knew she could handle this little storm. It would be unpleasant, but not so unpleasant as the apparition of briar and the gray-streaked child.

The rain let up, and Madeleine breathed a sigh of relief. She had time.

And then she noticed something out of place: a man.

The light was growing dim under the tide of thick clouds, but she clearly saw the figure of someone lingering along the west bank. She wondered who on earth would be out on the bayou in a storm. And this man was on foot. The dense swamp forest behind him was too thick for even the most zealous hunter or fisherman. *Another hallucination?*

But as she motored forth, Madeleine was stunned to see it was Zenon.

SHE WAS MOVING DOWN the center of a waterway perhaps thirty feet wide, and Zenon was standing at the outer edge of the west bank. He did not seem to notice her until she was right alongside him. He was absolutely filthy and disheveled, his shirt torn and streaked with rust. Their eyes locked.

She was dumbfounded. Why was he out there? Perhaps he was stranded. Before she could think what to do, he turned and disappeared into the woods.

Madeleine maneuvered a little further down the waterway and saw a boat moored a small distance beyond. A small fishing trawler, Zenon's trawler, and it appeared empty.

She turned east, away from Zenon and into a tiny channel that ended in her cypress cove. Crawfish Cove.

The skiff drifted inward until the cypress encircled it completely. Madeleine could advance no further, and cut the motor. Directly ahead, one of the cypress towered before her, its diameter spreading seven feet, triangles of roots jutting above the water.

In a blink, Severin appeared at the stern of the boat. And with her came the bramble.

Madeleine squeezed her eyes and tried to make the apparition disappear.

Put the layer back. Put it back.

But it seemed as if once flowing, the vision persisted. She wished she hadn't stopped. Severin stared at her with challenging eyes, and rain began to fall again. The sound of it filled the swamp and the trees all around, as if echoing applause in a grand theater.

"Did you come to shoot yourself, like your brother?"

Madeleine closed her eyes and breathed evenly. She knew that hallucinations could be brought on during moments of stress, and so she strove to make herself absolutely calm. Rain washed down her face.

"He shot himself after he tried to kill that man," Severin continued.

Madeleine opened her eyes.

"He tried to burn him up."

Madeleine knew the child was not real, simply a hallucination she should ignore. Nevertheless, Madeleine spoke directly to her.

"That isn't true."

"It is true, very very. I'll show you."

The briar stretched over her like a wave, and the cove grew dark. Madeleine screamed. Her vision faded to black, and then it seemed that she was no longer sitting in a boat in the rain, but was instead warm and dry deep within a tangled cave of thorny stems. To her right, an illuminated tunnel opened up. She could see movement in there. Walls and incandescent lighting. It looked like the basement of some kind of commercial building. And then she saw Marc, his tool belt slung around his hips. He and another man hovered around an electrical transformer.

"Marc!" Madeleine gasped.

She heard a titter of laughter, and saw Severin grimacing from the shadows.

It's an illusion. This isn't Marc, and Severin isn't real.

Marc's hands pressed against the wall on either side of the transformer. Wires protruded from an open panel. Behind him, a tall lean man was whispering. Madeleine did not recognize the man, but he had an unusual way about him. Then she realized what was different. The man had that strange, surreal grayness about him, much like Severin.

Madeleine shuddered. This was Marc's Severin.

Marc stood drenched in sweat. His back was to the stranger, and he was obviously trying to ignore him. From his hip, Marc's two-way radio crackled with the apprentice electrician's voice:

"You got the juice cut off yet, Marc? I been sittin in here waiting."

The stranger continued to hunker over Marc's shoulder, whispering. Marc reached up and touched a bundle of wire inside the transformer—a commercial transformer. The stranger leaned in closer and whispered more urgently.

Marc scowled at him and looked like he was going to close the panel door. Then he stopped and unhooked the bundle of wires. The apprentice's voice came over the radio again, sounding more impatient. Marc retied the wires to a different terminal, one where another bundle was already tied, so that now two bundles were sharing the same connection.

Marc picked up the radio and held it to his mouth. He shut his eyes and clenched his teeth, then sighed, relenting. He pressed the button on the side of the two-way.

"I'm done. Go ahead."

Marc stepped back from the transformer.

For a suspended moment, everything fell silent. The stranger had stopped whispering. He backed away from Marc. They looked toward the building, where the apprentice electrician was somewhere about to throw the main breaker.

"No," Madeleine whispered, and felt tears spill down her cheeks.

An explosion tore from where the two men watched, and the transformer burst with sparks.

And then, the bramble folded over them, and the faces of Marc and the stranger faded. Madeleine was once again sitting in blackness. The bramble kept twisting until it opened above her. Slowly, the sound of rain returned. It found her, soaked her, and she was once again crouching in the boat in the gray-shrouded cypress cove. An open space in the briar. Hot tears that spilled down her face were replaced by cold raindrops, steaming from the heat radiating from her body.

"Don't fret for your brother," Severin said. "He tried to kill that man because that's what he's supposed to do."

All around her, the rain sizzled. She turned her eyes away from Severin and focused on the garden of cypress knees that rose out of the water beyond.

Not real. Didn't happen like that.

She had to remain calm. The vision had been so tangible. So detailed. Marc never intentionally hurt anyone.

I need treatment.

She fixed her gaze on the contours of the tree's wooden root system, steadying her breathing. She had to return to the swamp house right away. She would be caught in the storm for sure, and to what end? She couldn't even escape Severin.

But something about the tangle of cypress knees prevented her from turning away. One of the larger roots was jet black and rounded, not brown and pointed like the others.

The wind picked up. The storm had arrived.

She looked at Severin, and then back at the jags of cypress knees which were now fading behind a curtain of rain. The large round root moved. It bobbed ever so slightly with the motion of the water.

Madeleine gasped and stood, rushing forward to look at the large round shape that was not a cypress root. A human head, hidden under a blanket of wet black hair.

"Oh my God!" Madeleine said, and then again with growing alarm, "Oh my God!"

Behind her, Severin began to giggle.

How could Madeleine trust her own eyes? She thrust an oar into the water and shoved the boat closer, trying to get a better look. She could see the rest of the body below the surface. She reached over the side of the boat and lifted the face, soft black tendrils falling away in wet clumps. The girl had long dark lashes to match her thick black hair, and her olive skin had gone ghostly pale in death.

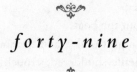

forty-nine

BAYOU BLACK, 2009

ADELEINE SHIVERED IN THE rain, unable to believe the dark-haired girl who swayed in the water below her was actually dead. Her young expression was so peaceful; she looked like she had simply fallen asleep. But no way could she be alive; she had been lying face down in the water.

With trembling hands, Madeleine put her fingers to the waxen throat, hoping to find a pulse. But she found no sign of life, and the girl's skin was as cold as the November waters that enveloped her. Her body rolled under the pressure of Madeleine's hand, and as it did, through the girl's torn clothing she caught sight of gray, bloodless wounds in her back and chest.

From behind, tiny hands shoved Madeleine's back. She lost her balance and went hurtling toward the water.

She screamed and grabbed at the boat, but too late. A shock of cold purple water swallowed her and pointed roots sliced at her flesh. She had fallen directly upon the dead girl, and the body lolled underneath.

Madeleine shrieked, floundering. The rain was now coming down so hard she was unable to tell whether her lips were in the water or out. Aquatic scavengers skittered across her body as they abandoned the corpse.

Madeleine flailed, swallowing foul liquid. The girl's body was now completely entangled with Madeleine's, and the cold, raw clay-like feeling of dead skin raised an instinctive panic. She floundered with her in a horrific water ballet until she was able to scrabble up onto the base of the tree.

Severin laughed from the boat.

Lightning tore through the sky, and the sound of thunder broke simultaneously. Madeleine shuddered, crouching on a ridge of inhospitable cypress knees. Bleeding, teeth chattering, she couldn't move, terrified of what lurked beneath the surface of the water. The skiff bobbed only a few feet away, but it was growing obscure behind the thick downpour.

The wretched body had gotten wedged in the cypress knees in the struggle, and the face was now tilted up toward the heavens. Even in the rain, Madeleine could see that she was very young, and lovely. Long, thick lashes and . . .

A sudden jolt of recognition: Anita Salazar. Madeleine cried out and reached for her, grasping at her face. She was so very clearly dead. Nothing to be done for her. Madeleine felt a ghastly uselessness.

What was Anita doing here? Madeleine's thoughts ran tilting and frenzied. And then: *I shouldn't be touching her.*

She realized this was a crime scene, and the police would want it left alone so they could gather evidence. Madeleine would go straight to Sheriff Cavanaugh. A team would come out to recover Anita's body and . . .

But no. It would be too late. The storm would soon bear down on the tiny cove and anything could happen. Anita's body would likely wash away into the Gulf, lost forever. Madeleine racked her mind for someplace—anywhere—here in the bayou where she could seek help. But this section was utterly wild. The only place she could think of was an empty fishing cabin with no phone lines and no electricity.

Zenon's fishing cabin.

My God.

Zenon killed this girl.

The cold rain penetrated to her marrow as she realized Anita must have gotten away from him somehow. He had been hunting her when Madeleine saw him on the far banks. Suddenly she knew that if the storm did not claim Anita's body here in the bayou, Zenon would.

If she left her behind and the body disappeared, what was she supposed to do about it? Tell the authorities that she found Anita's remains in the bayou, and then promptly check herself into some mental health facility? Her story would be met with a jaundiced eye. No, she had only one choice: She had to bring her back.

Madeleine wiped wet hands across her face. The storm was more violent than she had expected, and it drew the little cove into its maw. For the first time she realized she might not make it home. And yet, she had to try.

Slowly, gingerly, and with loathing, she lowered herself from atop the cypress knees, back into the chilling depths. The water stung the cuts on her arms and legs. She eased herself over to Anita and encircled her with her arms. The body slid without resistance. The boat had drifted further away, so she tucked Anita under her arm and swam over to it, clutching at the side.

Severin was leaning over, watching.

"Leave it here."

"Go away," Madeleine tried to say, but the effort of gasping for air in the rain and swamp water prevented her from speaking aloud.

She tried to heave Anita over the side of the boat, but whenever she raised her the effort caused her own body to sink below the surface, and she had to lower her again in order to catch a breath. She was unable to get enough leverage to lift her high enough.

Finally, Madeleine gave up and tried to pull the skiff in toward the cypress knees. She clutched Anita with one hand while trying to grasp the tether with the other, kicking out her legs in a frog swim. It was slow going, but she eventually made it back to the tangle of roots.

She wedged Anita into a crevice and pulled the boat firmly

toward her. Her arms and legs trembled from the exertion, and she was utterly exhausted. She planted a foot in the root system.

Severin scowled from the stern, arms folded. "I told you to leave it here. Now Zenon's gonna come for you too."

Madeleine gasped and looked back toward the mouth of the cove. No sign of his fishing boat, and anyway it couldn't fit through the narrow passage. But of course his boat was not there. She had believed the words of Severin, a hallucination.

But then lightning flashed, and she saw him.

He was swimming into the cove, a mere twenty feet away, his body camouflaged by the storm.

"Oh my God," Madeleine breathed.

She braced herself against the roots and heaved. Time slowed and her arms turned to lead. She despaired, knowing she would have to give this up and climb in alone. She could survive; Anita could not. But just as she was about to abandon the effort, Anita's body spilled over the edge into the skiff.

Zenon was just over ten feet away, thrashing closer. He had seen Anita.

Madeleine scrambled in after her and tore wildly at the motor, and it roared to life. Zenon's hands reached up from the water and grasped the side. He heaved himself, the boat tilting under his weight, and Madeleine knew it was too late to throw the throttle.

She grabbed the oar and bashed him full in the face, throwing all her weight into that single motion. Zenon fell back into the water, and Madeleine nearly toppled over the side after him.

She regained her balance and hit the throttle, roaring away as he grabbed at the side again. But he was unable to grip it, and Madeleine sped out of the cove. She felt the tug. An urge to turn the boat around and collect him. But Zenon's skill hadn't improved much, whereas Madeleine was getting good at letting his implanted thoughts pass through her like vapor.

The skiff entered the main waterway and was immediately broadsided by turbulent water. It floundered. The wind had intensified, white caps appearing and disappearing in winks on the surface.

The current pushed her sickeningly closer to the bank. She was forced to slow the throttle, and it took ages to point the nose in the proper direction. She cast furtive glances at the gunwale, half-expecting Zenon's fingers to curl around it. She finally regained control and began speeding south.

Nightfall was hours away yet, but the storm allowed only battleship colors in the dimmest light. Rain sliced at her, and water sloshed in the boat.

She wondered if Zenon had drowned. She thought of his body, that lithe, solid thing that had nearly entangled with her own. She was stricken with incredulity. He was a madman; criminally insane. He would have a head injury from the bashing she'd given him. Maybe he did drown. Was drowning, even now.

But more likely, he was out there somewhere, already aboard his fishing trawler, coming after her. She'd had a solid head start, but he had the more powerful vessel.

The gale and tide kept trying to force her back inland. She would have gladly turned around and headed that way, but this particular channel led to nothing but swampy wilderness. Her best bet was to head south toward the open sea, turn down the Intracoastal, and then inland again toward home. First opportunity, she'd telephone for help.

The skiff chugged forward. The water whirled, the storm having liberated it from the marsh. She could now see almost nothing. One dim light glimmered behind her, so faint it might have been an illusion, but she had to assume it belonged to Zenon's boat.

Her skiff rode the waves head-on, and the motor did not die.

fifty

*I*N THE MONTHS SINCE Chloe had sacrificed the Terrefleurs herd and they'd refined the sugar on the plantation, she'd had some luck in subsidizing cane through other smaller farms run by fellow black sharecroppers. She'd also put Bruce Dempsey to work for her in New Orleans, arranging for the transportation of liquors from those same sharecroppers' cellars to underground buyers in New Orleans.

This had helped narrow the financial gap caused by these rogues who now waited for her in the parlor. They were representatives of the Sugar Trust, and much as she loathed them, she needed their co-operation in order to keep Terrefleurs from imploding. These men were staunchly opposed to conducting any business with her. She was about to change that.

She stood in the pantry with Rémi, her hands on his arms.

"Rémi, listen to me. Did you see those men? When I came through the door just now, did you see the men waiting in the parlor with Jacob?"

Rémi's gaze chased through the pantry, sweat at his forehead. He

stepped toward the parlor door. Chloe grabbed his arm and stepped
in front of him.

"Rémi, no! They can't see you like this." She put her hands to
either side of his face and made him look at her. "Answer me. Did
you see them?"

Rémi's eyes found hers. He nodded.

She said, "Tell me something about them. Ask the river devil."

Rémi narrowed his eyes. "Ulysses. I will not go near him. Don't
you know what it means?"

"This plantation has a chance. We cannot continue refining sugar,
but if we can make the Sugar Trust work with us, we may survive.
You must tell me something about those men."

But he wasn't listening. His gaze had chased some drift of movement.

"Stupid man!" She slapped him across the face.

He caught her wrist and drove her against the wall. A jar of tepins
tumbled from the shelf behind and smashed to the floor.

He looked at her, confused, and then his eyes snapped. "Woman,
you must not do that. It's dark in the tunnels. I don't recognize you.
The child . . ." He put his hand to her belly.

She shoved him away. "Another child, yes, and I will take them
all away from here if this plantation dies."

She folded her arms over her chest and glared at him. "Oh, see?
Now suddenly you hear me so clear."

He stepped toward her. "Chloe, you could not do such a thing."

"No? If I must care for all these babies, and we lose our home,
what you think? I can look after crazy man too?"

He was staring at her, eyes dull. A despair that bordered on defeat.

She stepped toward him. She put her hand to his cheek, lifted her
face, and kissed him. He did not respond. She took his hand and put
it back on her belly.

"Rémi, the river devil pays no mind if he ruins us or saves us.
You must be strong for your family. You must make him save us."

She wrapped her arms around his neck and pulled him into her;
let him feel the force inside. She lifted her face again and this time he

kissed her back. His hands gripped her with restrained ferocity, as though he didn't dare let go.

He said, "It frightens me when I realize I've hurt you."

"But it does not frighten me. Now look. Look into the tunnels. Ask the river devil to show you."

❦

RÉMI THRASHED. HE FOUGHT against something Chloe could not see, something beyond the layers. He had told her what she needed to know, but she wanted more. There were secrets in there beyond stupid tattle-tales. The more lost in a fever he was, the closer he could get to real truth.

"Tell me, Rémi, what do you see?" She reached out to him.

He fought. Her fingers closed over his forearm. To touch him was like passing a hand through flame without getting burned, a wavering pressure that radiated from him. She felt it course through her. The door from the parlor opened. The room spun, and she felt herself falling. Rémi was swinging his fists.

"Damn your eyes!" he cried.

"Rémi!" Jacob Chapman lunged for him.

Chloe was on the floorboards. She saw the astonished faces of the men in the parlor through the open door. She reached over and closed it gently as they stared, aghast.

Jacob struck Rémi. He hammered him to the ground. Easy to subdue, because Jacob was only fighting one man. In Rémi's world, who knew how many attackers there were? He probably didn't even know Jacob existed at this moment.

"Put him outside," Chloe said.

"He wants me to kill the boy," Rémi said. "The one with the blood eye. I will not!"

Chloe rose to her feet and stretched against pain, one hand to her back and the other to her belly. She opened the rear door to the stairs. Jacob hoisted Rémi and heaved him through it.

"Just leave him be now," Chloe said, but Jacob had slung Rémi's arm around his own shoulders, and was dragging him down the rear stairs.

Chloe closed the door behind them. Her hand went to her lips and came back with blood. Jacob must have thought that Rémi had hit her. He might have—Chloe wasn't certain, but she suspected she'd injured herself as she'd swooned. So much power. She still felt a little drunk with it.

Beyond the window, Jacob was dragging Rémi toward the kitchen house. One of the workers joined them in the path and assisted.

The door to the parlor opened behind her, and one of her guests appeared.

"Madame! We are concerned for your safety!"

Chloe darted to him and stopped the door swing with her foot. "I'll only be a moment longer. Bernadette!"

Bernadette appeared beyond the man's shoulder.

Chloe said, "Please see that these gentlemen are refreshed with our best cherry bounce."

The man in the doorway gaped at her with a look of horror. "We've enjoyed your drink already. Refreshing after the silly ban on alcohol. But really, I must insist . . ."

"In just a moment," Chloe said, and closed the door on him.

She pressed her forehead against it. She had them, she knew it. Before she even stepped out and initiated the meeting, she had them. But already it wasn't enough. Terrefleurs' new crop, like so many other sugar plantations in southern Louisiana, was showing signs of mosaic cane-rotting diseases.

New Orleans. That was where she needed to look. The bootlegging with Bruce Dempsey had already yielded more than the sugar crop. She should focus on that. Use the warehouse on Magazine.

The back door opened and Jacob reappeared. "You're hurt."

"I am fine. *Ecoutez*, these men from the Sugar Trust, they have brought in cheap sugar from the islands and have skirted the tariffs."

"What? That ain't legal."

"If we make it known, the plantations will revolt and the government will put them in prison."

"Come now, Chloe, how could you possibly know this?"

"I have opened these secrets, and now we must use them to make these men resume business with Terrefleurs."

"But that's blackmail."

She threw him an impatient scowl. "You will help me with these men?"

"Of course, I'm at your service. Y'all know I'll help y'all out any way I can."

"Is that really so?" she said, her voice softening.

He blinked. "Of course."

She opened the door to the parlor.

"Wait," Jacob said, but she ignored him and joined her guests.

They had their hands on their tumblers of cherry bounce, and looked up at her with both wonder and terror. Jacob grabbed her wrist and put his handkerchief to her mouth. She jerked away from him, but saw that the handkerchief was covered in blood. She frowned and dabbed at her lips with the handkerchief, and settled herself onto the lady's chair.

fifty-one

BAYOU BLACK, 2009

*I*T SEEMED LIKE HOURS had passed, and Madeleine had kept checking over her shoulder for the glimmer from Zenon's craft. Hadn't seen it again.

She risked shining a spotlight at the shore and could see that the banks had fallen back and given way to another artery of water. She hoped it was *her* artery of water, though in the darkness it was impossible to tell. If she was wrong, she could get lost in an endless maze of cypress forests. She snapped off the light.

She angled the craft and let up on the motor, allowing the current to push her into the little waterway. Finally, the waves from the Intracoastal receded to the calmer whitecaps of the small channel.

The wind and the current were finally at her back, and they lifted and carried the tiny boat toward home. The knowledge that the journey would now get easier was a balm to her nerves. But she couldn't tell whether she was headed down the right path. It seemed like she should have at least reached the saltwater intrusion station.

Severin was looking over her shoulder. "He is angry, very, very."

Madeleine tasted bile. She knew she could very well be having paranoid delusions about everything. But she cut the motor and listened. The wind had lifted, but its steady breeze still chimed in the treetops on either side of her. Severin said nothing, watching in the direction where Madeleine was leaning. Madeleine strained her ears as her heart began to race. If he had made it down the channel, it would not be long before his superior craft overtook hers. Ever so faintly, she did hear the sound of another motor. Off in the distance. She drew in her breath, listening through the layers of wind and rain.

And then suddenly, the urgent pulsing of an alarm wrenched through the darkness. Madeleine jumped, causing Anita's body to loll to the side.

What is it? A hurricane warning?

But the alarm was not the kind of piercing rise-and-fall wailing of an emergency alert siren. This sound was more like a rhythmic kind of honking. It was—

It was the saltwater intrusion station. The storm must have surged seawater deep into the bayou, triggering the lock. The alarm was signaling that it was about to seal off the channel.

"Oh dear God!"

She pounced on the motor and ripped the cord. It roared to life and she sent it immediately into full throttle. She shined her spotlight down the channel, speeding toward the gateway.

If she could just make it through, she would be safe. It would close behind her and Zenon would not be able to follow. Even if she ran out of fuel she could make it to one of the tract houses before Zenon even set foot on earthen ground.

"Come on!"

But the small craft could only travel so fast, and she had already pushed it to its limits.

Then, finally, she could make out the lock ahead of her. The alarm pounded in her head. But even in the weak ray of the spotlight, she could see that the gate was closing.

Her motor was already maxed; the boat would not go any faster.

She watched in horror as the gate slowly closed. Her skiff was less than fifteen feet away but the lock was already too narrow. She frantically tried to reverse the throttle, but it was too late.

She was going to crash.

❧

fifty-two

❧

BAYOU BLACK, 2009

ADELEINE THREW HER ARM across her face as the vessel charged the saltwater intrusion lock. She had no sense of the impact itself, but in her next moment of awareness, she was completely submerged and could not breathe. A cold, black, airless void.

She began to flounder, slowly at first, and then with a growing wildness, trying to lift her head for a gulp of air. She was deep below the surface. She could see nothing, and thrashed upward with mounting panic. Pressure increased, crushing her ears. Her lungs contracted, and she feared she would involuntarily inhale.

But she realized she wasn't facing upward. She was at the bottom; she'd been swimming toward the bottom. The bayou felt silky down here. Even the sticks and debris were soft and smooth. She was sleepy, the urgency in her lungs fading. And she thought she might care to lie down. Wrap herself in the amniotic bath of Bayou Black and sleep on the broad, soft bed of clay that lay beneath the forest.

Madeleine lay down on her side, curling her head over her hands in the form of a prayer. The river bottom was black as the inside of a hollow oak. She closed her eyes.

Severin's voice whispered in her ear. "Wake up, Madeleine."

Tiny hands lifted her and tilted her face up. She opened her eyes. Still black down here. And she was so sleepy. But Severin was right.

Madeleine kicked, thrusting her body in a straight line for the surface, clawing at the water above. She broke through and gobbled blessed oxygen. Her throat convulsed, spewing a tide of water, and her lungs felt like they were full of crushed glass.

A tempest shrieked all around. She spun in the water, still sucking for air, when the sight of a small fire caught her eye. At first she was unable to identify where she was, and she watched the flames flicker and dance until they were finally extinguished in black water. She was treading in complete darkness, the sound of thunder rolling around her, and then she remembered.

Lightning flashed, illuminating the shape of some creature nearby, and she lunged in the opposite direction. She had the unreasonable suspicion that it was an alligator. And then in another flash, she could see that it was Anita, floating facedown in the water.

Madeleine swam to her and pulled her toward shore by the hair.

The rain began to spill again, though the wind remained stable. The bank was steep and tangled with brush. Ordinarily it would have been a vertical mess of woody roots, but since the water level had risen to flood stage, the bank was a miniature jungle of partially submerged shrubs that scraped at her skin as she swam in.

She managed to find a dubious foothold and dragged the girl up from the water. Fireworks of pain shot through her chest. Her shoulder wasn't functioning properly. She found no flat surface, no stretch of dirt where she could stand and get her bearings. Nothing but branches and logs and scrub. Every molecule of her body ached. Blood was flowing from somewhere at her forehead; she could taste the rusty liquid, diluted by rain.

Somewhere in the far distance came the purr of a motor.

Madeleine sprang to her feet in a crouch, animalistic, balancing on a log and tightening her grasp around Anita. She pulled the girl deeper into the woods, stabbing herself on sharp sticks. She staggered and groped, her right arm becoming less and less useful from whatever injury she had sustained.

Her body suddenly sank waist-deep into a pool of muck. She set Anita over a log and hoisted herself out of the fetid-smelling liquid, steadying herself with a thick branch.

She tried to take another step, but her muscles refused to obey. She began to tremble. And then to weep. The rain continued its deluge, and the woods hissed in blackness. It occurred to her that she had very little chance of making it to safety like this. She could see nothing, and the way was blocked by fallen trees, pools, and swamp debris. And to try to tackle it all while still carrying the girl . . .

The faintest glow of light appeared, and Severin's face emerged from the darkness.

"You'll die out here."

Madeleine's body would not stop shaking. "It's starting to look that way."

"The water will swallow this place soon."

Madeleine nodded. "I can believe it."

"I can lead you out."

Madeleine looked at her, an abomination of her own mind. Her brain must have manufactured Severin's statement in a desperate play at survival: *Keep trying.*

Well, if she was going to die anyway, she had nothing to lose.

"All right, Severin. Get me out, then."

The girl stood, and a wide halo of light glowed around her. Madeleine could finally see the cypress forest, and discovered she was closer to the channel than she'd thought. Then it occurred to her that it was because the banks were flooding. The water had followed her in, stealing into the forest even as she had struggled ashore.

Severin started walking, and Madeleine heaved Anita's body up and tried to follow her.

Severin stopped. "Not with that. You leave it behind."

Madeleine shook her head. "No."

"You won't be able to carry it that far. You'll die."

"I'll probably die here anyway."

If she could at least drag Anita deeper into the woods, maybe neither of their bodies would wash out to sea. Rescuers stood a better chance of finding them in the heart of the woodland.

"I'm taking this girl with me. Or I might as well stay here and drown."

Severin scowled. "I can show you a place where she won't wash away. They can come fetch her later."

Madeleine considered this. "I'd have to be damn sure it was a floodproof spot."

Severin turned and started walking in a slightly different direction. Madeleine hoisted Anita and followed, trying to ignore the eels of pain that shot through her shoulder.

SHE'D MADE EXASPERATINGLY SLOW progress. She'd had to lift Anita over enormous fallen logs and then climb over them herself. She'd stopped frequently to rest. Most of the time she was either slogging on her knees or scrabbling on her feet with one hand to the ground. She'd carried the dead girl on her back, or dragged her, or whatever it took to move her just a few more feet.

Rain was streaming without pause, and the wind howled. But finally, the muck and pools hardened and real earth solidified below Madeleine's feet. She could tell they were ascending to higher ground though the slope was almost imperceptible. Pine and oak replaced cypress and tupelo gum, and newly formed streams of water gushed by in veins through the earth.

Finally, they came to the highest point: a ridge, though the change in elevation was subtle. Severin pointed to a monstrous oak, and Madeleine could see that its branches would be sheltered from floodwaters. Her only chance.

She used the last reserves of her energy to hoist Anita's body into the cradle of the massive oak. She pawed at the tree with numb fingers, and wedged Anita into a section where the trunk divided into four huge branches. As a safety measure Madeleine removed the belt from around her waist and cinched the girl's body to a limb, hoping it would help keep her stable.

When she finished, Madeleine curled up over Anita in the arms of the great tree, closed her eyes, shivering, and released herself to exhaustion.

fifty-three

NEW ORLEANS, 1920

AT THE FAMILY'S WAREHOUSE on Magazine, where Chloe had quietly established a gambling ring, she began to rely more upon Bruce Dempsey. He was known as "The Brute." The nickname came about because when he introduced himself, his sparse front teeth caused him to pronounce his name "Brute Dempthey." Chloe knew Dempsey was not aware that this was the reason behind his nickname. In his mind, he probably thought they called him The Brute out of deference to his tough reputation, and so he seemed to like it.

Chloe realized the gambling hall itself had proved a brilliant move. She was entertaining the people of New Orleans with dice and cards and an opportunity to take home the evening's pot, so long as they tithed a standard cut to the house. She'd begun it as a small, dirty enterprise, but amidst the excommunication of the devil's drink, sin had come into fashion. She found that whiskey helped loosen gamblers' fingers from their money clips. So effective was the booze in separating cash from gamblers, that Chloe had begun arrangements to increase production. She'd heard that the agents of the Prohibition Unit,

the newly formed task force of the Department of Treasury were paid
laughably small salaries. This made them easy accomplices, and Chloe
had paid them less money for their cooperation than she'd paid the
police. A busy year.

Chloe had also given birth to a baby girl. She'd named her Marie-
Rose. But the infant had been greedy, and had turned Chloe's womb
inside out. Chloe bled for two weeks. Disgusted, she'd handed the
baby over to the capable hands of Tatie Bernadette and the wet nurse
to care for with the rest of the children. For Chloe, they were all
disappointments. The twins made little progress with their exercises
and Patrice had natural talent, but was obstinate.

Shortly after, Chloe left for New Orleans where far more urgent
affairs awaited. Bruce Dempsey had been getting carried away with
himself. He'd been skimming money and had taken to drinking the
newly produced liquor. He no longer wore filthy tattered clothing
but instead swaggered about in sharp suits and felt hats, and entertained boisterous women.

His superstitious fear of Chloe had faded. He'd continued to serve
her because he'd found it profitable, not because he'd feared or felt
indebted to her. He had forgotten that Chloe still possessed his ear.
So Chloe had to resurrect his deference.

She'd suspected that Dempsey had redirected some of the profits to
his own pockets, or to some of the women he'd kept on hand. Also,
although Chloe had forbidden Dempsey to drink, he'd been keeping a
bottle in the warehouse. But Chloe was dependent upon Dempsey's
roguish ways, along with a small crew of other street characters she'd
assembled over time to keep her business safe from other underground
gangs. Criminals, all of them, and greedy. Dempsey himself carried a
reputation as a ruthless murderer. In the days before Chloe had taken
him, he was said to have killed a man for making jokes about his sluggish wit. Since he'd gone to work for Chloe, gossip had churned about
the violent means Dempsey used to extract payment for gambling
debts. And more than one overzealous gambler had disappeared altogether when Dempsey sought his bounty. Rumors flourished.

Chloe's employees at the warehouse each remained loyal to her for one reason or another, and even Jacob Chapman had been a crucial ally as a liaison in legitimate business dealings, but mostly it was The Brute who helped her business grow. He saw to it that everyone performed his job, be it dealing cards or watching the door, and he always succeeded in collecting debts. And yet Dempsey himself was a difficult one to control.

At first Chloe started dropping hints that the spirit Ulysses had told her Dempsey was not trustworthy, and that Chloe should let Ulysses come eat his soul. Dempsey sneered at this, but he still valued his position at the warehouse, and so he assured Chloe that he'd been nothing but loyal.

"Then so be it," Chloe said to him. "But should you take a drink of alcohol, may your gut rebel against your body."

Chloe had shown Dempsey his own severed ear, now white and preserved in a jar of shine. "Do not forget, Bruce Dempsey, you belong to me."

Dempsey had stalked out of the Toulouse Street house with his heavy square jowls clenched, but Chloe could see the anxious wrinkle creasing his face. She'd learned where he'd kept his whiskey stash, and she'd slipped crushed powders into the bottle.

Later, when Dempsey had taken a drink, he'd grown ill and vomited so profusely that he'd been forced to leave the warehouse that night. For a full day, he'd wallowed with a cramping gut and hallucinogenic dreams.

The sickness had been enough to keep him in check, at least for the time being. But were it not for the pharmacist, Chloe might never have regained Dempsey's full loyalty. The pharmacist, Chloe's latest acquisition among her indentured souls, had run up an exorbitant gambling debt. Rather than send Dempsey to collect, Chloe had personally overseen the matter.

The pharmacist worked at a clinic designated as an official opiate dispensary. New Orleans had established the clinic in an effort to reduce the frequency of petty theft in the city, and to drive down the underground price of illegal opiates in hopes of eliminating the entire underground trade.

Chloe had extracted from the pharmacist a small payment on his debt, but also she demanded a supply of morphine. She had intended to take the drug home to Terrefleurs and administer it to Rémi in an attempt to keep him subdued, but when the situation with Dempsey had arisen, she'd decided that she might see what magic the morphine tablets could bring to him.

"You have demonstrate to me a loyalty and spiritual purity," Chloe had told Bruce Dempsey after a week had passed without dalliance. "I know this is difficult for you, because for so long you are a bad man. As a reward for your effort and for being my servant, I give you this tonic that will help purify your soul. Do not forget who take care of you."

Dempsey had eyed the tonic with suspicion. However, he seemed to have been amply spooked by his sickness and hallucinations, and did not seem inclined to provoke Chloe when it came to affairs of the spirit. And so he'd drunk the tonic, and even appeared glad for having done so; for he'd found the effects very pleasant. So pleasant, in fact, he would eventually lose his craving for alcohol altogether, and seek instead only that tonic that he could obtain from one source alone: Chloe.

Chloe had mastered the talent of getting people to do her bidding. Through Rémi, she'd learned secrets of the other world. She used a bend of her mind, the way a convex lens can pull light into a single, concentrated spot. But it took enormous focus. The morphine tonic proved an easier tool to get what she needed from Dempsey.

Tamed, Dempsey had again become Chloe's faithful attack dog, and tolerated no one who dared undermine her endeavors, least of all deadbeats who dawdled in paying their debts. Chloe's profits were soaring. For the first time in a while, Terrefleurs and the entire Le-Blanc estate were flush.

fifty-four

BAYOU BLACK, 2009

"MARC," EMILY SAID.

Madeleine could see nothing. She was in some sort of current, fighting against a river that flowed in darkness. She flailed, grasping at anything to keep her from getting swept away. But when she lashed out, her fingers closed around bramble. Nothing but bramble. It tore open her hands. She stopped struggling.

She heard Emily's voice again: "Marc, I love you."

A tunnel opened, and Madeleine could see silhouettes through matted briar. Marc and Emily.

"Em, you need to leave," Marc said.

"Leave? You can't mean that."

"I mean it!"

The water slowed to an eddy. Madeleine was gasping, spitting out fluid. She could hear their voices through walls of thorny branches that were always curling, always stretching. Marc and Emily's tunnel emitted the only light, and it filtered through to Madeleine in patches. But it illuminated enough that she could now make out gray shoreline. She swam to it and crawled up onto packed mud. She rolled onto her side. A clear view into the tunnel now. It looked like the living room of the Creole cottage on Bayou Black before she and Daddy had cleared it out. The couch and coffee table, the television. Emily looked strange, as though her skin were translucent and light shone from deep within her. A paper lantern of a girl.

Marc said, "You take what you can. You leave here. You get as far away from here as possible!"

"I don't want to leave you, Marc. I'm afraid you might hurt yourself. There's something wrong but you won't tell me."

Madeleine put her hand over her face. "Oh, God, please make it stop."

A face in the shadows. Severin was crawling across the bramble wall like a gecko, the branches snapping as she crossed over and jumped down onto the mud next to Madeleine. Madeleine leaned away from her. But Severin turned around twice on the mud and curled up against Madeleine's waist. Madeleine was too exhausted to react. On the mud, something round and smooth glinted. She picked it up. It felt like a little compact mirror. She held it up to the light and saw that it was a pocket watch. Daddy's watch.

"Hurt myself?" Marc was saying.

Madeleine looked up sharply.

Marc said, "I'm going to hurt *you*, Emily. Do you hear me? I'm going to hurt you *and* the baby. I already tried to kill one man. It wasn't an accident. I lied to you and everyone else about that."

Emily backed away, and when she did, the bramble seemed to recede from her. "You need help. Your sister, she's a psychologist. We should . . ."

Marc's face grew very dark. He took a step toward Emily, and she recoiled. Suddenly, the lights went out. Emily screamed.

"No," Madeleine whispered.

She heard Marc say, "I can make the lights go out without even flipping a switch."

Through the tunnel, the television blinked to life. A KJUN TV-10 journalist was talking about a meth lab bust in LaFourche. In the greenish light of the television, Madeleine could see Marc and Emily facing each other. Emily's hands were clasped over her middle.

Marc said, "I can turn on a TV and a radio, too. I can make a phone call without a telephone."

The radio came on, a metal band competing with the newscaster on the television.

Marc shouted, "Now you leave! You leave Louisiana, and you don't tell me where you're going. In fact, don't tell anyone in my family. And you pray to God we can't find you."

Severin rose to her feet. "Get up."

Madeleine obeyed, numb. Severin was climbing up over a network of roots and Madeleine climbed after her. The sound of Marc's radio went silent, and then the television. Emily was weeping. The light came on again in Marc's tunnel, but it was much more distant now, only shreds of light far below. Madeleine heard the sound of car keys being snatched from a table, and then a door slam. She climbed. Dirt and wood stung her torn hands. As in the swamp, a halo of light surrounded Severin as she led Madeleine up, up, and then they were scaling a tree. It didn't feel as though she were climbing it. She was weightless, and the upward movement was effortless, the way an ant may climb a tree. She heard the storm. Saw her own body. Climbed inside. It was cold.

MADELEINE OPENED HER EYES. Rain. Severin.

"Get up," Severin said. "You'll die up here."

The little girl was hovering above, scorning gravity in her sideways position in the tree. Her hair was wet and oily, her skin glowing silver.

"Go away," Madeleine slurred.

She felt so groggy it seemed that the tree wanted to absorb her into its heart. The pulling sleep was warm, intoxicating.

Severin snarled, and then Madeleine felt razor-sharp fingernails slice into her ear.

Madeleine jerked and sat up. She realized she'd been slumped atop Anita's body.

Severin scrabbled along the underside of the branch and leapt to the ground. She twisted her head and looked up.

Madeleine tumbled out of the tree, her chilled and bleeding fingers unable to close around the branches, and plopped to the earth below. Knees were stiff and slow to react. Madeleine rolled on wet leaves. Severin began to walk into the darkness with the ring of light around her. Madeleine staggered to her feet and followed stiffly.

They were walking along the ridge of one of the *cheniers*. She felt she could close her eyes and follow Severin along the ridge. Could even sleep and still be able to follow. She kept her eyes open, if only to deny credibility to what was happening. Shells crunched beneath her feet and she wondered how often floodwaters reached this height. Her muscles loosened. She was able to move more fluidly. Without having to carry Anita, she felt featherlight, and here on the high ground there were fewer obstructions. The oaks provided vast canopies to slow the rain and keep the ground clear of scrub. She began to harbor hope that she might make it the entire way after all.

The oaks fell away to open fields, and Madeleine was no longer protected from rain by a canopy of trees. The wind whipped at her back and stung her lacerated body, and she hunched forward with her arms folded tightly across her chest. So cold.

Finally, through the veil of rain, she could see lights. A house.

fifty-five

BAYOU BLACK, 2009

*T*HEY WERE ABSOLUTE TROOPERS, that poor, bewildered family who'd been the first people Madeleine came upon when she emerged from the woods in the dark of morning. They'd called the police and allowed her into their home though she must have looked a fright. When Sheriff Cavanaugh arrived a short while later, he insisted on driving her to the hospital himself, and on the way she told him all that had happened. She was careful, however, to leave Severin out of it.

"Did you see Zenon attack the girl?" Cavanaugh asked.

Madeleine shook her head. "When I found her, she was already dead."

"He followed you in the storm?"

"Yes. Well, I'm pretty sure it was him. Someone was behind me in a boat, but of course I couldn't see his face."

"Would you recognize the boat that followed you?"

She nodded. "Yeah, well actually, I saw the boat clearly when I was going in and out of the cove, but once it started to follow me, all I could see was the spotlight." She paused. "It was so dark, and with the rain . . ." She took a breath. "But yeah, I'd recognize it if I saw it again."

She was starting to feel uneasy. What if they found no proof of what Zenon had done?

Sheriff Cavanaugh patted her arm. "Don't worry, darlin. We'll get that sumbitch."

"Do you know where he is?"

"My boys are looking for him now. His truck's at his place, but he ain't there."

"Have you found his trawler?"

Sheriff shook his head. "It ain't docked anywhere so far as we can tell, but until this storm lets up, we won't be able to really look."

Once in the emergency room, the nurse told her to change into a hospital gown. She was splotched with blood, dirt, and the occasional leech. The doctor found she was suffering multiple lacerations, a broken clavicle, a concussion, and, incredibly: dehydration.

The nurse and doctor violated her with needles and sutures and the most uncomfortable shower of her life. None of it mattered, though; she fell asleep while they were still stitching her knees.

DADDY WAS GONE AGAIN. Somewhere around the time Madeleine had been pulling Anita's body from the swamp, there'd been some kind of screw-up on the psych ward at Tulane, and they'd let him out. He disappeared. Considering his going to ground among the homeless, he likely didn't even know what had happened to her.

The doctor had wanted Madeleine to stay overnight, but he'd released her when Ethan showed up to take her home. Sam had come along too, and bless her, she'd brought some fresh clothes. The police had collected Madeleine's belongings right down to the skivvies. They'd needed to send them to the lab for testing since they'd neither found Zenon nor recovered Anita's body by the time Madeleine had left the hospital.

Sheriff Cavanaugh had phoned her as a courtesy. "That storm

moved through and they's another one come up right behind it, and
it's flooding pretty good. We can't get anyone out there to recover
that body just yet."

"I see," Madeleine had said, trying not to acknowledge the twist
in her stomach.

"We goin out first light tomorrow morning though. Skinny little
thing like you can make it with no help, my boys damn sure better
get their asses out there and find her, storm or no storm."

On the drive back, Ethan wouldn't let go of her hand.

"We were so worried," he kept saying, and she felt like a fraud.

She'd told him only half of what happened. The same story she'd
told the sheriff: a recount of surface events. No reference to the world
beyond the veneer, where Severin had drawn her into the briar.

Madeleine would. She'd tell him. Just not now.

She checked the passenger's side mirror. Her truck followed back
there, but she couldn't see Sam behind the wheel through the rain.
Only the headlights. Couldn't see Severin, either. At least not at the
moment.

Madeleine unfolded the paper in her lap, a receipt listing her personal effects which were now in the custody of the Terrebonne Parish Sheriff's Department. Nothing special. Just an inventory of her
clothing, garment by garment, and whatever items had been in her
pockets:

One ball point pen (she'd used it to sign the listing agreement with
Nida);

$5.87 in cash;

One tube lip balm;

But her gaze settled on the last item on the list, the one thing she
hadn't been carrying when she'd first set off into the bayou:

One gold pocket watch.

THEY RECOVERED ANITA'S BODY the next day. But a week later, after a
Thanksgiving spent with Ethan and his family, Daddy still hadn't

appeared. Nor had Severin. Madeleine had no idea what kept Severin away, but she guessed it helped to avoid stress or agitation. Easier said than done. Zenon was still at large, and reporters had been leaving lots of messages. Madeleine honored the sheriff's request to keep quiet until the authorities could bring him into custody. Because Anita had disappeared in Texas and her body had been found in Louisiana, the FBI had gotten involved, and so Madeleine had to retell her story to their investigators and the U.S. Attorney's Office. Apparently, crossing state lines during a crime makes it a federal issue.

Madeleine had been grateful for the time off over Thanksgiving. The idea of working left her exhausted. She'd flatly refused to self-diagnose. Couldn't connect her scientific mind to what she'd experienced.

She just wanted to talk to her father. She had to ask him about the briar. She wondered how long she could keep her secret before it swallowed her alive.

fifty-six

HAHNVILLE, 1922

*T*O KEEP THE NONGAMBLING patrons interested in buying drinks, Chloe had allowed some of the streetwalkers to come into the warehouse and mingle with the crowd. They danced the Charleston in their underclothes and entertained customers in the back room, and they paid a kickback based on the tips they earned.

With money springing from every corner of the warehouse on Magazine Street, worries over losing Terrefleurs had become little more than a lark. If the crop produced not a single sprig of cane next season it wouldn't matter. Terrefleurs now provided a front for the New Orleans operations. If anyone were to ask, the function of the warehouse was to store and distribute cane; an odd explanation in that Terrefleurs was much closer to the sugar refineries than was Magazine Street, but an explanation nonetheless.

Chloe's trips to Terrefleurs had become increasingly rare. Between the country heat and the needs of the children and plantation, Terrefleurs left Chloe feeling like a catfish gasping in the mud. She counted each moment before she could return to New Orleans.

As for Jacob's part, he seemed to thrill at perusing New Orleans with Chloe. As if he relished the fact that he and Chloe were a spectacle in New Orleans, and people looked upon them with disdain. They did not like to see a white man and a black woman together, particularly among the gentler class, even if Jacob acted merely as a chaperone.

Jacob proclaimed to have had enough of the morality movement that had begun to seize the nation, nurturing laws such as the Volstead Act, and breeding activists such as the Ku Klux Klan who held public whippings for adulterers and gamblers. Ever since the day Rémi and Chloe wed, Jacob seemed to have undergone a transformation. He spent much of his time at Chloe's warehouse and in other speakeasies throughout town, countering the morality movement, and preferring to champion the sinner's cause—a much more exciting cause.

fifty-seven

BAYOU BLACK, 2009

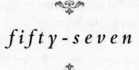 ADELEINE LAY GAZING AT Severin. Ethan was sleeping, his breathing even, his body warm. His hand rested over Madeleine's hip. When they'd made love she'd been able to forget. She'd thrown herself into the sensations of her body and had managed to escape the dread that had been closing in on her. But afterward, even though she'd exhausted her body, her mind had seemed to rebound, and it had turned back to that dread. Worries that Zenon would never be found. That he'd kill again. Sometime during the spin of those worries Severin had stolen back into her awareness.

Now, the little girl was standing in the doorway, staring. With her came a deepening of shadow. A stir beyond the corners.

Please go away, Madeleine thought.

Severin said, "You could not send me away so easily, verily. No more than you could send away your bones."

But what are you?

"I am you and you are we."

Madeleine squeezed her eyes shut. No use. She saw Severin even more clearly through closed eyes: the detail of her nakedness, gray and grimy, and the tunnels of thorns that waited.

Severin spoke again, but when she did she was muttering in Madeleine's own voice. A perfect facsimile. "Even if they catch him and bring him in, what'll they say when they find out we're crazy?"

Madeleine opened her eyes.

Severin was stepping toward her. She switched back to her own child's voice as if to argue back. "Not a shade of worry in that! He will not answer for it. Who would come to find him where he hides? He understands the ways of the bramble!"

And faster in Madeleine's voice: "He'll kill again, I just know it!"

Shooting back in her own voice: "So he will! He begins with us now, so surely! He plans our death even as we wallow!"

HUSH! The thought flew from Madeleine's mind with near-tangible fabric.

Severin went quiet. But only for a moment.

Her eyes brightened and she renewed her argument, but this time she spoke with both voices simultaneously, louder and with mounting hysteria.

Madeleine stumbled from the bed.

Ethan sat up. "What's wrong?"

But Severin was still shouting in two voices at once, and Madeleine could only look at him, blinking. His words seemed so lost behind Severin's chaos. He had no idea what was happening and she felt sick and distant from him. And even as a sense of estrangement swept her, Severin added new threads to her arguments.

—*What will Ethan say when he finds out . . .*

—*Zenon thinks to come for us and send you through . . .*

—*There's no way I can hang onto . . .*

—*He will leave not nary a trace, not nary . . .*

—*Certain to find the tastes to our liking if only . . .*

Madeleine whispered to Ethan, though she could barely focus on him. He was a distant ghost in the bramble now. But she pretended he was right there in front of her.

"It's fine, Ethan," she said, and she couldn't even hear her own voice. "I'm going to get some water. Go back to sleep."

She pulled on her bathrobe. It still smelled like smoke after many washings. She walked carefully toward the door, half-blind from the bramble that now choked the bedroom, hoping that Ethan was going back to sleep. Severin crawled along above her head and maintained the vigil. Other creatures shifted in there too.

Madeleine groped her way out into the flat. She saw tunnels of twisting vines across the walls and ceiling. The television and the couch were there. She looked where the kitchenette ought to be but couldn't see it. She reached instead for the front door and stepped outside.

Fresh air. She switched the automatic mechanism so that she could not lock herself out, and sat down on the landing. A distant sound of night birds. She pressed her mind toward those sounds, listening past Severin's cacophony, stubborn. Severin raged on a little but then seemed to tire, and she quieted. The bramble settled too. It lay still against the neighboring buildings on Magazine.

"All right," Madeleine said aloud to the little girl. "Is it true that Zenon wants to kill us? I mean me?"

"Yes, so surely. He knows the practice to send the living through to the other side. You must gain this skill too and learn—"

"Severin. Listen to me. Can you tell me where he is?"

"Ah! He lies in the briar!"

Madeleine shook her head. "No. In the real world. The physical world. Can you tell me where he's hiding?"

Severin grinned. "A little trip we take, across the thorns a little some. We shall see his hiding hole."

fifty-eight

HAHNVILLE, 1926

WHEN SHE HEARD TATIE Bernadette bustle out of the rear pantry, Marie-Rose pushed open the small door that concealed her within the cupboard. She peeped through the narrow crack and could see Tatie's heavy form waddle out toward the steps to the cellar. She would now be busy bringing elderberries to the kitchen house for making jam, but Rose still had to be mindful of her brothers. If either of the twins learned of the secret niche, well, it would no longer be a secret.

Rose made herself into a little brown bunny, quick and silent, and hopped out. Today being Saturday, no boat would be coming to take them down the bayou to school. She didn't even have to do pigeon exercises. Tatie thought them un-Christian and so she only made them do those when mother was around.

Rose scampered into her mother's parlor and snuck the key from her dressing table, then hurried to the rolltop desk in the great room. She stopped and listened, standing poised and still like a rabbit, prepared to bolt if anyone were to approach.

The house was quiet. The boys were probably out catching frogs, and Maman was, as usual, in New Orleans.

Maman was secretive, more so than Papa. Rose delighted in following and spying on Papa, because he always did such strange things. He, too, loved to spy. He spied on the workers, and Rose spied on him. He also walked with spirits in the woods. Though Rose could not see the spirits, she knew that Papa could, and he spoke to them, too. Rose always wondered what the spirits told him. She sometimes did very wicked things—like tie the twins' school shoes together even though they were always late for the morning boat—just to see if the spirits would tattle to Papa. So far they had not. Instead, Papa largely ignored her. She was a little brown bunny, blending in with her background, invisible to all but the most careful observers.

She closed her eyes and begged the spirits to watch over Papa, and to trust her with their secrets. She hoped they would tell her when there might be a pirate ship passing on the river, or perhaps buried treasure somewhere on Terrefleurs. She was very good at keeping secrets.

Tatie Bernadette would beat her good if she found out she tried to contact the other world. Tatie would think it was like praying, and she mustn't pray to anyone but Lord Jesus. But Rose knew that Maman prayed to all kinds. Not that Rose spied on her, too. Maman didn't come home much and when she did, Rose usually kept out of sight. She had spied on her only once, but had to stop because she was afraid that Maman would stew her in a pot and feed her to the whole plantation if she caught her.

Rose slipped the key into the oblong brass lock in the desk and turned it carefully until she felt, rather than heard, the latch release. She eased up the rounded wooden top to reveal the many drawers and pigeonholes inside, where Maman kept ledger books and personal letters bound with ribbon.

Rose moved the bundle out of the way, careful to remember its original placement. She pressed her hand to the center pigeonhole and pushed a wooden peg through the other side, and pulled out the molding that hid the secret compartment.

She peered into the dark niche and saw a tiny flask of hooch. Nothing else.

She heaved a sigh of disgust. Ever since she had witnessed her father placing the flask in the secret compartment years ago, Rose had been checking to see if someone might have hidden something else important in there. And yet, the result was always the same. Papa had stashed the flask when he heard Maman coming. And now, three years later, the flask still sat there, forgotten. Rose had held faith that one day she would peer inside and find a pirate's map, or an emerald, or at least a sacred root.

Once, Rose had mentioned to Papa that she'd heard it was wise to keep a diary of all your secrets. "You'd have to hide it in a special place, of course," Rose had said, trying to sound casual. "Although there probably isn't one hiding place in all of Terrefleurs. I wish I knew of a hiding place to put a diary."

She had hoped her father would start a journal of his visits with spirits and hide it in the desk. She could then sneak in and read it, and maybe learn about the strange world that captured both her parents' attentions. She might even become a voodoo priestess, more powerful than her own mother.

But it seemed this was a world that would always be hidden. Papa never started the journal, and no one else would speak to her about the spirits. Tatie Bernadette had once whaled the tar out of her when she caught her trying to tie a gris-gris. She had made Rose get down on her knees and pray for forgiveness, and beseech the Lord's protection from the false gods that surrounded her.

Rose scowled at the secret compartment. No hidden treasure. Only a dusty flask of hooch.

She unscrewed the cap and with heroic daring, took a sip.

Her throat seared shut, and her mouth threatened to spray the brew all over the bundled letters. She mashed her lips together with all her might, eyes watering, forcing it back down her throat. Finally, the liquid was in her stomach. She hoped it would stay there.

Why would Papa ever want to drink that? Another secret that ended in disappointment.

Rose slipped her own secret in the compartment, her own diary, and replaced the molding and the wooden peg. She had thus far only made one entry but had vowed to write in it once a week, recording whatever mysteries she could learn from her papa.

She placed the bundled letters in front of the molding and closed the rolltop, locking it with a click. Her face burned with pleasure.

As she ran back to her mother's room, though, her belly began to ache. She fretted that she might be coming down with a stomach flu. She replaced the key in her mother's dressing table and slipped out of the room.

"What are you doing!"

Rose spun around when she heard the sharp voice behind her. She was relieved to see her older sister Patrice standing in the hall, hands on hips.

Rose gave her a grin. "It's all right. Maman's in New Orleans."

"Marie-Rose, Maman catches you, she'll beat you nine ways from Sunday. You best be careful." She turned and started back down the hall.

Rose was elated. Patrice was now her accomplice!

"Don't worry, Patrice," she whispered. "No one will see me cause I'm a little brown bunny."

Patrice's spine went rigid, and she whirled on her sister.

"You hush up!"

She seized Rose by the shoulders and shook her until her teeth gnashed. "Why you talk like that? You know what they do with a little brown bunny? They kill it and eat it! Is that what you want? Be somebody's dinner?"

Rose's jaw went slack and a sob escaped her.

"Patrice," she wailed. "Patrice!"

Patrice released her sister's shoulders, and the little girl sank to the ground in a heap, tears rolling down her face.

"All right, stop that now." Patrice crouched down to put her arm over her sister's shoulders. "Don't you ever trust them, yanh? Don't you listen to Maman when she works those evil games with the pigeons. It's devil's work. She'll feed you to the devil for dinner."

Still weeping, Rose felt Patrice's cool hand smooth the hair from her face, and she allowed her older sister to lead her back to the pantry.

Patrice tensed her lips. "You got to stop that mess about being a bunny. Rabbits aren't clever. They're food. All that *Compère Lapin* shit is pure lies."

Rose halted in mid-sob and stared, astonished by the expletive. She'd never before heard such a thing coming from her sister. True, the stories of *Compère Lapin*, or Brer Rabbit, had inspired her wish to be a little brown bunny. *Compère Lapin* could do whatever he wanted, running free and escaping the fox through his speed and wit.

Patrice retrieved a short length of sugarcane from the cupboard and slipped the cool stalk into Rose's hands, clasping them together.

"You don't want to be somebody else's food, yanh? Better to be an alligator, with sharp teeth. You've got to be strong. And mean."

She basked in the sudden attention of her older sister. But Patrice was already leaving. She opened the outside door, filling the pantry with a fresh breeze.

Marie-Rose blurted, "I hide so nobody sees me. Maman hates me. She says I turned out her room."

Patrice paused and looked back. "You mean womb. You turned out Maman's womb because you came out feet first. You ought not to have done that."

"I'm sorry. Now she hates me because she wanted to have lots and lots of children and she can't no more."

"Any more. It's all right. She only wanted children for—different reasons."

"And Papa doesn't even know I'm here."

"Papa needs our help. Ask him to make you dolls, like the ones he makes for me."

Marie-Rose twisted the cane in her hands and stole a glance at her sister. "But I like the painted bisque dolls from the city. They're so much prettier."

Patrice rolled her eyes. Her skin was smooth coffee and cream. As she tilted her head, the sun caught in her lashes and the clean knot of hair above her long, graceful neck. Marie-Rose wanted to be like her, or make her angry, or both.

Patrice said, "It's good for him to make us the dolls. It keeps the river devil away."

"It does?" Marie-Rose took a step toward her sister, realizing she'd just revealed a secret for her new diary.

Patrice said, "And you shouldn't ought to show Maman your progress with the pigeons. Let her think you can't do it. The twins can't. She might as well believe none of us can."

Marie-Rose scowled. "You're just saying that because I'm the best of the four of us. You don't want Maman to favor me."

Patrice let out a long, slow breath. She put a hand to her hip and looked toward the garden. Marie-Rose watched her.

A pigeon burst onto the landing behind Patrice in a flutter of wings, causing Marie-Rose to jump. It darted past Patrice in the doorway, right into the pantry, thrusting its neck with each step.

Marie-Rose moved backward. "No!"

It spread its wings and came at her, flapping into the air, darting and pecking. Marie-Rose screamed and tried to beat it away. It kept at her. The stalk of cane tumbled to the floorboards. The bird swooped on it and took it in its feet, and then fluttered past Patrice and out the door.

Marie-Rose balled her fists and shouted, "Darn you Patrice!"

"You watch your mouth, young lady."

"But earlier, you said the word—"

"Never mind that. It's high time you think about growing up. You want to be mother's zombie slave you just keep pitching fits and playing like you're a bunny."

Marie-Rose was heaving, furious. But she was also slightly terrified of her older sister, and awed by her calm. Patrice retrieved a knife and a fresh stalk of cane, and peeled back the tough outer green. She handed it over. Marie-Rose accepted it.

Patrice said, "Only way is to try and outsmart Maman. Don't let her catch on to anything you learn, and keep out of her way. Understand?"

"Yes ma'am."

Patrice turned and closed the door behind her. A feather swirled among the dust motes from the wind in the door. Marie-Rose stood alone in the pantry. She put the pliable white wood at the heart of the cane between her teeth and gnawed, sucking the sweet juices.

fifty-nine

BAYOU BLACK, 2009

ADELEINE SAT IN THE living room of the flat, Ethan holding her hand and Jasmine dozing at her feet, while federal agent Gorman listened to her story. When she'd made the call, she hadn't expected him to get up in the middle of the night and come to the flat. Severin was there too, but she seemed uninterested, and most of the bramble had receded from Madeleine's field of vision. The clock showed half past four in the morning.

Madeleine explained to the agent that Zenon might be hiding in an abandoned industrial plant which sat along the Gulf of Mexico at Beaumont, Texas, near the Louisiana border. She'd provided the name of the plant along with instructions for getting there, and had offered up a lie about how she had been there before with Zenon when they were teenagers.

"There's a tall cylindrical structure that looks something like a corn silo," she explained. "You might find him in there."

Agent Gorman watched her face as she spoke. "Why would he be in there, as opposed to another building?"

"The lock is broken, and there's usually nobody around."

"I see." Agent Gorman paused, still watching her. "And why didn't you tell me about this before?"

"I didn't think about it until now. I couldn't sleep. I was thinking about Zenon, and then I remembered the old plant. It would be a perfect place for him to hide." The lies were tumbling more and more easily off her tongue. She shrugged. "I may be wrong, but it's worth a try."

Agent Gorman's gaze burned on her. Madeleine was certain he knew she was lying. Ethan listened, sleepy-eyed.

Gorman said, "Why would he go to a place you know about? Knowing you might tell us?"

"Like I said, I may be wrong. I'm sorry to have gotten you up in the middle of the night."

This was true; Madeleine could be wrong. She almost hoped she was wrong. She was placing a tremendous amount of credibility on something that was either a phenomenon or madness. But she knew better. Severin and her briar patch had revealed the truth.

Gorman continued to stare, expressionless. Madeleine did her best not to squirm.

"All right. We're checking it out. Anything else I should know?"

She flinched, remembering one other thing: In the vision Severin had showed her, Zenon had not been alone. She'd seen another male figure within the darkness of the industrial plant, about Zenon's height, broad-shouldered, chewing on a toothpick or something and wearing a porkpie hat. But how could she possibly tell Gorman that Zenon had an accomplice in such a way that Gorman would trust the information? Already he seemed to sense she was lying about how she knew about the plant.

"I can't think of anything else," Madeleine said.

"I trust you'll be available if we need you?"

She shrugged. "I'll be here."

HOURS LATER, AFTER MADELEINE had given up entirely on sleep and had made coffee while Ethan showered, she called Agent Gorman to find out whether they'd made any progress. He informed her that they'd picked Zenon up early that morning, and he was now in custody. Madeleine felt such relief that tears coursed down her face. Perhaps now she could stop focusing on the horrible murder and figure out what was going on with herself. Perhaps. Once she was sure they had a strong case against him. Then she'd be able to relax.

Gorman had, however, refused to divulge where they had found Zenon, citing case confidentiality. Madeleine suspected that he was just being obnoxious, though; no reason why he couldn't tell her whether they found Zenon at the industrial plant in Beaumont. She suspected he was playing mind games because he had guessed that she'd lied about how she knew the place.

Her stomach churned. She wanted so very badly to know whether what Severin had showed her was real. It would be one more piece of evidence to support the argument that she was not crazy. That something else was going on.

She caught a glance of herself in the mirror, already dressed for work in navy blue slacks and a white button-down. Even the bruises were faded. Almost normal-looking. The sound of Ethan's shower was soothing.

She switched on the TV and surfed until she found the news. They showed images of an armed robbery caught on a security camera. Madeleine chewed her lip, watching. And then came the next headline, "Manhunt Ends," and Zenon's face flashed. The reporter divulged that he'd been picked up early that morning at an industrial plant near Beaumont, Texas.

Confidentiality, my butt.

Madeleine listened carefully to every word, but no mention of a second man. She was worried, but what could she do about it? She sank onto the couch.

"Severin."

"Yes?"

"What about my father? Can you tell me where he is?"

"Another little look?"

"I'd rather you just told me."

"Ah! Would you just? Why would that be pleasing to me?"

"What is it that you want?"

Severin smiled, a slow, malicious expression that made Madeleine's blood grow cold. "A little sport. A game or such."

Madeleine didn't want to think what she meant by that. She recalled the way Severin had been toying with the rat in Bayou Black—her version of a game.

Severin pouted. "If we wish to see the father we must go have a look in the dark caves."

"I have to go to work in a few minutes. I'd better not."

"Yes, the ward. The people touched in the head. They love to listen to the whispers."

Madeleine stared at her. "You realize you can't come with me, don't you?"

Severin gave her a nasty look. "I come when I like!"

"Who are you talking to?"

Madeleine looked up, surprised, and saw Ethan dressed and ready for work.

Madeleine gestured a little unsteadily at the television. "They got him."

Severin was saying, "Touched in the head. We whisper to one to bite the other. A fun game, yes . . ."

The room grew darker as the bramble advanced.

"I . . . I think I'm going to stay home today after all," Madeleine said.

Ethan was looking at her with concern. The television rambled and Severin kept going with her nasty words. Madeleine couldn't make out what Ethan was saying. She wanted so badly to talk to her father about all of this. All her years of education and research seemed suddenly irrelevant. She needed to hear him speak about his experiences, and she would be listening with a new set of ears.

Madeleine said, "I have a headache. Can't concentrate."

She was barely aware when Ethan kissed her good-bye.

⁂

AGENT GORMAN SUMMONED HER to the FBI's Louisiana headquarters on Leon C. Simon Boulevard. Usually, he would come to her place or call her if he had questions, so the request to come to their offices was an unusual one. She wondered if he asked her there as a means to intimidate her.

She was dismayed to discover that the topic of the interview was Zenon's hideout in Beaumont. Gorman and another agent asked her to go over what happened in the swamp and how she came to know about the industrial plant. They stood over her, and asked her the same questions over and over again. Hours passed, and she began to feel like a broken record, repeating herself in that closed-in room.

Apparently Zenon had denied ever taking her there as teenagers, which is something she had expected. But, the agents had learned that the plant had not been abandoned until six years ago, when she was already in her twenties.

Oops.

Madeleine cleared her throat. "Their offices might have been active. But that silo-looking thing was abandoned. The lock has been broken for years."

A decent lie, she thought. She had no idea what else to tell them. Absolutely no way was she going to tell them about Severin.

Gorman exchanged looks with the other agent. "Why would Mr. Lansky deny having accompanied you there?"

She shrugged. "Zenon Lansky is out to get me. He'd probably say anything to discredit me."

"That's true." Gorman settled himself in a chair opposite her. "Except I don't believe you either."

She swallowed. "I can't help that."

Silence crushed in around her. She felt the urge to say something else. To prattle on in some wild explanation. But she guessed that's exactly what they wanted. The more she spoke, the more likely she was to expose her secrets.

She pulled back her chair and stood. "Look, we've gone over and over this, and I've helped you all I can. Now I'm going home."

"We're not finished yet." Gorman placed a hand on her arm to detain her.

She felt the temperature rise in her blood.

Lie or no lie, you'd think I was the murderer!

"*I'm* finished." She removed his hand from her arm. "And unless you're going to arrest *me*, I'm going home."

The door opened and a woman appeared.

"Please wait a moment, Dr. LeBlanc."

She had obviously been observing them somehow. She introduced herself as U.S. Attorney Kristen Jameson. Her strawberry blond hair held a tinge of gray, and she wore an expensive suit and very little makeup.

"I know you're tired, and it seems like you're repeating yourself," Ms. Jameson said. "I've asked the agents to be very thorough with this investigation."

She gestured for Madeleine to sit. Madeleine looked at the agents with suspicion, then sighed, and sank to the chair.

Jameson sat next to Madeleine. "We're trying to build a strong case against Mr. Lansky. But there is a serious lack of evidence. We have tested the blood found in the plantation house in Hahnville, and we have been able to match it to blood samples taken from Angel Frey. She's been missing for some time, but we still don't have a body for her yet."

"Angel Frey?" Madeleine's heart began to race. "I heard about her. My God. That was her blood in the plantation house?"

"The police are working very hard to come up with something concrete to connect him."

"Her blood in that house? That sounds like pretty strong evidence to me."

"It's a good start," Jameson agreed. "But Mr. Lansky asserts that he hasn't been to the plantation property in years."

"But I saw him there. And my father did too."

"We are anxious to talk to your father. *If* he can be located."

Madeleine bit her lip.

Mrs. Jameson said, "But even so, it's my understanding that your father has mental issues. Not the best candidate for a witness."

Madeleine swallowed, cheeks burning, and managed to nod.

"But either way, Dr. LeBlanc, right now it's just you. We can't prove Mr. Lansky was there. Anyone could have gotten into that old abandoned house. And," she said, watching Madeleine's face, "it does seem odd that you're the only witness we have, and you can put him both at the plantation *and* at the swamp. *And* you located him in Beaumont. You have to admit, it's quite a coincidence."

Madeleine's hands were going numb. "I guess that does seem strange."

The U.S. Attorney stared at Madeleine's face. Madeleine refused to move. Didn't dare flinch. She felt that if she so much as batted an eye, she would lose whatever reserve of calm was left to her and the bramble would take over.

"All right," Jameson finally said. "I will tell you this: It's beginning to look like the bulk of our case against Mr. Lansky will hinge on your testimony, and we want to make absolutely sure that you are a credible witness. That's why we have to ask so many questions."

"There's no other connection between Zenon and Anita Salazar?"

Jameson shrugged. "We do have witnesses that can put the two of them together. We were hoping to pull evidence from the victim herself, but due to the extreme conditions her body was subjected to postmortem, anything that might have been there is contaminated. We were hoping for something stronger."

"And you've searched Zenon's fishing cabin in Bayou Black, and his house in Plaquemine too?"

She nodded. "We found a stun gun and pepper spray at the fishing cabin, but he sells those at his store. It's looking like we've recovered as much evidence as we're going to get. You will be our key witness, Dr. LeBlanc."

Ms. Jameson drew a deep, tired breath. "I hope you're ready."

❧

sixty

❧

NEW ORLEANS, 2009

SHEILA PRICE PACED THE street, muttering to herself and wringing her hands. There had been a cold snap, and nobody was buying. She tugged at the lacy sheer black dress that barely covered her butt. Despite the brisk temperature, Sheila started to sweat. She needed a fix.

She walked back to the heart of Iberville as quickly as her high heels could carry her, and found Carlo working the corner. He wore a blue knit cap and a denim jacket lined with fleece.

"Carlo, set me up, baby," she said.

Carlo looked at her. "Mm hmm. You know the deal."

"Look, I ain't got jack right now. I'll bring it to you later."

"Yeah, right."

"Come on, baby, I ain't goin nowhere. I'll pay you as soon as I get it."

Carlo spat. "You won't be bringin in nothing you stand round here tryin to work me. Get on out there and find yourself a friend, then you come see me."

Sheila cursed and hustled away. She wrapped her arms around her thin body, more from agitation than from the cold. She joined Bea, who was already working the walk.

"How you doin?" Sheila said.

Bea shook her head. "Not too good, baby. Ain't nobody need a date on a night like this."

Sheila paced. "Bea, you got any money? I need to get a hamburger for my baby."

Bea laughed. "I heard that one before. Listen honey, if I had any cash, I wouldn't be standin out here on no street corner tonight. And if anyone gonna get a fix with my money, it's me."

"It really is for my baby," Sheila said.

"Your kid's stayin over at my mama's house, and she already feed him."

Sheila snorted.

FOR CARLO, BUSINESS WAS not so bad. The usual folks had been coming by his corner. Around ten o'clock, Avery came down from his perch atop the stairwell.

"What up?"

Avery shook his head. "Nothin good, man. The ambulance done come around here, picked up one of the customers."

"So?"

"I heard a couple a others went to the hospital, too. They all bought their shit from us. The good shit."

Carlo cursed. He knew all the regulars by name, but he didn't ask Avery who had gotten sick.

Avery looked Carlo in the eye. "You get your stuff from the same dude you always do?"

Carlo grunted. He managed to keep Avery in the dark about who his suppliers were, and he was not about to make an exception now. It was true that Carlo had found another supplier who cut him a good deal, and from the sound of things, the guy must have cut the stuff with some kind of filler.

"We can't sell that shit now. Word get out, ain't nobody gonna buy from us. They'll all go up the street."

Carlo gave him a hard look. "Oh? Well I guess you willing to give up your cut, then?"

"We done a little business already."

Carlo shook his head. "Ain't enough. I still got a load of that shit up there!" He pointed a thumb toward the brick building behind him. "The hell I s'posed to do, just throw it out?"

Avery shoved his fists in his pockets.

Carlo put a hand on his shoulder. "Aight, we gonna make this one quick. Any good customers come along, you tell them to come back in a few days. You see any a the real messed up junkies, send'm down to me, we'll make'm a real good deal. They probably won't even know if they get sick."

Avery nodded. "You gonna let'm get it on here?"

"Naw, make sure they stay in the empty buildings. Let'm ride it out where no one's around. You get back up there and keep watch for Task Force. We'll wrap it up quick."

Avery strode across back to his stairwell and wound his way up to the top where he had a clear view of the streets.

✖

SHEILA WALKED BACK AND forth, blessing passersby with her smile, but they were few and far between and no one stopped to talk. A police car approached and Bea and Sheila ducked into the liquor store until it passed.

Sheila could stand it no longer. "I'll be back in a little while."

Bea said, "Don't be gettin no fix from Carlo. I heard two people already done got sick offa his junk."

Sheila glanced back at Bea, but hurried down the street. She hoped Bea was wrong.

❧❦❧

DADDY BLANK STRETCHED HIS legs into the night and heaved himself out of the car.

"Nah, I didn't expect you'd want to come. God forbid you be seen out here."

He patted the extended hand, and closed the car door. Raindrops shimmered on black paint as the car disappeared into the darkness.

He was damned. They were all damned, he and his children. And now they were facing off, and the only remaining solutions were grim.

Better stay away from Maddy for now. Too dangerous for him to be around her.

The more effective medication was not available at the hospital. A gentle dose of China White would wrap him in a warm, tingling euphoria that made even the most troublesome questions of life and death seem unimportant. He'd already had a fix or two from the street corner pharmacist, and the effect had long since dissipated.

❧❦❧

"HEY, CARLO," DADDY BLANK said. "You got a good horse for me?"

"Nah, but I can fix you up with something else. You want blow?"

Daddy Blank frowned.

"How bout some Viagra?" Carlo laughed.

"Son, why don't you quit with the smart mouth and give me what I came for."

Carlo shook his head. "You better come back in a few days. I'm outta stock."

"Bullshit, you cretin. Why you giving me a hard time? Look." He fished in his pockets and pulled out all he had. "Take it all." He shoved the cash into Carlo's hand. "There, now be a good boy and make a damned sale."

Carlo tucked the money out of sight. He signaled for Avery to give Daddy Blank a double supply to match his double payment. The stuff was worthless anyway, and Daddy Blank was not really a true regular.

"Look, Daddy Blank, we almost out of supply and got some pissed-off customers." Carlo gestured toward the empty building. "You be cool and take that shit in there where no one can see you."

"Fine," Daddy Blank said.

"Hey, Daddy B." The two men turned and saw Sheila walking toward them.

"Hello there, Sheila, those are pretty shoes you got on," Daddy Blank said as he walked away.

"You want some company?" she called after him.

He shook his head and disappeared.

Sheila continued toward Carlo, trailing her finger along the chain-link fence. "Daddy Blank said I look pretty."

Carlo folded his arms. "He said your *shoes* was pretty. You find yourself a friend, like I told you?"

Sheila shook her head. "Ain't nobody out tonight." She leaned in close and continued trailing her finger from the chain-link up the expanse of Carlo's arm. "I was thinking, maybe you could be my friend."

Carlo looked her over. She was still pretty, though her lifestyle was taking its toll on her looks. Her features were turning hard, her mouth starting to pull back in a permanent clench. Nevertheless, still pretty.

Carlo took her by the elbow and steered her toward a battered railroad house a few doors down. His supply was worthless anyway.

"Tonight's your lucky night."

❧❧❦❧❧

sixty-one

❧❧❦❧❧

NEW ORLEANS, 2009

*T*HE POLICE PULLED DADDY Blank's body from an abandoned building in Iberville, a shadowed neighborhood between the French Quarter and the Garden District. A junkie was the one who'd called it in, but not until after he had had his own fix and was coming back down.

Madeleine's father was not the only drug-related death that week. She learned that a rogue supply of China White had hit the streets, killing Daddy and a prostitute, and putting several others in the hospital. As she wandered through the industrial flat, Severin followed her from room to room, sometimes whining or playing, and sometimes speaking sinister words.

Madeleine steeled herself. She had to work out her father's affairs, and knew that the act of putting things in order would help her maintain a little sanity, whatever that meant. She sat on the couch with the telephone, tears streaming, making the necessary calls to notify her father's friends and begin arrangements for a funeral.

Jasmine dropped a little red rubber ball into Madeleine's lap. Madeleine threw it and Jasmine fetched it, and they repeated this over and over again, and all the while Madeleine was talking on the telephone and trying to block out Severin's chatter of how she brought on her father's death because of her magnetism for bloodshed. It was like trying to listen to the radio and the television at the same time, but somehow the act of playing fetch with Jasmine helped Madeleine to focus.

When she hung up, she forced herself into the kitchen to make dinner. Though she was not the least bit hungry, she had to do something. It seemed that keeping active kept the bramble away.

She was cutting up some chicken, her hands glistening with its carcass, when the phone rang. She wiped her hands with a paper towel as she grappled for the phone. It was Sam, calling from her cell phone to tell her she was on her way. Apparently she had found out from Vinny. Madeleine told her that it wasn't necessary to come over, that she would be fine, but Sam was having none of it.

"Is Ethan there with you?"

"No, he was in with a patient when I called."

"You mean he doesn't even know yet?"

"Not yet."

Sam said, "You shouldn't be alone right now. I'll be there in a minute."

Alone. If only.

Madeleine glanced at Severin, who was sitting in the corner of the kitchen, gouging the wood of a cabinet door with her fingernail. She sighed. Perhaps it would be a good distraction to have Sam over. She agreed and hung up.

Madeleine folded her arms and looked at Severin, who had grown tired of scratching at the wood and was now sprawled out on the kitchen floor, lolling around like a typical bored child. A triangular gouge scarred the cabinet door where she had been clawing at it. Madeleine stared at it for a moment, then leaned over and fingered the mark.

The surface was smooth, and the image of the gouge disappeared even as Madeleine moved her finger across it. She admonished herself for having fallen for the illusion.

Suddenly, Severin leapt up and dug her fingernails into Madeleine's leg. Madeleine jumped back in a flash of pain. But in doing so, she inadvertently knocked the knife off the cutting board. The blade tumbled to the ground and she managed to sidestep it just before it would have skewered her foot. It bounced off the hard tile floor and back up again, where its tip sliced into the cabinet door.

Severin threw herself backward on the floor, giggling with delight. "Lovely, lovely!"

Madeleine smoldered. The mark in the cabinet was no longer an illusion. She saw the same little triangular gouge, exactly as Severin had formed it with her fingernail, only this time it really existed.

Madeleine stared at her. "Why would you do something like that?"

Severin stopped laughing and looked up, then began to wail.

"Oh, quiet down," Madeleine muttered.

The child's voice rose an octave, reverberating throughout the flat. Madeleine pressed the palm of her hand to her forehead. *My God, how am I supposed to function with this?* She wrung her hands and glanced at the door, knowing Sam would be coming over any minute.

"Stop it, Severin." Madeleine tried to keep her voice calm.

But the tantrum only escalated, and the wailing transformed into piercing shrieks. Severin threw herself back on the floor so that her skull bounced against the tile, and began kicking at the cabinets. She beat at them with her bare, filthy feet, kicking so hard that Madeleine's teeth chattered, and she squeezed her hands over her ears.

From the couch in the living room, Jasmine raised her head and looked over toward Madeleine. Severin continued pounding with her feet. Jasmine woofed. *Could Jasmine hear Severin on some level?* Madeleine thought suddenly. Jasmine woofed louder and leapt off the couch, trotting toward the door.

It's not the door, Jazz. It's in here. In the kitchen with me. Please hear it. Please see it.

Severin's shrieking and kicking intensified. "Stop talking to that dog! I'll send it through! I'll kill that dog the same way I scratched the cupboard! And I'll kill all your friends! I'll whisper them dead! Just like your brother! Just like your daddy! I'll send them through to the other side!"

Madeleine's throat clenched. Was it possible Severin had something to do with their deaths? Her fear tumbled backward and flipped into rage, so pure that it striped her vision in black and white.

"Oh no you won't," Madeleine said through clenched teeth. "If I find out you had anything to do with my father or my brother's death, *I'll* kill *you!*"

And then, somehow, Madeleine was the one screaming. "I'll kill *you*. I'll find a way, you disgusting little fiend, and I'll kill you!"

She drowned out the demon girl's shrieks with her own rage, her throat going raw, thorny branches snaking in around her.

Madeleine stopped, panting. Something behind the black tendrils caught her eye. As she stood over Severin, she saw a flicker of movement in the window. Her head snapped toward it, and she saw her own reflection. Behind it, another face. The pale face of a woman. *Oh, please, no.* Madeleine thought. *Not another one like Severin. I can't take this.* It happened because she had lost her temper, she reasoned frantically. Her anger brought on another apparition. She had to calm herself.

But when Madeleine spun around, wheeling wild-eyed at the figure, the sight of it caused her to freeze. She recognized it. No, she knew her. And she was not an apparition. She was Samantha.

"Maddy?" Sam's face was deathly pale, and she had Jasmine tucked under her arm.

Severin rose to a sitting position, grinning.

Madeleine stared at Sam with wariness, not able to trust what she was seeing. She took a shaky step toward her and reached out a trembling hand to touch her shoulder. Madeleine's fingertips met the fabric of Sam's shirt and the warmth of her skin beneath. No illusion; Sam was indeed standing there. Madeleine felt a rush of relief, but she retreated a few steps and folded her arms, looking at the floor, turning away from Sam's bewildered gaze.

"Maddy, are you all right? Didn't you hear me knocking?" Sam set Jasmine down on the floor and Jazz padded back to the living room couch.

Madeleine thought of Severin's feet beating against the cabinets. The sound would have drowned out Sam's knocking. Deliberately? A tear rolled down her face.

"I heard screaming, so I came in." Samantha's voice began to waver. "Maddy, who were you yelling at? I saw . . ." she trailed off. The room filled with silence.

Severin tittered.

Madeleine wrapped her arms around herself and turned nervously away from Sam, unable to look at her.

"Maddy," Samantha whispered. "It's me, Sam."

"I know who you are," Madeleine sputtered.

She stood regulating her breathing, struggling to regain composure. She racked her mind for some kind of explanation, some lie that she could offer up to Sam to deflect her from the truth of what was happening, so she would stop looking at her that way. But no such explanation existed.

Finally, Madeleine just began to speak.

"There is a person. An entity. An evil little . . ." Her words tumbled out in a halting staccato. Her throat stung from screaming. She took two more deep, slow breaths, and began to speak again, this time with complete calm and control.

"I don't know what she is, really," Madeleine said matter-of-factly, keeping her eyes on the floor. "I think of her as a kind of spirit or an imp. Maybe even some sort of curse. She has come to me in the form of a little girl, and she speaks to me and sometimes acts out."

Madeleine took on the tone of a schoolteacher, and was gaining confidence. "She has a negative quality about her, and she may even be dangerous. I have reason to believe that a similar such entity had visited my brother, and possibly even my father. But the bottom line is, I'm not crazy."

Those last words hung limp in the air, and Madeleine realized that she had somehow faltered. *I'm not crazy.* It sounded so very, very feeble. She made the mistake of stealing a glance at Sam, whose face was ashen.

"She reveals things to me." Madeleine's words poured out faster and with a higher pitch. "I sort of learn about things before they actually happen. Or she'll show me something that happened to someone else, like Marc, and I know what happened. Even though I wouldn't ordinarily know . . . what happened."

My God, I sound so crazy!

"All right." Madeleine forced herself to slow down. "Perhaps there have been symptoms that could possibly indicate the beginning stages of schizophrenia. A touch of confusion, difficulty in concentration. The good news is, I'm quite confident I can control that." She waved her hand dismissively. "What you should know is that this entity has made me privy to some special information."

Oh, for the love of God! Madeleine heard her own words, and she was sounding crazier and crazier with every breath.

Samantha's eyes glistened with tears, and the sight made Madeleine's stomach turn. Sam obviously was not going for it. Madeleine was losing her.

Madeleine whirled on Severin, who sat hugging her stained legs to her naked body.

"Give me something! Tell me something about Samantha."

"No," she said. "I don't think to do that. You never do what *I* say. Let her suppose you're crazy. It amuses."

Madeleine moaned with frustration, pulling at her hair. She grabbed a knife from the wooden block on the counter, wishing for a way she could plunge the thing into the demon child's black, shriveled heart.

"Is this what you want?" Madeleine raged at her. "Is this what you crave? Blood?"

She drew the blade down the center of her hand and let the blood run to the floor.

Sam screamed.

Severin giggled.

"Is that what turns you on, Severin? Give me something, damn it!"

"Maddy stop! Please!" Sam cried, moving toward her with her arms outstretched.

"Stay away," Madeleine pleaded, waving her off, and Sam recoiled. Madeleine realized it must have looked like she was threatening her with the knife.

She turned back to Severin. "Please, Severin. Please. Just help me."

Severin's face was pinched into a nasty little pout. Finally, she said, "Her first pet then, see. The first pet she had when she was a little girl. It was a kitten."

Her first pet was a kitten. So what? "Come on, Severin. Give me something better than that."

The child scowled, but remained silent.

Samantha watched fearfully with her fingers pressed to her mouth and sparkles of moisture dotting her lashes. Madeleine's blood throbbed at her temples. Severin was toying with her, and she knew Sam thought she had completely escaped her senses.

"You had a kitten," she finally said, resigned. "Your first pet when you were a child was a kitten."

Sam did not move, but her tears brimmed over and spilled down her cheeks.

"Well?" Madeleine's voice rose. "Am I right?"

With her fingers still covering her mouth, Sam slowly shook her head. "No," she whispered. "No, honey. My first pet was a dog. A puppy, when I was about ten years old." She reached out to her. "Maddy . . ."

The blood boiled in Madeleine's head. She wheeled on Severin, who was laughing.

"Ha, ha, ha! Maddy is a daft old frog!"

"Damn you!" Madeleine shrieked. "You evil little beast! Damn you to hell!"

She sank to her knees, her entire body quaking with rage.

Sam was immediately at Madeleine's side, arms encircling her and tears streaming. "It's OK. Maddy, it's OK. It's all right. It doesn't matter."

Sam smoothed back her hair. The knife clattered to the floor, and Madeleine cradled her wounded hand, now slick with blood.

The room went dark.

Madeleine looked up.

The kitchenette was choked with bramble but for a pool of light in the living room beyond. In the haloed glow, a small girl played with a tiny gray kitten. Madeleine watched.

Still crouched in the center of the kitchen, Madeleine sat back heavily on the tile. She gave Severin an icy look.

That was very ugly, she thought.

"I gave you what you wished on!" Severin said.

Madeleine reached out with her good hand and held Samantha's, her arm resting on her knee where she sat on the floor.

"You were very young, Sam. Two or three years old. You had a little gray kitten that you loved, and you hugged it. You squeezed it . . ."

Sam's face froze.

"It was an accident," Madeleine continued softly. "The kitten died."

Now Samantha sat back on the floor, her hand still gripping Madeleine's. Her eyes were unfocused, gazing into the distance. Madeleine's glanced back to the vision in the living room, where a young Samantha now sat sobbing over the little cat. Mercifully, the scene faded away and the kitchen was once more bathed in natural light.

"Now don't you feel bad for being mean to me?" Severin whined.

Madeleine shot her a look, and she lowered her head in a silent pout.

"I'd forgotten." Sam stopped, then swallowed. "I'd forgotten all about that."

She looked at Madeleine, eyes confused, and then her gaze wandered back to the vague distance.

"My mother and I had gone to the grocery store," Sam said. "Where they were giving away free kittens. She let me pick one out. I felt so bad when it happened, I cried all night. And we never talked about it again. I . . ." She swallowed. "I guess I somehow purged it from my memory."

"I'm sorry, Sam."

Samantha looked at her fully, searching her face as though she were a stranger. "Tell me exactly what's going on. What's this—person?"

sixty-two

ADELEINE HOISTED HERSELF UP from the floor, and Sam did the same. Together they bound Madeleine's wound as she began to describe the events that led to Severin's first appearances. She put on some coffee and they sat at the kitchen table. Severin crawled under the table and sat at Madeleine's feet.

Samantha listened carefully, offering no words of judgment, though Madeleine was certain she was not convinced. Sam gently asked Madeleine what she meant earlier about having exhibited "beginning signs of schizophrenia," aside from Severin and the visions.

Madeleine told her about the little indications, such as losing the ability to tolerate radio or television, and wandering concentration. She confessed that schizophrenics are prone to grandiose delusions, thinking they have been "specially chosen" by the alien ship or the CIA or whoever was communicating with them. In Madeleine's case, Severin provided glimpses into the lives of others, or little hints of events that had not quite happened yet, such as the gouge on the cabinet.

"You have to understand," Madeleine told Sam. "She guided me out of the bayou in the middle of a storm the night I found Anita's body. And she showed me where Zenon was hiding. How could that be a figment of my imagination?"

Sam's face held no expression. She was obviously still making up her mind.

"Have you seen a doctor?" she asked quietly.

Madeleine shook her head slowly. "No. And if I do, it won't be until after the trial. I have to appear clear and in control of my faculties until it's over."

"Maddy, I think you should see a doctor. To hell with the trial."

"No. I can keep a lid on this. The only reason you found out is because you walked in on me when I thought I was alone."

"The doctor can put you on medication and keep this at bay."

"I know that better than anybody. And I also know medication won't keep Severin away. Daddy told me as much before he died. But if they find out, I've lost all credibility as a witness. I won't risk that. And besides, Sam, *she showed me where Zenon was hiding!* There is no way I could have otherwise known that. These aren't just random hallucinations. Don't you want to find out what this is about?"

"I just don't want anything to happen to you. Whatever it is, I just want it to end."

"I know. Me too."

"Where is the little girl now?" Sam asked. "Can you see her?"

Madeleine looked down at Severin under the table. "She's sitting right here at the table with us. Oddly enough, she's been behaving since we sat down. Probably because we're talking about her. She likes to be the center of attention."

Severin's brow furrowed. Sam followed Madeleine's gaze to the floor where Severin sat, and then looked back and shivered.

She asked, "What have you told Ethan?"

Madeleine's mouth went dry. She could only shake her head.

"Nothing?"

Madeleine lifted her shoulders helplessly. "I wanted to. I'm going to. There just hasn't been the right moment. I was going to maybe tell him tonight. But then Daddy . . ."

Samantha nodded and squeezed her arm. "If you want, Maddy, I can tell him first. I can tell him about this, and about Daddy Blank too. It might make it easier for you to discuss it with him."

Madeleine looked at her, thinking it over. "Yes, Sam. I'd like that."

She nodded, tears still flowing freely down her face. "Anything."

"But I want to tell you," Madeleine said. "That you've been such a good friend to me. I can't imagine what I would have done if it weren't for . . ."

Her words caught, and the muscles seized in her face as tears spilled afresh. Sam leaned over and wrapped her arms around her, and together they wept. They clung to one another for a very long time.

MADELEINE SAT ON THE couch, sipping water and listening to the endless ringing of the telephone. Jasmine slept stretched across her lap. Severin sat on the floor and sang softly. Madeleine rubbed her hand over her raw, wet eyes. Her stomach churned.

"It gets easier, a little some." The little girl hugged her legs. "People going through. Sometimes it's fun."

Madeleine looked at her. "What makes you think I would ever enjoy watching people die?"

Severin shrugged. "That man who sent your father through, you wish on him to die, yes?"

Madeleine stared. "My father died of a drug overdose. He did that to himself."

Severin pressed her lips together and cast her eyes downward.

"Well . . . some yes, but not very." She looked up at Madeleine. "You wish to see?"

Madeleine felt a blanket of cold settle over her, emotions turning to crystal. She nodded.

The room transformed into that now-familiar dark, tangled cave and Madeleine recognized a section of the Iberville ghetto. She saw Carlo Jefferson selling his wares. She watched her father emerge from a black car with gold hubcaps, and wondered who might have driven him there. She watched.

She saw.

Rage mounted inside her. While her father lay unconscious in filth, his face streaked with his own vomit, she watched Carlo go through his pockets to see if he had any more cash on him. Apparently he was angry at having lost money on a bad supply of China White.

Madeleine saw Carlo walk away, leaving her father alone in an abandoned building, even as the very life drained from him.

❦

SHE FELT A COLD anger permeate her blood, spidering through her veins until it crackled in her throat. Of the awful things that had occurred in the past year, here was one event where she could pin blame squarely upon a single person's shoulders. The sensation grew inside her, an almost delightful hatred that she explored and coddled as if running her tongue over a canker sore inside her mouth. Carlo. He had done more than enable her father's death; he had made it certain.

Violent fantasies flickered through her mind.

In the kitchen, her cell phone stopped ringing.

"See?" Severin said. "Now you wish on him to die, yes?"

Madeleine looked at the little girl. "Yes, Severin, as a matter of fact I do wish him dead."

Severin looked satisfied, and she nodded with a smile. "And so you have a chance. To send him through, yes. A good exercise to start."

But as Severin spoke, she conveyed the full embodiment of her thoughts, not just by means of her jumbled speak. Madeleine saw a crisp image of the shotgun inside her mind. Severin communicated in 360 degrees, and speech and imagery comprised just one segment of that.

Madeleine had to chuckle. So this was it. This was madness. Pure, simple, tongue-wagging insanity. About to become criminal insanity. She had always been on the outside looking in, the lofty daughter or aspiring psychologist, passing judgment. And now it was she who was insane, knocked off her pedestal and into the abyss.

Severin was real; Madeleine believed that. But the devil-child brought with her a miasma that distorted and spun the filters that looked out to the rest of the world. More than ever before, Madeleine understood her father's clarity beneath the confusion and violence.

But it didn't matter. Severin was right; it had gotten easier already. Maybe being insane wasn't so bad. Madeleine felt her conscience turn to granite, and there was freedom in it. She could dance across that shelf of granite and act upon any inclination without moral care.

Severin went back to singing to herself in the corner.

Madeleine's upset stomach threatened to become a handicap. She went to the bathroom and purged, brushed her teeth, and washed her face. From the cedar chest in the living room, she retrieved the shotgun her brother had used to kill himself.

She walked out the door with the shotgun tucked neatly within the folds of her long coat.

Behind her, Severin whispered in a sickly sweet voice: "I'll come with you."

SIXTY-THREE

sixty-three

HAHNVILLE, 1927

HERE HAD COME A day when Ulysses began to drift away. Not completely at first; he would linger nearby as Rémi carved dolls from alder wood or tupelo gum, but he'd let him alone. Sure, he'd call over to Rémi from time to time, interjecting an opinion or unsolicited advice, but nothing like his usual taunts. The moment Rémi finished carving one doll, Marie-Rose would beg him to carve another. He could not deny her. And so in one stretch, he'd carved enough dolls for Marie-Rose to match Patrice's collection.

Gradually, Ulysses's presence had become sporadic and more distant. Rémi would catch sight of him wandering the avenue of field workers' cottages, or standing in the shadows outside a bonfire. Rémi would be working the fields with Francois and the other laborers, and from time to time, he'd catch sight of Ulysses harvesting cane in the distance. Rémi had no idea what caused this freedom.

As Ulysses's presence faded, so too did the anxiety and confusion that had plagued Rémi for the past several years. He found himself once again able to concentrate on his surroundings, and he even found he could attend to several things at once; he could put on his shoes and talk to Patrice at the same time, even if a radio was playing nearby.

In fact, he found he loved the radio. It brought him amazing news such as the Intracoastal Waterway undertaking, a path of artificial and natural canals that ran from New Jersey to Florida, and around to Texas, a massive toll-free shipping channel that had been under construction since Rémi and Chloe were wed.

He was mystified when he realized that private civilian groups, not just the government, now occupied the radio waves. Rémi had heard that the radio stations would become available to private industry after the war, but he could not remember whether the war *was even over.* He had a vague memory of discussions of its coming to an end around the time he married Chloe, but that had been several years ago, and he could not well remember anything that happened outside the bramble in the interim.

At some point over the last year, Patrice had purchased a brand new radio with vacuum tube receivers. It could pick up signals from both Baton Rouge and New Orleans, and beyond. Rémi had previously not allowed the radio to play while he was nearby, as the sounds would send him into a tailspin of confusion, but now he was fascinated. He listened to news, music, editorial commentary, and even the Sunday night program that broadcast children's stories, a favorite of Marie-Rose.

Indeed, Rémi was fascinated with the world around him. It felt as if he had been away on holiday for a very long time, or had slept for years like the mythical Rip van Winkle, awakening in a world he did not recognize. He was shocked to see his own reflection in the glass: His hair was unruly, he had lost more teeth, and he was sharply thin.

When he came across a chest full of relics from the Great War, he realized that his last surviving brother was dead. Tatie Bernadette informed him that it had happened nearly ten years ago, on the night he and Chloe were married.

"Why didn't you tell me?" Rémi asked her.

"Chloe told you," Bernadette replied. "You don't remember?"

It wasn't so much that Rémi did not remember; he simply had not been listening.

Rémi, your brother is dead. You are the only LeBlanc now. You and your children. You are the sole heir. I have helped you.

Chloe's words had been a tiny filament in a vast tapestry of sights and sounds that enveloped him, most prominently the face and voice of Ulysses. Constant noise; constant distraction. And the more he struggled, he would slip further into that place. The place where the trees grew black and the earth wobbled beneath him when he walked, as if the weeds formed a blanket over water. The place where the indigents lived, drawing him away, deeper into the woodland of eternal night.

But the most amazing aspect of Rémi's awakening was the presence of his children. Patrice, Guy and Gilbert, and little Marie-Rose seemed to spring to life before his very eyes. When Rémi was under Ulysses's bewitchment, the children scuttled about his periphery like spring hatches over water. With his newfound clarity, they became little people to him, with individual personalities and boisterous manners, and they were thrilled to have his notice.

Indeed, it was Rémi's pleasure to notice them, but he feared he might at any moment lose himself in Ulysses's world again. And so he savored every hour. He tilled the fields of sugarcane with worshipful hands. He fished and trapped with his sons in the swollen river, for it was a wet year, and he listened, mesmerized, as Marie-Rose read aloud from her books, in both French and English.

And Patrice—sharp-witted and already a striking beauty—with Patrice he could converse through the night, until dawn misted the river. They discussed the radio programs, how the Johnson grass threatened the sugarcane crop, Rémi's state of mind, the rumors of a bad flood year, anything and everything. She was now a young lady of fourteen, and though Rémi had lived in the same house as she, he had missed half her childhood. But Patrice was strong, wise beyond her years and with a baffling intelligence. She reminded Rémi so much of Chloe.

And in those weeks of awakening, Rémi longed for Chloe. Tatie Bernadette had told him that Chloe had gone to New Orleans to manage business affairs. She was in the habit of staying in the house on Toulouse where his brother used to live, and tending to the new distribution venture that had brought Terrefleurs back into financial buoyancy. And so, Rémi waited for Chloe to return. In the meantime he delighted in the company of his children and the serenity of Terrefleurs, which was, for the moment, innocent of her demons.

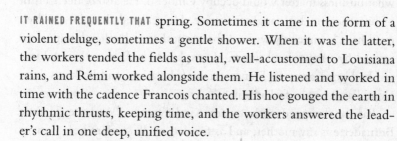

IT RAINED FREQUENTLY THAT spring. Sometimes it came in the form of a violent deluge, sometimes a gentle shower. When it was the latter, the workers tended the fields as usual, well-accustomed to Louisiana rains, and Rémi worked alongside them. He listened and worked in time with the cadence Francois chanted. His hoe gouged the earth in rhythmic thrusts, keeping time, and the workers answered the leader's call in one deep, unified voice.

But when the rains poured with intensity, the fields lay silent. The workers confined themselves to more domestic chores, making repairs on their own cottages, or telling tales and singing in the dining hall. Rémi was surprised to see that Chloe had outfitted even the workers' cottages with indoor plumbing, another testament to the wealth she had brought Terrefleurs with her keen business sense. She had also greatly improved the plantation school so even the workers' children, who could not afford to take the boat down the bayou to the school in Vacherie, were now well-learned.

How Rémi longed for Chloe, and wished she would return from New Orleans. With the rains confining him to the main house, he was left with little to do but think of her. And wonder how long before Ulysses would return.

What kind of life is this? Why do I bother?

It occurred to him that were it not for his wife and children, he wouldn't.

RÉMI SPOKE WITH PATRICE one afternoon as they sat in the shelter of the gallery while rain shrouded Terrefleurs in curtains of gray. He smoked tobacco while Patrice sipped her first taste of cherry bounce, though it seemed not a taste that agreed with her much.

Patrice told Rémi that her mother had expanded the distribution end of the business, and that she was routinely needed at the warehouse. Rémi listened and nodded, though he could not imagine what business matter would occupy Chloe so. He also noticed a hint of bitterness in his daughter's voice. He realized that the children must have been lonely with an absent mother and father, being raised instead by a nanny and tutors. He explained to Patrice that he himself had gone away to France for his education, and he knew how alone Patrice must feel at times.

Patrice shrugged with apparent indifference. "As I see it, Tatie Bernadette is my mother, and as for you, well, you are here now, at least."

Rémi was surprised and disturbed.

"Your mother loves you very much, Patrice. She has saved this plantation from financial ruin. The only reason she has not been here with her children is because she is working hard to keep Terrefleurs strong."

Without turning her face to him, Patrice looked at her father from the corner of her eyes, and then focused again on the drumming rain.

"Is that the only reason, Papa? How can you know that? Don't you know that to her, you are no more than a pigeon in the garden?"

He did not answer, for his thoughts were captured by the wailing sound of cadence drifting from the avenue of field workers' cottages.

"Listen to that!" he laughed. "They are calling cadence in this storm! They must be working together on something."

He peered out toward the small cottages, but could only see dim shapes behind the sheets of water. "Fixing somebody's house, maybe."

Patrice smiled but knit her brows. "What's cadence?"

"Have you not ever gone to play out by the fields?"

The rain hissed all around, and just beneath it came the lone voice, sounding off in rhythmic Creole.

Rémi gestured toward the sound. "Cadence is the songs we sing while we work. There is a leader, and he sets the pace, and the rest answer back. It keeps the work going, and everyone moves together." He shrugged. "It makes the time go by."

"Oh, I have heard that," she said, narrowing her eyes blindly into the curtain of gray.

Thunder crackled and obscured all other sounds.

"I just thought those were songs." She shook her head dreamily, not being accustomed to the effect the cherry bounce had on her young constitution. "I don't hear anything, Papa."

The atmospheric rumble continued, and when it passed, Rémi strained to listen beyond the rain. But the singing had stopped, and now he heard nothing but the pattern of rain and occasional bursts of thunder.

❧❧❧

THE NEXT DAY THE rain continued with the same intensity, and again the field workers could not tend the cane. As Rémi and the children gathered around the radio in the late afternoon, his head turned once again toward the call of cadence from the field workers' cottages. He listened to the rhythmic Creole words, but the babble of the radio interrupted and gave him a headache.

He excused himself early and went to bed. The taunting cadence droned through the afternoon and all through the night. When the rooster crowed at dawn, he was still lying awake, listening to the ceaseless rise and fall of the field worker's voice. His body lay tense with dread.

Grim-faced, he rose and opened the door, stepping out onto the gallery where the drizzle had stopped and the engorged black body of the Mississippi rushed beyond. He circled the gallery to the rear of the house that looked over the field workers' row. A lone figure stood in the center of the avenue, working the mud with a hoe and calling out into the dawn with the working man's poetry.

Ulysses.

sixty-four

EVERIN HAD HELPED HER to picture the face of the man she was about to kill. The child had laid a corridor of bramble that wound from Magazine, past grand houses, out to where the structures became shabbier. Madeleine hadn't even had to think. Along with Carlo, Severin had repeated images of Daddy Blank dying alone amid garbage in the condemned building. Madeleine let the acid of it etch her resolve.

She could have taken the truck, but she hadn't. Too difficult to drive like this. She'd walked the entire way, primed and ready to commit murder. She turned into Iberville, where people lingered in the streets and on stoops despite the chill, sipping from paper bags. Children playing games. Neighbors gossiping.

She found the street where Carlo conducted his trade. She could see his watchman at the top of the exterior stairwell of a decrepit building. He paid little notice to Madeleine. His duty was to watch for police.

On a nearby porch, a little boy was playing alone. A breeze blew

Madeleine's coat open, exposing the weapon, and she tucked it back inside. She looked over at the little boy and knew he had seen the shotgun. He watched with round, dark eyes, but made no effort to move from the porch or alert anyone. Madeleine steeled herself.

She stood for a moment, looking for Carlo.

Severin was calling for him: "Come out, come out, wherever you are."

Madeleine held the weapon tightly between her arm and torso, the steel barrel warm with her body heat. The little boy was watching.

She stepped onto the sidewalk and saw Carlo standing on a far corner where he conducted his dealing.

A car pulled up. A Lexus hybrid. Ethan's car. Madeleine stared at it, bewildered. It looked out-of-place in this neighborhood, and severely out-of-place in her mindset.

Severin was saying something. She repeated the final exchange between Daddy Blank and Carlo, speaking in their voices.

Ethan stepped out of the car. "What are you doing here, Maddy?"

She didn't answer. She took a firm hold on the gun with both hands, pulling it out from under her coat.

The watchman was looking directly at them now from atop the stairwell. His eyes grew wide and his posture taut, but he took no action. The little boy had both hands wrapped around the metal spindles under the porch rail, watching as if from behind the bars of a jail cell.

Ethan said, "Maddy, would you please put that thing away, and go for a drive with me?"

"Can you cover him?" she asked.

Ethan said, "What?"

But Severin pulled on the thorns, and Ethan disappeared behind a wall of bramble. Madeleine drew closer to Carlo until she knew he would be an easy mark, then raised the shotgun and sighted down the long, gleaming barrel. She fixed her aim on the son of a bitch, right between the eyes.

An unspoken alarm erupted in the neighborhood around her. Children were snatched off porches and stuffed behind doors. As if she and Carlo were in a stadium, all around them people were watching. Creatures watched from the thorns, too.

Someone shouted, "Do it! Get him!"

She had a clean shot. She could see his face clearly under the courtyard lights. The man was a parasite. He was not worth the oxygen he breathed.

Somewhere behind her, Ethan was speaking, but he was beautifully hidden. Severin demonstrated the next few seconds. She coaxed them forth with a barrage of sensations. She showed Madeleine what it could look like. God, what it was going to *feel* like. The intense satisfaction. The taste. Vengeance.

And yet deep inside, Madeleine was sensing something else. Something broader than the outer world and even the strange world beyond it, deeper than her own mind. A question arose from that space:

Is this me?

A simple question. One that was so small and subtle that it should not have survived through the bombardment of senses that Severin had created for her. It certainly shouldn't have been able to sprout amidst the hatred. But the question was there, all the same. And when it arose, it sabotaged her hatred. It caused it to shrivel like salt on a slug. She recognized that stillness as part of what had helped her to thwart Zenon.

She lowered the gun.

ETHAN PULLED HER QUICKLY into his car and they drove away. Severin was raging. She was crouched on the floorboards by Madeleine's legs. She screamed and clawed at her face, drawing blood. But Madeleine herself felt strangely calm. She watched the little girl as though she were observing any patient at the psych ward. Perhaps because the combination of grief and rage had been so intense she no longer felt any emotion. At least not for the moment. And in her calm, the bramble seemed to recede. She realized, then, that Severin's presence was not necessarily related to the presence of the bramble.

Shots rang out behind them.

"Get down," Ethan said.

Madeleine looked over her shoulder, dazed, and saw flashes of light from the landing above. From where Carlo's lookout was camped.

Madeleine felt Ethan's hand on her shoulder, pushing her down. She crouched over as they sped away.

She thought of the little boy who'd watched her through the metal bars along the porch rail, and she made a silent vow to never again contribute to the chaos. Any chaos.

They turned a corner and she rose back up. "Thank you."

Ethan shot her a sideways look. She caught the heat in his face and started to tell him—

But what could she say? She turned her face and stared out the window.

But he reached over and rubbed her neck. She pressed her cheek to his hand. They turned right, and Madeleine realized they were heading in the opposite direction from Magazine.

"Where are we going?"

"To a hospital, Maddy. We need to get you some help."

"Ethan, I'd rather just go home."

"I understand why you'd feel that way. But it's just too risky right now."

She shook her head. "Ethan, I'm not going to check myself in."

He glanced at her, lower face framed in the reflected headlights of the rearview mirror, and his jaw was set. "Madeleine, you are a danger to yourself and to others."

She closed her eyes. Her pulse was quickening, alarms ringing. She would not give in to emotion, no, because that would allow Severin to beckon the thorns, and Madeleine wouldn't have the cognizance to avoid going to the hospital. As it was, Severin was carrying on in an endless stream; a myriad of overlapping voices:

Danger to yourself—

The only witness is a paranoid schizophrenic—

Too weak to make your first kill—

. . . not enough evidence to hold him—

Trying to concentrate across all of Severin's blathering was like trying to count raindrops. And yet she had to hold on.

Ethan said, "Now we can go to whichever facility you like. Doesn't have to be Tulane. I can understand why you wouldn't want to go there."

She opened her eyes.

He said, "Hell, it doesn't even have to be New Orleans. I'll take you to Baton Rouge, honey, if you want. No one knows you there. You wanna go to Baton Rouge? I'll take you on over and get a hotel right next door."

Madeleine said, "It's not that. Listen. I understand your fear. But I need you to hear me when I say that I am absolutely not going to seek treatment right now."

"You're a danger—"

"Honey, Zenon's the danger." She pulled her hair back from her face. "Zenon's the danger."

As they wound through the neighborhood, the little houses were decorated in electrical snowflakes and wire reindeer. She'd forgotten that it was going to be Christmas.

She said, "You have every right to be angry."

"It's not about me being angry. OK, I'm a little angry. But I'm mostly worried."

"I know I didn't inspire confidence just now. If the circumstances were different, I'd say I need treatment too. But I need to avoid that because it's literally a matter of life and death."

He was silent.

She said, "You got a first-hand sense of Zenon's ability. Put that with the fact that he's a murderer. He's killed before, Ethan, and he'll kill again."

"This isn't about him."

"I wish it weren't. Yes, I'm in a terrible position to try to stop him, but the truth is I'm the only one who can."

"Madeleine, you nearly shot a man just now!"

"Nearly. There's a whole lot of difference between nearly and actually. Yeah, I was tempted. Carlo Jefferson killed my father. I felt the most intense hatred I've ever known. But I did stop myself. You didn't stop me, the police didn't stop me, no one stopped me but me. And now I've got to stop Zenon."

"We can't just pretend everything's fine! What are you supposed to do until the trial? Hide?"

Madeleine was silent for a moment, thinking, and then she said, "Well, to use one of your words: neuroplasticity."

"What?"

"Neuroplasticity. I'll change my brain. When I'm calm, things seem to be more manageable. So I'll practice keeping my emotions even, reinforce that, and build up the neurons that send calming signals to my body."

"And if it doesn't work? If things get dangerous?"

"I'll give it up and go straight to a hospital. But I need you to help me to try and make it work, at least until the trial."

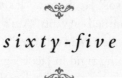

sixty-five

CHLOE WATCHED JACOB AS he regarded the satin-lined valise that lay agape before him, stuffed to absurdity with money. Large denomination notes that collectively totaled a small fortune.

"I told you before I want none of this," Jacob said.

"For your services," Chloe replied.

The soft evening light shone through the window of the small sitting area off the master quarters. In it, her skin glowed amber; his was scarlet. Chloe would ordinarily never dream of allowing Jacob into her private rooms, but her mistrust of the servants compelled her to conduct this transaction away from their prying eyes.

"It is only fair that you enjoy your share of the bounty in this business venture," she said.

"I got my own damned money!"

He flung his arm across the valise, sending bank notes fluttering into the air and across the small table. "Do you hate me so much, Chloe? Do you really believe you can just own me like one of your brutes?"

Chloe's eyes widened in surprise.

Jacob leaned toward her. "I might as well be Bruce Dempsey, your paid dog!"

"I do not see it as that."

"Don't you?" He was clenching his fist. "I think you do, Chloe. You can't stand that I've helped you out. You want to pay me off and own me like you own everyone else."

For a moment, Chloe thought he was going to strike her. She watched him warily, holding her stance, saying nothing.

"If I'm wrong, say so," Jacob said. "It's true, ain't it? You think I'm one of your goddamned servants. Ain't that true?" He grabbed her shoulder and shook her. "Ain't it true?"

Chloe stood tall, going rigid in Jacob's grip. He relaxed, but still held her shoulders with his right hand and his stump. Slowly she turned her head once from side to side.

Jacob let the stump arm slide to her elbow, but pulled in closer with his hand. "Well, what is it then? How do you see me?"

Chloe watched him, dark eyes wide and solemn. His breath was labored, and a sprinkling of sweat had formed on his upper lip and brow.

"Tell me," he said, his voice hoarse.

Still, she did not answer, not with words. She looked past his eyes to what watched and listened inside of him. The thing at the center of every human that she'd come to know by learning from Rémi's time spent in the world beyond. She let that part of herself address that part of Jacob.

He looked confused. But he bent his head, hesitantly, leaning in to her. She tilted her face up to meet his. Their lips touched.

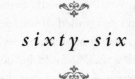

sixty-six

NEW ORLEANS, 2009

THE BRASS BAND PLAYED a slow, mournful dirge. Madeleine decided to walk in the foot procession instead of driving behind the hearse. She marched with Samantha on her left and Ethan limping to her right, all the way from the church down the scarred, narrow street, following the Dixieland jazz band leading the mourners toward the cemetery. Severin was smiling and prancing as if she were in a Mardi Gras parade, clearly enjoying the funeral that was meant to honor Daddy Blank.

When the police questioned the neighbors in Iberville, no one admitted to having seen anything. No mention of Madeleine's name or anyone else's.

Madeleine looked over her shoulder and saw lots of other people moving solemnly in the funeral procession. Most she knew, but still plenty were unfamiliar. She wondered, were they all real, or were some phantoms like Severin?

They entered the cemetery and proceeded to the LeBlanc mausoleum that would be Daddy Blank's final place of rest. Madeleine watched as Ethan, Vinny, and some of her cherished friends carried her father's coffin to the platform. *Are you really at peace, Daddy?* She wondered whether he might continue to walk this earth in another form, like Severin. *God bless the poor bastard who is haunted by Daddy.*

Someone was talking, speaking fondly of her father. Severin crawled inside the mausoleum vaults, like a child playing hide-and-seek, and then crawled back out again. Madeleine glared at her. Finally, they relinquished Daddy's body to the new resting place.

The band kicked up again, but this time the tempo was upbeat, almost jubilant. They played "When the Saints Go Marching In." Madeleine looked around and smiled. It sounded nice. They formed a procession again and began marching toward the museum on Chartres Street where the wake would be held. She offered up a prayer of gratitude to whoever decreed that the latter part of a Dixieland funeral should be a celebration for the passing from one world to the next.

"Let me get you something to sip on," Ethan said when they reached the museum.

"Thank you."

He squeezed her wrist and then strode toward the refreshments. She watched him go. Wondered how much of this insanity he was willing to weather.

The crowd in the museum was swelling to capacity. Politicians, judges, waitresses, street people; hundreds of folks had turned out to honor Daddy Blank. She spotted Oran moving in her direction, pushing Chloe in her chair.

"Hello," Madeleine said to them.

Chloe grunted and produced a small paper bag which she passed to her great-granddaughter. "Put it under your bed."

Madeleine accepted the parcel and looked inside. She saw only muslin wrapped around something, with a single black ant crawling across the surface. Whatever it was, it smelled like swamp rot.

"What is this for?"

"The child. She is here now, yanh?"

Madeleine stared at her. She realized her jaw had gone slack. She licked her lips, lowering her voice. "When I first saw her I thought she lived with you and Oran. You humored me. You knew all along what was happening."

Chloe said, "If I had told you, you would not have heard me."

Madeleine watched her face, listening.

Chloe said, "If she misbehaves, try lulling her."

"Lulling her?"

"A song. A rhyme. Not a gentle song. Something that reflects the place of the river devils where she came from. She won't stay there now that she has you. But when she goes back, she'll try to bring you there with her."

"How much do you know? Can you tell me how to manage this?"

"I can help you. You have now a key to unlock the greatest secrets of the mind. And its darkest shadows."

Chloe looked away, and Madeleine followed her gaze to where Ethan was heading toward them with two bottles of water.

Chloe muttered something in French that Madeleine couldn't catch, and then said, "You distract yourself. A waste, yanh. You would have done better to join with Zenon instead of treating him as your enemy. He would be a better match for you."

For a moment, Madeleine wasn't sure she'd heard her right. But before she could reply, Chloe made a sound that erupted from within her throat. She waved toward Oran, and he wheeled her away toward the door. Just like that.

Madeleine regarded the little paper bag still in her hand and folded the top over, then tucked it inside her purse.

Ethan joined her. He stood by her side as the mourners approached. She shook hands, embraced, and kissed dozens of people.

"I'm sorry, Madeleine . . ."

"Your father was such a dear man . . ."

"He'll always be remembered . . ."

A cross-dressing singer, Strawberry Chiffon, kissed Madeleine and offered condolences in French through tear-streaked makeup.

The mayor and former mayor greeted her. All of her father's friends were there, and even some who were not his friends.

Joe Whitney was there.

He was the closest thing to an enemy Daddy Blank had, but when Madeleine looked into Joe's eyes she saw that he was genuinely stricken.

"Miss Madeleine," he said, with both hands clasping hers. "I'm so very sorry for your loss. This city will miss one of its finest advocates. Your father . . ."

No sign of his usual persona. His eyes held nothing but sadness.

"He didn't think much of me, I guess. But I truly did admire him. I'm sorry."

He patted her hand, but did not release it. He had a strange look about him, like he wanted to tell her something.

"What is it, Joe?"

"Miss Maddy, this may not be the time or the place." He coughed. "But I feel I should tell you that I have taken a new client."

The poor man was ruffled. Madeleine had no idea what he was getting at, or why it would pain him so to tell her about his business affairs. But then she suddenly remembered seeing him at the police department the day Zenon was arrested, and her hand went cold inside his grasp.

"I have been quietly representing Zenon Lansky since his arrest. It'll be in the papers tomorrow."

Madeleine withdrew her hand. "I see."

Ethan said, "You've got to be joking."

Joe's fists dropped awkwardly to his side. He hunched his shoulders in a helpless gesture. "I wanted to tell y'all myself before it came out in the papers. I—I'm loath to cause you any more distress, Miss Maddy, I'm truly sorry."

She stared. So Joe Whitney would defend Zenon at trial. Weird, but OK. It seemed a plausible move for Joe's career, and it might help dilute the press regarding the mega-center scandal. But what of it? When she looked at his face, Madeleine could see that the man was battling a guilty conscience, and for Joe Whitney, that took some doing.

"Is there something else, Joe?"

He looked at her and then averted his eyes. "No, my dear." He patted her arm. "Just . . . you have my heartfelt condolences."

He looked at Ethan and nodded. "Ethan." He shuffled away.

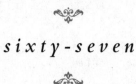

sixty-seven

NEW ORLEANS, 1927

*J*ACOB FELT A TIDE of elation. He would do anything for Chloe, anything. As he stood with his arms wrapped around her, he wanted to convey all that was in his heart through that one kiss. She intoxicated him. She had a core of intense, magnetic burning.

Despite the suffocating heat of the upper room, their bodies pressed together. He kissed her again, his mouth opening to drink her in. It stirred something within him, something that he'd only thought to enjoy with parlor maids and paid companionship. He never dared believe he might taste the purity of Chloe's kiss, feel the taut curve of her back. He could feel sweat through her dress. He moved his lips down and tasted it at her neck. His own sweat soaked through his shirt.

She leaned into him as if they could interlink their very bones. Her hands at his face. At his neck. And then unbuttoning his shirt. A heat overwhelmed him so fast and with such intensity that it stole the very air from the room, causing him to gasp. One by one, they tore each garment free, discarding them. The afternoon sun filled the room with light and burning.

With nothing between them, they strained their slick bodies at each other, until Chloe was pressed against the wall as Jacob lifted himself in toward her. She threw her head to the side and bore down, groping for him while he searched with his hands on her thighs and along her downy center, stretching to enter her.

He grew frustrated, and scooped his arms under her thighs then and carried her, anchoring her with his mouth on hers, and kicked the door open to the adjoining bedroom. He laid her on the white lace bedspread, and paused, heaving and struggling over her.

A stillness spidered across his conscience. To take Rémi's wife, Rémi who had helped him and his family, who had loved and cared for his sister Helen—to take his wife now while Rémi was incapacitated—it was the act of a scoundrel.

And yet, in the echoes of his mind, doubts hinted at absolution. Rémi was beyond reach. It had been too long. He was naught but a burden to his family now, especially to Chloe.

"Jacob, come to me," Chloe breathed, and she clutched at him with her knees, arching her back to lift her hips and belly.

"Chloe."

He sank to her, pressed his mouth to her ear and breathed her in, tasting her skin, gripping her hips, wearing her sweat. He slid his mouth down the curve of her neck, to her breasts, and then her abdomen. She rocked with him, twisting against the pressure of his tongue as it found its way to her center. Her hands gripped the bedspread and coiled into his hair. He tasted her, needed to taste her, and he held strong until she rocked and shuddered.

She fell limp into the mattress, and then he lifted himself up and slid over her. He gripped the now supple muscles of her thighs and entered her. She gasped, struggling against him. He bucked, every muscle in his body taut, thrusting deeper and harder until she was crying out. She pinned his legs with her knees, and squeezed her circle tighter around him, as if seeking more of his skin, his muscle, his sweat, his spirit. She *did* want to own him, to possess him, and he knew it.

He watched as her body rippled with a new wave of sensations, and she shouted and rocked. And he could hold back no longer. He thrust at her, his body uncoiling in release. He threw his head back with a wrenching groan, and he strained his hips at her for a long, stretching moment.

Finally, he slumped. The room grew still.

❧

HE LAY ATOP HER, listening to her breathing as it gradually smoothed. He could hear sounds beyond the door, the agitated bickering of servants. Jacob ran his fingers along Chloe's skin, savoring the feeling and the smell of her, and the scent of their sex. His breathing matched hers.

Just beyond the door, the quarrel escalated. Angry voices raised almost to the point of shouting.

"*Qui est là?*" Chloe said, annoyed.

He rolled off onto his back. She reached for a linen.

Jacob smiled. Few servants dared raise her ire. She rose, donned her house robe, and opened the door.

Rémi stood at the stairwell.

sixty-eight

W HEN SHE HAD BEGUN rebuilding the house on Esplanade, Madeleine had pulled the necessary permits through the city of New Orleans. The
Historic Preservation Society was pleased to learn that she wished to
build a close replica—double-gallery Creole Victorian—of the original house. The only relevant changes to the layout were to add
modern-sized bathrooms, closets, and a kitchen. Unfortunately, some
of the details that had made the old house such an amazing work of
art, such as the carved marble fireplaces and elaborate moldings,
were not in the budget. It had taken a coup of bureaucracy to get the
permits through, but she'd managed. After that, the crew had laid
the foundation and begun framing.

It all required a great deal of money.

Madeleine learned that the estate she'd once shared with her
brother and father would indeed be liable for the other burned
houses on Esplanade. The financial drain left her short of breath. She
considered halting construction, but after assessing the market, she

determined the only sensible course would be to finish construction and sell the property.

Between that, the family trust, and the house in Houma, she hoped to break even. Madeleine wished she could return to work and start generating an income, but the idea of returning to a career in psychology now seemed hypocritical.

She strolled Esplanade, observing the swarm of workers as they sawed and nailed, erecting the frame of her home. Severin strolled with her. Madeleine found that so long as she included Severin in what she was doing and kept her occupied, the outbursts were fairly minimal, and Madeleine was able to function without others becoming aware. And yet, there were days when she didn't dare leave the flat, because she was lost in the bramble.

"Those men have hammers," Severin observed.

Madeleine nodded. Though she avoided speaking to her openly in public and looking like she was talking to herself, subtle acknowledgments such as nodding or changing facial expression seemed to be enough.

"That one killed another." Severin pointed to a worker above who was nailing ceiling joists. "No one knows. Another man is in jail because of it, but *he* sent him through, truly."

Madeleine glanced at her, then looked back up at the worker. "Time to go."

They got in the truck and pulled into the street.

Severin scowled. "I just thought to tell you something of that man."

"I know, Severin. I don't really know what to do about that."

The girl had revealed many such injustices; things Madeleine wanted desperately to correct. But she felt powerless to do anything. And as the list of Severin's revelations grew longer each day, Madeleine was feeling more and more overwhelmed.

Severin kicked at the dashboard. "You don't much listen to me! Listen! Listen! Listen!"

Madeleine continued to drive, hands firmly on the steering wheel, trying to think of something to do to calm her down. Severin kicked, and then she turned and sank her teeth into Madeleine's arm. Madeleine wrenched away, causing the truck to swerve. Pedestrians leapt and scattered in alarm.

This had to stop.

Madeleine pulled over and removed the keys from the ignition, hands shaking, and turned to Severin.

"Why would you do that?"

Severin gave her a hard smile. "It satisfies."

Severin swung her legs and kicked the dashboard again.

My God, she is relentless.

Madeleine remembered Chloe's advice about lulling, and began to sing.

Ring around the rosie
A pocket full of posies
Ashes, ashes
We all fall down

Severin stopped kicking and looked at Madeleine with interest. "What's that you sing?"

"It's called 'Ring around the Rosie.' It's a nursery rhyme. Haven't you ever heard a nursery rhyme before, Severin?"

She shook her head.

"Well, here, I'll teach you. Repeat after me. Ring around the rosie . . ."

Severin looked down at her feet, losing interest. "What does it mean, all that?"

"It's from the Great Plague." Madeleine emphasized the word *plague*. She started the truck and turned onto Rampart Street. "They called it the Black Death, because the victims' bodies turned black when they died."

Severin turned back toward her with eyes full of wonder.

"They would develop sores. Red rings on the skin. That's why it goes 'Ring around the Rosie.'"

"Ring around the rosie," Severin repeated. "What about the rest?"

"*A pocket full of posies,* because they thought bad smells caused the disease, bubonic plague. They carried posies to hide odors. *Ashes, ashes.* They used to burn the bodies."

A shiver tickled Madeleine's spine. She had gotten the girl's attention, but it was such a macabre subject. She wondered if she was placating the child by talking to her this way, or taking one more step toward her own madness. The sick, violent kind of madness that Severin craved.

"*We all fall down,*" Madeleine finished. "Dead."

The child was smiling. "How does it go again, please?"

They repeated the words of the old nursery rhyme together. She wondered *how on earth it had come to be a children's game.*

"Ring around the rosie," Severin announced.

"I thought you'd like it."

ZENON'S TRIAL BEGAN.

Madeleine stayed away from the courtroom, keeping interactions with others to a minimum. She feared she might slip and do or say something that revealed her secret. The case was high profile, and Madeleine glimpsed the highlights as Ethan watched the news at night. When the time approached for her to testify, Ms. Jameson called her back into the U.S. Attorney's Office at the federal building.

The receptionist led her to a conference room and offered her a refreshment, which she refused. Ms. Jameson appeared, explaining that they would be going over her testimony just as if she were on the stand. She began by telling how she had gone out in the little boat to the place she used to go with her brother.

"A storm was on the way," Ms. Jameson said. "Why did you go out there in a boat that afternoon, knowing that you'd encounter severe weather conditions?"

"I . . . I . . ." Madeleine had had this answer ready before, but suddenly could not remember what she had said. She couldn't very well tell her she was running away from Severin. Good God, she thought, and it's such a simple question.

Severin swung her legs, kicking at the table. Madeleine could feel sweat forming at her hairline.

Ms. Jameson gave her a quizzical look. "Is something wrong?"

Madeleine shook her head.

"Why were you out there?"

"I, er, was depressed. My brother had committed suicide. Out there." She gulped. "I was selling the house. I suppose I was feeling sorry for myself, and I went to that spot because we used to go there together. I didn't care about rain. We were raised with it."

The lawyer's eyes narrowed, her chin resting on her hand. Madeleine squirmed.

"Dr. LeBlanc," Jameson said. "What are you looking at?"

Madeleine's eyes snapped up from the seat next to her, where Ms. Jameson doubtless saw nothing but an empty chair.

"Nothing. I guess I'm a little nervous."

"Dr. LeBlanc, is there anything you'd like to tell me? Because if there's any information you left out, now's the time to let me know."

Madeleine's heart thundered, and she was sure the attorney could hear it. Sweat snaked from her brow to her ear.

"I can understand your being nervous," Jameson said. "But the jury may interpret that as not being truthful. Our case is not as strong as I'd like it to be, and your testimony is the best evidence we've got. It is crucial that you appear calm and simply tell the truth." She paused, and then said, annoyed: "Why are you humming?"

Madeleine strangled off the nursery rhyme—she had not even been aware that she was humming it aloud. *Get it together.*

"Habit." Madeleine drew herself up and looked directly into the attorney's eyes. "Ms. Jameson, I think I might help myself to some of that water after all."

She stood and filled a paper cup from the water dispenser, then settled back down. The lawyer's eyes continued to drill into her.

"I'm glad we're doing this," Madeleine said. "Because I didn't even realize I was so nervous about the trial until now. There'll be reporters in the courtroom, won't there?"

Jameson nodded. "Are you sure there's nothing else you have to tell me?"

Madeleine shook her head, maintaining eye contact.

"Please go on," Jameson finally said.

Madeleine continued with the story, and Ms. Jameson stopped her at every turn to ask questions and prod for hidden information.

THE INTERVIEW HAD CONTINUED for another two grueling hours, but Madeleine had held fast, maintaining composure and answering matter-of-factly. They'd hashed out the details of that night to exhaustion. The U.S. attorney relented, and she stopped looking at Madeleine as if she were a kernel of dried corn about to pop.

Finally, Ms. Jameson indicated that the interview was over. "Dr. LeBlanc, I'd like to reiterate that it is of the utmost importance that you relax and tell this story as simply and truthfully as you can. If you're telling the truth, you have nothing to worry about."

Madeleine nodded.

"I'd also like for you to attend the trial for the next few days until it's time to give your testimony. I think it would help if you got used to the courtroom environment."

The color drained from Madeleine's face. She knew the courthouse would be swarming with reporters, and if she did anything conspicuous . . .

But she knew Jameson was right. It was crucial that Madeleine maintain composure on the stand. She agreed.

Jameson seemed to have caught Madeleine's hesitation, and assumed that hawkish look once again.

"And, I'd like to go over your testimony one more time before you take the stand."

Madeleine stood tall and tried to sound confident. "That sounds fine."

"We'll give you a call to set a time."

⁂

MADELEINE WAS GLAD SHE had agreed to attend the trial, because she was not prepared for just how imposing the courtroom turned out to be. More importantly, it gave her a chance to practice keeping Severin in check. Madeleine discovered that she could maintain entire conversations without saying a single word. She simply had to organize her thoughts into sentences, and Severin would reply as if Madeleine were speaking aloud.

Thus she managed to keep the child occupied, though it left little room for her to concentrate on what happened on the stand. As an observer, that wasn't really an issue. But when on the stand, Madeleine would have to be able to concentrate, which meant ignoring Severin for a period of time. She had no idea how she would handle that.

As the time drew nearer to her testimony, Madeleine's face had been in the papers and on the news. They had resurrected the details of how she found Anita in the water and later led the police to Zenon.

"All eyes are going to be on you," Ethan said.

"I know."

"Are you ready?"

"I think so. It's been months, and no real incidents."

"Yeah, I wasn't so sure that was going to work. But you seem OK."

And then Madeleine said, "I'm not sure what I would have done without you here."

He stepped toward her. "You would have made it. You're tough. But I'm glad you're letting me be here for you."

"It's all right, you know. I wouldn't hold it against you, if you decide . . ."

He stopped. "Decide what?"

"You know. If my condition gets too weird. It's a lot to ask of someone if . . . I'm just saying it could get much worse. In fact it'll probably get much worse."

"Are you giving me permission to leave you?"

She looked away.

Ethan said, "Good God, Madeleine, I work with the human brain for a living. If anyone can handle this, it's me. The only time I get second thoughts is when I get the feeling you're trying to get rid of me."

She shook her head. "I'm sorry. You're right. I've just seen first-hand where this can lead, when Daddy was at his worst. I can hardly stand the thought of you seeing me like that."

"I told you I'm willing to take this on. The question is, are you?"

IN THE MORNING, SHE awoke very early. Ethan was still sleeping.

Between meetings with the U.S. Attorney and familiarization with the courtroom, Madeleine felt she could tackle just about anything Joe Whitney had in store.

She just wished Jameson would stop harping about being truthful. Madeleine had no desire to stand before the court and lie. She would tell them the entire saga exactly as it happened, and only leave out those parts that pertained to Severin.

The problem was, when getting sworn in, the oath is to tell the *whole* truth. That was the part that Madeleine did not want to think about.

She went to the kitchen and made coffee and toast, paying attention to each smell and sensation. Cleared her mind in preparation of her testimony. Severin fussed about the room, but her mood seemed stable. Madeleine sat at the table and stared at the wall, letting the silence settle in, listening to nothing but the space around her.

"Severin," she finally said. "I have to go to court today."

"We've been going there almost every day."

"Yes, we have. Only this time I have to take the stand, which means I have to testify."

Severin wriggled on the couch.

"I have to talk to the lawyers for a long time," Madeleine said. "And I may not be able to speak to you. Do you think you can be a good girl and behave while I'm up there?"

Severin's eyes shimmered in the pre-dawn light, and she smiled with magnanimity and sweetness. "Of course!"

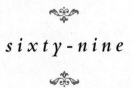

sixty-nine

NEW ORLEANS, 1927

ÉMI STARED UP AT them, his feet rooted to the landing. Chloe pulled the door to narrow the opening, but he had already seen into the master bedroom, where Jacob Chapman had been in his bed.

Rémi's mouth went dry. Even in the dim light, he could see Chloe's expression. Her eyes searched Rémi's face as though wondering if he even recognized what he saw. Rémi felt sick. Ulysses began to laugh.

Rémi was moving again, so rapidly that his mind moved more slowly than his body. He lunged spiderlike up the staircase and burst through the door. Jacob was hurriedly dressing next to the bed. Rémi pounced on him, knocking him to the ground and wrapping his hands around his throat.

Jacob gagged once and then grimaced, gripping Rémi's forearm with one hand and hitting at his face with his stump. Jacob's tongue began to protrude.

Behind him Chloe was shrieking. *"Non, Rémi! Non!"*

She gripped his shoulders and tried to wrench him away. With one quick movement, he backhanded her, sending her sprawling to the floor.

He turned back to Jacob who had managed to take a breath and struggle free, though he made no move toward counterattack.

He could kill Jacob now. Kill him with his bare hands. And what a satisfying way to elicit death.

The damnable pipe smoke. It stole his rage. Molded his thoughts. He realized, then, that the sensation didn't seem to come from within him. It came from . . .

He raised his eyes to Chloe. She pulled herself to her knees and wiped blood from her mouth with the back of her hand. The three of them were heaving on the floor, blinking and gasping.

Rémi thought to kill them both.

And in the next instant, he thought instead to throw himself over the handrail.

He gripped the roots of his hair. This turmoil of thoughts, these warring notions.

He did neither. Instead, he rose to his feet and escaped.

ULYSSES HOUNDED RÉMI THE entire distance back to Terrefleurs. With sour breath and vile words, he spoke of Rémi's doom, chiding him for not having sought vengeance on the adulterers. Had he not warned Rémi about Jacob? Had Rémi not foiled Ulysses's efforts to kill Jacob? And how could Rémi expect Chloe to remain faithful after all these years? She had only taken Rémi as a lover and a husband out of pity. She had no real loyalty to him. Ulysses told Rémi he had only one choice; he must take revenge on those who had betrayed him. If he did not, it would mean his ruin.

"Take your knife," Ulysses said, lisping French through sparse teeth. "Go back to the house on Rue Toulouse. Remember it is your house, your own house where they fornicate. Kill them both. Burn the house down."

"Get thee hence, you devil!" Rémi shouted in despair, but Ulysses only railed the louder.

The children delighted to see their papa when he returned to Terrefleurs, but quieted when they realized his state of mind. Rémi confined himself to the men's parlor where he sat, damp and filthy with mud.

In the evening, Patrice quietly entered her father's room with a tray of supper.

"Was it mother?" she asked, hands folded at her apron.

Rémi sat in silence, barely able to discern his daughter's words through Ulysses's droning.

Patrice sighed. "Whatever mother did, I'm sorry. She's quite— careless."

She busied herself at the vanity. "Papa, won't you carve me a new doll?"

Water poured from the pitcher into the basin. Patrice was using a linen towel to wash mud from her father's face.

The feel of soft cotton roused him from his reverie for a moment, and even Ulysses paused in his diatribe.

"A new doll would be nice," she said.

"But I just carved so many."

"Papa, they keep you in this world with us. Haven't you noticed?"

Rémi looked up at his daughter as she washed his face. "You're talking river magic."

She smiled at him. Such a soft expression; such tenderness.

Ulysses spoke again, breathing his sickness into the room: "She is a beauty, is she not? She truly cares for you. You should take her as your wife once you have gotten rid of her mother. You heard what she said. She hates her too."

Rémi jumped to his feet and knocked the basin of water to the ground.

"Leave me, Patrice!"

She stood frozen for a moment, then calmly gathered the broken pieces of porcelain and left the room.

Rémi was alone again with Ulysses. He had nearly drowned Chloe in the river once because of Ulysses's words. And what the beast had said now about Patrice was grossly unthinkable. It filled him with revulsion to think that the eyes of this demon had fallen upon his daughter.

He became frantic, fearing that Ulysses might harm Patrice or his other children with the same tricks he had used to take Jacob's hand. He escaped to the work shed, only vaguely aware of Marie-Rose and the twins as they scurried into hiding at the sight of him. He stumbled on an abandoned game of marbles and fell sprawling to the soft earthen floor of the shed. The dirt became affixed to his soaking hair and clothes, dotting his lashes. The way the children hid, he must've looked like a wild beast. The children huddled under a workbench with wide eyes, hands pressed to mouths. They seemed to melt into the shadows as if in hopes that he not see them. And indeed, the shadows were creeping forth.

Rémi snatched a hammer and a bucket of nails, and ferried timbers from the wood pile back to the house, and the rain bore down all the while. When he had assembled enough lumber, he withdrew to his room, nailing the boards across both doors and sealing himself inside the men's parlor.

Ulysses smoked Rémi's tobacco, watching.

"This is your doom then, you know this?" He blew a cloud of smoke toward Rémi. "Shall I make it easier for you?"

He watched with large, deep-set eyes, as he took another puff from the cigarette. He leaned forward and blew the stream of smoke onto the tangle of boards nailed to the door. "Get this over quick, eh?"

The wet boards steamed, and then the steam became smoke. Rémi heard crackles of flame.

He dropped his chin, still heaving with exertion. "So be it."

The sound of crackling subsided, and the smoke vanished from the boards.

"Coward," Ulysses said, and then sighed. "And so tell me, what is this? You barricade your doors, and what does that do?"

"It will keep everyone out of here so that you cannot touch them."

"Ah." Ulysses shrugged, then began to laugh. "And what makes you think I cannot get out? For that matter, *you* can get out. What is to keep them safe from you?"

He laughed more deeply, the brown stumps of his teeth gaping. "You may not listen to me now, but eventually you must if you are to save yourself. I give you good advice."

Rémi gripped the wood and closed his eyes. He pressed his face into the smoky, splintered boards. No escape. No refuge. He knew Ulysses's words were true. When he wandered the briar, deep in a dark bayou with the black trees and wavering ground, he often knew not what the self he left behind might be doing. A husk of a body while his mind was elsewhere. His children likely were *not* safe in the company of that other self.

He ground his teeth and wrenched the boards from the door, leaving the wooden frame pocked and ragged.

⁂

FROM BEYOND THE WALLS of the men's parlor, Rémi could hear the popping sound of the radio. It was time for Rose's storybook program. Rémi tried to shut his ears to the confused buzz of sound, hideously tangled with Ulysses's relentless drone:

"Your children, and the children of the plantation, they call you the *loup-garou*. You are their bogeyman, not me. You creep the woods and hide and spy in the shadows. When the children are naughty, their mothers tell them that the *loup-garou* will take them down to the bottom of the bayou."

He knew of no escape from Ulysses's incessant taunting. Even if Rémi sought the quietest corner of the woods, there would still be Ulysses and his venom. Never silence.

"Listen, Rémi," Ulysses was saying. "Do you hear it? Listen to that radio."

And then, mercifully, Ulysses fell silent. So conspicuous was his silence that Rémi *did* listen. He turned his head toward the wall where the radio announcer's voice filtered into the room.

Rémi caught the broadcast in bits: "Mississippi River . . . torrential rains . . . bursting levees . . . Missouri . . . northern Louisiana."

Rémi opened the door and walked into the great room where the children and Tatie Bernadette sat assembled around the radio. The twins looked up at their father with round eyes. Rose's radio program had been preempted with the news of flooding that had already saturated Missouri and Arkansas, and was beginning to tear through Louisiana.

The announcer spoke of rains that had begun to fall last October, and now returned with force. From Canada to the southern United States, creeks and streams overflowed their banks and overwhelmed the rivers they fed. The spring floods coursed into the Mississippi River from Minnesota and Iowa down through Mississippi and Louisiana. Since January, a serious threat of massive flooding had begun to loom, and as the winter progressed into spring, the situation was becoming disastrous.

Already the northern states along the Mississippi River and one of its biggest feeders, the Ohio River, had been overwhelmed, and that torrent was working its way south. Scientists predicted that New Orleans would soon disappear under the Mississippi.

The announcer's voice, otherwise so devoid of any emotion, was strained. He spoke of discussions to destroy the levee below the city; sacrificing St. Bernard and Plaquemines parishes in order to save New Orleans.

Rémi was amazed. So fleeting had been his mental respite that he did not attend much to the threats of flood. His levee was sound enough, or so he thought, and although he charged Francois to organize the reinforcing of it, Rémi did not fret much over the possibility of minor flooding. It was a regular occurrence on River Road.

If the river was already swollen beyond flood levels, then regardless how strong the Terrefleurs levee was, water could crest over the top of it.

Ulysses was speaking again. "Think of this, Rémi. Because of you, Jacob Chapman has the biggest levee for miles around. Now Glory Plantation will stay dry while Terrefleurs is washed away. He will have nothing to do but laugh at you while he screws your wife."

"*Tais-toi,* filthy pig!" Rémi snapped. "You think I do not know this?"

Marie-Rose started to cry, and Tatie Bernadette hustled the children from the room.

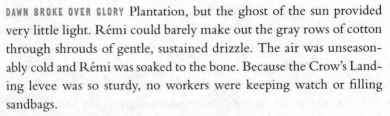

DAWN BROKE OVER GLORY Plantation, but the ghost of the sun provided very little light. Rémi could barely make out the gray rows of cotton through shrouds of gentle, sustained drizzle. The air was unseasonably cold and Rémi was soaked to the bone. Because the Crow's Landing levee was so sturdy, no workers were keeping watch or filling sandbags.

Except for Ulysses, Rémi was alone.

Relics of the Great War, mementos stashed in an old trunk as remembrance to a lost brother, would serve one last purpose. Rémi's hands were numb and clumsy as he positioned the six petard grenades at the base of the levee.

Beyond the wall of earth, the Mississippi River raged. During the night she had risen by another fourteen inches. And somewhere downstream, perhaps miles away, she carried the pull-ferry Rémi had used to cross her. It had broken free just before Rémi reached the far bank. He had had to spin untethered on the platform until it lurched near enough to the north side so he could jump across to the banks of Glory. He was sure that the ferry was now in splinters scattered along the Mississippi's path.

He had watched the torrential flow and wondered whether downriver, the Terrefleurs levee might already be gone. But what did it matter now? No turning back. If Terrefleurs was to flood, so be it. Rémi could do nothing about it now. He had had time enough for one task only: either to blow up the levee at Crow's Landing and flood Glory, or scramble to reinforce the Terrefleurs levee. But the best hope for Terrefleurs *was* to burst the levee at Crow's Landing. Diverting the torrent to Glory would mean less strain on the Terrefleurs levee.

Rémi might not be able to concentrate long enough to fully deal with Jacob, but at least in this one quest, Ulysses would gladly assist.

Despite the roar of the river and the hissing rain, Ulysses's voice came loud and clear, not only to Rémi's ears but inside his very mind. Ulysses was calm and solid. To be working alongside him after struggling against him for so long was a relief.

"We will flood his land," Ulysses said. "He will lose the new house."

Rémi picked up one of the old grenades and examined it. Water beaded on the paraffin wax, and Rémi wondered if his brother's relic French grenades would even explode. On one of them, the paraffin had worn away and rust bloomed along the iron cylinder.

"We will ruin him, and then we will kill him."

Rémi turned the grenade over in his hand. Wire lashed the iron cylinder to a block of wood, and a smaller block lay on top. Inside were two shotgun cartridges positioned in front of the fuse. He crouched and laid the petard next to the others.

"Line them up. Strike the nail in the hole. Six in a row, bom bom bom bom bom bom! And then you throw. There and there." Ulysses pointed to the top and center of the levee. They had positioned sandbags as targets where the explosions would cause the most damage. "You have five seconds. Aim well; you will not have a second chance. Do not strike the first until you are ready to strike them all. No good to try to make careful aim with the river coming at you."

For just a moment, Rémi imagined the faces of his children, and his throat grew thick and numb. Could he survive on vengeance alone? How long before his children turned away from him as Chloe had? How long would he continue to inflict pain upon them all?

"You hit them fast, and then throw them fast. Five seconds from the time the first one hits. Then you must run."

Rémi pushed away thoughts of his sons and daughters. He picked up the hammer and hefted it in his hands. No good stalling.

He tapped the nail in the first grenade and then in each one in the line, quick as his numb hands could manage, activating them all. The blood rushed in his ears, and the raindrops seemed to slow their descent toward the earth. Rémi threw the first grenade, and it landed on the first sandbag near the top of the levee. The second grenade bounced off its target and then tumbled down the incline to the base, and Rémi paused.

"Keep throwing!"

He launched the third, fourth, and fifth grenades, and they each came to rest on their marks. Before he could throw the sixth and final grenade, the first grenade exploded. With the debris of the levee still surging heavenward, he threw the last grenade but could not tell where it landed.

"Now come!"

Ulysses stood just upriver on the levee beyond the site of the explosion, his hand stretched toward Rémi.

The second grenade exploded.

Debris from the first grenade hailed from the sky, and a rock pelted Rémi's shoulder in a burst of pain. A surge of water began to gush from the wounded levee.

Ulysses called: "Come!"

Rémi covered his head against the hail of earth and wood, but he did not move toward Ulysses. Two more explosions sounded, and then only the sound of rushing water. Even as it surged toward him, Rémi noted that two of the grenades had not exploded, but instead lay impotent where they had landed.

"Rémi! Come! Now!"

The four active grenades had inflicted only superficial wounds upon the levee, and water pooled sluggishly toward Rémi's feet. But the Mississippi fixated. She surged at the fissures and pried at them until they gave way, dividing earth and wood until Crow's Landing crumbled into brown frothing torrents.

Despite the tremendous force, one need only to stride for higher ground to avoid her wrath. Downstream, people would see the water coming from far away, and would have ample time to escape to safety. Even Rémi, standing before the disintegrating levee, still had adequate time to sidestep the waters. To save himself.

"Rémi! Come!"

But he did not. He chose instead to stand with widespread legs and embrace the furious river.

The water knocked Rémi from his feet. It swallowed him, drowning out all sounds, including, for once, the voice of Ulysses.

seventy

NEW ORLEANS, 2010

ADELEINE SAT DRESSED IN a new fitted suit, watching the trial. Sam was on one side of her and Ethan on the other. Previously the courtroom had been about half full, but today people were jammed in to capacity, and Madeleine felt a queasy suspicion that this unusual attendance was because of her scheduled testimony. She saw Sheriff Cavanaugh, and also Shawn, the reporter from the *Times-Picayune*. Sheriff had been testifying that same morning. Now they were waiting for court to resume after a late afternoon recess, and Madeleine was wondering if they'd ever get around to calling her to the stand. Chloe was sitting several seats down in the same row. Madeleine nodded at her and she nodded back.

"Have you been seeing much of Chloe lately?" Sam whispered as people continued to shuffle toward their seats.

Madeleine shook her head. "Been kind of avoiding her. From what I read in Mémée's diary, I don't want to get Chloe involved. I'm just trying to make it through the trial."

"Relax," Ethan said.

"Trying to."

"Come on," Sam whispered. "Joe Whitney couldn't possibly hold up against you. Anyway he'll be too busy staring at your boobs to be able to concentrate."

Madeleine rolled her eyes with a chuckle. "You are so very wrong. But thanks for the laugh. I needed it."

Sam smiled. "Well, Joe Whitney's such an easy target. The way he's always pawing at the ladies and flashing those gold hubcaps."

"Gold hubcaps?" Madeleine said, puzzled. "He doesn't have gold hubcaps on his BMW."

"On the Beamer, no," Sam said. "But he's got'm on that other car, the black Jag."

The bailiff called out from the front of the courtroom. "All rise."

Madeleine rose to her feet as the judge entered in long black robes, but in her mind she remembered Severin's vision of the night her father died. When Daddy'd been dropped off in Iberville, he had gotten out of a black car with gold hubcaps. Joe's car.

Anger flurried in Madeleine's stomach. Joe Whitney was the one who drove her father to the ghetto. Never said a word about it. Joe Whitney.

She felt the temperature rise in her neck, but she forced herself to be calm. Today was too important a day to let herself get swept away with anger. She breathed in slowly, and exhaled with deliberate restraint.

The bailiff called Madeleine's name.

She rose and strode to the stand, taking a deep, cool breath. Her heels clicked across the floor. She took the stand and looked only at the bailiff who approached her, with her gaze carefully avoiding the vast sea of people who were all staring.

Madeleine raised her right hand and swore to tell the truth. Her palm was clammy, and she was certain she left a wet print on the Bible. Jameson approached.

MADELEINE EXPLAINED IN DETAIL how she and her father had seen Zenon at the plantation house, and the pool of blood she found there. And then, she explained what had happened that night on Bayou Black. The opening questions were the same ones she'd answered in the pre-trial interviews, and Madeleine's responses were as honest as possible without mentioning Severin. Her confidence was building. In fact the testimony went even more smoothly than it had in Ms. Jameson's office, because Jameson was not stopping her to explore weaknesses as she had before. Madeleine knew that would most likely occur during cross-examination, when Joe Whitney took his turn.

However, by the time Ms. Jameson finished asking questions, the judge adjourned court until the next day.

Madeleine was disappointed. She had hoped to get it over with that afternoon. She would now have to endure another sleepless night, followed by another day of testifying, with the worst part yet to come. And she had already worn her lucky suit.

After the judge left the courtroom and people began to move toward the exit, Madeleine felt a cool hand on her arm. She turned to see a handsome dark-haired woman in her fifties, and she recognized her grief-stricken expression from the news. She had the same long nose and thick, dark lashes as her daughter, Anita Salazar.

Madeleine gasped. "Mrs. Salazar!"

Around them, conversations rippled to silence.

Mrs. Salazar regarded Madeleine with heavy, red-rimmed eyes. "Dr. LeBlanc. I want to thank you for your courage. For bringing my daughter back."

She leaned forward and kissed Madeleine on each cheek.

Madeleine was speechless. Mrs. Salazar took her husband's arm and he held her with care. They slowly left the courtroom.

❧❦❧

THE FRONT PAGE OF the morning newspaper led with a picture of Mrs. Salazar kissing Madeleine's cheek. That kiss invoked renewed confidence and determination. Madeleine would see that Zenon paid for what he did.

Once again, she resisted the reporters' questions as she entered the courtroom with Ethan and Sam. She settled herself, waiting to be called. And once again, the courtroom was jam-packed. The trial picked up where it had left off, and Madeleine was called to the stand for cross-examination.

Joe started off by asking small details about Madeleine's testimony from the day before, referring to the old plantation on River Road. "You entered private property in Hahnville, Louisiana, without permission?"

"Yes."

"So you were illegally trespassing."

"Yes."

"Did you perhaps think that the property was open to the public?"

"No, there were 'no trespassing' signs posted."

"But you went in anyway?"

"Yes."

"What did you expect to find there?"

Madeleine took a breath. "I was curious about the place. I had uncovered documents that indicated the old plantation had belonged to my family in previous years."

Whitney nodded and scraped his teeth along his lower lip. "Still does."

She looked at him, confused. "I beg your pardon?"

"The property is still owned by your family, Dr. LeBlanc. Were you not aware of that fact?"

"I—no. No, I wasn't."

"Are you saying you did not know that Zenon Lansky owns it?"

Madeleine was stunned. "*Zenon* owns that property?" She stole a look at Ms. Jameson, and could tell that the news was no surprise to her.

Why didn't she tell me?

And then she wondered if perhaps she had, and Madeleine was so absorbed with appearing sane that she had somehow missed it.

"I didn't know he . . ." Her voice trailed off, because in that moment, she realized that Joe had said that the property was owned by *her family.*

Whitney retrieved a piece of paper from his desk and presented it to the judge and to Jameson. Jameson objected and the two lawyers approached the bench while Madeleine sat on the witness stand trying to absorb what Whitney was saying.

Whitney returned and handed Madeleine the paper. "Dr. LeBlanc, will you please examine this document and tell the court what it is."

The blood throbbed in her ears. "It, uh, it looks like a property deed."

"That's correct. And can you tell me whose names are on it?"

The paper was trembling in her hand. "It says that my father, Gaston Rémi LeBlanc, deeded the property to Zenon Lansky in 1980."

A murmur rippled through the courtroom, and the judge had to bang the gavel to restore order. Madeleine gripped the stand. Joe retrieved the paper from her hands and asked another question, but her mind was racing. She didn't know what to do with this information, and had to force herself to focus on what he was saying.

"What was the question again?" she asked him.

"I said, did you know that Zenon Lansky was your half brother?"

"Wh . . . what?"

"Are you asking me to repeat the question yet again, Dr. Le-Blanc?"

Madeleine felt nauseated. Felt even that she might faint. Each and every person in the room was staring at her.

"I . . . no I don't . . ." she tried to say, and it came as a whisper.

"Beg your pardon, Dr. LeBlanc?"

Madeleine filled her lungs, and it came as a shudder. "No. Zenon is not my half brother. He grew up in a house near me."

"Shall I produce the paternity test?"

Whitney strode to a stack of papers and selected one, showed it to the judge, and then handed it to Madeleine. Madeleine couldn't even read it. She made a show of sweeping her gaze across it as it wilted in her grasp.

"Well, Dr. LeBlanc?"

"If Zenon Lansky is my half brother, it's news to me."

"That so? Because by all accounts, you and him have been running around together since you took your first steps."

Madeleine shook her head. "Marc and I—I mean, my brother, my real brother . . ."

She paused, steadying herself. "We knew Zenon's parents when we were kids. Zenon *had* a father. A different father."

Whitney grunted, signaling to the jury that he doubted her veracity. "Were you aware that your father deeded the plantation over to his son, Zenon Lansky, when Zenon was still an infant?"

"No," Madeleine said. And then, "I had no idea Zenon owned that property, let alone that my father had given it to him."

"So, your father never mentioned *any* of this to you?" He spread his arms wide.

"No!" Madeleine said. "I had no idea!"

"Since your father is deceased, Dr. LeBlanc, I guess all we have to go by is your word."

Ms. Jameson piped up with an objection, and the judge sustained it.

The memory of that night in the flower shop crept over Madeleine. Disturbing on its own, but in light of this news it was an absolute abomination. Her gaze stole to Zenon. He was watching her. And on his face there lurked the ghost of a smile. He must have known all along. There was another person who would have known about it as well: Chloe.

Madeleine's blood coursed with outrage and mortification. She closed her eyes for a moment, but she knew the bramble was stretching from the shadows. From beneath the seats, curling from the corners, reaching higher, up toward the ceiling.

I'VE GOT TO CALM *down*, Madeleine told herself. *It doesn't change what happened to Anita. It's a separate thing.*

"Now, Dr. LeBlanc, let's go back to the night when you found

Anita Salazar in the bayou. You claim you saw the defendant wandering along the banks, near where the body was found."

The courtroom was filled with briar, ebony, and snaking.

But Madeleine managed to say, "Yes, that's true."

"How close would you say he was to the body, about twenty feet?"

"No, he was probably about forty yards from the actual spot where I found Anita. He was on the opposite bank of the waterway and down a ways."

Whitney's eyebrows lifted with feigned surprise. "Forty yards? Did you say forty yards?"

"Thereabouts."

"On the *opposite* bank?"

"Yes," her voice was beginning to sound weak even to her own ears.

"That can hardly be considered near the body."

"I assumed she'd gotten away from him, but then died from wounds he'd already inflicted."

"Objection, your honor!" Whitney bellowed.

What did I say? Why is he objecting?

"Sustained," said the judge. "The witness will confine her response to only answer questions posed by defending counsel."

Joe Whitney tented his fingers to his mouth. "And you say he was wandering in impenetrable wilderness."

"Well, yes. I suppose it wasn't completely impenetrable," Madeleine said. "Because he was there."

"And later, *you* were wandering impenetrable wilderness."

"I—yeah."

"But you saw him clearly."

"Oh, yes." Madeleine said. "I was surprised to see him, because I'd never seen anyone there on the banks before. I'd never known anyone to attempt to go out there on foot."

"So you were surprised to see him standing there in the rain."

"Yes. I mean, no, it wasn't raining. Well, it *had* been raining. But it stopped raining just before I saw Zenon."

"And then it started again?"

"Yes." The word tumbled idiotically into the courtroom.

Joe Whitney threw back his head and laughed. "So you say it was raining cats and dogs. Then it stopped, and you got a good look at Zenon, and then it started pouring again?"

She gritted her teeth. "Yes!"

He laughed and clapped his hands together. "All right, all right. Now let's talk about the boat. You saw a boat near the body."

"That's correct."

"And you assumed that it was the defendant's boat."

"Yes."

"And later, after you retrieved the corpse from the water, the storm hit, it was dark and raining, and you were pursued by that same boat?"

She could feel the blood pulsing in her neck. It was clear what he was getting at. She took a deep breath.

"It was difficult to see due to the rain and darkness, but on the way back, I could hear a boat's motor and see a spotlight. I assumed that it was Zenon's boat chasing me, because there had been no other boats around. And Zenon had already tried to board my craft."

Joe looked annoyed, and Madeleine felt that she had scored at least one small victory.

"But you can't be sure that it was his boat, correct?" he said.

"Like I said, no, I couldn't see to be sure."

"All right Dr. LeBlanc. You testified that you ferried the body of Anita Salazar from one end of the bayou to the other."

"Yes."

"In the middle of a severe tropical storm."

"Yes."

"And when you wrecked your boat, you carried the corpse bodily."

She paused. It was sounding ridiculous. Macabre, even.

"Yes, that's correct."

"You're stronger than you look, Dr. LeBlanc." He winked at her and walked toward the jury, then turned back and spread his arms wide. "She was already dead."

"Yes."

"You testified that you feared for your own life, both from the severe weather and because you thought you were being pursued. Is that true?"

"Yes."

"And yet you risked your life to lug around the body of a woman you barely knew, and whose life you could not save?"

"Yes, I did."

He lifted his shoulders. "Now why would you do that?"

This, at least, she could answer with confidence. "Because of the storm, I was afraid her body would get swept out to sea, and no one would know the truth about what happened to her."

"The truth about what happened to her," Whitney repeated, scratching his chin. "That's what we're trying to figure out now."

She folded her arms.

"Dr. LeBlanc, did you know that your blood was found all over the victim's body?"

An uneasy sensation wormed through her stomach. "No, I did not. But of course that would make sense, because I'd injured myself in several different ways, and then carried—"

"Carried her body all around the swamp. We heard all that. Do you know how much of the *defendant's* blood was found on the victim's body?"

She looked at Jameson, who was on the edge of her seat, but did not assert any objection.

Madeleine looked back at Joe. "None. I was told they found no evidence like that. They said that any blood or tissue from Zenon would have been destroyed during the storm."

"Yours wasn't."

She straightened her back. "Yeah, but she'd been completely submerged in the water twice since Zenon got at her."

"Objection."

"Sustained."

"I bled on her after I'd already pulled her out of the water!" Madeleine blurted.

The courtroom had gone so dark from the briar. Severin shifted from deep in the thorns.

Joe put his hands up in a calming gesture. "All right Dr. Le-Blanc, all right. You bled on her after she came out of the water." He sighed and folded his hands, shaking his head. "Dr. LeBlanc, you admit to being there in the swamp the night Anita Salazar was killed."

"I wasn't there when she was killed, but I was there soon after."

"And you admit to being in the house on River Road where detectives found a profuse quantity of Angel Frey's blood. Enough blood to draw the conclusion that Angel Frey had died there. Seems to me you're the one most likely committed the murders. What do you have to say about that?"

"Objection, your honor!" Ms. Jameson interjected.

Finally!

Again the judge ordered counsel to approach the bench, and the trio hissed at each other. Madeleine's gaze swept the courtroom. Jurors cut her with suspicious looks. Ethan and Sam seemed alarmed. Reporters were scribbling furiously on notepads. All of their faces looked strange in the briar, eyes glinting silver and faces drawn in shadow.

From somewhere above, Severin laughed.

Madeleine looked up and saw her sitting atop thick molding that ran a few feet below the ceiling. Perched the way a carved cherub might look down upon a Victorian parlor.

"You're in trouble!" Severin chided. "You frightened up when it was your turn to send someone through, but you're in trouble anyway!"

The lawyers returned to their positions.

"The witness will answer the question," the judge said.

"I . . ." Madeleine stammered.

Every single eye in the courtroom was trained on her. Severin continued to swing her legs and giggle.

Madeleine tore her eyes from her and focused on Joe Whitney. "I—What was the question?"

Joe Whitney sighed deeply and leaned against the witness stand, speaking sideways to Madeleine so that he was still facing the jury.

"Dr. LeBlanc, you admit to being present at the scenes of both murders. The defendant, Mr. Lansky does not. You are the only one we can be sure was there. What do you have to say about that?"

"I saw him! I saw him there. Both times. And my father, if only he'd . . ." She stopped.

"Dr. LeBlanc, did you kill Angel Frey?"

"No!"

"Did you kill Anita Salazar?"

"No, my God, I did not! Why would I do such a thing? I've never even met Angel Frey!"

The courtroom erupted in turmoil, and again the judge had to bang the gavel. This time, he threatened to clear it.

Whitney continued.

"That's right. Why would you do such a thing?" Whitney's voice became soft, almost kind.

And then Whitney turned and looked her full in the face for a moment, and the strangest expression came across him. As though she could draw a line down the center and recognize fear on one side of it, and avarice on the other.

He said gently, "Dr. LeBlanc, have you ever had a conversation with an invisible little girl named Severin?"

Madeleine's heart stopped.

SHE SAT FROZEN, UNABLE to speak. Ms. Jameson balked, and was silenced by the judge.

"Dr. LeBlanc. Have you ever had a lengthy conversation with an invisible little girl named Severin?" Joe repeated.

"No, I have not," Madeleine croaked.

"Dr. LeBlanc, may I remind you that you are under oath."

"She's not invisible!" Madeleine snapped.

Joe looked at her, genuinely surprised. Her mind reeled. What had she said? What could she say?

Joe Whitney gave a condescending smile. "The *whole* truth, Dr. LeBlanc. Have you ever had a lengthy conversation with *anyone* named Severin?"

Madeleine sat mute. She could think of nothing to offer in explanation. She knew her silence was damning, but she simply could not speak, truth or lie.

"I—she's . . . Yes."

"Can anyone see Severin but you?" Joe asked. "Because if not, I would call her invisible, wouldn't you?"

Tears streamed down Madeleine's face, and she started to shake.

"Is she in the courtroom right now?" Joe asked delicately but loud enough for all to hear. "Won't you point her out for us, Doctor?"

She was speechless. *How did he know? My God, how much did he know?*

"What kind of conversations have you had with this invisible girl?"

Madeleine could say nothing. She tried to speak, but failed.

Whitney sighed. "Permission to treat as a hostile witness, your honor."

"Proceed," said the judge.

"Dr. LeBlanc, is it true that in your conversations with the invisible girl, the topic was usually about death and violence?"

Madeleine remained mute, tears streaming.

"Your honor . . ."

"Please answer the question, Dr. LeBlanc."

Oh, dear God. "Yes," she whispered.

"Forgive me, Dr. LeBlanc. Did you answer yes to the question, that the topic of conversation between you and the invisible little girl, was usually death and violence?"

She shuddered. It was over. Too late. No sense fighting.

"Yes," she said, louder.

Melee broke out in the courtroom. Joe raised his voice while the judge banged in frustration.

"Is there a history of schizophrenia in your family?"

Schizophrenia. Well, Madeleine was no longer convinced of that. As long as she was going to be compelled to speak the *whole* truth, she might as well tell it all.

"No," she said. "I don't believe that's true now."

"You mean to tell me your father was not diagnosed schizophrenic?"

"Yes, he was diagnosed as having schizophrenia. Improperly diagnosed. As a licensed psychologist, I now believe that diagnosis was an erroneous—"

"Please just answer the questions, Dr. LeBlanc. So you are having conversations about death and violence with an invisible little girl. And you also just happened to be present at the scene of two murders. Would you say that was a fair statement?"

"It didn't happen the way you're implying!"

"Dr. LeBlanc, have you yourself engaged in any violent acts over the past year?"

"No, I have not! I am not a violent person!"

Ethan stared. Sam was ashen. Chloe, even Chloe, looked on with anxiety. Madeleine caught the look in their eyes, and her last words hung stiffly in the air.

"Dr. LeBlanc," Whitney said, leaning in. "Did you know a man named Carlo Jefferson?"

Oh, no. How could this be? How could he know all of this? She covered her face.

Ms. Jameson cast futile objections at the judge, and once more the two lawyers approached the bench and whispered furiously. It all seemed so conspiratorial. Half the courtroom was lost to bramble. The judge once again directed Madeleine to answer the question.

Severin grew bored again, and lowered herself so that she was hanging from the molding. She reached her arm up and walked herself along the rail, swinging as if she were on a set of monkey bars, though her agility defied gravity. She swung in close to Madeleine and jumped, landing near where Joe Whitney stood. A grimace on her face.

"I knew of Carlo Jefferson, yes." Madeleine said softly.

"Did you attempt to shoot Carlo Jefferson the night of November fifteenth of last year?"

Madeleine said nothing.

"Were you aware that Carlo Jefferson died of gunshot wounds on that night?"

This couldn't be. Madeleine trained her thoughts with pinpoint focus.

Severin, help me!

"Are you aware," Whitney growled, "that you were seen carrying a gun near Carlo Jefferson's residence on the very night he was killed?"

The courtroom erupted, and the judge was livid. Madeleine wished he would make good on his promise to clear the court.

Severin, do something!

"What do you wish on me to do?" Severin asked.

Tell me something that will help put Zenon away! They're going to blame it on me!

Joe Whitney was shouting. "Tell me about the gun you were carrying the night Carlo Jefferson was killed. Was that the same gun used to kill your brother, Marc LeBlanc?"

"That was a suicide!" Madeleine sobbed.

"Zenon does right," Severin said. "Why should I help cage him? You've never sent one single person through. You never listen to anything I wish on you."

Madeleine could barely absorb what Whitney was implying. Worse than anything she had feared. But it was too late. She had now told so many lies that she could hardly remember what was the truth. She wept with horror and humiliation.

Ms. Jameson was valiantly raging at the judge and Whitney, trying to salvage the situation, and the judge was banging the gavel again, calling for order.

Severin. Madeleine formed the thought carefully and deliberately, and looked directly at her. *If we can get Zenon convicted, he could get the death penalty. That means they will send him through.*

"Dr. LeBlanc," Joe Whitney was saying, had been saying, and he waved his hand in front of her eyes to get her attention. "Hello? Dr. LeBlanc, did the invisible little girl instruct you to shoot Carlo . . ."

The courtroom disappeared. All around was bramble and nothing more. Madeleine began to feel an unnatural sense of motion, and below her, a tunnel of thorns yawned open. She gripped a witness stand she could no longer see. Severin laughed and dove down the center of the tunnel. Madeleine was slipping after her, falling, and then the bottom of the tunnel fell away to an openness that seemed to stretch forever. It looked as though she were tumbling toward the earth. It lay in azure sparkles, land and sea. Above her was bramble where there ought to have been clouds. Her stomach dropped.

The great river was below, drawing nearer. It stretched in a long, thin, snaking line from far beyond where she could see, and then spread into a fan as it greeted the ocean. She felt herself fall deeper toward one of the arteries. She was closing in without feeling the cold, but she could smell the thin ionic atmosphere. She could see trees now, and swampland, and she could smell pine and moist earth. She had to grip the witness stand to maintain balance. A plantation below, and she recognized it as Terrefleurs on River Road.

". . . Jefferson?" she heard Whitney say from a distant corner of her psyche.

She realized that time in the briar didn't sync with time in the real world, as the fugue felt like it had already been transpiring for several minutes though it could have only been seconds. Joe had only just finished stating his question, *Dr. LeBlanc, did the invisible little girl instruct you to shoot Carlo Jefferson?*

"It's not schizophrenia," Madeleine said aloud, keeping her eyes focused on the plantation house. "I've had clairvoyant experiences. They're not hallucinations."

Whitney was blathering in protest, but she ignored him. She felt as if she were dropping toward the plantation house, and the scene moved so rapidly she gasped, sure she would feel the impact of the roof as she careened toward it. But at the last moment she swooped forward and rushed past the main house to a tiny structure just beyond. A miniature building with several rows of round holes in it, pegs positioned below each hole. The pigeon house. She saw inside the hole. Saw clearly though it was pitch black in there. Pink nail polish and blood that had turned black with time, and a glimmer of precious metal.

It was what she needed to know.

Take me back, Severin!

Back in the courtroom. And though the briar still corroded the veneer of the physical world, she could see Joe Whitney and most of the others.

She looked Joe straight in the eye. "Zenon Lansky murdered Angel Frey at the house on River Road. And after he killed her, he took a keepsake."

Whitney opened his mouth and Madeleine could hear him suck in wind as he was about to bellow.

She trained her eyes and balled her focus onto Joe Whitney.

You. Keep. Still.

She thought this without speaking aloud. The same focus and direction she used with Severin. Whitney's open mouth froze, and no words came out. He held motionless for a moment.

She turned and threw the same gaze at the judge, and he paused with that cursed gavel in midair.

She knew she had one moment, and for that moment, the room belonged to her.

"If you look inside the pigeon house at Zenon Lansky's property in Hahnville, you will find Angel Frey's finger, along with her ring."

She wrenched her eyes from Joe Whitney and searched the crowd until she saw Sheriff Cavanaugh, who looked appalled. "You'll have to clear away the brush to get to it," Madeleine said. "Please look, Sheriff."

Whitney released the frozen breath that had caught in his lungs. "Ob-JECTION, your honor!" The sound reverberated from deep within his jowls. "I call for an immediate mistrial, and I demand that you place Dr. Madeleine LeBlanc under arrest for the murders of Anita Salazar and Angel Frey!"

seventy-one

HAHNVILLE, 1927

*T*HE TWINS HAD SUPPOSEDLY gone out to help with the refugees, but more likely they'd taken a slingshot and frog gig and headed for the woods. Mother was back from New Orleans and was speaking to Francois outside. Marie-Rose huddled with her older sister in front of the rolltop desk.

"Patrice," Marie-Rose whispered. "But what if Papa is dead?"

"Don't talk that way. We don't know what's happened, and until we find out we must continue to hope."

"I can find out."

"No!" The vehemence of Patrice's reply caused Marie-Rose to jump.

"But—"

"Don't you go looking." Patrice switched on the radio.

The announcer was droning with no emotion. Rose tried to listen, but he spoke of what was happening in faraway places, no mention of her father. The man was saying that the Cabin Teele levee had burst, and the water now covered everything to the west. The river had also claimed McCrea, and then the Glasscock levee above Baton

Rouge, and with each breach the water had stretched a hundred miles or more into the land. Several miles of the levee at Bayou des Glaises had crumbled, flooding the area they called the sugar bowl. The river had swallowed the homes of more than 100,000 people there.

"But what about Papa?" Marie-Rose said.

"Hush."

The announcer spoke of levees that folded even as workers were stacking them with sandbags. In Melville, the surge from the Mississippi collided with that of the Atchafalaya. Together the two waterways had devoured the town.

Marie-Rose said, "I don't understand. What's happening?"

"People thought they could tame the river. Now she's gotten up from her banks and she's out there walking the earth."

"She's walked the earth before!"

"But now she's hungrier."

The announcer continued to speak in an even tone, as though reading nothing more engaging than a harvest forecast. With the crest of the river looming ever closer, New Orleans had lobbied to dynamite the levee at Saint Bernard in order to divert the water flow away from the city, but the residents of Saint Bernard and Plaquemines took up arms in protest. Miles away, a molasses tanker had rammed the levee at Junior Plantation. An investigation was underway to determine whether this had been an intentional act. Many believed that the destruction of the Crow's Landing levee had also been deliberate.

Rose and Patrice looked at one another. Marie-Rose knew that the Crow's Landing levee bordered Glory Plantation, where Monsieur Chapman lived. Patrice's clear blue eyes shifted away. She was sitting in the window, the sunset washing over her dark skin, and she looked like a living statue of tarnished brass.

The people of Plaquemines and Saint Bernard had posted guards at the levee to prevent their New Orleans neighbors from taking matters into their own hands. When a skiff had drawn too close to the Saint Bernard levee, guards had fired upon it, killing one of the pilots. Residents had also fired upon another skiff carrying a reporter and photographer from the Associated Press.

Marie-Rose closed her eyes.

The announcer said that now, New Orleans has secured the government support it needed, and officials were planning to dynamite the levee. The residents of Plaquemines and Saint Bernard had only forty-eight hours to clear out before their homes would be sacrificed to the river's flow.

The man on the radio was saying nothing about Papa. Rose pushed his voice to the far corner of her mind, drawing on the skill she'd learned. She let the vines come forth.

"Rosie, stop it!"

Patrice shook her until she opened her eyes.

"The lady said—"

"Don't you listen, Rosie! They trick you to go chasing in there, and one day you'll find out you can't come back."

"I can come back!"

"You might think so. For Papa it got harder and harder. Now sometimes he's in there for years at a time."

"It's not fair. I finally learned how to do it. Maman says we're supposed to go in there and bring back secrets."

Patrice lowered her voice. "Never you mind what Maman says."

"But she says we could all die."

"Not die. Become extinct. It means our lineage won't continue."

"Creole?"

Patrice shook her head. "No. People like us who can work the river magic. But Rosie, you mustn't trust what Maman says."

"I just want to find Papa."

"The briar patch is ruled by your pain, Rosie. Those spirits you see, they live inside of you, they are your pain, and they make more pain for you just to keep themselves in existence."

"You don't know!"

"I do know. I've spent my entire life watching Papa, and Maman too. She treats him like an otter. Sends him deep into that wild to fetch back secrets. She wants to do the same with us. Worse. Sometimes I wonder if she wants . . ."

The words halted at her lips. She was staring at something beyond

Rose's shoulder. Marie-Rose turned. Their mother was standing in the doorway to the pantry.

Chloe's eyes bored into them. Marie-Rose wondered how much her mother had overheard. Chloe walked toward them, boots making slow clicks across the wooden floorboards, and switched the radio off. Patrice lowered her gaze.

Chloe said, "Marie-Rose, you were going to look for your father."

Marie-Rose gaped at her, suddenly both excited and frightened. Patrice said nothing.

Chloe said, "Go, then. Tell us where he is."

Patrice kept her gaze on the silent radio. Marie-Rose wished she would look at her, give her some sign as to what to do.

"I'm waiting," Chloe said.

"Yes ma'am." Marie-Rose closed her eyes again.

The vines returned, curling, black, with dark tiny leaves. Creatures were skittering in there. And river devils. Lots of them, Rose knew. Maman had said one day she would have a river devil too. Rose wondered which one. They were all scary. Maman had said it was better to seek them out first.

She moved through the tunnels, trying to be silent, trying to go unnoticed.

The sound of a chair moving, and then her mother's voice: "No Patrice! You stay here."

"I will not sit and watch while you send her into that place!"

"You obey me!"

Rose tried to adjust so that she could see her sister, but she could no longer see anything in that world. She'd already gone so deep, so fast. She tried to concentrate on Papa. If she had a river devil of her own she could have found him immediately. Tormentors in the physical world; guides in the bramble.

Suddenly, water enveloped her, and she gasped. It felt thick like fresh milk, and smelled foul. The vines opened up to a place she did not recognize, but she knew it from an internal sensing that comes easily in the briar. The Locoul Plantation. She saw an older woman and a younger man with an ugly scar that criss-crossed his throat. Papa was not here.

Patrice and Maman, so distant were their voices, but Rose could still hear them.

"Then let me go instead," Patrice was saying.

"No! She should go on her own."

Patrice pleaded, "Rosie's too young. What if they find her?"

"They will find her eventually. All of you. It's part of who you are."

Rose turned away from Locoul Plantation and followed a pull that led elsewhere. In the bramble, places did not follow rules of location. This was also true of time. Things existed outside of linear patterns.

A new tunnel opened up, at once vast and spreading and yet still contained within the thorny maze. Unlike in the physical world, here things appeared as they were, not as they looked. The river imparted her true nature—a concentrated energy that was not really alive, but somehow had a life force. She'd grown tired of the structures meant to tame her, had shaken loose and arisen, crushing all to her bosom, leaving mud-silken trails of her caresses.

Papa was close. Marie-Rose dipped down beneath the surface, feeling the fetid water envelop her, but she could see nothing but blackness and could only hold her breath for so long. She lifted her head above the surface again.

Rose knew she was looking at Glory Plantation though nothing was recognizable. All of it underwater. A hog, long dead and puffed into a grotesque balloon, lay wedged atop some rubble. The levee stretched long and otherwise solid, but a crater bisected it. The water seemed still as glass. Like a sleepy bayou where rooftops rose instead of cypress trees. And yet Marie-Rose felt the power of it. A steeple rose above the surface. It stood tall and pious on a plane of glass, no hint of the small chapel supporting it.

But as Marie-Rose watched, the steeple groaned and then leaned away from the breach in the levee. It burst into splinters. The water boiled around it for a moment, the steeple's cross bobbing momentarily before being dragged under, and then: silence and stillness again.

Rose knew her father was very close. And yet, the feeling was different from what it ought to be. A sense like Papa, but not quite the same.

Hands closed around her wrists. She gasped. A woman rose from the water, eyes silvery and shining, teeth sharp, her hair black, long, and thin.

"You wish to see your father, you ought not be looking up here."

Rose tried to shake loose from the grip, but the woman held tight. And then she dragged her down beneath the surface. Marie-Rose screamed. She felt the water, tasted it as it filled her mouth, and yet she was letting loose clear screams in her physical body, she knew. She could feel the hands of her sister and her mother on her, but the river devil had the strongest grip.

She couldn't breathe.

"I'll show you where he is," laughed the river devil.

She went down, down into that unholy water. All silver and shining. It felt like she was inside a pool of mercury. It might have been pitch black to her eyes, were it not for the river devil. Marie-Rose kicked, trying to free herself. But she knew she was coming close to the place where Papa was. She felt her strength waning. The river devil dragged her into the depths, silver eyes shining with the river itself, her grin wide and hungry.

Hungry for what, she didn't know, but the river devil seemed to delight at Rose's panic.

And then she saw Papa. The husk that had once been her father. He was that same ghastly silver-gray as the water and mud, illuminated by nothing but the river devil's whim. His body lay wedged in a window. He was not recognizable beyond the knowing sense that comes inside the briar. He looked as though he'd become one with the river, his clothing and skin streaming like the green, feathery coontail that roots itself to the river bottom.

Marie-Rose flailed. She tried jerking away from the river devil. She felt herself growing weaker. Warmth at her seat—perhaps in her physical body she had wet herself. And with Maman looking on.

But her vision here did not dim. It only grew brighter.

Even through her panic, she wondered what had happened to the rest of her father. The part of Papa that had nothing to do with his physical body. She could still feel that sense of him somewhere.

"Breathe, Rosie! You can breathe down here!"

Patrice. She was there, gripping her by the waist, right next to the river devil. But Patrice was wrong, Marie-Rose couldn't breathe. She couldn't fill her lungs with that thick, silver water. And she could no longer move. Couldn't fight.

Patrice pressed her lips against Marie-Rose's and blew. Rose saw bubbles flash before her eyes. But her sister's breath did enter her lungs. Thin with oxygen, but it calmed her. They were moving up again, toward the surface: Patrice, Marie-Rose, and the river devil.

seventy-two

NEW ORLEANS, 2010

ADELEINE PUT A HAND to her forehead as she stared out the window of the Mercedes. What would they find at Terrefleurs? Were they even looking?

She'd begged Severin to shed some light on what had happened, to give some scrap of information to use against Zenon, and it had backfired. Should they find nothing in the pigeon house at Terrefleurs, then she was publicly exposed as a raving lunatic, continuing the madness handed down from generation to generation.

And yet, if they uncovered a severed finger from the pigeon house the way Severin had showed her, what did that mean? To Madeleine, it meant further evidence that whatever was happening was something beyond schizophrenia. But to the rest of the world, it was evidence that incriminated her. Zenon would be free to kill again, and Madeleine would go to prison for the murder of the two girls.

In a closed courtroom tomorrow the judge would rule on whether or not to grant Joe Whitney his mistrial.

She ran her finger along the dark upholstery. Oran was driving. It occurred to Madeleine that this might be the first time she noticed any color at all to his skin. As she sat behind him, his ears were red.

If she hadn't had to fight her way through the bramble and the equally daunting reporters, Madeleine might not be sitting next to Chloe in the backseat of the old Mercedes. She'd have escaped the courtroom with Ethan and Sam. But the reporters were everywhere. Those pointed questions. Mrs. Salazar's appalled stare. Madeleine had felt sick after her disastrous testimony when she'd spotted Chloe's Mercedes waiting outside the courthouse. She might as well have chosen a cannibal's stew pot as a getaway car. But no choice, and no time to find Ethan. The reporters had been so voracious she would've probably accepted a ride from Joe Whitney himself just to evade them.

Her cell phone was turned off. She hadn't wanted to talk to anyone. But it wasn't fair to just leave Ethan and Sam hanging. She powered it up and called Ethan.

"Hey," she said. "Just wanted to let you know I'm OK. Had to get out of there."

"Where are you?"

"In Chloe's car. I'll let you know when and where I land."

"You sure you're OK?"

"Yeah, all things considered. Look, I'm going to probably turn my phone off again. Reporters."

He let out a long breath. "All right. I was worried. Sam was too. I'll tell her you're OK."

"Thank you."

"And Maddy . . ."

"Yeah?"

"I'm glad you called. I wondered if you were just going to disappear."

She nodded, even though she knew he couldn't see her nodding, but her throat was too tight to say anything.

Ethan said, "Just let me know where to meet you, OK?"

"I will."

"Love you, Maddy."

"Love you too."

But when she hung up, she felt such a stark flash of self-loathing that it made her stomach roll. She saw herself as she must have looked on the stand. All the strangeness and humiliation. Hated that Ethan had seen it. She let the feeling run through, and then run out of her. Ethan had said he was up to the task. This would be his chance to either reaffirm or rethink his loyalty.

Madeleine took a breath and said to Oran, "Why don't you let me off at the next corner."

"Oran will drive you home," Chloe said.

"My place will be crawling with reporters."

Chloe waved a hand. "Then you come to my house."

And Madeleine felt the tug. But this time, there was no mistaking its origins. She gave a harsh laugh.

"What are you doing, Chloe? You think you can use that trick to manipulate me?"

Madeleine threw her gaze at those burning red ears in the front seat. "Oran, stop the car right now!"

He pulled over and slammed on the brakes. And his response was so sudden that Madeleine knew he was reacting to something deeper than the vocal command. Chloe teetered in her seat belt, and Madeleine instinctively grabbed her shoulder to steady her.

Chloe placed a hand over Madeleine's as she regained her balance. "What I do, I do for the better. A mother tells a child to stay away from the stove when the pot is boiling over, and that is not manipulating."

Madeleine shook her head, marveling. "You trick people for the better? The better of *what*?"

Madeleine was shaking now. "You knew! All this time, this entire time, you knew Zenon was my brother, and you wanted me to *make a child* with him!"

"Do not believe in cultural superstitions. He is right for you to make a child. You have your own devil now, Madeleine." Chloe flung her arm at the window, beyond which stood the quiet homes of the Garden District. "Do you think you can live like them? Marry some foolish bull and breed mundane babies? You are nothing like them."

"I'm the only one who knows what's right in my life."

But Madeleine did feel a sense of loss as she looked upon one of the gracious, stately homes beyond the window, its green shutters and white columns almost drowsy in the afternoon heat. A bicycle with streamers on the handlebars leaned against the porch, and along the sidewalk stood a wrought-iron gate, closed with a pretty latch.

Madeleine curled her fingers around the door handle. "Chances are I won't ever have a life like that, I know. But at least for right now, I'm not completely alone."

❧

SHE'D WALKED FOR A timeless expanse, unsure where to go, disbelieving there might be anywhere *to* go. She'd been afraid to stop. The longer she walked, the more the black vines receded.

She steadied herself and trudged along the sidewalk. She was somewhere at the boundaries of downtown. She realized she'd somehow gotten herself headed back in the direction of the courthouse. A doorway gaped from a brick building, and a gust of stale air brushed her face as she approached. A tavern. Not necessarily an appealing place, but the simple darkness and quiet of it beckoned her inside.

She stepped in, blinded by the contrast in lighting from the street, and worked her way to a table in the back. The tavern was mostly empty. Not quite time for the five o'clock rush though a couple of barflies dotted the counter.

Madeleine reached into her bag and powered up her cell phone as she sank into the farthest chair. She eyed the bartender, who was engaged in conversation with someone at the near end of the bar, a white-haired businessman. Madeleine thought if she'd ever wanted a drink, the time was now. Something good and strong.

But first she sent a text message to Ethan, telling him where she was and asking him to come get her.

Then to her surprise, the bartender walked around the counter and set a glass of some kind of hard alcohol in front of her. She looked up inquisitively.

"From Joe," he said, hitching a thumb toward the near end of the bar.

The man she'd mistaken for a businessman was now turning toward her. She grit her teeth. Joe Goddamned Whitney.

❧❧❧

MADELEINE SHOULD HAVE PICKED a bar that wasn't so close to the courthouse. Come to think of it, she was half surprised that Ms. Jameson wasn't here tossing back a few herself.

Joe lifted a hand toward her from where he sat at the bar. "I'd've brought that drink over myself, hun, but I figured it'd just end up right back in my face."

He chuckled, but Madeleine was already calculating the velocity of pitching the drink in his face from where she sat, distance be damned. He must have seen the savagery in her eyes because he lifted his hands.

"Now hold on there, before you get to thinking too hard, I got something to tell you. All I ask is that you hear me out."

She glared at him. "I can't imagine we have anything to discuss."

But she was battling a sensation of defeat that was slipping toward despair. She exhaled, sagging as she let out her breath. Joe took this as a signal to indulge him, and he wrested his body off the bar stool and sagged into a chair opposite her.

She folded a shaky hand over the drink and raised it to her lips, draining the glass.

Joe grunted. "Me too." He motioned to the bartender for more drinks.

Madeleine's throat burned, eyes filming. She was not used to hard liquor. The result was an instant and welcome numbing in her lips that slowly filtered through her body.

Her cell phone buzzed with a text from Ethan: *Be right there. Worried. You OK?*

As the bartender brought over another round, she sent Ethan a message stating that she was fine. Joe lit a cigarette and waited for the bartender to leave. Madeleine put her cell phone back in her bag and looked into the fresh glass, but felt no further compulsion to drink.

Joe said, "All right. I'll get to the point. Just a few minutes ago, authorities recovered evidence from the plantation house on River Road. They found . . ." his face twitched. "They found . . ."

He sucked in a breath and then downed his glass.

Madeleine listened, tides of her own blood pounding in her ears.

Joe licked his lips, and she could see that his hands were shaking, too. She waited for him to continue.

"This has been one goddamned helluva case," he said, his voice gruff. He looked at her, and for a moment, she saw a flash of shame in him. "I want you to know Miss Madeleine, I took no form of pleasure in what happened in that courtroom today. I did what was necessary to defend my client, as is my duty by law."

"Tell me what they found, Joe!"

"They found a digit. A single human finger wearing a ring. The ring matches descriptions of the one worn by Angel Frey. In the pigeon house at Terrefleurs Plantation. Just as . . ." He gulped. "Just as you said."

So it was true. She felt relief rushing through her, but at the same time she recalled Whitney's final plea to the judge: *I demand that you place Dr. Madeleine LeBlanc under arrest for the murders of Anita Salazar and Angel Frey!*

"They'll be coming to arrest me, then. They'll think I did it. I told them where to find it."

Joe pursed his lips. "I doubt that'll happen, Miss Madeleine. There is visible blood and tissue beneath the fingernail. They'll do DNA testing on that tissue, and my client—" He coughed. "Well, if you repeat this to anyone, I'll deny it, but my client has deep concerns over those DNA tests."

My God. Madeleine laughed out loud, or maybe it was a sob. She took a trembling sip of the whiskey, fighting back the emotion that threatened to carry her away.

Joe said, "They had to use a boon or they'd've got it out hours ago. I can't for the life of me figure out how he got it into that pigeon house in the first place."

"Maybe he got a bird to carry it up there for him."

Joe looked at her as though he took her comment for sarcasm. If he'd read Mémée's diary, he would have understood just how serious she was.

He lowered his voice. "Miss Maddy, how exactly did you know about the pigeon house?"

She stared at him.

"It's all right, you can tell me," Joe said. "Anyone else, I'd say they had something to do with the crime. But you do have a kind of a sight, haven't you? Just between you and me, what exactly did you see?"

Her lips pulled back to bare her teeth. "Just between you and me? Are you my buddy now, Joe?"

Joe's hands went up. "I had no choice in the courtroom today." He waved a hand and took a drag from his cigarette. "Doesn't matter. You have a sight, just like Daddy Blank."

Madeleine's gaze flickered over Joe's face.

"Your father been a pain in my ass for many a year. Had a way of knowing things. Every time I think I might do a little something on the side, make a little money under the table, there go Daddy Blank, ringin my bell. And I'd think, there's no way he could know about this. Over the years, I figured it out: He had a sight."

She listened intently, unable to say a word. *My father's enemy knew him better than I did.*

Joe went on. "Even when we were at school together, he was already on my ass. I had a buddy who had a talent for getting his hands on exams before the actual test date come around. My buddy'd get the tests and I'd sell'm. Your daddy somehow knew every detail of our game. Made me split some of the profits with him to keep his mouth shut."

Madeleine had to smile. That did sound like her father.

"He was already a little whacko by then, and I thought maybe no one would believe him, but I couldn't take any chances. Over the years, whatever I got into, he'd either call me out publicly just to piss me off, or he'd come by in private if he wanted a cut." Joe took a final drag from his cigarette and crushed it out.

"Then his mind really started slipping, and I was safe from him a while. Big Brother was off duty." Joe regarded Madeleine for a moment. "God forbid you should start to slip that way."

Her back stiffened. God forbid.

Suddenly Joe's eyes grew shiny. "Miss Madeleine, I have to tell you something."

A stillness settled over her. He was about to make a confession. "I know, Joe."

He spoke as if he had not heard her. "I was there. The night he died. I was with him."

❧

JOE'S LOWER LIP BEGAN to tremble as he spoke. "Your daddy was harassing me. Of course he was. I harassed him back some. And then, we went on and took a little drink together. We was talking and remembering old times. He was down. He was really down."

Joe looked at Madeleine through moist eyes. "Your daddy and me, I know it looked like we always warrin with each other, but we're friends too. Were friends."

He paused, eyes glimmering with the same light as the whiskey.

"Then it was time to go on home, and your daddy asked me to drop him off." Joe's breath hitched, and he gestured in the general direction of Iberville. "Out there. I want to tell you that I didn't know what he was about to do there."

Joe caught his breath and blinked wet lashes. "But I can't say that to you, honey. Because I *did* know. I knew what he was after. I thought of taking him to your place instead, even though I know he wouldn't have stayed, but I didn't do that. And I even thought of calling you after I'd dropped him off, letting you know where he was."

Madeleine's hands trembled, and she felt her eyes fill.

"But I didn't do that either. I didn't do that either." He swallowed. "Because," he said, and the word emerged like a choke. "Because, I thought maybe it'd keep him quiet a little longer. Keep the heat off of me. I wanted him to keep his mouth shut about that goddamned mega-mart until the thing blew over some."

Tears finally spilled over and tumbled freely down his face, and they streamed for Madeleine as well.

"So I let him go on over there," he whispered. "And I didn't call you. And that was the last time I saw him."

"I see," she murmured. "But that didn't stop you from representing Zenon."

Joe wiped his eyes. "I swear to you honey, I had no idea what I'd gotten myself into until it was too late. I didn't know he was your half brother. All I knew was that you were a witness and I didn't really think nothing of it. Later, I quietly asked to be removed from the case. Twice. Both times the judge refused." He shook his head. "I don't know what I'm asking of you, Miss Madeleine. I can't ask you to forgive me. How could I?"

She was indeed angry. This was not a good man. But as much as she wanted to, she could not hold Joe responsible for her father's actions. Nor could she provide whatever absolution he sought—she felt it was not hers to give. And so she said nothing.

Joe sat motionless, his lips parted, eyes downcast, his shoulders lifting with each drawn breath. Then he looked up.

"But you knew, didn't you?" he said. "You knew I was there. Already knew it."

The bartender appeared again with a third round of drinks, though Madeleine hadn't touched the second one. The first had left her blessedly numb. But as for Joe, she could see that he was getting swept away.

He lit another cigarette and took a long, deep pull. "Your brother got the sight too, you know." He gave her a sidelong look. "Not your brother Marc, God rest his soul. I'm talking about your half brother."

Madeleine bristled.

Joe watched her, continuing. "After they pulled that evidence out of the pigeon house—and it didn't take them long, by the way. Your sheriff friend made some calls and that place was crawling with badges. Had a boon truck out there within an hour."

God bless Sheriff Cavanaugh and his tireless troupe.

"Anyway," Joe said. "I'd had a long talk with my client. Seems he got himself a special friend who feeds him information."

Madeleine's face remained expressionless, knowing Joe was watching her, but inside she was spinning. He was confirming what she'd suspected.

"Joe, isn't there some rule about attorney-client privilege? I'd hate to have to bear witness against you in front of some kind of ethics committee."

Joe made a grumbling noise into his glass, and otherwise chose to ignore the comment. "I must say, defending someone like Zenon Lansky, makes me rethink my chosen profession."

"Oh, there's always hope. The judge could declare a mistrial and Zenon could go free, and then your work here would be done."

He shrugged, missing the sarcasm. "A mistrial would just buy some time, that's all. U.S. attorney would have Lansky's ass back in jail awaiting a new trial before sundown. She can't afford to let this one go. It's a real high-profile case, thanks to you. The biggest one this city's seen in a long time."

"If this weren't such a high-profile case, you wouldn't have taken it."

Joe laughed with genuine mirth as he shook his head. "Just like your daddy. I have to say, I do miss him, your father." He regarded her. "We were always at odds, but we loved each other too. Well, I loved *him*, anyway. When my wife was in the hospital with lung cancer, he was there the whole time. And he didn't just make appearances. He was really there. He held her hand. Hell, he held my hand through it all. He was a good man. You just never knew what to expect."

She softened. "I am sorry about your wife, Joe."

Joe nodded. "I didn't deserve her. Since she's been gone, I've turned into some silly old fool, making passes at women half my age."

He sighed, holding his drink with both hands and staring into the amber liquid. "Well, I'd better get back to my client. You take care of yourself."

She watched him gather himself from his chair. As much as it would have pained her to admit it, she was grateful to him for telling her what he knew about Zenon and the police discovery. Certainly the bureau detectives and Ms. Jameson would have preferred to watch her sweat a while.

Joe paused at the bar and dug out his wallet to pay the bartender. Madeleine remembered the moment in court earlier that day, when she was able to silence Joe with sheer concentration. The bartender glanced at Madeleine, and she focused her thoughts: *On the house.*

As Joe handed the bartender some folded bills, the bartender put up his hands.

"No charge today, Joe."

Joe looked surprised. "No *charge*?"

"Nah, it's on the house."

Madeleine's pulse quickened.

Joe stood for a moment, then tucked the money back into his wallet, more confused than grateful.

"Thanks," he muttered, then shuffled toward the door.

As he left, Madeleine saw a little girl's silhouette in the door, framed by the late evening sun.

"Madeleine works the little trick, yes," Severin said.

Madeleine stood and retrieved her wallet from her purse, and offered a wad of bills to the bartender.

"On the house today, Miss," the bartender said, waving off the money.

"No, not today," she said, and dropped the bills on the bar in front of him.

As she left with Severin, she heard another customer ask if his drinks were on the house too.

"Hell no, you pay up," the bartender said.

Madeleine smiled. She blinked at the sunlight, leaned against the brick wall, and waited for Ethan.

seventy-three

NEW ORLEANS, 2010

*I*N THE CASE OF The People vs. Zenon Lansky, the good judge had declared a mistrial. Though not as a direct result of Madeleine's courtroom outburst. In that, he had ruled that the trial should continue. Later, however, it had come to light that some members of the jury were discussing what the newspapers had said about Madeleine.

The judge interviewed the jurors individually, and found several who had ignored his orders to stay away from news media, and were therefore "tainted." One juror had said that she read in the papers that Dr. Madeleine LeBlanc was a "seer," and that if the doc said Lansky'd done it, then he done it.

Just as Whitney had predicted, Zenon's freedom had been short-lived, and the U.S. attorney did indeed have his ass back in a federal holding facility before sundown.

Letters to Madeleine rolled in. People from all over the U.S., and then all over the world, had something to say. Mrs. Salazar had even sent a note of support.

Eventually detectives had released the results of the DNA tests from the remains at Terrefleurs, and the frenzy reached a crescendo. The lab had determined that the pigeon house remains belonged to Angel Frey, and matched the tissue scrapings underneath the fingernail to Zenon Lansky. This of course exonerated Madeleine in the eyes of the public.

And, false reports abounded, especially in the less-than-reputable publications. Some even stated that Madeleine was holding séances to determine winning lottery numbers.

MADELEINE MET WITH ETHAN at the PJ's Coffee at the uptown campus. She smoothed out the crumpled steno paper, light greenish-beige with a line down the center, with cramped script covering two sides in thick black ink that bled through.

"It came in the mail?" Ethan asked.

Madeleine shook her head. "No. Someone slipped it under the door."

"At your place?"

She nodded, handing it over to him.

Dear Madeleine,

I think about you every moment since arriving here. I can't imagine why you haven't come to visit me yet, you being my sister and all. I guess you probably blame yourself for getting me locked up. The guilt must be a lot for you to handle. You don't have to feel too bad, though. I'm pretty sure I'll be out soon. Seems if I concentrate real hard, things happen the way I want them to. Family trait, I guess. I know it must be hard for you to come to this place to see me. I'm really trying to understand that. I wish I could make it easier on you and come visit you instead. But of course that ain't going to happen just now. The next best thing is if one of my buddies came to see you. There's an old boy in here who's going to be let out soon. I showed him your picture on the TV, and he already thinks very highly of you. He says you looked real pretty on

the TV. He's a nasty son of a bitch but he's been rehabilitated.
Anyhow, don't be surprised if someone pays you a visit. The burden
to make social calls shouldn't just be on you. Fair's fair.

Your brother,

Zenon

Madeleine waited while Ethan read the letter. She understood
Zenon's meaning: He was not willing to go quietly to prison, and
would get at her in the only way he could. Already he had somehow
gotten someone to deliver this letter to her door. She wondered who
could have done that. Someone on parole? A guard? She wondered if
whoever it was might still be out there, watching.

Ethan looked up from the letter and pressed his lips together in a
tight line. "That son of a bitch."

He looked at her and took her hand in his. "Don't worry. I won't
let anyone get near you."

She squeezed.

He said, "Have you shown it to the police?"

"No, but I will. Can't imagine it'll do much good."

"You get yourself a handgun and keep it with you."

She arched her brow.

He said, "I don't like this one bit."

"I can't exactly pick off released prisoners like ducks in a shooting
range."

Ethan balled his fist and slammed the table. Madeleine's empty
paper coffee cup fell sideways. She watched it, let it rock back and
forth. His left hand was still clasped in hers.

Ethan said, "You're going to see him."

"I can't think of a better idea."

"Tell the police, carry a gun."

"That's just reacting. It won't solve the problem."

He was staring at their joined hands, his thumb moving over her
knuckle. "I'll go with you."

"I think he'd just shut down if you were there."

"Damn it! You drop this bomb on me and I'm just supposed to sit here and do nothing?"

Madeleine said, "Quite frankly, my instinct was to not tell you at all."

"That would have pissed me off worse."

"And so here I am."

"Well. At least you're not shutting me out." He breathed out through his nose. "I'll drive you there. I guess it's the only thing I can do."

"You don't have to—" But she saw the flicker of intent in his face and she stopped herself.

Instead she said, "Thank you."

He put his other hand over the one that already gripped hers and held on. Students wandered in through the glass doors, carrying on conversations with unseen people through microphones clipped over their ears.

"All right," he said as if accepting and moving on. "But I still don't think you should go alone."

"There's no one else he'd respond to."

"Yes there is."

She looked at him inquisitively. His dark eyes held steady.

He said, "Chloe."

"Oh, God no."

"Think about it, Madeleine. Who else on the planet knows more about all of this than she does? She's probably the only person who can help you."

"I don't trust her!"

"So don't trust her. But bring her along."

seventy-four

HAHNVILLE, 1927

ATRICE WALKED ALONGSIDE THE twins as Chloe led them through the woods. Guy and Gilbert were almost as tall as Patrice now though they were two years younger. Marie-Rose was not present. She was back in the nursery where she'd been ailing since the day Maman had sent her into the bramble to find out what happened to Papa. Patrice had done what she could but she hadn't been able to bring Marie-Rose back. Her sister would have to find her own way. It could take days. Or longer. In the meantime, Marie-Rose lay strapped to her bed, lest her physical body try to wander the way Papa used to.

Papa, at least, would not be wandering anymore. Patrice felt her throat tighten.

She looked over her shoulder. Behind the children, two field workers took up the rear of the small procession. One of them, a hunter from Terrefleurs named Ramsey, carried a shotgun with the barrel resting on his shoulder. He'd been born deaf and could read lips if you spoke very slowly. You didn't even have to make a sound, so long as you didn't say anything too complex: come to supper, time for work. But Ramsey couldn't really carry a whole conversation. Mostly, he was a loner and spent his time hunting along the bayou, bringing back his catch to share at the kitchen house. No wife, no children. He accompanied Maman for many secret tasks.

The other worker was someone Patrice did not know very well. He had once lived at Locoul, but had been working for Chloe in the bayous. Fishing, Patrice supposed. He made her very uneasy. Perhaps because of his appearance. He had an ugly scar; an X crisscrossing his throat. And one of his eyes was red as though half-covered in a splotch of blood that never dried, and never blinked away.

Patrice slowed and mouthed to Ramsey, *Where are you going?*

She had actually wanted to ask him "do you know where *we* are going," and whether he knew why Chloe was leading them into the woods, but she didn't think she could communicate all of that.

As it was, Ramsey just shrugged. He cast his gaze away so that if Patrice tried to say anything to him again, he wouldn't even see it. The twins kept stride ahead with their long, gangly legs snapping through the woodland. She could see the outline of Gilbert's slingshot through his shirt. He wouldn't have dared to tote it along openly, but Patrice knew he was loath to go anywhere without it.

The worker with the blood eye leaned toward Patrice and whispered, "We are going to the bayou."

Patrice shot him a look. She hadn't wanted her mother to hear. But her curiosity was now piqued.

"I can tell that much on my own, thank you," she whispered, and then: "You can read lips?"

"No. It was easy to guess what you asked. I am Ferrar."

"Patrice."

She neither curtseyed nor offered her hand. Maman was now a fair distance ahead.

Patrice asked, her voice low, "How is it that you know Maman?"

To her surprise, Ferrar grinned at her with genuine warmth. "We go way back, your maman and me. I work for her now. Carry the hooch from the pirates. Least I used to."

"Pirates!"

Guy and Gilbert turned to look over their shoulders, and Patrice bit her lip. It seemed Maman hadn't heard, though.

Ferrar said, "They make rum and whiskey in the islands, where no one'll find them, and bring them to the bayous. I know those places real good. Cocodrie, Bayou Black, Big Hellhole Lake."

Patrice was vaguely aware of her mother's New Orleans operations, that she was selling alcohol, but she had no idea that her enterprise was so far-reaching. "I never heard of any of those areas you mention."

"Lafitte? Bayou Bouillon?"

"I've heard of Lafitte."

"In Bayou Bouillon the water likes to boil. And you can hide real easy in Bayou Black. They ain't nothin but places to disappear. I don't do it no more, though. As of yesterday."

"Why not?"

Ferrar nodded toward Chloe, who was now so far ahead that she was just the occasional flash of fabric through the woods. Only Ramsey kept pace with her, and Patrice kept her eyes on him instead. The twins had fallen back as well and were now listening to Ferrar with interest.

Ferrar said, "Your mother don't want me workin for her no more. Says I got a flaw."

Patrice eyed him sideways, noting his scar and his blood-shined eye.

He caught her looking and put his hand to his eye. "I don't think she meant this flaw."

"I'm sorry, I wasn't . . ." But she was. She shrugged.

Ferrar said, "Doctor said it was supposed to go away in two weeks. But that was fifteen years ago. 'Fore you's even born. My mama says it ain't gonna ever go away cuz it's a mark from your mother, Miss Chloe. I owe her a life."

"A life?"

Ferrar nodded. "She saved mine when I was just a *piti*. Stuck me in the throat when I couldn't breathe. That's why I ran the bootlegging for her in the islands and all the lakes and streams. Wouldn't've done it otherwise."

Guy said, "I wanna be the new pirate if you ain't doin it no more!"

"Me too!" said Gilbert.

"Shush!"

But it was too late. Chloe had paused and was already turning back. She cut hands at Ramsey and he stopped walking. He shifted the shotgun to his other shoulder.

"You!" Chloe said as she approached, pointing at Ferrar. "Wait here! *Ici!*"

She grabbed Patrice by the arm and thrust her forward into the woods. Patrice didn't dare look over her shoulder at Ferrar. Chloe signaled Ramsey, and he resumed walking again.

Chloe was pinching Patrice's arm. "I have told you not to fraternize!"

"*Oui madame.*"

"You disobey me again and again!"

"I'm sorry, I didn't know . . ."

"You know. If you watch my intent you know exactly how to act."

Patrice bit her lip, afraid to say anything lest her mother's temper escalate.

Chloe said, "That boy, he is bad. These years, I put him to work in the water where he would stay far away. But he is too flawed! I should have let him suffocate years ago. I was young and did not understand."

Patrice gasped. "How could you say such a thing?"

She looked over her shoulder. Ferrar was obediently waiting a distance back, leaning against a mulberry. She couldn't tell whether he'd heard Chloe's words. Despite the ugliness of his appearance, he seemed such a gentle soul. Why had Maman brought him along, only to make him wait in the woods?

Chloe grabbed Patrice by the chin and made her look at her. Patrice stumbled, and had to clutch her mother's wrists to keep from falling. Ramsey and the twins stopped.

"*Allez!*" Chloe shouted at them.

Ramsey lowered his head and continued on through the woods. The twins stole worried glances at Patrice, but they followed after Ramsey.

Chloe whispered, still gripping her daughter by the chin, "You silly and stupid. He is making a fool of you, that boy. He will turn your line to rot."

Chloe released her. Patrice put her hands to her burning face. She didn't dare turn to see whether Ferrar had been watching.

How long before she was old enough to leave home? With Papa gone, the children were now fully at the mercy of their mother. Even if Patrice could leave now—go off to boarding school abroad or enter a convent—she didn't dare leave her sister and brothers behind. Already, look what had happened to Marie-Rose. She wondered if she could ever travel far enough to escape the river devils. Rosie was now attached. That horrible grinning woman. One day Patrice would become part of a pair, too, mother had promised. Maybe years from now, or maybe tomorrow. Or maybe today.

Patrice saw a glimmer ahead and realized they'd reached the bayou. A remote corner of it, far away from the fishing and swimming holes where the plantationers spent their scant idle hours. Patrice realized that was the reason for coming here. This cove was the farthest point from Terrefleurs and any of the neighboring plantations; and they were sure to be alone, out of sight, out of earshot. It made Patrice nervous.

She reached a searching thread into her mother, and found the intent: exercises. But not exactly pigeon games. They were far away from the garden and the *pigeonnier*.

Patrice wondered about the new exercises, but she couldn't bear to keep seeking inside her mother's intent. So much hatred there. That hatred found its way into Patrice's own heart, too. Hatred for

Chloe. Yes, she would call her Chloe from now on, not Maman. Chloe was nothing a mother should be. The trees stretched higher, blacker, and formed thorns.

For some reason, this acknowledgment of hating her mother caused her to raise her head. She walked taller.

Ramsey and the twins were waiting by the bayou's edge. And to Patrice's eyes, the cove existed inside the briar. But for once she didn't fear it. She realized that her hatred was a powerful tool to bring to the world of thorns. Chloe reached the bank and turned. As Patrice approached, she gathered up the black feeling that had formed in her breast and streamed it toward her mother. Chloe's eyes opened wider for just a moment. She must have felt it.

Chloe gestured toward Ramsey's gun. He loaded it with shot.

Patrice joined her brothers and folded her hands, waiting to learn the new exercise.

❧

THE CHILDREN'S EYES WERE closed. Easier to see this way. Even with her lids sealed, Patrice could see the cove, the bramble, the truth of light and shadows, and, most importantly, the unseen. The full spectrum of senses. Patrice, the twins, Ramsey, and Chloe were all standing on the banks facing the woods, their backs to the bayou.

They began with a simple exercise of intent. Chloe directed them to seek inside of her, which they did. Patrice found that their mother wanted them to use the pigeon exercise on Ramsey. Patrice joined with her brothers to implant the suggestion according to their mother's will. Patrice knew that her mother was not strong enough to move Ramsey on her own. Patrice was. But her mother didn't know just how strong she'd become. Let her believe that it took the three children to join together in order to move a grown man.

Under the influence of the children, Ramsey laid his shotgun against a tree and then knelt on the sandy bank. Chloe took a kerchief from her pocket and blindfolded him. And then Patrice and her brothers followed through with the next directive that they found inside Chloe: causing Ramsey to rise to his feet and take up the shotgun once again. He stepped back into line next to Patrice and faced the woods.

Patrice realized then that they had become so efficient that they did not even have to concentrate. The children controlled Ramsey without conscious thought of their own. Chloe was effectively manipulating Ramsey by proxy, magnifying her intent through the lens of her children. As much as she hated her mother, Patrice felt excited by the ease of it.

She continued to relay her mother's intent alongside her brothers, eyes closed, sight more vibrant than ever. She felt the presence of river devils. Male, female, small and large. They were drawn by the cluster of children, the race of humans that could conduct them into the physical world, and accelerate their purpose. And then Patrice realized that Marie-Rose was there too, standing between herself and Ramsey. The silver-eyed river devil hovered behind Rosie, hands wrapped around her waist. Patrice opened her eyes and the two faded to colored shadows. Ramsey was standing there, deaf and blindfolded.

She closed her eyes again and could see Marie-Rose and the river devil looking just as solid as the rest of them. Patrice reached out and squeezed her sister's hand.

A rabbit appeared at the woods. It paused at the tree line before stepping out toward the banks. Patrice knew that she had called it. She saw a second rabbit, and then a third. All four children calling them forth.

Something stirred inside of Patrice. In the briar, the inhibitions receded, and base intentions came forth. Primal feelings. A hunter's lust. The quick movements of the rabbits excited her. She wanted to grab one of them. She wanted to feel it go still in her grasp. And yet . . .

And then Ramsey, acting on the implanted suggestion of the children, shot the first rabbit. He could see nothing, but the children guided him with their minds. The rabbit fell.

Patrice felt a mixture of horror and elation. Marie-Rose tightened her grip in Patrice's hand. Patrice knew her sister was thinking the same thing as she: The tale of *Compère Lapin*, the little brown rabbit who lived in the briar patch. A second shot rang out, and a second rabbit fell. The others jumped but did not run away.

"Take their fear," Chloe said.

Patrice concentrated on suppressing the fear reaction in the rabbits. She found it in a tiny corridor inside their heads.

Ramsey reloaded. Continued to shoot them down one by one. He shot and reloaded in a continuous motion like the machination of a clock. But the rabbits kept coming forth. They emerged from the trees in obedience to the suggestion, and they waited to be shot.

Patrice stopped calling them.

Chloe said, "Do you see how powerful you are? No one can do these things but you. That is why you have power. The hunter and the rabbits are one in the same. No more than pigeons, both of them, and they must do as you wish. . . ."

And Patrice thought, *But they are following your wishes, Chloe, they aren't really my wishes.*

She sensed the excitement among the river devils, and knew that the intent belonged to them as well.

"You are all calling the rabbits, and you are all shooting them through Ramsey. In this way, you do not know which of you has killed which rabbit. It is easier for you at this stage, but you will grow bolder. . . ."

The rabbits kept coming, called by the other three children, and Ramsey shot them each between the eyes. The tail ends of his blindfold stirred in the breeze.

Chloe said, "These rabbits, they are like all humans. You can move them to your will. But there are those who naturally oppose you. Those others would bring our secrets to the entire world. They show people how to unlock the triggers within their own minds. So then all the people everywhere become the same as you. You are no longer any more powerful than the fools of the world."

Patrice turned her focus to her brothers and her sister. She implanted the suggestion to cease their calling. Ramsey continued to shoot the remaining rabbits, but no more came forth.

Chloe paused, and scanned the children. "The other one is here, yanh? Marie-Rose?"

Patrice said nothing, but the twins nodded. "Yes ma'am."

Marie-Rose gripped Patrice's hand. Their mother's gaze swept over them, wide and searching. Patrice realized Chloe could only dimly sense the things that were so apparent to Patrice and the other children. Chloe grabbed Patrice by the wrist and shook it until the girls let go.

Chloe said, "Marie-Rose. There might have been more of your race but for the way you were born. You broke my womb. Now you are alone, the four of you. You must stand against the other ones by yourselves."

Marie-Rose started to protest, "But Maman!"

She stopped, realizing that Chloe couldn't hear her. The river devil bent her head and whispered into Rosie's ear.

Marie-Rose turned to Ramsey and spoke, and Ramsey also vocalized Rosie's words in unison with her: "But Maman, who are these others?"

Patrice gaped. She had never heard Ramsey speak before, and any utterance he'd made had been little more than a grunt. But now he spoke Rosie's words with perfect clarity in his own croaking, unused voice. It sounded impossibly deep and Marie-Rose sounded small and light as they spoke together: "How will we know them?"

Chloe nodded. "I will show you. See my intent."

All four children concentrated. They called. Patrice felt her fingers curl into fists. She sensed the briar growing thicker. The trees of the physical world stretched higher, blacker, more vast, pushing the sky away and forcing the enclave deeper into the tangled world.

Patrice followed her mother's intent along with her siblings. They searched, and found the presence in the woods. They sent their will forth. Unlike with the rabbits, there was resistance. They locked their minds together and pulled. And then Patrice felt a sense of yielding to her call.

Sounds in the woods—snapping branches. From the shadows, Ferrar appeared.

FERRAR LOOKED DIFFERENT THROUGH the lens of the briar. He emitted almost a golden shimmer, just the faintest trace, but he also emitted something much more powerful than the visual phenomenon. Patrice realized that she might have distantly sensed it when she'd walked alongside him, but now it felt like a tidal wave of energy.

Ramsey kept his shotgun trained on the woods. Trained on Ferrar. It sat at Ramsey's shoulder but through the blindfold, there was no need to lean in and peer through the sights. He saw and heard nothing, and in acting on the children's intent, or Chloe's intent, he had no awareness of shooting a rabbit or a stump or a human being.

Ferrar resisted them. He was slow to advance. It caused the children to reflexively pull harder at him. The exchange was electrifying. Ferrar stepped from the trees to the bank.

Patrice felt a stirring of such savagery that her lips fell open. But this sensation danced at the top of her head, and it warred with another part of her psyche, deep within her skull, one that tried to neutralize the viciousness. Like lightning dancing over the ocean. She felt that if she wanted to, she could expand or shrink that ocean, depending on whether she wanted to tame the lightning or let it dance. And that war within her psyche was equally as exciting as Ferrar's resistance.

Ramsey reloaded.

"Hold back," Chloe said sharply.

Patrice saw the X at Ferrar's throat. The splotch of blood at his eye. Either point made an excellent target.

But Ferrar's gaze was fixed upon Patrice. In it lay the vastness of that ocean, and at once Patrice understood. People like Ferrar could bring that vastness forth. It could soothe the turbulent energy. Swallow it up. And it acted as a roux for human evolution.

Chloe said, "See my intent."

Patrice searched inside her mother, terrified of what she would find. But the result was a simple thing. She wanted only for Ferrar to kneel. Ferrar would be blindfolded too. Cover that gaze that seemed to penetrate deep into the ocean within Patrice's psyche. And then, the children would turn their focus back to Ramsey. . . .

But Patrice didn't want to think about that. She joined her brothers and sister in making Ferrar kneel. She felt him resist. A warping, rolling wave of resistance. Too flexible to push against, because he seemed almost to bend with their will. Ferrar's gaze never left Patrice. Sweat beaded his brow.

"You see the flaw," Chloe said. "You see how these kinds may oppose you. *Les lumens.* Even with all of us in focus, he is obstinate."

Ferrar exhaled slowly through his lips. And then at once, the waves of resistance dissipated. The children actually lost balance for a moment. As though they'd been pulling a cart with a rope that suddenly snapped. But Ferrar remained on his feet. Patrice felt the lovely chaotic lightning snap through her mind and then disappear. She knew that she could not conjure that lightning back to life, that delightful, primal savagery, as long as Ferrar kept his gaze on hers. She could not bear to join her siblings in the pigeon game with Ramsey and his shotgun.

And suddenly, she didn't want to. Couldn't remember why she would ever want to in the first place.

But this was not true of her brothers and sister, they still drank from the intoxicating pool of Chloe's intent. They were heady with the power. They weren't trained in Ferrar's gaze.

"It doesn't matter," Chloe said. "*Le lumen* cannot oppose us all."

Patrice looked at her hands. She saw just the farthest hint of Ferrar's shimmer. His ocean had seeped into hers, and helped her to broaden the vastness. Even her own hatred for her mother seemed to have dispersed like mist on the ocean.

But Chloe's intent still accelerated. It passed through Patrice like vapor, but it rested inside the other children. Not in words, but in an awareness and solid but artificial desire. To not shrink in fear and weakness, but to strike Ferrar down, naked-eyed, and preserve the power of their line.

No!

Marie-Rose turned her face toward Patrice. Patrice focused her mind on her sister, and on Guy, and then Gilbert, pushing her mother's intent out of them. Leaving them open.

Ramsey and all four children turned away from Ferrar and faced the bayou. The sight of it soothed Patrice. No longer looking upon the litter of dead rabbits. The river devil looked from child to child and began to babble. She spoke in a language that Patrice did not understand. No; she might not have been able to identify the words, but she felt the river devil's full intent. The hatred for Ferrar. The conjuring of that exhilarating chaos.

"What is this?" Chloe said. "Turn around."

She yanked Gilbert's arm and he turned to face his mother. The other children looked over their shoulders. They seemed uncertain. One by one, they turned back, casting confused glances from Chloe to Ferrar. Patrice turned too.

Chloe said, "Now! The hunter, turn Ramsey around."

But the children, in unison, turned instead and faced the bayou again. Patrice could feel her mother's gaze boring into their backs. The vastness inside kept her calm, preventing her from fighting or resisting, while somehow bolstering her strength. The river devil stepped away from Marie-Rose and pounced at Patrice, her silver eyes flashing. She lashed out with a sharp claw at Patrice's arm. Patrice flinched.

Chloe yanked Patrice by the hair and threw her backward onto the bank. Patrice cried out. She felt the skin abrade down her forearm as she tried to break her fall.

"You do this!" Chloe said.

Rosie's river devil railed and babbled. The strange conjuring filled the bayou. Patrice pushed against the packed mud and looked back over her shoulder at her mother.

Ferrar stepped forward. He leaned over and put his arms around

Patrice, and lifted her to her feet. She looked down at the dirt and blood scraped into her hands and forearm. Her skirts were mottled with filth.

Chloe said, "You disobey me! You fraternize! You poison your brothers and sister!"

Patrice took a shaking breath. "No Madame, I think it is you who are poisoning us."

Chloe slapped Patrice across face. Patrice gasped and felt a momentary resurgence of electricity. But she saw the surge in the river devil's eyes, and she let the crackling pass through and out of her.

Chloe turned to Ramsey. Her face was hard. Patrice observed what lay inside her mother's heart. Chloe implanted the suggestion to Ramsey to shoot Ferrar through the throat. Chloe's ability was much weaker than that of her children, but Ramsey was an easy vessel to navigate.

Ramsey turned, the shotgun aiming back toward them. Patrice threw her gaze on him and made him swing the weapon away, but too late. A shot rang out. It caught Ferrar. Patrice turned to look.

Ferrar sank to his knees. But the scar at his throat was untouched. Blood poured from his shoulder. It had spattered Patrice.

Ramsey was reloading.

Patrice trained her focus on Ramsey. He paused, chin down, the blindfold tails at his back. She could sense her mother's doubled efforts. But Ramsey heard Patrice's suggestion with much more resonance than anything Chloe could send forth. He turned back to the bayou and threw the shotgun into the water.

Chloe flew into a rage. She struck Patrice, a hard cut across the mouth, and Patrice tasted blood. Chloe struck again and again, pummeling until Patrice stumbled and fell back to the packed wet earth. A tuft of fur from one of the fallen rabbits drifted on the breeze. Chloe kicked.

Patrice reached inside to that shimmering ocean that seemed to wash through herself and Ferrar and to a smaller extent, the others; even Chloe. She used her mind to push Chloe back. Chloe stopped.

Patrice said aloud, "Children, turn and see."

Guy, Gilbert, and Marie-Rose turned around to face them.

Chloe's face twisted with rage, but Patrice formed a tight net around her, and Chloe seemed unable to move against it.

"Ferrar," Patrice said.

Guy and Gilbert stepped forward and went to Ferrar, who was now lying on the edge of the woodland, leaking blood with the rabbits. The twins put their hands to his shoulder and compressed the wound. The river devil shrieked. Marie-Rose pressed her hands over her ears, weeping and screaming.

Patrice rose to a sitting position. "Make a doll, Rosie. In the mud."

Marie-Rose looked at her older sister. She knelt at the edge of the water, tears streaming, and traced an outline of a figure in the banks. Marie-Rose's physical form still lay strapped in the nursery at Terrefleurs, but her projected self worked with the water and mud to form a small creation. The shape emerged from lapping water that trickled through channels of dirt. The river devil quieted, watching the little girl, and seemed mesmerized by the activity.

Patrice turned her attention to her mother.

"We need clean cloth." She crystalized the thoughts that showed exactly what she wanted.

Though Chloe fought, she followed the motions of Patrice's implanted suggestion. Chloe reached under her skirts and pulled a knife from a belt around her thigh. With shaking hands, she tore shreds from her skirts and then gave them to the twins. The boys pressed them into Ferrar's wound and held.

"Now kneel," Patrice said.

Chloe's mouth was pulled into an angry grimace. She sank to her knees in front of Patrice. Patrice rose to her knees to face her. Mother and daughter stared eye-to-eye.

Patrice said, "You're going to leave us alone now. You're going to leave Terrefleurs for good and live in New Orleans. You're not welcome here anymore."

Chloe quaked before her.

"Do you understand?"

Chloe was grinding her teeth. It seemed that she fought harder against this than when she had torn her own clothing. Patrice saw the turmoil of intentions inside her mother, and she sensed the determination.

But Chloe answered, at least for the moment, "Yes."

✧

seventy-five

✧

NEW ORLEANS, 2010

ADELEINE AND ETHAN SAT in the drawing room at Chloe's home on Rue Toulouse while Chloe peered through heavy spectacles at Zenon's letter, dust motes drifting in a shaft of sunlight. Severin crouched on all fours, her spine making dragon ridges down her thin, bare back, and she crawled along the floor. Beyond the wall, reporters milled somewhere on the sidewalk. They'd been following Madeleine around like ducks. Severin settled in under the curtains, layered with a thin white sheer and then a heavy brocade, and a third layer of drapery seemed to form from the dust itself. It looked like you could peel it off like a sheet of plastic wrap. Madeleine remembered that first day when she'd come to call on Chloe. Back then, she'd come looking for answers. But each answer she'd uncovered led to a host of more questions.

The old woman grunted and laid the letter on the tea tray beside her. "That is bad."

Ethan nodded. "He'll use the trick, the implanted suggestion."

Chloe looked at Madeleine. "You taught yourself how to do that."

"I suppose I did. Did Zenon learn it from you?"

"These secrets come from the other world. You have the ability to inhabit that world, and bring secrets back. Zenon can too."

"Are you saying that he taught himself as well?"

"No, I did teach him. I showed him the beginning. He is continuing from there."

Madeleine didn't like the sound of that. If Zenon continued to learn secrets like the implanted suggestion, each discovery could be another weapon to add to his arsenal.

Ethan said, "What other secrets are there?"

Chloe regarded Ethan with thinly veiled distaste. "Do you know how old I am?"

"You'd said you were a hundred and fourteen years old," Madeleine said.

"Now one hundred and fifteen. I was born in 1895."

Ethan said, "My God. You've learned the secret of longevity. That's amazing."

"Why do you speak!" Chloe snapped. "You have nothing to do with this."

"Chloe! What's the matter with you? Ethan has every right to speak."

"Then I have nothing more to say!"

Chloe curled her claw-like hand over the arm of her chair and turned her face to the window, lips curled inward. Severin laughed.

"I have nothing more to say!" Severin repeated in Chloe's voice. "He can't make the kind of babies Zenon can so we don't like him!"

Madeleine made a noise of disgust. She'd had enough and rose to leave, but Ethan put his hand to her shoulder, easing her back into her chair.

"It's all right. I'll go wait in the car."

"No," Madeleine said.

"Really. I'll see if I can send some of them reporters on a wild goose chase. Don't forget why we came here."

He planted a kiss on the top of her head and walked his uneven steps to the door, then left.

"That was very rude," Madeleine said.

"The secrets are only powerful as long as they are kept secret. Once the masses learn them, we are no better than anyone else."

"These abilities don't make us better, Chloe, just different."

"Ah, but you are wrong! My children were better. But they left me. They taught their own children to consider me as poison. I watched you grow, you and your brothers, and waited for you to come to me."

"I don't understand why you watched from afar."

"You, and Marc, and Zenon, your parents were absent. You learned to fight and survive. The masses, they know no hardship and therefore are weak."

Madeleine shook her head.

Chloe said, "But I would not do that again. We lost Marc Gilbert because he did not understand. The next child of the briar, I will be there. I will teach."

Severin said, "Marc had a child, so surely! At the mirror end of the river it lives!"

"Hush!" Madeleine snapped, realizing after the fact that she'd spoken aloud to Severin.

Chloe looked surprised by Madeleine's outburst. The old woman didn't know about Marc's baby, and now more than ever, Madeleine wanted to keep it that way.

Chloe's gaze went to the curtains and down to where Severin sat crouched beneath the window. "Your devil is here too, yanh?"

"Severin is under the window."

Chloe's eyes brightened. "Do not fight her, Madeleine. I can help you. I can teach you the ways of the other world. I cannot see it as you, but I have seen my husband and my children and their children. I know the ways. I will teach you."

Madeleine looked away. She wanted so badly to learn how to tame this phenomenon. Any knowledge Chloe could share was invaluable. But leaning on Chloe seemed about as sensible as leaning on a guillotine.

Madeleine asked, "Hasn't anyone ever escaped the river devils?"

Severin cried out, "I'll never leave! I'm your pair, and I stay with you forever, truly."

Chloe said, "Once you have opened that passageway, it is always there. I helped my daughters and sons to open it early. But, you children of the briar, you must not see it as a sickness. You are frightened because the river devils bring chaos."

Madeleine said, "Zenon doesn't seem to experience the . . . what are they, fugues? He always seems to be in control of his awareness."

Chloe leaned forward. "Ah, you see? It is because Zenon is faithful to the cause of the river devil. It is powerful, yanh?"

"But what is that cause?"

"You learn the secrets. Bring them out. Obey the wishes of the river devils."

"But . . . murder? He obeyed by committing murder."

Chloe gave a cough that might have been a laugh. "You are so pious. What Zenon does, it is culling. He helps to remove those that would oppose us."

Madeleine felt the hair rise on her skin. Hard enough to understand Zenon's taste for murder; even harder to believe that Chloe should support it.

"And now he wants to cull me."

Chloe's face clouded.

Madeleine said, "I want you to come with me to see Zenon."

"No."

"I want to talk to him. See if we can call a truce."

"I will not go. Zenon is the strongest warrior of all the children. It would be wrong of me to oppose him."

Severin rose and approached, her face softening to a kind of sincerity. Her thin, naked form streaked with gray.

She touched Madeleine's hand. "We're going to be together for eternity."

Madeleine flinched.

Severin said, "You should think toward it, a little some. We're the ones who can select and cull. That means everything, yes truly."

Madeleine's heart filled with sand. Select and cull. After all, she had wished to cull Carlo Jefferson. A faithful descendant of Chloe; one of her warrior-children of the briar. Madeleine disliked the sense of being just a cocktail of traits handed down through generations. Her life having been preordained in the DNA scriptures inside each of her cells.

Madeleine said to Chloe, "Zenon intends to kill me. Is that what you want too? Is that part of this?"

Chloe shook her head, and perhaps the faintest hint of emotion played at her brow. "Of course not. I do not wish for your death, or his. I have watched you all these years."

"Then come with me. Let's talk to Zenon together."

Chloe looked away. "I will not go."

Madeleine sighed, exhausted. She opened her hands and drew a slow breath.

"All right. I'll go alone."

Chloe still did not look at her. She kept her eyes fixed on the wall, and Madeleine was surprised to find a faint tremor at her lip.

"Use your skill," Chloe said. "When you go to see him, use the same skill he would use."

❦

seventy-six

❦

NEW ORLEANS, 2010

LUORESCENT LIGHTS GLARED THROUGH a caged lens. Madeleine's fingers dug into the arm of the plastic chair as she debated whether or not she should stand up and walk out of this soulless room before it was too late. Severin was not present, at least. There seemed no rhyme or reason to when she appeared or when she was gone, and Madeleine wondered if she'd ever know why.

She tried to remain calm. At the next booth, a prisoner in an orange jumper was talking to someone through a telephone, but he kept eyeing Madeleine and making lascivious gestures. She did not look at him, and instead kept her eyes on the words someone had carved into the booth. Filthy words. She closed her eyes.

Zenon appeared. He too was in an orange jumpsuit, looking like any other prisoner. Madeleine reflexively looked away from him, suppressing the urge to bolt. He walked to the booth and sat down, separated from her only by a sheet of glass.

He smiled, and his mouth seemed to twitch strangely. It occurred to her that he might be as nervous as she. He deflected his gaze and pulled out a cigarette which the guard lit for him, then began to smoke, inhaling deeply. She lifted the handset and he did the same on the other side of the glass.

"Thanks for coming to see me, *Sis*," he said.

She looked at his wide gray eyes and realized for the first time how much they resembled her father's, even her own. His skin was much lighter, though. The African blood in him was not so apparent.

The prisoner who had been eyeing Madeleine said something to Zenon, and Zenon shook his head.

"Sick bastard. This ole boy got sent up the river for grand theft auto." Zenon leaned toward her and lowered his voice. "But I happen to know he also raped and killed half a dozen women. Two of'm were mother and daughter. Says to tell you he thinks you're cute."

Her eyes involuntarily darted to the prisoner, and he winked. A scar cleaved his cheek. Madeleine sighed. She had worked in a mental institution long enough that such antics had lost their shock value on her.

"I received your letter," she said.

Zenon smiled as if they were discussing a mail-order box of chocolates. "Oh, you got it. That's good to know. I wasn't sure whether it had gotten to you or not."

"Oh it got to me. You definitely got to me Zenon. Is that what you wanted?"

"It's a start."

"Zenon, listen. I came here today because I want to call a truce."

"A truce?"

"I don't want a war with you."

"Getting too hot for you, baby? I understand that. Play with fire, expect to get burned. I guess you thought you were immune." He shook his head. "Don't think I'm interested in a truce, baby. That all you come here to say?"

She shook her head. "Not really. I have some questions. Hoped maybe you'd answer them for me."

"All right," he said. "Shoot."

"How long have you known that I was your half sister?"

He smiled and looked at her for a long moment, weighing whether or not to indulge her. Finally, he shrugged.

"Found out about Daddy Blank on my twenty-first birthday. Got a letter from a lawyer along with the deed to the plantation on River Road. I was surprised, but it didn't really mean nothing but extra property taxes to pay at the time. Always meant to sell it." He shrugged again. "Other than that, I never heard a damn word from him about it, or you. Thought maybe I'd bring it up sometime, but then brother Marc'd already decided he didn't like me no more."

Zenon crossed his arm under one elbow. "My turn. How long you been having conversations with your secret friend?"

She was startled. Somehow she never anticipated that he might want information from her, too.

"It started, I guess, that night on the bayou. When I found Anita Salazar." She swallowed. "And you? Have you had conversations with . . . unusual people or things?"

"My lawyer would probably object to the direction this conversation's taken. He didn't want me to meet with you alone in the first place."

"Tell me the truth, Zenon," she said aloud, and in her mind she made certain he would.

Zenon did not speak again immediately, but instead fixed his gaze on her.

"You fuckin with my head, ain't you, baby?"

Her breath caught in her throat, and they stared at each other while prisoners and guards milled nearby.

"That's all right," Zenon said, his voice just above a whisper, and then he continued with an almost casual air: "Tell you what. I'll answer you because I see fit to do so, and not because you trying to pull some shit on me. That might work with my lawyer, but you think you can use it on me, you wrong."

Her face and hands grew hot, but she said nothing.

"There's someone that I see," Zenon began carefully, letting his gaze drift.

Madeleine waited.

"He's a . . ." he shrugged. "I don't know. Seem like just another good ole boy. But no one can see him but me. I call him Josh."

She nodded.

He paused, checking her face. "Well, maybe he'll go away. Since I've been in here I've been seeing a shrink, and he keeps me pretty medicated."

Madeleine narrowed her eyes. Zenon was sharp, alert. "You haven't been taking meds."

Zenon leaned in and lowered his voice, as if that might hinder any eavesdropping by the authorities. Madeleine knew their conversation was probably being monitored, and it made her uncomfortable.

"Why no, Madeleine, you got me. I have not been taking them. Why should I take pills from somebody who don't know nothing about me? You know me better than anyone else on this planet, now, don't you?" His voice was intimate, and she shifted in her seat. "Yes ma'am. We know each other real well, you and me."

He took a long drag from his cigarette. "Well anyway, yeah, maybe I been hangin out with old Josh some. We got this little game goin. I ask Josh about some of the other prisoners, and he shows me what crime they committed—or ain't committed; some of'm're actually innocent, can you believe that?" He shrugged. "Passes the time. Like watchin TV. That's how I come to know about your new boyfriend here." He gestured toward the prisoner in the next booth. "Kind of funny, him goin down for stealing cars after he did all that rapin and killin."

Madeleine looked away. As she held the phone to her ear, she noticed a strange prattle in the background. A radio. But the language was unfamiliar.

"Is there a radio there with you?"

Zenon motioned his head toward the guard. "He carries it around for me. Don't really need it here while I'm talking to you, but it's best to keep them guards in practice. They practice listening for you inside their heads, and they don't even know it. I keep'm exercising. You let'm go too long they get rusty."

Madeleine felt sick, knowing she'd been one of his pigeons. "What language is that on the radio?"

"Hungarian."

"Why do you listen to languages you don't understand?"

"Well that's my own exercise. Jiujitsu for the brain."

She looked at the shortwave. The sound of the announcer's voice sounded eerie somehow, if only because it didn't match. But at the same time, because she didn't speak the language, it wasn't as distracting as an English-speaking program. It almost soothed her, and her mind danced across the plane of words with gentle oblivion, pausing to collect the odd intonation that sounded familiar. *Ház* sounded like "house." And she thought she caught the word "carton."

The radio snapped off. Nobody had touched it.

He was watching her with a leer. "Enough radio. Maybe I'm sharing a little too much, yeah. Gettin hypnotized by those devil blue eyes."

She lowered them, afraid to look at him, but then steeled herself and returned his gaze. "What about Anita Salazar? And Angel Frey?"

His face grew hard and he leaned in close. "Listen to you, bringing that up. Kind of personal, don't you think? But hell, what can I say, baby, it's in my genes. That's what Joe Whitney thinks. This new trial, I'm pleading not guilty by reason of mental defect."

"What are you talking about?"

"Bad genes, baby. Predisposed to kill. Ain't nothing you can do if it's in your genes."

She sat dumbfounded. "You've got to be kidding me."

"Got it on both sides of the family. My mama killed my stepdaddy. Didn't you know that? Made me help get rid of the body. She never thought twice about doin what had to be done in that sense. And Daddy Blank, hell, you know what I got runnin around in my genes from that side."

She was mute. She could only stare at him.

"Daddy Blank used to smack you and Marc around when he was out of his senses. He was a violent bastard. And Marc was too. Hell, I remember when Marc went after Daddy Blank with a two-by-four. Worked him over good, didn't he, yeah? And what was that shit about Marc frying that electrician worked for him? You and I both know that weren't no accident. And then Marc killed his own self."

He leaned back in satisfaction. "Predisposed, baby. And you, hell, I don't need to bring up the thing with Carlo, do I? We can't help it, it's in our genes. We're violent people. One big happy family."

She swallowed hard. It sounded like he was rehearsing for the new trial.

"You'll never pull this off, Zenon. People don't just get away with murder on a 'bad genes' defense. That sort of thing doesn't happen in the real world."

"Yeah, it's a long shot, ain't it? Joe Whitney says it'll be a landmark case. Josh seems to think so too. Josh also thinks I can persuade a jury to do anything I want them to do."

She deliberately kept her voice soft. "But what's the real reason you did it? Why did you go after Angel Frey?"

He shrugged. "What do you want from me? I was under orders. Josh is a bossy fucker. I didn't have no choice."

"You didn't have to follow any orders."

"Yeah, I did. This shit's still new to you. But for me, Josh been coming around almost ten years now. You can't hold out forever."

"Ten years," she murmured. "There were others then, weren't there? These two girls weren't the first ones."

"Don't get all high and mighty. You follow orders and that's that." He shrugged, and looked genuinely puzzled. "Don't you know? Hasn't your little parasite friend been working you? They start you off slow, I guess, but you'll catch up. You ask me, they're threatened by certain kinds of people. And those people are a threat to us, too."

"How can people like Angel Frey possibly be a threat to us?"

Instead of answering, he said, "She was golden inside. Just like all the others. You seen it yet?"

"Golden? I don't know."

"Oh, you'd know. Lumens, they're called. It's contagious, too. You and me, we're already paired up. And we're paired with the wrong kind."

"I'm paired with Severin. And you're paired with Josh."

Zenon's gaze traveled elsewhere, just over her shoulder to a blank zone where he probably saw the shapes in his mind more clearly than those around him. "I don't think people like Angel Frey even know what they are. Just like you and I didn't know. Till it's too late."

He said, "Least that's as much as I can make out from the mile-deep pile of grass turds Josh keeps feeding me. It's the culling, yeah. When you cull, you shape what's left."

He took a drag from his cigarette, gaze still diverted. "You think you got a choice, baby? You ain't got no choice. And it dudn't make a difference anyway once you got blood on your hands. You're just a damn mouse in a maze. Your little parasite friend gonna tell you how to get where you're supposed to go, and you're just fuckin yourself if you don't listen. Take it from me."

Madeleine didn't believe it. Couldn't believe she could ever become a killer like Zenon. But then she had come very, very close to killing Carlo. And when Severin led her through a labyrinth of swampland on a stormy night, Madeleine had felt an awful lot like a mouse in a maze.

Zenon took a deep breath, and for a moment, he looked like the boy she remembered. Vulnerable. Maybe even frightened. "We should have had this conversation a long time ago, I guess. I wanted to. But you kept avoiding me. Chloe's right, you know. About you and me."

She drew in her breath, shaking her head. Beyond unthinkable. "Zenon, that's just wrong. That will never happen."

His stare crystallized to ice. "Oh, that's right. You're too busy wrapping your legs around that gimp of yours. Faithless, that's what you are. No loyalty at all."

Madeleine lowered her voice and spoke through her teeth. "Why in God's name would you ever want to lay your hands on your own sister? You knew about all that but you still . . ."

"You want the long answer, you go see Miss Chloe. But here's the short answer: I wanted to touch you ever since we were kids, before I ever even knew anything about Daddy Blank and his dirty secrets. I kept my hands off out of respect. I loved you and Marc both, even then. Before any of it. Before I found out respect was just another little trick people use to manipulate other people. But I have learned my lesson, sister-baby. You're a faithless fucking whore and that's how you're gonna get treated."

He cocked his head, and suddenly Madeleine felt the urge to unbutton her blouse and reveal her bra. The force of the thought was overwhelming, stronger than Chloe's trick. Strong as she remembered.

"Stop it," she said through a clenched jaw.

He laughed. "Oh, come on, baby, it's what you're made for. It's how you end. You ain't got a shred of loyalty to you, not even for your own blood. You'd just as soon see me fry."

"This isn't doing either one of us any good."

He puffed, a single expulsion of air. "Maybe not for you, but I'd just as soon watch you go home to meet your maker. You think they'd take you in up there at the pearly gates? With a devil on your back? Or maybe they send you down below where your daddy and other brother gone, yeah?"

Her hands began to shake, but she held the receiver fast to her ear.

"I can't really do much while I'm sitting in here, but this one," he nodded at the prisoner who'd been leering at her, and lowered his voice. "I bet you he can pull it off, yeah. What you think, baby?"

The prisoner with the scarred cheek paid no attention to them now, but instead continued to chat on the phone with his visitor. Zenon was watching Madeleine's face.

"Yeah baby, he's a wild one. They gonna let him out in a few days, I expect."

She tried to steady her voice. "I thought you said they convicted him for grand theft auto."

"No, baby, he ain't convicted yet. This here's just a holding facility. Looks like he's gonna be free as a bird. Prosecutor doesn't have a case."

Perhaps the prisoner overheard Zenon talking, because now he looked at Madeleine and winked again.

Zenon grimaced. "He's one that doesn't even need any encouragement. He already got his eye on you. I s'pose you best start lookin over your shoulder once he gets out."

She'd heard enough. She hung up the phone under the leering gaze of that awful prisoner. Zenon rose and swaggered toward the door, and the guard offered him a fresh cigarette and a light. She supposed that he probably had them tending his every need. They were his pigeons, just like the prisoner he was dispatching to come after her. Just like the twelve jurors he would eventually have at his new trial. All of them part of Zenon's pigeon games. "Not guilty," the jurors would surely say. Zenon would go free. Free to kill and cull for as long as he lived.

Zenon blew her a kiss as he disappeared through the heavy metal door.

She stood to leave, and realized the pigeon-prisoner was massaging his crotch as his gaze followed her.

No way was she going to let Zenon get away with this.

She turned and stared directly into the prisoner's face. She formed her mind into one single thought.

His expression changed ever so slightly, and he removed his hand from his lap. His gaze drifted back toward the door where Zenon had exited.

Madeleine repeated the idea in her mind once more. Allowing for the violence to stir in her imagination.

And she knew she had gotten through to him.

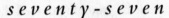

seventy-seven

NEW ORLEANS, 2010

ADELEINE LEARNED THAT ANOTHER prisoner had attacked Zenon on the night she'd gone to visit him. Without being told, she knew who the other prisoner was. She'd unleashed him herself. But in the attack, Zenon did not die; he was, however, left in a catatonic state. He could breathe on his own but was otherwise unresponsive.

Madeleine's intention was not that Zenon should suffer injuries in that particular way. When she had used the trick on the other prisoner, she had bent her mind around the concept of killing Zenon. And probably, that's what the prisoner intended to do. He'd broken Zenon's neck with his bare hands, and then proceeded to beat him nearly to death. Madeleine learned that he had acted suddenly and without provocation. And when the guards caught up with him, he was trying to remove Zenon's jumpsuit, and they suspected he'd intended to sexually assault him.

An important thing to remember when cross-pollinating suggestions into other people's minds: The thoughts that grow will sometimes be hybrids.

Zenon had left a living will. In it, he'd provided for the situation that he might become incapacitated. In such a circumstance, Zenon had appointed power of attorney to his sister, Dr. Madeleine Le-Blanc. He also deeded the old plantation, Terrefleurs, to Madeleine.

She wondered if she would ever understand him.

MADELEINE LED ETHAN INTO the foyer of her new old home on Esplanade, looking up at the staircase that swept in a curve to the mezzanine above. The railing, made of a smooth polished cherry that seemed to glow from deep within, beckoned her to touch its surface. The steps arced around the foyer in contour to the crystal chandelier dropping into the heart of it.

"It looks exactly how it did before the fire," Ethan said.

Madeleine nodded. "They've done an amazing job. But, it isn't really *exactly* the same. There are new details. Step lights hidden in the stairs so you can see your way in the dark. Modern kitchen and bathrooms. Things like that."

Some things simply had to change in order to accommodate a new era. Now, at this point in her life, Madeleine understood that better than anyone.

Jasmine bounded ahead, her furry tail standing with recognition as she leapt from one new-but-familiar room to another. Severin, too, explored as if in a giant doll house. An instant ghost to haunt the halls.

It was a bittersweet tour; Madeleine would sell the house. She could not afford it. She had agreed to a settlement that drained almost everything, including the rest of the trust fund and the sale from the cottage in Bayou Black. But, she still held the warehouse on Magazine and the apartment within it where she lived.

She looked through the window of the grand hall, beyond which reporters were assembled along the street.

Ethan followed her gaze. "Let's get away from prying eyes."

She gave a rueful smile and looked up to where Severin was running along the top of the landing upstairs. "If only it was just them."

Madeleine led him to the rear courtyard, the little hidden garden nestled against the crook of the house, and Jasmine trotted along with them. Jazz found a stretch of shade beneath the gentle, lacey honeysuckle, and lay down.

Ethan looked around. "Is the girl here right now?"

Madeleine shook her head. "Inside."

"It amazes me how you handle it."

"Thanks, but I'm not so sure I am handling it. Just trying to make it through each moment."

The courtyard still had some construction rubble. Leftover ends cut from sheetrock, a square industrial pencil, a screwdriver, and other odd bits that lay piled in the corner. Madeleine would have to see about getting it all hauled away. Her old wrought iron bistro table and chairs still rested in the sunshine, and on the table lay a construction worker's forgotten paper cup with coffee and cream and about half a dozen cigarette butts.

Ethan cleared the cup and sat on one of the chairs. "The truth is, Madeleine, you're one of the most amazing people I know."

Her urge was to correct him, argue about the "amazing" part, but she stifled it. She sat down opposite him, not meeting his eye. She thought of Zenon and all the things she wished she'd done differently.

Ethan said, "And I know how hard it's been, but when you think about it, you really come from a brilliant family legacy. Me, my family's got genes that breed athletes and scientific minds. That's nice and all, but your family, it's like you're a step ahead of evolution."

Madeleine looked over her shoulder toward the French doors, as though the house itself were a reflection of that legacy. "I suppose. I haven't made up my mind yet. Can't figure out whether we've all been cursed or are just unlucky."

"Or gifted."

She looked at him. "Chloe called them gifts, too. But gifts aren't supposed to come with a price."

"It's just part of it, baby. Any time a change comes along, it's just the natural human condition to react with fear. But fear ain't nothing but what you get when you've yet to understand."

"Or accept."

"Yeah, or accept. The disconnect in your family is just that you're all out of sync. None of y'all understood the other one's deal until it was too late."

"Now it's too late for Zenon."

Ethan turned away for a moment, his gaze following a golden butterfly lighting upon the fresh greens climbing the side of the house. Those vines looked so different from the black thorns that had become her inner garden.

Madeleine said, "I can't figure out why he deeded Terrefleurs to me. But I think I might try and fix it up."

Ethan looked back at her. "I'll help you." And then he said, "You're the last of them, you know."

She shook her head. "Technically, there are two of us. Zenon's still alive."

"I don't know, Madeleine. I've seen a lot of neurological trauma before, and I don't think he'll ever be anything but catatonic."

"I'm going to look after him. Make sure he's comfortable in the hospital bed, at least."

"You know you didn't have a choice."

"I didn't. But there are so many what-if's." But then she recalled her brother's secret. "Actually, you know, Zenon and I aren't the only ones left."

Ethan thought for a moment. "Marc's child."

She nodded. "It's not too late for the baby."

"It's not too late for you, either. You can be the one who tries something different."

"But what? Just make it from day to day without getting overtaken? Seems that's what we've all done."

Ethan rubbed his jaw. "Me and Sam both wanted you to get treatment at first, but now . . ."

Madeleine shrugged. "What treatment? There's no existing therapy for this."

Ethan considered this. "Maybe it's not so much a matter of treating. Maybe it's about training."

"You mean old Chloe's briar university."

"She does know more about this than anyone there is."

"But she's liable to lead me into a spider's web."

"You don't have to follow everything she says, and you don't have to buy into her philosophy. Just be the scientific observer. See what she shows you. Keep an open mind."

Madeleine thought this over. "Maybe. Just so long as she never finds out about Marc's baby."

Ethan said, "Yeah, no kidding. And aside from Chloe, you could look at other ways to figure things out. See if you can get a new handle on it."

"Like what?"

"We oughtta be able to figure something out. You and I both know a thing or two about the power of the human brain."

"Physician, heal thyself?"

He grinned. "Something like that."

"But this is different from anything that has to do with my training. I wouldn't know where to begin."

"How about neuroplasticity?"

Madeleine lifted her brows. The adaptable brain. The brain that can be trained. After all, she'd managed to make it to trial (though not quite *through* the trial) by following her own brain-training regimen.

She said, "I suppose it depends on the objective. I need to figure out what I'm training *for*. I guess the top of the list is to keep the wildness and chaos under control."

"And also, tap into all that potential that the rest of us know we have, but can never seem to get at. You actually have real access."

She flipped it over in her mind. She wasn't sure, but she was warming to the idea.

"Neuroplasticity," Ethan said again. "What do you already know about keeping the chaos under control?"

"Well, when I'm relaxed, the briar seems to stay manageable."

"Good. So you build up those relaxation neurons. What else?"

She grinned. "There's, um, you know, sex. Seems to be an excellent bramble tamer."

Ethan raised a brow. "Well, we will most certainly have to study up on that one. Consider me your devoted training partner."

She laughed. "And that's another one: laughter. I suppose because both are kinds of escape."

"OK, good. So far we're going to make super neurons for laughter, relaxation and sex. I can think of worse methods. Walking, too."

She remembered Monkey Hill, and laughed again, a shaking, exhilarating release.

"Anything else?" he asked with a grin.

She thought back over the past several months. "For some reason, when I'm in the flower shop with Sam, helping her make arrangements, it calms Severin and me both. And in my grandmother's diary, she said her father used to carve dolls, and that helped to heal him somehow. But Mémée's last entry was when her father had gone missing after a flood, so I don't know much more after that."

"Dolls?"

"Yeah. I thought it was some kind of a voodoo practice. But now . . ." She frowned. "Anyway, I tried carving on a stick but only managed to cut my hand."

Ethan gazed at her a moment. "Maybe it's the creativity."

She considered this. "You know, I think you might be right."

He said, "The creative brain undergoes a shift in chemical and electrical activity. Maybe that environment is ideal for your particular brain requirements."

"Brain requirements. Ha."

"It's worth a shot."

"You're right. I'm not terribly creative, but I can work on that."

He said, "All right, so we have a neuroplasticity plan of action for the chaos part. What about the other part? The part about tapping into your potential?"

"Well, I would say that the creative practice helps with that, too. Otherwise, it's just a simple matter of exploring in there."

"You can literally find things?"

"Well no, it's not like hunting for Easter eggs. But as I wander through, there are certain senses that awaken."

Severin's voice came from behind. "I can show you much, much!"

Madeleine wheeled around. The little girl was standing by the French doors. Her eyes were gleaming.

Ethan asked, "Is she back?"

Madeleine nodded.

"Ask her where she comes from."

Severin answered him directly. "I am what is Madeleine, and Madeleine is we."

Madeleine said to her, "But can you show me? Show me exactly where you come from?"

"Hang on," Ethan said, and he stood and patted his pockets, then limped to the pile of rubble. He grabbed the construction pencil and a cut piece of sheetrock. "We're going to do this right. Recorded sessions. All right now, go ahead."

❧

MADELEINE CLOSED HER EYES. It began as it had before. She felt as though she was spinning toward the earth, and yet it still occurred within the bramble. A wide, dizzying cavern. She was both falling and weightless at the same time. Severin was leading the way. But as they traveled, Madeleine realized she was not falling toward the earth, though it did seem to have a similar shape, this place.

"What do you see?"

Ethan's voice. He sounded far off and unreal. Inside the briar, he was the hallucination and Severin was reality.

Madeleine replied, though she could not see him: "I can't tell yet. Some kind of heavenly body. I thought it was earth, but it's not."

But as she drew nearer, she said, "Tangled lines. Looks almost like a giant clod of hair. I'm trying to get closer."

Severin led her deeper toward the mass. They both seemed disembodied in this strange corner of the briar. She felt Severin's presence but could not see her, and she could not see her own body. The convoluted lines that comprised the mass were very fine. They stretched much longer in proportion to hair, unless a strand of hair could span the length of Lake Pontchartrain.

Madeleine said, "It looks like . . . wait a minute. Give me the pencil."

She felt Ethan pressing it into her hand. The sheetrock rested in her physical lap. She drew what she observed. Easy enough, as it was only a matter of scribbling.

"You come from this thing?" she asked Severin.

"Deep inside, yes, truly. I'll show you."

Madeleine watched, and the deeper they plunged, the easier it was to determine the individual shapes, though they were impossibly tangled together. So much like the briar itself. But here, each strand thickened to a jumbled mass at one end and frayed splits at the other.

"Keep drawing," Ethan said from so very far away, but the sound ricocheted all around her.

She jumped, watching. She strained to see better as they closed in on one of them. All around, sparks. Flashes.

"I can't draw it all, I . . ."

"Do what you can."

And so she moved the pencil to what she hoped was a clean corner of the sheetrock, though she couldn't actually see it, and drew the nearest strand. She ran the line down to show the length first. Long and direct, but with miniscule curves along the route. The fanning end where it splayed.

She said, "My God, it's a . . ."

But then her own voice echoed around her, like Ethan's had, reverberating through all the tangles and twists and byways. Flashes of light, too. Reflections. She could see Jasmine dozing. She could see

Ethan watching her. She realized she was straining so hard that her physical eyes were open, and she was seeing what she would have seen there in the courtyard, but in thousands of fractals. A hologram that extended beyond sight to include sound and touch and other senses, too.

"It's a neuron. I'm looking at my own neurons inside my brain."

SHE RETURNED TO PRESENT awareness. Jasmine was still dozing under the honeysuckle. Ethan was still sitting opposite her at the bistro table. No longer reflections and reverberations, but once more singular shapes and sounds. Severin had curled by her feet.

"You see now that I am we," the little girl said.

"It's true," Madeleine said, rising to her feet and disentangling Severin. "She's part of me."

"What, the river?" Ethan said, rising with her and looking at the sheetrock drawing.

"They were neurons. Severin occupies the neurons inside my brain. See there?" Madeleine pointed to the more detailed portion of the drawing, where two neurons joined in a cluster of dendrites.

He looked up, intrigued. "Well, this particular neuron looks an awful lot like the Mississippi River."

He handed it to her and reached into his pocket. "Here, I'll show you."

"You talk to him much so much," Severin said, scowling.

Madeleine took the tablet from Ethan. He was right about the drawing. The snaking axon could be compared to the path of the great river. And at the end, where the length took a sharp turn and then fanned out in an axon terminal, it bore the same pattern as the Mississippi delta, splayed fingers gripping the ocean floor at Plaquemines Parish below New Orleans. Ethan was scrolling on his Blackberry.

"I suppose most rivers look like neurons, in a way," Madeleine said, puzzled.

"Yeah, but your drawing looks *exactly* like the Mississippi. Have a look." He handed her his Blackberry.

She regarded the display. He'd called up a satellite image of the great river, so that you could see the exact contours of land and water, and even the soft, sandy shallows that rimmed the coastline. She'd seen this before. When she'd journeyed through the briar to find Zenon, she had a sweeping perspective from above.

"You call on me and now you have nothing to say!" Severin cried.

"Look," Ethan said. "Even at the top. The axon tangles up in an area that looks like the Minnesota wetlands, and the cell body looks like one of the Great Lakes."

Madeleine panned the satellite image to the top of the river and saw, just as the crude lines in her drawing showed, a field—almost a dendritic field—of reaching, branching water and land that made a sort of synaptic jump to the Great Lakes. From there, more rivers sprouted, the largest of which was the Saint Lawrence, stretching through Quebec. It emptied into a vast estuary that cradled Prince Edward Island, New Brunswick, and Nova Scotia. Madeleine felt a surge looking at the pattern. Interesting coincidence that the paths in her drawing mimicked these exact waterways; interesting coincidence that these waterways connected the Acadia of the north to the Acadia of the south.

Madeleine turned to Severin. "Which is it? Neurons inside the brain, or the Mississippi and St. Lawrence Rivers?"

"Parts in same! You wish so much to divide! The networks of the mind cannot end at flesh. I am a thing that is you, and we are a thing that is the river. Nothing divides!"

"What is she saying?" Ethan asked.

Madeleine put her hands to her temples. "I don't know. Sometimes she gets so angry when she can't have my full attention. She says that it's all the same, me, her, the brain network, the rivers."

Ethan thought for a moment. "Humans are made of water."

Madeleine looked from Ethan to Severin.

"I think we have a lot to learn," Ethan said.

"I think we do."

Madeleine examined his face. It had become so familiar to her. The way he looked, the way he smelled, his crooked gait—everything. She'd never leaned on anyone else before in her life like this, and somehow Ethan made it seem as though her burdens were not even burdens.

She said, "And I think . . . I think I'm very lucky. I'm so glad you're here."

Ethan smiled at her. "I'm the lucky one."

He took Madeleine's hand and pulled her toward him. The late afternoon sunlight played on the honeysuckle, and a light breeze ruffled Jasmine's fur. Ethan slipped his arm around Madeleine's waist. She leaned into him.

"You turn away from me!" Severin said, her voice sounding strained and menacing.

Madeleine regarded her. "Severin, I'd like to be alone with Ethan for just a little while."

"No!"

"If you'll give me an hour, or better yet, two hours, I promise to give you my undivided attention for the same amount of time."

Severin's eyes glinted. "Only us then? None other?"

"Yes. Just you and me."

Severin seemed to think it over, though her eyes narrowed. Madeleine wondered whether she'd made a mistake in trying to barter. The briar seemed a dangerous place, one where you could get lost, with creatures that waited and whispered. Memories and reflections and endless passages.

Severin said, "Then so. Alone with him for now, and then with me, to find the delights in the thorns."

Severin turned, looking back toward the French doors, and then she was gone.

Ethan smiled at Madeleine, and put his hand behind her ear. "You're going to be all right, Madeleine. You know that, don't you?"

"I think so. You really think neuroplasticity is going to work in managing this?"

"Neuroplasticity, baby." He kissed her ear. "Neuro-plas-badass-sticity."

Two hours alone with Ethan. Two hours with Severin. And tomorrow she would see Chloe about understanding this strange new world. Maybe they'd look in on Zenon together. She didn't see it as a matter of obligation, but as a way of honoring her own spirit, and that of the generations that intertwined them.

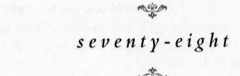

seventy-eight

HAHNVILLE, 1927

*I*N THE NURSERY, PATRICE washed the blood from Ferrar's shoulder. Her sister's body lay strapped in the next bed, but Marie-Rose's consciousness was watching Ferrar. Patrice was not in the briar, so she could only sense her sister, not see her.

"Where is your mother?" Ferrar asked.

Patrice replied, "She left. She's gone to New Orleans. You're safe."

"Will she be back?" Marie-Rose's voice asked from a distant corner of Patrice's mind.

Patrice sighed. "I'm afraid she probably will, 'tite. I don't think she'll stop until she's turned us all into living devils."

She felt a tremendous anguish coming from Marie-Rose. Living puppet-beasts for Chloe. The possibility was horrifying, and far too real.

Patrice added, "But I think she'll stay away for now. We just have to be ready in case she finds a way to come back."

Ferrar was watching Patrice in what must have appeared to be a one-way exchange.

Marie-Rose whispered, as though Ferrar could hear, "Patrice, the river devil don't like this man none."

"Mind your grammar. And I know. Just let it alone."

"But there's a thing in him that's leaked into you!"

"Leave it be, Rosie. Go back to your body and I'll release you."

The younger sister sighed and climbed back into her physical form. There, she opened her eyes. Patrice untied the straps that kept her in the bed.

"You're still in the briar," Patrice told her. "So be careful where you step. If you get to wandering I'll have to tie you down again."

Patrice turned to Ferrar. "The doctor should be here soon. Guy and Gilbert went to fetch him."

And then she paused, looking him over from his blood-shined eye, to the X at his throat, to his bandaged shoulder. "You'll have a third scar now, I expect."

"A third mark from Miss Chloe," he said.

Patrice took a step forward, examining him more closely. She shut her eyes so that she could see better. The river devil was curled over Ferrar's shoulder, whispering into his ear.

"Scat!" Patrice shouted.

The river devil bared her teeth and rose toward Patrice. Patrice opened her eyes, and the creature vanished from her vision.

"Patrice! You mustn't provoke her!" Marie-Rose cried.

Patrice turned to Ferrar. "You've got to be careful. You're one of the others. The river devil's been whispering to you. She's probably planted some ideas that could get you killed. Some reckless act. Drinking foul water or crossing an old bridge."

Ferrar heaved himself up onto his good elbow.

Patrice said, "These wrong ideas, they'll feel like your own. But they're just whispers. If you watch carefully, you can tell the difference. The river devil isn't strong enough to do anything to you but whisper."

She cast a meaningful look toward her sister. "And none of us are going to help her get her way, are we Rosie?"

Marie-Rose watched with wide, terrified blue eyes. Her coarse hair was askew, and she looked like a dark corn husk doll. Patrice knew that the briar's point-of-view made it difficult to resist what the river devil wanted.

But Marie-Rose whispered, "No ma'am."

"Thank you for helping me," Ferrar said.

Marie-Rose looked up at her sister. "Patrice, what if Maman does come back? What'll we do?"

"Then we'll have to leave, 'tite."

"But where will we go?"

"I don't know." Patrice took her sister's hand and led her to the stool. She took a wide-toothed comb and brushed the little one's hair, tying it back from her face.

Patrice said, "We'll go somewhere we can disappear, that's all. There are all kinds of places out there. Cocodrie, Bayou Black, Big Hellhole Lake."

Marie-Rose closed her eyes and relaxed into her older sister's gentle touch.

Patrice cast a tentative smile toward Ferrar. "There's even a place called Bayou Bouillon, where the water boils."

"But Maman has ways of finding," Marie-Rose said.

"Then we'll go where it's too far for her to get to us very easily. We'll go all the way to Paris if we have to. That's where Papa's family came from."

"I can hide you," Ferrar said. "If you need anything, you come to me. I will help you."

Patrice thanked him, though she would never dare accept his offer. A man like Ferrar, with the hated golden shimmer and vast ocean of stillness inside, would never be safe around the children of the bramble.

Epilogue

NEW ORLEANS, 2010

H E WAS AWARE THAT she was entering the room. His eyes were closed, but he knew. And he could sense Chloe, too. He tried once again, as he had countless times before, but failed to open his eyes.

"You can see with your eyes closed, you know," Josh said.

And when Zenon tried, he found that Josh was right. There. He saw Madeleine. Tall, slender, blue-eyed, her black curls tied back from her face. She'd brought along a quilt which she was unfolding, and a riot of shapes and colors glared into the room. The patterns made his head throb. He closed off the circuit that had allowed him to see.

"Come on, don't be a wuss," Josh said.

But then he sensed Madeleine floating the quilt over him. The wind from it chilled his already cold body even further, but the captured air caressed him with such softness that it brought anguish to his throat. The quilt settled over him, and he felt warm. He opened the circuit again and could see once more. Madeleine was talking with Chloe.

To Madeleine, he was probably lying there in complete oblivion.

After all, his eyes were closed, and he did not move. But he was far from oblivious. And neither was Josh.

"Ain't that sweet," Josh said. "She sends some thug over to kill you and now she tucks you in for beddie-bye."

"I didn't exactly leave her a choice," Zenon said, wishing his words could break through the barrier of his own mind and actually form on his lips.

And then Madeleine murmured, "I wish things had been different."

Zenon watched closely, but it seemed apparent that Madeleine hadn't overheard them. She was just speaking from her heart.

The two women were talking. Chloe spoke about her children, of the strange paths where their lives led. Alienation. Zenon knew a thing or two about that. And now all he could do was lie in this bed, mute and motionless.

Then, to his surprise, Madeleine flipped the quilt and smoothed it over him. He once again felt the caress of air, and also her touch. But now the quilt's crisp white underbelly showed and the dizzying patterns lay hidden.

"Yeah, she's my sister all right," Zenon said.

"Don't be foolin yourself over Madeleine, now," Josh said.

"Those two women standing there are the only ones who know me."

Josh folded his arms. "Bullshit. I know you. And unlike them, *I* can hear every word you say. Don't you see this is the best thing that could've happened?"

"What're you talking about?"

"Before, you weren't listening to me. You'd do what I told you, then you'd haul off and go your own way. Watching Madeleine. Keeping souvenirs. The way things were heading, it was sure to end in disaster."

"It did."

"Quit feeling sorry for yourself, and listen up." Josh glanced at Chloe, then turned back to Zenon. "This time you need to listen, and do exactly what I tell you."

"Do what? I can't do anything but hole up in this goddamned bed!"

"That ain't so. You can still use the trick."

Zenon looked at Madeleine and Chloe. From Chloe he could learn. And Madeleine, how he would love to guide her. To have one more chance to hone her into a trained warrior. Together, they could shape the path of human kind.

Josh said, "You know she and her beau are talking about fixing up the old plantation house, Terrefleurs?"

"What?"

"Yeah, ain't that the sweetest? Funny that you gave her that place. Maybe she'll screw him ragged on over there."

Zenon listened, and felt as though a ball of molten tar was bubbling beneath his rib cage. Faithless. He should have gotten rid of her and that smirking rich sonofabitch when he'd had half a chance. Josh's face was hard.

"There now. You done wallowing yet? You ready to get serious and take things to the next level? We can start with the trick you already know."

"What good's the trick when I'm stuck in this bed? What the hell'm I supposed to do?"

"With my help?" Josh leaned in, and though his brow was furrowed, his lips formed a slow smile. "Plenty."